An Untilled Field

By Dennis Carey

Published by Dennis Martin Carey

An Untilled Field

Copyright © 2015 Dennis Carey
Published by Dennis Martin Carey

Dennis Carey has asserted his moral right under the
Copyright, Designs and Patent Act, 1988,
to be identified as the author of this work.

A CIP catalogue record for this book is
available from the British Library.

ISBN 978-0-9931943-2-0

For Joan

PART ONE

Chapter 1
Lecarrowanteean, County Mayo, Ireland, 1879.

Imagine.

You're four.

You don't know why it happened, no-one explains things to a four-year-old.

Yesterday, the person you depend on most in the world, the one who feeds you her milk, the one who pats your back when you can't breathe, was dragged away in chains. Bleeding and bawling. Your father was hit with a stick until still, his blood flecking your feet. Your house was knocked down.

Today you've walked. Barefoot. All day. With Liam. On stony tracks and across wet fields. You've climbed ditches twice your height.

You've not ate since yesterday morning, before your life of smiles, stroking and stories was smashed into pieces.

You sit in the corner of a field, far from home.

The dark of night-time is on its way.

How do you feel?

Aiden feels cold.

"I code, Ee-am," Aiden says. The fabric stretches as he draws up his thin legs and folds them inside his petticoat.

Liam gnaws at a dirty fingernail, deep in thought. Aiden's been quiet since it happened. You're usually telling him to shut up with his childish, eejity blithering and endless four-year-old-boy questions, but he has few words now. And he can't say 'Liam' anymore. "Here, cuddle in t' me."

Aiden shuffles sideways and nestles his curled body in the warm armpit of his brother.

Liam draws him in close.

"Where's Mammy?" Aiden says, worming deeper.

More words.

"With Da. Do ya not remember?" Liam says. "We'll find her... Me and you'll go to Ballycastle to find Mammy and Da. We'll be like the brothers in the stories Da told us. Remember the stories? The two brothers? Goin' off to find the chieftain to kill Theron, the big Vikin' invader fella with the axe. His ships, full of army."

1

Aiden tenses as he coughs. The ferns around them flutter. He collapses his thin, malleable body back against his brother. "I do," he says.

A day of a thousand short, small-boy steps and no food takes its toll. Aiden's eyelids fall closed, long lashes pointing out at the field, and his round mouth gapes. He slips towards sleep.

There's blood on Liam's shin. His father's blood, wiped to a smudge by the rushes of the fields, stretched like the tracks of shooting stars. It's too dark for Liam to think about his father's blood. He licks two fingers and wipes at the marks. They dissolve into the pale scar below his knee, an old scar from a safer time. His father was there for that, too.

Except for the dew that carpets the sloping grassy field, the evening is dry. The ditch bank protects them from the cool north-westerly breeze, but the makeshift shelter of gathered fern affords no protection from rain.

"No rain, with th'elp o' God," Liam prays, as he shifts to settle.

The last time he spent a night in a field, his father was with him. Liam had felt safe. "We'll be makin' shelter outside tonight, the sky for our roof," his father had said. After Da set his fishing line in Lough Cloonagh, he shaped a shelter in the midst of a spindleberry bush. His father filled the space with fronds of fern, enough to put under and over you.

His father's shelter was warm. Warmer than this one. And comfortable. And lovely. His father pointed out the sprigs of spindleberry to Liam, masses of rose-red capsules emerging from crimson-pink cocoons. He had warned against eating the berries, as enticing as they were. "They're deadly poisonous, a ghrá, and they taste bitterer than sloes."

That night, Liam didn't want to sleep, afraid the night would run away whilst his eyes were closed. He forced them to stay open, watching the stars inch between the twigs of the bush. More stars joined in the longer he looked. By the time he gave up, lulled to sleep by the lapping of the lough, the sky was full.

This night, he wishes for sleep. Before it gets too dark. He wants this night to run away. He's not scared, he's sixteen years old, born twenty-ninth of June, 1863. Nearly a man. He's not at all scared, he reminds himself, he's sixteen.

He stares at the darkening field and listens. Apart from Aiden's nasal breathing and the breeze brushing the damp grass, he hears nothing. No fox. No horned stag. No banshee. No boy-eating Viking invader with an axe to split them both into pieces. Nothing to be scared of. Except the dark.

He wriggles a hand down and cups Aiden's feet. The toes are cold. He squeezes him closer and parks a cheek on top of the round head.

"Always have a plan," he remembers Da telling him. "Need teaches a plan." Liam didn't know what that bit meant. "Think what could go wrong and be ready." Yesterday something went wrong that his father was not ready for.

Before he crawled out from under the roof this morning, he, Liam Walshe, formed *his* plan. Look after Aiden, find Mammy and Da, then pay Cuffe back for what he did.

He closes his eyes, and hopes for sleep.

"Who's Ba-ee Cass?" Aiden says.

Liam smiles. "It's a place," he whispers, into Aiden's hair. "Ballycastle's a place. We're going there t' find Mammy and Da. Sleep now, little man."

Liam wonders where Ballycastle is.

Chapter 2
London, England, 1876.

A cloth-wrapped fist crashed into the side of Bernie's nose. He heard a crack in his face.

Adrenaline coursed his veins. It helped him breath, fuelled his muscles and anaesthetised his body. He was surprised it all still worked at his age. He felt old. *Too* bloody old for these damn shenanigans.

The nose bled but there was no pain. Bernie knew the hurting would come. When it did, more drink would help.

The crowd yelled obscenities of encouragement at the fighters. Bernie didn't know what was being said, the shouting an indecipherable wall of static.

The fighters danced on the balls of their feet. Bernie thought it a polka swinging dance. Peggy came to mind. She was there, in the crowd, they could dance. Polka with abrupt syncopation, lively with brutal, vicious variances from the rhythm.

Break your partners, please.

Concentrate.

Bernie stepped to the side - a chassé movement - and lashed out with his left. It was fast. He could still be fast. The fist passed around Crimson Corner's guard and clattered an ear, jolting sweat from his hair. The ear swelled raw-meat red as the younger man teetered backwards.

The fighters readied their stances and prowled the ring. No conceivable step pattern - freestyle.

Bernie pushed a punch between Crimson Corner's wrists catching him on the brow. The head snapped back. It set up a follow through with a swinging right that Bernie leaned into. The big punch missed, throwing Bernie off balance.

Crimson Corner capitalised with an uppercut to the underside of Bernie's chin.

Bernie's head sprung up, nose blood arcing into the air. As Bernie fell away, his opponent advanced, swinging. A blow missed Bernie's upturned chin, landing square on the breastbone. The blow forced Bernie backwards - a fallaway - into the sacks of hay. He rocked back onto his feet, in the fashion of a wooden-horse, and grabbed his attacker around the head. He pulled him in tight, concerned, hoping for respite. Bandaged knuckles pummelled his ribs.

A tall black man, with a wide neck and a door-knocker beard, barged into them. He wore a blood-stained shirt strapped tight to his body by a set of thick braces. "Break loose!" Door-knocker said, and prised the brawlers apart with muscled arms.

The crowd shouted and punched the air in frustration.

Bernie sucked air into his lungs, it hurt to breath, and stretched his stance. He leaned back and stared between his hovering forearms. The wrapping on his left hand was loose.

"Fight on," Door-knocker instructed.

Stepping, swaying. Weaving, waiting. The pugilistic dance resumed.

Bernie staggered, exhaustion setting in. Blood and sweat blurred his vision. His arms were heavy, his ribs ached. A blow buffeted his left eye. Another blow, the same eye, knuckles penetrating deep into the socket. He winced as he twisted away.

The fighters returned to stance. Bernie's eye swelled shut. He threw punches but hit nothing, Crimson Corner had lost a dimension.

The fighter from the crimson corner relaxed his guard, backed off and taunted Bernie.

Chapter 3
Lecarrowanteean, Ireland, 1879.

"Liam, here with yer brother. Now!"

Liam jerked himself away from the window and stared wide-eyed at his mother. His ears flushed scarlet. He was a lad who acted older than his years, it was unusual for his mother to shout.

Maggie Walshe had a hand on her hip, the other to her forehead, her face full of torment and anguish. She turned and paced the earthen floor. A straight-body waddle, her hands rubbing the bulge of the baby in her stomach. The sharp turns of her bare feet kicked up black dust.

Liam resumed his vigil at the window.

Jimmy Walshe nailed planks of wood to the inside of the half-door. The clouts reverberated within the confines of the cottage.

Aiden Walshe held podgy fists to his ears. He rocked his head and squalled back at the noise.

Maggie whisked Aiden into her arms as she passed. The pregnant belly made it awkward, but he clambered astride her swollen stomach and she swaddled him in her shawl.

"It's alright a ghrá," she said. "Mammy's here."

There were four miscarriages before Aiden. She knew she was not the only woman to lose a baby. There was Mary McGloughlan, Mary's sister Breege, the wife of the fellow Jimmy buys the manure from in Coolcran. No, losing a child was not unusual, just devastating in a way that ripped the heart out of you and cast it onto the riverbank stones. She gave each a name. Names she didn't share with her husband. As far as he was concerned they were all called God's Will. She remembered their birthdays. They are still with her. Her dreams tell her that.

Aiden didn't announce his arrival kicking and caterwauling like Liam had. His arrival was peaceful, silent even, the baby exhausted from completing a journey that several before him had failed in. He's sickly. Small and sickly. They say his size comes from her side of the family, her father was slight. But it could be because he's sickly. Coughs and fever led to many long nights of reassurance at the breast. Then there's the blood, of course. Coughed into her palm as she stroked his back. "It's alright a ghrá," she'd say, "Mammy's here."

It made him all the more precious.

"Let's see them get through that," Jimmy said, stepping back from the door. He dropped the hammer. "Liam, what's goin' on outside?"

6

"Makin' somethin' big, Da," Liam said, staring out.

"That's it 'til the others get here," Jimmy said. "There's nothin' else can be done."

"What others?" Maggie said, her voice raised a pitch, her eyes wide and blinking. "Until who gets here?" A palm pressed Aiden's head into her neck.

"No doubt Billy Cuffe will be down," Jimmy said, his voice calm. "With a Magistrate. They have t' have a Magistrate with them t' carry out an eviction sure they do. That's the way of the law."

"So who're them out there?!" she screamed, pointing to the door. "And what're they at?"

Aiden raised a fist to his round mouth.

"Whisht now Maggie, a stór. You'll scare the boys," Jimmy said. He moved towards her, "Shhh," and wrapped his long arms around his son and pregnant wife.

"I hate that damn Cuffe, God forgive me for cursin'," Maggie said, into his chest. "The way his eyes eat into yer skin. Makes ya want to scratch."

"I want Liam," Aiden said, pulling his face clear.

"Mammy, let me go out t' them," Liam said, joining his family in the centre of the room. "I'll take Da's hammer and–"

She held a finger to his lips. "Enough," she whispered.

It's a gesture Liam dare not ignore.

They stood, swathed in each other, as though saying goodbye to a condemned relative.

The hammering outside drew Liam back to the window.

"Da, come see. What're they buildin'? It's like a tepee tent thing."

Jimmy moved to the window and stooped to peer out. As his mind made sense of the contraption, the colour drained from his face and his head drooped. "Holy God," he said. His thumb made a small sign of the cross in front of his face.

"What is it, Jimmy?" Maggie asked. "What is it they're buildin'?"

Aiden wriggled from the crush of his mother's arms.

The men had built a tripod using three of the poles. A fourth pole was slung horizontal underneath, its broad, flat end pointing with menace towards the cottage.

Jimmy turned from the window. "It's a batterin' ram, Maggie. They've a batterin' ram with them."

Chapter 4
London, England, 1876.

"Hit the bar-stud! What you waitin' for?" The crowd were testy.

The fighters danced. Hopping, swaying, ducking.

Bernie drove forward with a right. It was off target.

His opponent grimaced and deflected the fist.

Bernie edged closer and swung with his left.

His opponent read it, danced to the side - chassé - and poured punches into Bernie.

Blow after blow buffeted Bernie's face, wounding, cutting, getting heavier as his defences were prised apart and his opponent had time to swing. He forced his tired arms up. The blows pushed him away, clear. Wrapping hung off his wrist down to the straw-strewn floor, as if attempting to wriggle an escape from the ring.

The pinch of the match had arrived. They coaxed their shapes into proud stances and edged closer for a last dance.

Bernie swayed to and fro, his feet no longer leaving the ground - an exhausted, stuttering mazurka step.

Leading foot drew up beside leading foot. They swung punches. A flurry of tangled arms.

Bernie looked for an opening. A narrow gap. Through it he thrust a clean, powerful blow.

Crimson Corner flinched. His arms dropped.

Bernie punched again, without retaliation. His confidence rose. Another blow. Had Crimson Corner punched himself out? The fight swung to Bernie. They stood heels to toes and traded blows towards exhaustion, a spectacle.

The crowd roared and cursed and roared. Well-dressed gentlemen, flanked by well-dressed working women, looked on approvingly. This was what they came to see. Man against man in brutal combat. Someone might die here tonight.

The mighty Door-knocker stepped forward and stopped it with an arm. Like Samson at the Temple of Dagon, he heaved the fighters apart.

The crowd, in pandemonium, yelled and pointed and yelled.

Bernie's bandage had entangled their arms and trailed across the floor.

Door-knocker shoved Crimson Corner away and grasped Bernie's wrists. He tore at the blood-stained strips.

Bernie glared at the referee for stopping the fight but he didn't resist, he had no strength to resist, he barely understood what was happening.

There was confusion inside and outside the ring. Amongst the melee, he heard Door-knocker bellow an instruction. He blinked blood and sweat from his eye. A blurred image of a jacketed man clambered over the hay-filled flax sacks and crossed the ring. The 'ring' was set out about twenty-four foot across, though no-one measured it. Each fighter had a post, in diagonally opposite corners, their handkerchief colours tied to it. The blurred image worked at the strapping on Crimson Corner's hands.

'Bare-knuckle Boxing' is a misnomer. In most bare-knuckle fighting circles, the knuckles are not bare. The wrist and hands are wrapped in a six-foot length of cotton crepe bandage.

In an attempt to regulate 'bare-knuckles' out of the sport, The Marquess of Queensberry commissioned a set of rules to be drawn up. Yet an illegal, underground circuit of bare-knuckle pugilism still thrived in the warehouses of 1870s London. Fight rules were by agreement.

Bernie rocked from side to side. Fatigue enveloped him. He felt numb, adrenaline and alcohol inducing analgesia. He needed to rest and ready himself for the pain to come and work its healing. He gulped hot air as he waited for Door-knocker to finish with the bindings and announce the draw.

The referee cast Bernie's strapping aside and gripped a wrist of each fighter.

Partridge will be disappointed with the purse, thought Bernie, but damn Partridge. There is better money from a draw than from a defeat. Bernie felt old. He swayed, his legs uncertain, grateful that Door-knocker had a hold on his wrist. He pushed back his head, his working eye gazing up through the smoke and steam into the criss-cross metalwork of the warehouse roof. His head spun. His body hurt as it repaired itself.

Door-knocker turned his head and winked an eye at Crimson Corner. "Fight on!" he yelled, and threw an arm of each fighter into the air.

The crowd thundered its approval.

Before Bernie realised what had happened, a red-knuckled fist smashed into his left eye. The swollen eyelid exploded on impact, splashing blood like a slapped puddle. A punch struck him in the liver and emptied his lungs of air. He doubled over, his chin exposed, its underside hanging in the air like an expectant punch-mitt.

Door-knocker grinned, the finale had arrived. A keen student of pugilism, he appreciated a clean execution of the knockout blow.

Crimson Corner drew back his right fist to his side and twisted at the waist. Planting his left leg, he rotated the entire right side of his body towards Bernie. The movement was fluid and forceful. He tightened his body, blowing out a breath, just before impact. He struck the underside of Bernie's jaw with the palm heel of his hand, following through with his arm in an upward curve. Sweat spun from his body.

Bernie's head snapped up and back, pinching the nerves at the top of his spinal column.

The second from the crimson corner stepped over Bernie's prostrate body as he crossed the ring. He plucked the green handkerchief from Bernie's post.

Two men rolled Bernie 'The Cat' O'Malley onto a tarpaulin sheet and carried him from the ring. They tipped him into the alley that led to the canal wharf, bleeding, broken-boned and unconscious.

Chapter 5
Lecarrowanteean, Ireland, 1879.

Light from the small window reflected off the whitewashed walls. A piled-high basket of turf cluttered the corner. The fire threw up licks of flame, and the damp, unseasoned firewood in the hearth hissed and sizzled. The chimney, black from almost a decade of smoke, drew the air. Worn wooden chairs sat either side of the fireplace, the hand-woven rush-seats sagging from long evenings of storytelling.

In the back-wall corner, a thin blanket curtained off a narrow cot bed for husband and wife. Next to this lay a smaller crib for the boys. The crib would be a challenge to fit three children when the third one arrives, but they'll deal with that when the time comes. Experience has taught them not to expect all their hopes to be fulfilled.

A mahogany chest of drawers, on finely-turned legs, stood near the door, its stately ornateness at rude variance with the poverty of its surroundings. Her mother had dowered the heirloom, and Maggie cherished it. Farm tools leaned up against the chest.

Maggie deposited Aiden on the crib. She grimaced with the ache in her back as she bent and straightened. She crossed the floor and snatched turf from the basket. A flurry of sparks were sucked up the chimney as three sods landed in the grate.

"There's always something else can be done," she said. "No-one'll take my house so long as I'm standin'." The edges of the turf frazzled into flames as she stretched backwards, pushing the heels of her hands into the small of her spine, elbows wide like goose wings. She dragged the gruel pot from beneath the chest of drawers and emptied a pale of water into it.

"Maggie, what're ya at?" her husband asked. "We'll be needin' that for drinkin'. I have it planned out."

"No-one'll take my house," she repeated.

She carried the pot to the fireplace, loaded it onto the cooking crane and swung it in over the flames. She drew back the screen of the bed and reached underneath. She withdrew the half-full chamber pot and, without pausing, emptied the dark-yellow liquid into the warming water.

Liam stared, his jaw gaping.

The chamber pot pinged as it landed on the floor.

"Maggie?" Jimmy said. "Holy Mother of God." He tutted but didn't argue her down. He went to the window.

People from Kincon town gathered at the side of the house. He recognised Pat Lacey the butcher, his lad Vincent and the Brown brothers, identical twins he found impossible to tell apart. Spinster Kennety, from out the road in Rathoma stood there. Others were arriving.

The sound was faint at first and difficult to identify. Crunching steps on a stony track. Marching. He heard the sound of marching. The quick-time-cadence, military-marching of a large, organised body of men. He pressed a cheek to the pane for a better view. His breath fogged the glass.

"What in God's name?" he said.

"What is it?" Maggie asked.

"Holy God."

"Jimmy, what's goin' on?!" Maggie shouted and wrapped an arm around Liam's waist, pulling him to her.

Aiden winced at the shouts.

Maggie stamped a foot into the ground. "For God's sake Jimmy!"

Jimmy turned from the window and said, "The *others* are here. They've brought the constabulary, Maggie. Hundreds of them. Must have every sub-constable in Mayo with them."

"Why're the constables here, Da?" Liam asked. "What'll they do? Will they take us t' the barracks, Da? Why have they come t'our house?"

Aiden whimpered and trembled. Through tears that matted his long eyelashes, he eyed the chamber pot lying on the floor, turned over on its side. Warm liquid wet his thighs and seeped into the crib blanket beneath him. He sobbed salty tears that lined his pale cheeks as they made their way to the dimpled corners of his mouth.

Twenty-five uniformed sub-constables of the Royal Irish Constabulary, the guardians of the peace, marched in off the main track. They pushed between the small crowd of onlookers and regimented in front of the cottage. Two lines of men in pillbox caps, rifle-green tunics and broad, black belts fastened with shiny 'S' clips, faced the cottage. Most carried batons. Leather handcuff pouches hung from their belts. Some carried Mark I Martini-Henry rifles with two-foot sword bayonets fixed to the four-foot barrels. The shiny, sharp surface of the bayonets glinted sunlight over the wall of the cottage as the men settled.

Two riders on horseback followed the sub-constables in and dismounted.

Whilst Aiden sobbed in the damp crib, his family grimaced through the small window.

"Da, they've rifles," Liam gasped. "Are they goin' t'–"

"It'll be fine, Liam," his father said. "I've a plan. We'll sort everythin'," The hairs on the back of his neck bristled.

"What're ya goin' to do, Da?"

Jimmy moved away from the window, hands drawing down his cheeks, his mouth open as if he hoped to inhale the answer. The Walshe gene made him tall, with long legs, lean arms and strong shoulders. "Wiry," people said of him. "Strong, long and wiry." He had no plan, and he no longer felt strong. The constabulary had assembled outside his house armed with batons and rifles and a battering ram, and he had no plan. His stomach churned. He stared down at the backs of his hands. The grimed fingers quivered.

There were shouts outside. He rushed to the window. A squat, uniformed officer in a stiff-peaked cap shouted out orders.

Chapter 6
London, England, 1876.

"You're an angel from heaven above, ya know that?" It hurt to talk, hurt to breathe, but he was with Peggy Deagan and he had his pride. "And your smile is as wide and as beautiful as the glorious River Shannon." Bernie O'Malley, at his most poetic.

"Are you suggesting I've a big gob on me?"

"No. The smile. It's the smile that's big."

Peggy had rescued Bernie from the alley and half-carried him back to her room.

"Angel from heaven?" she said. "A bloody old fool from Ennis, more like. I don't know that I'm able to pick up the pieces of your broken body every time you fight, Bernie O'Malley."

"Will ya do it 'cause ya love me, Peggy Deagan?" He spoke slowly to avoid any unnecessary movement of his bruised jaw.

"You must be the worst fighter in London," she said, shaking her head. "And you the age you are. Old enough to have sense. The lad in there with you tonight was young enough to be your own son. And what's with all this 'Cat' shite anyhow?"

He didn't want to be the worst fighter in London. "What cat shite?" he asked.

"You know. 'The Cat'. What's all that about?"

The music of her voice made him smile again. "I could stand in the snow listenin' to the sound of ya talkin'?"

He raised his shoulders off the couch and coughed blood into the towel across his chest.

"Go easy," she said.

"Me teeth don't fit prop'ly no more," he confessed.

As Bernie lay his head back down, Peggy resumed cleaning the wounds on his face, rinsing out specks of dirt and embedded grains of bloodied hay. She hesitated before going near his left eye with her swab. "I'd say you've permanent damage to that eye."

"How does it appear to ya, Nurse Deagan?"

"Like an apple crushed under the hoof of a horse suffering a bladder infection."

He creased his brow.

"The horse must've pissed on it. It's the only way I can account for the green and the blue and the red, and more blue... It's a doctor you need, not a nurse. It's rightly bad enough to be needing a priest."

"Wouldn't thank ya for either the two of them. A doctor tendin' a wound is like a priest hearing confession."

"Is that right?" She humoured him.

"Neither can afford their feelin's to show when caring for their fellow man. Them fellas can't afford to burden themselves with genuine empathy. No, as with the religious worker, so with the physician, the feelin's must be blunted. Whilst appearin' to feel all, they feel nothin'. But a nurse? A nurse feels everythin'."

"Will you listen to yourself? Not sure I'd agree, but I'm telling you, this eye looks beyond the help of a nurse."

"Give it time. Time's a better healer than all them," he said, hoping.

"You haven't told me yet. This 'Cat' business. Explain."

"I noticed you didn't deny ya loved me, Peggy Deagan. Ouch!"

"Oh, I'm sorry," she lied, "I didn't mean to hurt you." she smiled at him. "Now are you going to answer my question or not?"

Whilst she spoke, a craving entered Bernie like a ghoul. Sudden and invasive. He was well-acquainted with the sensation. The familiar symptoms of dry mouth and quickened pulse manifested. He counted the beats as they resounded in his head and then faded. He returned to her.

"It rhymes with O'Malley," he said. "Alley. From there he came up with Alley Cat. I wouldn't let 'im call me Alley Cat so we settled on The Cat."

"I've not a clue what you're on about."

"Ya need a handle for the ring. Brian 'The Mallet' Mathews. David 'Gee Gee' McCabe."

"Gee Gee McCabe?"

"Hung like a stallion, maybe? I dunno."

She gasped in mock shock.

The pulse again. Too many to count.

"Who was the *he* that came up with this?" she asked.

"Partridge, the gobdaw. T'was his idea."

"The fella in the posh frock coat? I don't know him."

"You'll meet him soon enough," Bernie said.

"I think 'Alley Cat' suits you better."

"Ya do?"

"Oh God, yes. It's where you end up isn't it?"

"Laughin' hurts, Peggy Deagan."

The pulse grew stronger. A rhythmic throb of blood passed along his carotid arteries either side of his neck, the pounding loud in his ears.

"I was handy in me day," he said. "You're tending the wounds of the man who knocked out the mighty Walter 'Crowbar' Cornwallis inside four minutes. Twenty-fourth of November eighteen-sixty-one."

The pulse, the craving, the desire. He wished it was only for her.

"Is that right? And who's Mr Crowbar Cornmarket when he's at the races?"

"Crowbar *Cornwallis* was good. Strong. Well, he was once. Prob'ly fair to say he was in his de-ascendancy when I came up against him. Still packed a punch mind. A blow like a tidal wave goin' up the Shannon." The needing had reached the front of his brain. "Listen," he said, "Thanks for lookin' after me tonight. I'd still be in that alley if it wasn't for you. So much for Mr Gregory bloody Partridge, the–"

"I won't come to see you fight again, Bernie." She stopped swabbing and stared into his working eye. "I've done it twice now. I won't do it again."

"Twice? I don't remember–"

"No, there was no other time. This time was two times, the first and the last. I want you to stop the fighting, Bernie." She tucked a small curtain of hair behind an ear.

His good eye stared back at her. He watched her lips move as she spoke, noticing the roundness of the face, the high nose peppered with freckles. He heard the sound of her voice, the tonal inflexions he loved so much, but he had stopped listening. He needed a drink.

"I'm scared you'll get hurt. Wounds that won't go away. Killed even. I can't live with that fear, Bernie. I'm deadly serious now, I can't cope with you and the fighting. I don't want to be losing you. Not now."

Her red hair fell forward, slipping the ear, enshrouding his face, its softness returning sensations to his numbed skin. It smelled sugary sweet. She leaned a little more and kissed his swollen lips.

He was back with her again.

"I'm just grateful ya were there tonight," he whispered.

It felt as if his brain was throwing itself against the inside of his skull, raging inside its cage, screaming for alcohol. He could bear it no longer.

"Will ya help me up, Peggy? I need a drink."

"You don't want a drink, Bernie."

How casually she dismissed his need. How easy it must have been to say those words. He needed a damn drink!

"You just need to heal," she said. "Look, I've done all I can here, you get some sleep. You're fine to stay here tonight if you want."

Her room was small and cramped, with black mould pushing the wood-pulp wallpaper away from the corners. Floral curtains hung from a pole held in place by two inadequate pins and, Bernie presumed, the prayers Peggy breathed as she knelt by her bed each night. Her clothes, a mix of pastels, sage and dead-leaf, draped a line strung across a corner. The couch he lay on filled almost half the space. A twisted candle, much of it wept to a lumpy pile of wax at its root, stood on a table by the bed and filled the room with a dreamy, yellow glow. Against the wall with the door, sat the single bed. He willed his mind to run away with salacious scenarios involving him, Peggy, a more heavily burdened clothes-line and the bed. But his mind was in the grip of something stronger.

"You'll be on the couch," she said.

"Peggy, I need a drink."

"And be gone with the twilight, or I'm in trouble."

His brain thumped, the beat emanating from deep inside his emotional centre where the most basic of needs germinate.

Peggy asked, "Why do you do it, Bernie?"

"Drink? It eases the pain is all. Nothing more than that. Can ya get me some, Peggy?"

"Not drink. Fight. Why do you fight?"

"Why do I fight...? My God. Fighting for as long as I can remember and you're the first to ever ask me that."

He drew a long breath and stared up at the bowed ceiling. Why did he fight? It was, what some people called, a 'good question'. If he understood things correctly, 'a good question' was one that did not have answers, or at least none that were obvious. Did he know the answer? He had known possible answers in the past. They were many and varied and were right or wrong depending on when they visited him. So he kept them locked away, in a labyrinth of cells in his head. It was safer to incarcerate them. Roaming loose, they were difficult to control. Answers can hurt you. These answers hurt. Like only the flawed love of a father can hurt.

"I'd like to know," she said.

At Peggy's behest, he visited them. He searched the lightless labyrinth, passing along its corridors, hugging the walls, wary. At each cell, a door creaked open and the contents spilled out into his consciousness like a fleeing felon. But which was the right answer? The wrong ones dissolved into the distance. Meaningless. Let them go. As he lay battered and bruised on Peggy's battered and bruised Victorian fainting-couch, the right answer fled its dark enclosure. It rampaged through the corridors of his mind, walloping off the walls. He had known the answer all the time. Not a 'good question' after all.

"Prob'ly the same reason, Peggy," Bernie said.

"What do you mean?" she asked, staring down at him.

"I fight... because it eases the pain." He tried to lighten the mood. "There's a saying we have back home. 'An Irishman is not at peace unless he's fightin'."

For the first time in his life he thought he had found someone with whom he could share his pain.

Chapter 7
Lecarrowanteean, Ireland, 1879.

"Attention, now. Everyone. Straighten up them lines, men." Constable Thomas Neild was the commanding officer.

The ranking of the Royal Irish Constabulary was a source of frustration to Neild. His next in line was titled 'Acting-Constable'. Acting? What on heaven and earth did that even mean? Below Acting-Constable, it got worse, it was the realm of the Sub-Constables. Substandard? Substitute? He had tried to look up the reasoning in the *RIC Standing Rules and Regulations, Third Edition*, but ended up having to consult a dictionary. "Sub: a prefix meaning near or under." Peace in Ireland was being maintained by under-constables! There were even two classes of Sub-Constable, second class for new recruits, first class for those in their second year of service.

If he were back in the army, his three chevrons would entitle him to be called 'sergeant'. Sergeant: a commander of men. He should be a sergeant, commanding constables. He had written to the County Inspector detailing his recommendations, but he knew well it'd probably be five years or more before he even gets a reply to his letter. The rules and regulations of the RIC are not altered overnight.

Rank was important to Neild. The more distinctive titles would provide a certain rank-authority, valuable now his physical-authority had abandoned him. He was short, no longer making the five-foot-nine-inch minimum, his waist-belt straining on its last two available eyelets.

"JJ, straighten yourself up like you're told," Acting-Constable PJ Huddy said. "Or I'll kick your shins for you."

Sub-Constable Jeremiah Jackson checked his alignment, stiffened and stared straight ahead.

Huddy, with physical authority in abundance, dabbed at his right eye with a handkerchief. Constable Neild's lack of control frustrated him.

"Right, men, listen," Neild said. "We are to play no role in this eviction other than to keep the peace. The Magistrate, Mr Hogan, here, will serve notice on behalf of the Land Agent, Mr Cuffe." Neild pointed out Hogan and Cuffe with an arm, both busy tethering their horses to the rear of the empty cart.

Cuffe turned, touched the rim of his hat with the tip of his blackthorn stick and nodded towards the men. He wore his usual mid-length sack coat, with its notched lapels. He liked to wear it buttoned high at the front, to ward off the Mayo chill.

The constable smiled, a proud smile, as though savouring this opportunity to demonstrate his leadership credentials. "Now listen to me carefully men, we are to play no part in this eviction other than to keep the peace."

"Ya said dat already, Peeler!" It was one of the Brown brothers.

Those standing next to the Browns sniggered.

Neild glared at the twins. It was not obvious which one shouted.

The brothers, their hands stuffed in their pockets, met the glare.

Huddy sniffed at the goings on and dabbed his eye.

"I happen to be a constable in the Royal Irish Constabulary, and you should address me as such," Neild said. "And I know it was you who shouted, young Brown." The constable turned back to his men.

"A disgrace to yer country is what y'are!" a Brown said, to laughter.

Neild ignored the remark.

"It's ashamed ya should be, sir, throwin' out a family onta the road."

"Are you not hearing me?!" Neild's face reddened as he roared. "This eviction has nothing to do with the constabulary. Our role here is to keep the peace. Now I'd thank you to hold yer tongue, whichever of ye shouted, or I'll have you confined to barracks for incitement of disorder."

Some in the crowd stifled a giggle.

Huddy pocketed his handkerchief and frowned at the exchange between his superior officer and the Browns. He wouldn't worry about which of them shouted, he'd give them both a kick in their scraggy pants and send them on their way to a night or two in a barrack cell.

Neild continued his instructions of deployment. "When I give the order, I want ye all to form an arc in front of the house. You are to let no-one through your line unless I authorise it. Now, does everyone know what an arc is?"

Huddy tutted and turned away in disgust. He estimated there were fewer than a dozen people in the crowd. Twenty-five sub-constables, six armed with rifles, to control a dozen villagers? He sniffed in disdain. The incompetence of his superior officer appalled him.

"Stations, men!" Neild called.

As the men shuffled to their positions, Neild said, "Magistrate Hogan, I hand proceedings over to you."

Magistrate Brian Hogan nodded his thanks and strode up to the door of the cottage. It was the first eviction he had served for Mr Cuffe on the Farmhill Estate. That morning, he told his wife he wanted it to go well, explaining to her that Cuffe seemed the type of land agent who might keep a magistrate busy with evictions.

In County Wexford, in the south-eastern corner of Ireland, sits the small town of Shillelagh. They say *shil-lay-lee*. The town is famed for its ancient oak forest. Wood from this forest has built sailing ships and held up the ceilings of great buildings, Trinity College library and Westminster Hall amongst them.

From the branches of its oak trees, men also fashioned fighting sticks, lengths of wood thicker than a man's thumb with a root-knob cudgel at one end. Fighting sticks have been created from other woods, ash, crab-apple and holly amongst them, but none are as famous as those fashioned from blackthorn. Blackthorn's ready availability, from hedges and forests all over Ireland, made the blackthorn fighting stick ubiquitous. Yet, in deference to the quality of the oak from that ancient forest, they all bear the description 'shillelagh'.

Cuffe won his fighting stick in a card game. His opponent failed to service his debt with notes, so Cuffe relieved him of his blackthorn shillelagh. It was as long as his arm and tipped with a bright, gold ferrule. According to his debtor, in its making, its knobbly length had been dressed in the blood of magpies and burnished until it shone brownish red. The fist-sized root-knob, which glistened like polished brown marble, had been seasoned for months in butter and hot ash. The root-knob's grainy bulk fitted Cuffe's large hand perfectly. It was exquisite. He had been entranced by its utilitarian beauty.

Cuffe flicked his blackthorn shillelagh under his arm and followed Hogan.

The magistrate unfolded a letter and addressed the door.

"James Walshe, by the powers invested in me by the County Courts of Ireland, I hereby serve this civil bill of ejectment, for non-payment of rent, where one year's rent is due. I must inform you, this notice has immediate effect. Now open the door so that I can hand you the notice in person."

"We're not leavin'!" Maggie Walshe shouted from inside. "We've no place to go. I have two childer here and another due. We've no place."

"By Christ, that obstinate woman frustrates me," Cuffe said, under his breath.

"Hold on, now!" Jimmy shouted, through the barricaded door. "I've said I'll make the payments, I just need time. What have ya all the

21

constabulary for? And the ram? What do ye intend t' do with the batterin' ram? Is it breakin' in the door ye're at?"

"Are you going to open the door, Mr Walshe?" Hogan said. "If not, we will be legally obliged to take the necessary action to gain access to this property."

"All I ask of ye is patience and forbearance. I'll get ya yer–"

"Mr Walshe, are you going to open this door or not?"

"I've a right t' me property. Ya can't evict us like this. I've the door barricaded. Yer not comin' in."

"Walshe. It's Cuffe." He spat the words at the door. "You have no rights, now open the door, Walshe, or I'm coming in through it."

A few sub-constables turned to look.

Magistrate Hogan had more to read. "I must, therefore, invoke the powers of the bill, to forcibly evict and eject you, and those with you, from the property and plot. Men, do your duty."

"That's enough," Cuffe said, and pushed the Magistrate clear. "Break down the door."

The magistrate cast the eviction notice to the ground and the workmen each lifted a leg of the tripod, shuffling the battering ram forward.

"Do it!" Cuffe shouted. "What delays you?"

The men drew back the horizontal post that hung from the apex, the tripod groaning from the weighty movement. They heaved, and the ram smashed into the thin door, splitting it down its middle.

Inside the house, planks and dry wooden splinters sprayed across the floor. A thunderous boom filled the room. Beams of light burst through the gaps as if it was the daylight battering down the door to enter.

Aiden yelped and shook, his arms held out in supplication.

"To one side," Cuffe instructed.

The three men each lifted a leg.

Cuffe kicked at the broken door.

The sound of a crying child carried to the front yard. Glances passed between the sub-constables.

Cuffe kicked again, sending planks of wood spiralling into the house. He hit at the bits of door with his fist and feet. The light wood fell away. He placed a leg over the remains of the door and stepped across the threshold. A wave of scalding liquid washed over him, knocking his hat from his head. His arms went up, too late to protect the side of his face. The scorching liquid sizzled on the skin.

Sub-constables turned at the roar of pain.

With a swing of her arm, Maggie flung the empty gruel pot at Cuffe. The metal kettle bounced off his hip and he recoiled in agony.

Cuffe wiped his face and flicked hot liquid from his fingers. He pushed himself erect in the dull room, his thick-set frame silhouetted by the rays of sunshine. He smiled at Maggie through the wisps of steam rising from his cheek. The smile was loathsome and terrible. He lashed at her head with the blackthorn stick.

The bulbous handle crashed into her jaw, spilling her sideways over the chest of drawers. A skilfully-turned leg fractured under her weight, and the chest collapsed forward.

Cuffe dabbed his face and sniffed at his fingertips. He moved over the sprawled Maggie, blood seeping from her mouth, her skirts in disarray. He leered at the bare white legs and sighed. The powerful hands of Jimmy Walshe clamped around his throat.

His head was driven hard against the wall, rough fingers squeezing his windpipe. He beat with the blackthorn, the blows of the root-knob landing about Jimmy's back and legs. But his attacker gripped on, crushing his airway.

Jimmy's nostrils flared, spittle built up in the corner of his mouth. He flexed his legs and heaved Cuffe's head up the wall.

The heels of Cuffe's boots left the ground. He tried to shake his head, but the grip wouldn't loosen. His eyes bulged and shot red with blood. The blows with the blackthorn waned. Life was being throttled out of him.

Jimmy's thumb located the Adam's apple. He pressed.

Cuffe rasped a choke as his tongue was pushed out of his mouth. His bloodshot eyes rolled back in his head. His arms fell limp. The crush on his windpipe ceased.

He dropped back down the wall.

Acting-Constable Huddy was beside him, the wooden constabulary baton suspended in the air.

Jimmy Walshe crumpled, senseless, to the floor.

Huddy withdrew to find his superior officer. Neild could deal with this.

Cuffe coughed life back into himself. He tore off the collar around his neck, gulping air. He rubbed at his throat as it swelled and tightened and glared down at the man lying at his feet. He checked for Acting-Constable Huddy and, despite the pain, he smiled. He gripped the ferrule end of the blackthorn with both hands, raised it to shoulder height and swung it down upon the side of Jimmy's head. He lifted the fighting stick and struck again. And again, driving down blows, the upstrokes flicking blood into the air.

"'eave h'm!" Maggie screamed, staggering to her feet, her voice distorted by the disfigured jaw. She spat blood and teeth onto the back of the cabinet and pressed a hand to the side of her swelling face.

Cuffe pointed the bloodied root-knob at her. "Don't move, witch," he croaked. "I'll bury you beside him."

As he raised the blackthorn to strike another blow, Maggie lunged at him. He checked and redirected the blow. The cudgel swung into the swell of her stomach.

The thud halted her. Her eyes bulged and red spit sprayed from her mouth as she folded and collapsed over her husband.

"Cuffe! Enough!" Huddy shouted, reappearing in the doorway.

"She went for me," Cuffe squeaked, clasping his throat. "Defended myself."

Huddy stared at the two bodies lying on the floor of the cottage, shrouded in his grey shadow. There was the blood in her hair, on her clothes, coating his head, splattered over the earthen floor.

"Good God!" Neild said, as he entered and surveyed the carnage. He turned to his acting-constable and barked out orders. "Cover up that opening before anyone sees in. Arrest them both. We cannot take them to the barracks in this state. Jesus, God... We'll take them to Ballycastle out of the way. Get rid of the crowd. I don't want these two seen, or you will have need of that baton."

Liam stood in front of the fire, holding his brother's hand.

Aiden cried and shook.

Chapter 8
London, England, 1876.

It was three o'clock in the morning, Peggy's heavy eyelids drooped and her shoulders slumped. She was due in the milliner shop downstairs in another four hours, but she wanted Bernie to talk. She had known Bernie for over half a year, but he had never talked like this.

On the night she met him, he had wanted her to do the talking.

The Bunch of Grapes public house on Narrow Street was a thin pub, with a rear terrace that drooped, almost to the point of collapse, into the River Thames. Peggy had been in London for the best part of two years, but the tall, slim building was the first public house she had ever entered.

She strode through the door with two friends from work. Agnes grew up in County Mayo, and Nora was only two-years-old when her family emigrated from County Cork. It was Nora's fortieth birthday, and the small group was out to celebrate.

The narrow pub brimmed with loud, boorish people, stevedores and watermen amongst them, drinking and arguing with marketers and dredgermen. Nora looked for, and received, a nod of permission to enter from the owner, before he descended through a hole in the floor to the cellar. Peggy's warm coat immediately felt unnecessary. They ignored the smell of stale ale-breath and sweat as Nora threaded them past the squeeze of the counter to the rear room. Men turned to look, noticing the properly-tailored clothes, the sugar-watered hair and the fragrance of homemade violet-scented infusions.

Peggy had thought entering a public house the most outrageous thing in the world to do. But London seemed to be like that, a city of the outrageous, permitting the single woman, should she wish, to live outside the modern, Victorian conventions. Not at all like Ennis, back home in County Clare.

Peggy sent letters home to her brother, telling him of her neighbours, families of French Huguenots and whole communities of Jews. "Cosmopolitan," someone called London. Peggy wrote her brother that she felt cosmopolite. She hoped he'd have to ask someone what it meant.

"West Clare," he said. "That's the music of a West Clare accent, or I'll throw meself into the river."

She turned to face him.

"Name's Bernie," he said. "Clare has a shoreline on Lough Derg, the largest and most beautiful lake on the River Shannon?"

Peggy looked shocked.

"But I'll stop talkin', say nothin'," he said. "I want you to talk. Say anything, I don't care what. I'll just stand here and listen."

He had moved away from the company he was with and stood beside her at the counter, blocking the access to a tight staircase. He stared into her bright-red hair. She wore it curled and shoulder length, real follow-me-lads style, dipping over a peach coat.

Her companions raised eyebrows at each other. He was handsome, in a mature, beaten way, his face slightly pocked with what looked like old scars. There was a more recent cut on the flat bridge of his nose. His hair was slicked back, exploding in a mass of curls behind his head. His features were strong. His eyes were green and gentle. They liked his Dublin accent.

"You can buy these drinks for me and my friends if you like," she said. She sounded outrageous.

"T'will be my pleasure, if ya promise to keep talkin'."

"We'll see."

Here in her flat, it was him doing the talking. Was it time, in the rawness of their relationship, for this kind of talk? Was it the 'this is who I am', talk?

It was the talk she thought she wouldn't hear for a long time, perhaps never. It was the talk that she needed to hear before committing herself to him completely.

He told her everything. He talked about his father, his mother, his brother. But mainly about his father.

"A big, drunken, abusive bastard," he said.

She learned that his father, Michael Kelly, was one of a rare breed in Dublin in the late 1830s. Reared a Catholic, he dissented to Protestantism and gained a good job and comfortable wealth. An aptitude for numbers in school led to him becoming the Chief Accountant for the City of Dublin Steam Transport Company, an import-export firm working out of Kingstown, near Dublin.

The company grew in prosperity through the 1840s. They secured the lucrative Royal Mail contract between Kingstown and Holyhead in Wales. Four new steamers were commissioned to service the contract, each named after a province of Ireland.

His father was a ruthless strategist in the company's expansion and was well remunerated for his talents. He had engineered a repayment scheme for the four new vessels that saved the company hundreds of thousands of pounds. He was well known and highly regarded in business circles as a shrewd financial expert. He was feared and despised at home.

It was always on a Thursday night, Bernie told Peggy. His father liked to take a drink on a Thursday. After work, he would visit the Temple Bar area of Dublin. In those days, Temple Bar exhibited the early signs of urban decay, but you could still get a drink there. And a whore. Bernie wasn't sure if his father ever partook of the prostitutes. But he partook of the drink.

On Thursday nights, Bernie and his younger brother Philip would lie awake, waiting for the sound of their father's arrival home. They'd listen for the equine clop and snort, and the mechanical rattle of the carriage as it approached and drew up outside their window. Huddled beneath the blankets in their bed, their hearts would fill with dread.

"We'd lie there and listen," Bernie said. "We'd know from the pattern of his footfall how drunk he was. Strident and crisp we might be safe. We'd relax. But if the steps was staggerin', or his shoes scraped the stones, God. I'd wrap an arm around me little brother to protect 'im, though both of us knew that was useless. I couldn't protect 'im at all.

"The oul' man'd sometimes argue with the carriage driver over the fare. That was always a bad sign. If ya heard him argue about a fare that was the same every bloody Thursday, 'twas bad. We'd be for it. Jesus, when I think of the look in Philip's eyes."

Bernie shielded his face with a battered hand.

Peggy, propped on a rigid arm, looked down at him, the cloth in her hand now redundant. "Go on, Bernie," she said. "Tell me."

It wasn't every drunk Thursday, but on a drunk Thursday when it was, his father shouted Bernie and his brother down from their bed.

"We'd be stood before him in the back parlour. The bare feet of us freezin' on them red-clay quarry tiles we had. He'd be shoutin', in the middle of some argument. An argument that started earlier that evenin' but only existed in his head. We wouldn't know if it was somethin' we'd done, or what. We soon learnt that we didn't need to know. He'd shout, and shout, on and on. It sometimes felt like he'd forgotten we were there. Then he'd start on Philip."

Bernie closed his eyes.

Peggy stroked the back of her fingers up and down his arm as he took a slow, deep breath.

"'What about you, Philip?!' he'd shout, his face stuck in Philip's, his beer breath all over 'im. 'What would *you* do if I wasn't here, bringin' in the money? If I was to quit this family. Fecked off and left ye?' We never bothered replyin' to the questions in the end, he had all the answers. 'You wouldn't be at that posh school!' he'd shout. 'I pay for all that you little tramp. With my money.' That's what he'd call us, tramps. His own children. Jesus, it's over forty years and I remember it word for word."

"Bernie, if this hurts too—"

"We knew what was comin'. We knew where this argument led. The argument that only he was havin'. 'And you have damn all thanks on me!' he'd go. Having 'damn all thanks' must've been a mortal sin, 'cause that was his justification to commence the beatin'. The first few times we'd be hopin' the mother'd come down. With all the noise. Save us. But she never did. Then we stopped hopin'."

According to Bernie, his brother got the worst of the beatings. He told Peggy about how, anticipating what was in store for him, Philip often wet himself standing in front of their abuser. Warm liquid pooling around cold toes.

"He had this bloody belt," Bernie continued, wiping a tear from the side of his face with the back of a wrist. "A thick, leather belt. He was a big man, well able to wield a belt. The back of the head or the body were his favourite targets. He caught Philip once with a lash on the back of the legs. I'd never seen welts like them. It crossed from the back of one knee to the back of the other. I remember it looking like two tracks of the same red road, the adjoining bridge washed away in a flood of piss. Me mother complained about them marks. The next morning. 'See how you've scarred the child?' The only time I remember her protestin'. It didn't stop the bastard."

"Lord bless us and save us," Peggy said. "And you only children."

Bernie sniffed and blinked his eye. He had more to tell. About the bad Thursdays.

On a bad Thursday, his father used the poker.

"Long as his arm, burnt black at the business end and as soft as pig iron. Philip got the worst of the poker, though I got enough of it. The poker scared us. Thought he'd kill us with the poker."

"Bernie, stop."

"Then we had, what I regard as *worst* Thursdays. On a worst Thursday, it wouldn't end with the beatin's. The ultimate disgrace was always reserved for me brother. Don't know why I escaped it, but it was always Philip. Smaller? Weaker? Or just prettier? No idea. Doesn't matter really. We knew it was coming when he'd start apologisin'. Ya didn't want 'im to start apologisin'.

"'I'm sorry, Philip,' he'd go, in this squeaky, pathetic voice. That voice scared us more than anythin'. Down on his knees, crying into Philip's face. Cryin'. Jesus when I think of it. I should've lamped 'im on the back o' the head with the poker stand. 'I'm so sorry,' he'd go. 'I've taken drink. Too much. I didn't mean to hurt ya. I love ya too much. It's the drink that made me.' He'd blame the bloody drink! 'Forgive me, Philip?' God, I hate that I remember these words. After the forgiveness part, he'd deliver the killer punch and Philip was doomed. 'You're my favourite, Philip John,' he'd go. 'You and me'll sleep in our special room tonight. Just you and me'."

Bernie hid his face again and sobbed. He sobbed the same way he sobbed when his age was still a single digit, when he returned to bed alone and sobbed for his brother.

Peggy brewed tea. Bernie's first tea in England.

Chapter 9
Lecarrowanteean, Ireland, 1879.

Aiden sat perched on the upturned mahogany chest of drawers, biting on a curled knuckle, an arm wrapped around Liam. His leg twitched beneath the petticoat dress. He had no more tears and his throat pained from screaming.

The men worked the tripod around the house, pausing to heave the ram into the next upright piece of wall.

Liam gazed over the head of his brother. He flinched at each dull thud, not wanting Aiden to hear, but feeling powerless to protect him. A pain grew in the pit of his stomach. Not a pain of hunger, which he would have recognised, this was new to him. A pain of despondency.

His home came apart, stone by stone, reduced to piles of scattered rubble. The familiar furniture of bed, crib and chairs lay broken about the ground, like fractured family friends. A small fire of clothes and blankets smouldered near the gable.

When a group of the sub-constables had entered the house, there had been several hushed Holy-be-ta-Gods and What'n-the-hells. These men hadn't enlisted in the constabulary to witness carnage like this. Liam read the shock in their faces. They lifted his mother off her bloodied husband and left her curled and whimpering on the floor. A cloth was placed to her mouth to staunch the flow of blood. A blue lump the size of a robin's egg had grown on her cheek. But it was her stomach she caressed. Rocking and lowing like a traumatised, wounded animal, incapacitated and rendered incapable of caring for her young.

The sub-constables were unable to revive his father.

The two boys watched.

The men had stood their mother up and locked her wrists with handcuffs. Standing straight was difficult and she faltered a number of times, clutching the swell of her belly. Drying blood masked her face and her hair stuck out from her head. Her shawl and blouse were torn and blotched red. They sat her on a stool, shackled.

She wept as she rocked.

There had been a delay whilst the small crowd outside was sent away to their homes. Liam heard a Brown brother shout something but couldn't make out which brother, nor what was said.

With a sub-constable at each limb, they carried his father from the house and loaded him onto the cart that delivered the ram posts. Handcuffs were unnecessary.

When the sub-constables tried to remove the boys' mother, she refused to leave her children. There had been more screaming and scuffling, her shouts unclear and stifled. It took three constables to drag her away, doubled over in pain, yelling back at Liam and Aiden. Her hair was wild, veins bulged on her bruised face, blood drooled from her mouth.

The horse that pulled the cart that carried their father was led away. Their father didn't raise a hand to wave, nor did he call out a 'so long'. He rocked in the jolting cart as it mounted the track.

The Royal Irish Constabulary had left, including the one that struck their father with the baton. The one that answered to 'Acting-Constable'. Before he left, he came and stood beside Liam and Aiden. Liam thought he'd arrest them or order them away. Instead he stared at Liam, and said nothing.

The acting-constable's face was hard, bony and incomplete. One cheek sank so deep into his face that Liam imagined the man biting its inside when he chewed. Above this crater sat a troubled eye. The eye scared Liam. The lower eyelid rolled out over the cheekbone, its insides out on show to the world. The bloodshot eyeball looked like it sat burning in a grate of peaty embers. The man wiped the eye frequently, with a white cloth, as though continually crying. He wasn't crying, Liam knew men like the acting-constable never cried. He had trudged off, without saying a word, with his unfinished face, his baton tucked under his arm.

"You'll see me again one day," Liam said. "You and that land agent, Cuffe." Only Aiden heard him.

He hoped Cuffe was crying from his burns. His mother had pulled the crane from over the fire when the battering ram first hit the door. She wrapped her hands in her shawl and lifted the big pot off its hook, her face grimacing from the burn of the handles. Liam remembered her rapid waddle towards the door, arms extended, straining, the pot in front of her big baby-belly. She launched the boiling piss and water over Cuffe as he stepped through the doorway.

Liam had expected Da to do nothing, to stand back and watch. Like himself. But Da didn't do nothing.

The departure of the constabulary was sullen. Gone was the uniform, quick-time-cadence. Each man walked his own stride. Cuffe and Magistrate Hogan rode off behind them.

Only the old woman, Spinster Kennety, from out the road in Rathoma, remained. She stood near the edge of the track, unmoving, in a black shawl wrapped over her head and around her body to a knot at the front. The shawl made her invisible. The constabulary hadn't moved her away, nor spoke to her, nor even glanced at her.

Spinster Kennety was not invisible to Liam. She had the glassy, trance-like expression on her wrinkled face that Liam remembered from the time she read the cards for him.

She stirred and shouted, "Care for the baby!" before giving a slow wave and shuffling off. Her shout triggered the memory of something she had said during the reading. Had she foreseen all this in the cards?

Liam called after her, but she didn't turn.

Spinster Kennety disappeared, leaving Liam and Aiden with the workmen.

"Stay away from Spinster Kennety," Da told him. "She's with the fairies". Liam knew the 'fairy' power was given to her by a traveller woman who had stopped in a make-shift camp a quarter of a mile from Rathoma.

It was in the year of the big snow, the year before Liam was born. A traveller woman was pregnant, and the family made camp whilst they waited for the baby to arrive and the weather to clear. His father told Liam of the worry in the villages at the time. "People were bridled like frightened cats," he said. "Their tails were up and the fur was risen on their back. Everyone locked the door at night. I made sure the hens were in and I gathered the eggs before dawn."

Whenever they spoke of travellers at home, his father tried to scare him with gossip from the men from Kincon. "They'd slit yer throat and steal the eye out of yer head," he told him once. "And in the mornin' they'd come back for the socket." It was enough for his father to get a swipe across the head from Mammy with the tail end of an apron.

His father said everyone was scared to go near the traveller camp for fear of trouble or a curse. No-one wanted them hanging around longer than they had to, everyone anxious for the baby to come and for them all to go. If you weren't interested in buying any of their tinkerings, you were better off keeping your distance. Everyone thought that. Everyone except Spinster Kennety.

His father didn't know if it was curiosity, devilment or just good-natured neighbourliness that drove her, but Spinster Kennety called to the camp soon after they arrived. It wasn't something Da would ever do. Da was devastated by what happened next.

Spinster Kennety befriended an elderly widow in the camp who claimed second-sight and knowledge of ancient Irish charms. Whilst the baby gestated in its mother's belly, the widow shared a gift with Spinster Kennety, passing on to her the ability to read a person's past, present and future from a deck of playing cards.

Da didn't approve. No, sir.

"It's unholy divination," he said, on more than one occasion.

According to his *Catechism of the Catholic Church*, all forms of divination were to be rejected and cast aside. "She'll end up with the Devil in hell if she carries on with it."

Mammy took a different view. She was not alone. By the time the baby came, Spinster Kennety was practising her divinations for people throughout the parish.

The baby's arrival softened hearts. Women flocked to see the child for themselves, keen to know the name and "if it has a prickeen". A small gift for the baby brought you good fortune. All agreed it was a fine, big baby. Fine and big enough to live. The baby was named Christy, after his grandfather. Christy Sherridan.

Mammy invited Spinster Kennety to read the cards for herself and Liam a couple of years back. Aiden was still a baby, just able to crawl with two teeth in his head. Da was at a neighbour, explaining the merits of four-field crop rotation.

"God save all here," Spinster Kennety said, on entering the house. Da would have approved of that. She immediately fussed over Aiden.

When they settled down for the card reading, Liam went first. Spinster Kennety told Liam to deal fifteen cards over the floor, in three neat rows of five. She revealed a column of three cards at a time, caressing each card with a bony, trembling finger. Liam and his mother were captivated, Aiden was indifferent.

Each column told her something new about Liam. When she turned the first three cards, she saw that Liam was going to grow into a tall and handsome man. His mother was pleased but said she knew that already and that it wouldn't be difficult for anyone with an eye in their head to know that too.

The next column, "What you rule," she called it, told her he was to meet his wife "within a three". Liam's mother asked what 'within a three' meant. Spinster Kennety explained it can mean within three days, three weeks, three months or three years, "but it will happen within a three". His mother seemed content with that. Liam thought the explanation vague and wondered if it was any sooner than 'within a four'. He knew better than to ask the question.

She passed her finger over the next three cards and said, "Now. What rules you... It'll happen within a two..." Then she stopped. She looked at Aiden, crawling near them on the floor. "It's the lovely baby, missis... the baby..." Liam remembers her poking a finger at Aiden as if they didn't know who the baby was. "The lad'll be carin' for the baby, missis."

She looked back at the cards, but she was hesitant, frightened even. Her finger hovered, but she didn't speak. At the fourth column, she snatched her finger back as if the cards were about to bite through its wrinkled flesh.

"What's wrong?" his mother asked, reaching for Aiden.

Spinster Kennety turned to Liam. Her eyes, glassy from the heat of the fire, stared deep into his. "I see danger, missus. Torment and danger. He'll have help, but. And I see there's a tall man, made evil by his own kin. There's badness here. Badness in the cards, missus... I've to go, now." That was it. Despite protests from his mother, Spinster Kennety gave up no more information, claiming she'd no more to give.

His mother was unconvinced. Spinster Kennety gathered the cards. His mother tried to stop her, appealing for more. "What about mine?" his mother asked. But after pausing to fan her frail fingers around Aiden's chin, Spinster Kennety left the house, refusing to speak another word.

Liam stayed well clear of Spinster Kennety after that. It had been the most terrifying experience of his life. Until today.

Liam watched the men lift and move the battering ram. "Aon, dó, trí, suas!" A man who answered to the name McManus counted, and up, the contraption shifted sideways, landing in front of another piece of wall.

With half the front of the house demolished, the thatched roof hung bent and twisted and sagging. It was clear to Liam that breaking the door down was only part of the reason for the battering ram. They intended to demolish the house. His family would never live here again, ever.

By dusk, two walls lay broken in stone heaps, the house bludgeoned open. Delft and pots lay shattered and crushed under rocks. An old newspaper flitted apart in the breeze. A neglected stool lay wounded beyond use in the corner. Tools were tossed into a tangled mess. The roof clung on to the top of a remaining wall, reluctant to collapse.

The chimney put up a resistance to the ram. Liam remembered helping his father build it onto the side of the house. It was he who knocked a hole through the wall to form the hearth and make it part of the room.

McManus called a halt to their work. The light in the day had faded, so they left the battering ram erect and walked back into town to collect their horse and cart from the barracks. Liam overheard them agree to come back for the wooden poles in the morning. The men didn't speak to, nor look at, the two brothers. They too had become invisible.

Minutes passed, hours passed. The red of the setting sun illuminated the ruin of their home. Aiden remained on top of the drawers, his cheek against his brother's chest, the steady heartbeat bobbing his head. Wisps of smoke from the smouldering fire curled up and drifted over the broken house, fleeing the devastation below.

Before it was completely dark, Liam lifted Aiden down. "Come on, little man," he said.

They ambled over to the house and crawled in under the corner of the roof. A dirty dress-collar lay abandoned on the floor, trapped beneath a stone. The boys settled, unaware that a single rusty four-inch cut-nail was all that prevented the roof from collapsing down on top of them.

Bernie told Peggy that he and his brother, Philip, attended Wesley College in Dublin. They worked hard as scholars and enjoyed all the sport the school had to offer. They excelled in athletics, handball and competitive wrestling. He tried to impress her by declaring a love for art, ignited by a visit to Wesley by a bearded, upright French artist called Théodore Rousseau. Rousseau brought along some of his landscapes to show off to the boys.

Respite from the barbarity of their father came once a year, for a four-week period in the summer. Their father sent them to Roscommon, west of the River Shannon. He never attended, citing too much work. Nobody minded. The boys and their mother boarded a horse-drawn Bianconi coach in Dublin and two days later arrived in Roscommon town. They stayed with their mother's elder brother, Frank Huddington.

"Fond memories of that man," Bernie said, putting down the bitter tea. "A bachelor, me mother's only survivin' relative. He'd have the liniment ready for us to rub into the blisters on our arses after the coach ride down. Taught us to fish, off the banks of Lough Ree. He'd paddle us down the Ree in his little rowboat, past these tiny islands with people livin' on them. If the weather was up to it, we'd go down as far as Athlone. He'd want to show off the new bridge he helped build. Then we'd row back home. That wasn't the easiest, with the River Shannon coursin' through the middle of the Ree in the wrong direction. The uncle'd tease us, sayin' we weren't goin' to make it back. He'd say we'd have to live on one of the little islands forever. We wouldn't have minded."

Peggy smiled.

"I can see you're enjoyin' this happy bit," he said.

She nodded. "It's a pleasing enough change."

"Frank died the first year of the famine."

She slapped him hard on the arm.

"Ouch!" he mocked. "I'm afraid it's true. Roscommon was one of the worst affected."

"I know that," she said. "My father had kin there."

"Me mother wrote him, tellin' him to come up to Dublin. But he had no time for me father. No more than any of the rest of us, anyhow."

By the time the brothers gained entrance to Trinity College in Dublin, the Thursday night beatings had ceased. Both had grown into strong young men. As if his body knew he was in the greater danger, Philip outgrew his elder brother in height and stature. His broad shoulders an effective deterrent to his father.

"Philip changed. I'll tell ya now when he was young, he was gentle. Carin'. I couldn't've asked for a better brother. But when he grew up." Bernie shook his head. "A bitter, angry young fella. Fists always in the air. He'd no friends. No-one close. Took to gamblin'. Cards mostly. And fight? He'd fight the Archbishop. Dangerous to go out with, always end up in a fight with someone. Man or woman, Philip didn't care. A rage in the head drivin' 'im to madness. I'd enjoy watchin' 'im fight the lads, he was good. But when he'd go for the women... couldn't abide it. It was handy knowin' how to execute a half-nelson wrestle hold when out with Philip. More often than not, it was on him I'd have to do it. The wrestling thing came in handy alright."

"Is that why you came to England, to get away from Philip?" Peggy asked.

"No. No, it wasn't runnin' away from Philip I was. The atmosphere in the house was oppressive, always was, as long as I can remember. But as we got bigger it became confrontational. Likely explode into violence at any time. Especially the way Philip was. Me mother would shuffle around the house with this shroud of fear over her face, as if she were scared she'd be dumped at the door of the workhouse any day. So she said little, other than to enquire what her husband wanted readying for his dinner. No, the reason I came to England was to bring Philip with me. Get him out of Dublin."

"Is Philip hereabouts? In London? Why did you not–"

"Whoa. Hold on, me lovely Peggy. It was you who got me started on me little story, you'll have to wait 'til ya see what happens. There's an order to things."

"Bernie, I've work in about three hours and I've had no sleep. I must know all this, so will you hurry up for Christ's sake."

Bernie took a slow sip of tepid tea.

"Bernie!"

"We were still in Trinity, but things were gettin' worse in the house. One day, me father had been chastisin' Philip about losin' all his money in a card game. I came home to find Philip with his foot on me father's throat. I wasn't sure I wanted to stop him, but I did. I knew then I needed to get Philip away, before he ended up killin' the oul' fella."

"You were concerned about *him* after what he did to you both?"

"Yes, I was. Plus, I suppose, I didn't want Philip getting' arrested for murderin' the oul' bastard."

"My God, Bernie."

"I called it 'Flight to Freedom'."

"Pardon?"

"The plan I hatched. I called it 'Flight to Freedom'. Philip liked that."

"You hatched a plan?"

"The plan was to stow away on one of me father's new ships to Holyhead."

"You raving–"

"In Holyhead, we'd change our names, assume new identities and start our new lives. We loved the irony of stealin' away on our father's vessel. We'd money to buy a chartered crossin', and it would've been a lot more comfortable, but that ship wouldn't be our father's ship. And it wouldn't've been stealin' from 'im."

"Your irony's not lost on me," she said.

"Philip was delighted with the plan. As the designated evenin' drew near we barely contained our excitement. Philip, especially. He was always thankin' me and tellin' me about how he was goin' to do *this* in England and do *that* in England. He was especially lookin' forward to changin' his name. The more he talked, the more certain I was we were doin' the right thing."

"I sense doom here, Bernie. By the way you're talking."

"Nineteen I was, Philip a year younger, both virginal and innocent, both givin' up the Trinity College education. We headed for Kingstown in the pourin' rain. When there, we entered the port easily enough and as it was my plan, it was agreed I'd go first. I made me dash for it and sneaked onta the boat alongside a covered wagon laden with grain for export. I remember it pissin' from the heavens, the rain bouncing off the canvas into me ear and down the neck of me shirt."

"And Philip?" she asked, the doom bearing down on her.

"When Philip made his run, wasn't he spotted by a group of patrollin' Kingstown Harbour Police? They likely mistook his intention to be stealin' the grain so nabbed him. He fought well, knockin' two of them onta their arses, but there were plenty left and sure they pulled him over and gave him a liberal taste of his own medicine. The batons were swingin' and the boots and fists were flyin'. I can remember the odd flash of red cuff from under their raincoats as they laid into 'im. He used to admire the police an' all. That night changed his tune, I know. And d'ya know what I did? Whilst all this went on?"

She shook her head.

"Nothin'. I did nothin'. Should I go back? Shouldn't I go back? All this goin' through me head. I hesitated. Then it was too late, they dragged him away, kickin', and shouting at me."

"Shouting? Shouting what?"

"He said... He told me go ahead with the plan. 'Go on, Bernie', he said. When he shouted that, the police were looking round like boars after a truffle, tryin' to see who 'Bernie' was. But I was safely on the boat."

"Then that's what he wanted. You to go ahead with the plan."

"I'm not so sure... Anyway, the Royal Mail ship *Connaught* steamed out of Kingstown without Philip, and with me drying off in a small cupboard near the mail-sorting room. I was headed for Holyhead on me own."

"I thought you told me you arrived here via Liverpool?"

"There was a big flaw in Flight to Freedom. We thought we were headed for Holyhead, but the ship went to Liverpool."

"But then... what about Philip? You'd be waiting for him in Liverpool, whilst he'd be thinking you were in Holyhead. That's a calamity."

"I think y've the measure of it."

"You were clever enough to get into Trinity College, the pair of you, but stupid enough to catch the wrong boat?"

"I think y've the measure of it, again."

"Holy God in heaven above. And did Philip try to get to Holyhead, or Liverpool, or anywhere?"

"I haven't seen nor heard from him since."

Chapter 11
Lecarrowanteean, Ireland, 1877.

It included a single-roomed, stone-built cottage with a chimney fireplace, but Jimmy Walshe always described his tenancy as "a close-to-thirty-acre field". To find it, he'd advise, you must ask for the townland of Carrow. No-one ever uses its full and proper place name of Lecarrowanteean (and many will never have heard of it). Carrow, Jimmy Walshe told everyone, is the loveliest little townland in the civil parish of Rathreagh, about an English mile and a half from Kincon town.

There is a turnoff on the Killala to Kincon road, where a wilful Cloonaghmore River turns away from its eventual estuary in Killala Bay and heads back inland. Take the turnoff and follow the stony, cart-wide track up its gentle incline a short distance. There you will find the Walshe cottage.

They survived off a sloppy-triangle shaped plot of land, bordered on its longest side by the track and on the other two sides by the sinuous course of the Cloonaghmore. The tenancy includes access to a fuel-providing peat bog, but for Jimmy Walshe, the field was everything.

As a 'tenant at will', all that bound him to his farm was the consent of the landlord. No formal contract or lease existed. The benefit of any improvement went to the landlord without recompense. For Jimmy's father, this was deterrent enough to ensure his family struggled to eke a living from the poor quality soil all of his father's life. Jimmy didn't think that way.

To him, the thirty-acre field was his salvation. If they nurtured the field, he reasoned, the field would nurture them. From day-one of him inheriting the plot, he made his plans and set about a life-long programme of land improvement.

Early on in his governance, he adopted a system described to him at length by a Scotsman he met at the Ballina Fair. The Scotsman called it 'four field crop rotation'. It was a new thing from England, and the Scotsman convinced him that by rotating his crops, as one crop depleted the soil of nutrients, the next replenished it. He also enriched the soil with manure bought from a neighbour in Coolcran. The steaming cart load, dumped trackside, was spread over the field from a wicker creel lashed to Jimmy's back.

The tilling, harrowing and sowing of each quarter of the field was carried out to a strict schedule, regardless of weather. Rain, hail or snow,

Jimmy worked the field. Liam thought it work to break the back of a stallion, but to his father, labour in the field was labour of betterment.

"The land *must* be nurtured," he'd say to Liam. "Ya must allow it to be as good as it can be."

No affordable improvement was too onerous. Two years previous, Jimmy embarked on utilising the field's natural slope to the river to drain excess water with underground ducts. Though costly in time and resources, many runs were now complete. Jimmy would confess his sinful pride to Maggie, who would reassure him the sploshing of the channelled water as it trickled into the Cloonaghmore, was the sound of God saying, "Well done".

The north-western edge of Ireland is predominantly set to a peaty soil. It is a natural phenomenon, determined during the ice age ten-thousand years earlier. The black soil is acidic, prone to water-logging and stubbornly infertile. When tilled, drained and fed, it changes its composition, becoming an excellent soil for planting. Through his nurturing, Jimmy Walshe turned the soil a nutrient-enhanced brown crumb that stood out from the darkness of surrounding acres. A bird of the air would see the contrast. He transformed the field into one of the richest patches of tillage in the whole of County Mayo. As fine a field as ever a crow flew over.

Chapter 12
London, England, 1876.

Bernie told Peggy he lasted almost twelve months in Liverpool. He survived amongst other Irish immigrants, living in black and baneful slum cellars. The same cellars that had earlier been condemned and bricked-up under prescription from Dr William Henry Duncan, Liverpool's first Medical Officer of Health.

It was whilst breaking into one of these pestilent cellars that he got into his first fight in foreign lands. A group of Irish Gypsies were about the same business and took exception to his interference. They tried to intimidate him away. A brawl ensued and, as can happen when a conflict ends in mutual respect, Bernie ended up befriending one of the men.

"He said I fought well. Ya see, I was good, once." Bernie coaxed a smile from his aching face. "Fast hands, he reckoned."

"Is that right, now?" Peggy said, raising an eyebrow. "I'll have to watch out for them."

"'Ya might come in useful,' he said to me."

"Oh, Lord."

He explained to Peggy how he spent much of his time calling to the dock each day. He learned the arrival times of incoming steamers and, in the vain hope of finding his brother amongst them, scanned the flood of frightened, hungry-looking passengers as they descended the gangplanks.

He did a lot of fighting in Liverpool. He fought with the police and with gangs of Orange Lodge men whose Saturday night entertainment was to come around and launch attacks on 'the Micks'. And he fought with the Gypsies.

As he finished his tea, Bernie said he thought himself lucky to have survived it all. "Those cellars were riddled with cholera, typhus, everythin'. They were fishin' corpses outta the River Mersey on a daily basis. Whites, blacks, Chinese, everyone. Those that weren't murdered and thrown in, had jumped in themselves."

Bernie said he became a "handy" fighter. He was light on his feet, lean and fast and broad shouldered. In anticipation of exploiting his skills, the Gypsies put him to train with their best fighters. He even represented his adoptive clan in a bare-knuckle fight to settle a dispute over the ownership rights to a Liverpool street of prostitutes. He won.

Long after the futility of the wait for his brother had caught up with him, Bernie left Liverpool. The failure of the potato crop had prompted an invasion of Irish, some of whom stayed, and some of whom transitioned their typhoid-ridden bodies onward across the Atlantic to America or Canada. The reception for new arrivals at Liverpool was, in the main, hostile. The city was ill-prepared for the influx and the British Government determined the best way to deal with the flood of immigrants was to recruit thousands of extra constables and draft in extra soldiers from London. It was following a conversation with a petrified East-end squaddie that Bernie decided to go against the flow of the infantry and head for London.

During that journey, he adopted the surname of his Liverpool Gypsy patron, Matty Cooper O'Malley, self-declared 'King of all Gypsies in England'. He thought Matty would be pleased by such a show of regard.

"I went ahead with that part of the plan," Bernie said. "I changed my name. Called meself O'Malley. But I brought more than a new name to London. I also carried the shame of leaving Philip in Kingstown."

"You did what he wanted you to do," Peggy said, gathering the cups.

"I often wonder if he attempted another escape. I hope not. As bad as Dublin was, Liverpool was worse."

"And in London you carried on fighting for money?"

"Seemed to suit me."

Peggy held his stare.

He managed a shrug. "Won some, lost some. Met Partridge. Won more than I lost. Made a bit o' money. Prob'ly not as much as Partridge."

"It's nearly six o'clock," she said, stretching. "There's no point in me taking a sleep now." She threw swollen shadows over the walls as she moved towards the bed. "Would you look at the mess of the candle? Nearly extinguished, like meself."

"So that's the answer to your question, Peggy Deagan."

"My question…? That seems a while ago." She ruffled back the blankets. "It's guilt is all. But you know that. Guilt's why you fight. A Trinity education and you end up fighting? A wonderful waste. But the guilt has ate into you. Every man you go up against is your father. Every blow you take is your share of the abuse. And you think punching their heads off will give you your redemption."

Bernie drew a deep breath, pursed his lips and sank into the arm of the couch. He'd never told the story to anyone before. He felt lighter for it. Peggie, somehow, brought him respite from his troubles. His shame became insignificant, his pains became tolerable and his anger melted. She eased it all. She cared. For the first time in his life, he was with someone who cared.

"But let me tell you, Bernie Kelly-O'Malley," she said. "Fighting won't ever work for you. Look at yourself. You've beaten your body into a wreckage for thirty years and you're still feeling guilty. You're still angry. Your body can't take any more. You have to find another way." Peggy flopped herself onto the bed and closed her eyes. "You have *me* now."

And she was all he needed, he realised. She healed him. It dawned on Bernie that he had got through the night without a drink. "I'll speak to Partridge about quittin'," he said, but Peggy was asleep.

Chapter 13
London, England, 1876.

"I'm supposed to be a cat, too," Bernie O'Malley said.

Its wheezy, droning purr and the lumps of shaggy fur gathered around its rump, gave it the presentation of an asthmatic, feline ragamuffin. The scrawny tomcat wound itself around his ankles.

"The dead arose and appeared to many!" Mr Gregory Partridge announced. He dipped his head as he entered the back room from the small corridor. "Isn't that what you Irish say at a long-awaited meeting of an old friend? Or have I it wrong?"

The Gun, sited close to London's dockside iron foundries, was a favourite hostelry of Lord Horatio Nelson. Partridge appreciated the pedigree of the clientele.

He looked resplendent in his grey, three-piece Scotch-stripe suit. There were velvet covered cuffs on the frock coat. He placed his top hat on the counter with his gloves and cane, careful to avoid landing them in a spill of ale, and ran his fingers back through the generous mass of hair. His round head was a snowball of white. He repaired the hat-flattening and tweaked his neat moustache and beard into alignment.

"My God man, you look worse for wear," he said. "Where on earth have you been? I was beginning to think you were dead my good man. You didn't die did you? And have come back to haunt me like some pugilistic Jacob Marley? I must admit you took some beating. How are you? Are you alright? It's been almost a week and I hadn't heard from you. I was beginning to worry about you. Where have you been?"

Bernie waited for Partridge to stop asking questions. "I believe you owe me some money," he said. The cat at his feet padded off.

"Two halves of ale, potman," Partridge said to the podgy publican who had appeared behind the counter. "And make sure they're full measures." He turned to Bernie as the publican shuffled away. "Yes, yes I do. Unfortunately, not nearly as much as I'd hoped. You were supposed to win that fight, Bernie. Quite a considerable payday for both of us had you floored that monster. No matter, something else is arranged. You'll be glad to know that whilst you have been sitting around, licking your wounds, I have been working. I am your manager after all, that's what I do. I'm here to take care of you."

"Talkin' about which," Bernie said. "Where the hell did you get to after the fight? I was left lyin' in the alley bleedin' to death, and *you* were nowhere to be seen."

"Yes, well, sorry about that my good man, but I was involved in an altercation of my own following your spectacular knock out. I had some important people betting on your victory, which I more-or-less assured them of, and they were none too pleased when you went spilling backwards over the bags of hay. One even sent his man over to remonstrate with me. Bladdy sore losers those Members of Parliament. So that's where I was, sorting that little mess out. Where the bladdy hell did you get to anyway? When I got around to seeking you out, I was pointed in the direction of the alley door and you had vanished. I feared they had thrown you in the wharf to hide the evidence of a murder. I'd make sure they would lock them all up and throw away the key if they had bladdy killed you, you know?"

The publican placed the half-filled pint pots of ale on the worn counter and glanced at Bernie's face.

Bernie noticed the 'stock-take'. He was used to it. Customers with smashed up faces tended to worry publicans. He picked up his drink and gulped some down.

Partridge peered in over the rim of his jug to check it was a reasonable measure before he lay down his money. Immune to such shows of distrust, the podgy publican gave no reaction, scooped the coins off the counter and left for the front bar.

They sat at a table.

"A friend rescued me," Bernie said. "And a good job she did 'cause I'd've died in the alley waitin' for you."

"Ah. Would that friend who rescued you be the lovely Peggy Deagan? What's her story, Bernie? Is she divorced or widowed or something? Can't believe she wasn't snapped up long ago. You're a lucky man, Bernie, old boy. I would love to have found myself a woman like her. A lovely bit of jam alright, even if red hair is not quite vogue. I can only imagine how she looked when she was younger. I picture a Goya painting of a reclining model from the turn of the century, its title escapes me."

Bernie was unsure how he felt about Partridge imagining how Peggy looked when she was younger. He knew of two reclining-model paintings by Goya, both of *La maja*, who had black hair. He hoped Partridge meant the clothed version.

Partridge clasped his tiny hand onto the jar of ale.

"I did see her, shall we say, at the fight," Partridge said. "I can't say she was watching the fight, because I don't think she saw much of it at all. Hidden behind those beautiful slender fingers of hers she was, most of the time. Is that where you've been these last days, convalescing beneath the beautiful slender fingers of the lovely Peggy Deagan?"

Bernie didn't answer.

"No matter," Partridge said. "That is all in the past and we must consider the future. I have your career to think of. I have the next bout–"

"I must talk to you about that," Bernie interrupted. He directed his good eye at Partridge. There was no easy way to tell him. "I've had enough. I won't be havin' any more bouts. I can't continue. I finally admit I'm too old. It's time I got meself proper work. London's full of proper work. I'll look for some that says 'Irish need apply'."

Partridge blinked as the statement sunk in.

"I see. Has the lovely Peggy Deagan been turning your head, Bernie? I can well imagine she has. And I'm not surprised, quite frankly. I would imagine she has a low opinion of the noble art of bare-knuckle fighting after watching your recent display. What the hell was wrong with you by the way? You were fighting as if you were drunk." He paused, waiting for a response. "You weren't drunk were you? You bladdy were. You bladdy fool, Bernie. We've spoken about this, you and I. Blast, I knew I should have checked you over before you went out. I would have smelled the alcohol and stopped you."

Bernie snorted and smiled.

"Don't give me one of your smirking snorts, I certainly would have stopped you. You're no use to me dead, are you, Bernie O'Malley?"

"No matter," Bernie said. "I won't be carryin' on with the fightin'. I'll find another way of exorcisin' me demons. No more fightin'. With immediate effect. That's what I came here to tell ya. And to collect me money."

"Of course, of course, don't worry about your money. You know I'll be good for that." Partridge took a small swig. "Not bad stuff at all," he said, looking into the dark, amber interior of his beer for signs of floating sediment. "Bernie, I want you to consider one more bout. I've been–"

"Hey, whoa-up there. Are ya not listenin'? Lookit, we've done alright out of each other these last few years, you and I. But I'm comin' up on fifty years of age. I must be the oldest scrapper in town. I took a beastin' last time, I reckon on losin' the sight in me left eye, me head hasn't stopped thumpin' in the last twelve months and I've still got broken bones floatin' around in me hand. I can hardly pick up a pot of ale without pain up as far as me earhole. This work will be rid of me, once and for all. I must take my leave before it's too late. And I've found someone worth leavin' for."

Partridge leaned back in his chair.

Bernie noticed him survey the eye, now a puffy, purple slit. It was clear Partridge had spent time arranging this next fight, so Bernie expected him to put up an argument. He was ready to refuse every offer.

"I see. She has turned your head hasn't she?" Partridge said. "I fully respect what you're saying, but hear me out. I cannot hide from you the fact that you are older than every man you fight, but it is also a fact that you are better than most of the men you fight. I will restrict your bouts to an older age group if that's what you want. There are plenty of aged fighters out there still eager to turn a coin in this noble art but, if you are serious about giving it all up, then that's what we'll do. We will close the partnership down, terminate our agreement, end our association... But I do have one last fight for you."

Bernie looked away and shook his head.

"It would be the perfect way to end your pugilistic career. The biggest payday of your life."

"Yea, yea, I heard all this be—"

"No, Bernie please, my good man. Do hear what I've got to say. When you've listened to me, you make your decision and I will accept it. Either way."

Bernie swigged the last of his ale and placed the pot on the table. "Talk then."

Partridge stood and rapped his cane on the counter. When the potman arrived he ordered a full pint for Bernie.

"Thank you," said Bernie, as Partridge placed the pot down.

"Is not sláinte the salutation of choice for you Irish?" Partridge raised his beer pot without drinking. There was no-one else in the small bar except the thin tomcat, preening itself in front of the lively fire. He leaned in towards Bernie. "This next fight is against Thomas Eldridge, under London Prize Ring rules, or at least a variant of it."

"'Steam Engine' Eldridge? He's a bit above my—"

"I know he's good, Bernie. Or at least he was good. But his pre-eminence is on the wane. I'm afraid he was beaten in his last two bouts. Now two losses do not a tomato-can make. Two defeats could be one of those unfortunate coincidences that will not happen again for a long time. Or, and this is what his people are concerned about, he is in his de-ascendancy."

"Like Walter 'Crowbar' Cornwallis," Bernie muttered.

"Who? My word, you're going back to when God was a boy with that name. Big Ben was only a pocket watch in his day. What about old Crowbar?"

"Nothin'," Bernie said, and took a slug of ale.

"To return to the point, then, Eldridge's management team are looking for a big payday before it's too late for them all."

"He has a management *team*?" Bernie said. "And I've you? You're not even in my corner when I need ya."

"I will take that as a compliment on my ability to do for you, what it takes a team to do for Thomas Eldridge. As you know Bernie, Eldridge is a *name*. He's a *big* name. He is one of the biggest earners in the illicit fighting business, so he can afford a team. However, and here's the angle, our Mr Eldridge has been profligate with his finances, squandering it all on gambling and on the upkeep of his own personal harem. As, of course, is his entitlement, I am not here to judge. But I suspect the hangers-on that make up his *team* are an even greater drain on his resources than his gambling and his harem put together. It pleases me not one bit to report it, but Thomas Eldridge has not one penny to his name."

"And you know all this how?"

"Let me finish, please. His financial embarrassment presents us with an opportunity. He is managed by his brother, Connor, who is older, wiser and more astute. Not unlike my good self, don't snort. And I believe he, at least, has the lad's best interests at heart. He wants this bout to be a pay-day for his brother. Something substantial that he can put aside for his retirement. Which, sadly, could be any day now."

"Why London Prize Ring rules? It might be a pleasant change to fight under Queensberry. Aren't they the future?" Bernie asked.

"Oh come now... Nobody is interested in seeing men fight with padded gloves, Bernie. This three-minute round nonsense is a complete distraction. Do you think for a moment that people are interested in watching fighters sit down and take a whole bladdy minute's rest after every round? Not at all, it completely disrupts the contest, breaks up the action too much. The Marquess of Queensberry may be a perfect gentleman but, I regret, the clientele we cater for is not. No, we draw the confidence trickster, the pornographer, the pimp, the cabinet minister, the full panoply of felons, Bernie. Keep fighting underground, I say, where it belongs. It avoids all the absurdity of interfering regulatory bodies."

Partridge paused to watch Bernie take a generous sup from his drink. "Anyway, not everyone makes the transition from fist to glove successfully," he said. "Take Tom Sayers, from Camden Town. In the sixties he beat men twice his size with his fists, lost to men half his size with gloves. God rest his soul. I'll be your cornerman for this last fight, how's that?"

"Except you're bloody hopeless. For a start, you're never—"

"Steady now, Bernie. Let's not get objectionable. I think it wholly appropriate that I take on the duties of your second for your last and final bout. I consider it the least I can do."

"The least you can do is turn up. It'll make a change for me for anyone at all to be in me corner. Aren't them the rules, that I have a man in me corner?"

"Rules are only for measuring a man's reach with his fist, Bernie. As I say, keep fighting underground, that way you make up your own rules. Much more exciting that way."

Bernie scoffed. He didn't want to be involved in any of this. He'd given his word to Peggy. "Thomas Eldridge up against me won't draw much of a purse."

"You are right, Bernie O'Malley, you are absolutely right." Partridge nodded his head. "And I am only too aware of that. We intend to make the money not from the purse, but from our good friends in the thriving and illegal, bookmaking business."

"You'd only get decent odds on me beatin' Eldridge and that won't happen."

"We will get the best odds on you, that is also right." Partridge looked around the empty bar again and lowered his voice to a whisper. "But what if I told you, Bernie O'Malley, that you *will* beat Thomas Eldridge?"

"I wouldn't believe ya."

"Now Bernie, I need you to listen to the rest of my proposal without any histrionics. I don't wish to offend your sense of fair play. In fact, I would rather like you to suspend your sense of fair play for a while." Partridge paused. "I want you to bear this one thing in mind. This fight game is a dirty business and gambling is a dirty business, too."

After stating what Bernie thought was the obvious, Partridge sat back in his chair as though he had said something profound. Ignoring the confused glaze on Bernie's face, he leaned in again.

"If one group could gain an advantage over the other and in the process prise a few pound out of it, then they would do so. It goes without saying, my good man. It's dog-eat-dog. I shouldn't have to explain this to you, you've been at the sharp end of this fight game too long for me to—"

Bernie put down his pot. "You haven't told me how I'm going to beat Thomas Eldridge."

"Bernie, wait, I'm getting to that. You will be pleased to learn that the outcome of this fight has been predetermined. It will be a fixed fight. Thomas Eldridge will take a dive. No, don't turn away, listen to me. This is the perfect way for you to retire out of this sordid industry. Bernie, I have recently acquired a considerable inheritance, which, quite frankly, I have no interest in operating. It will likely fall to ruin in time, but meanwhile, I do intend to put its value to work."

A fixed fight? Putting one over on the bookies? Partridge had been busy, but his plan was making no sense to Bernie.

"I intend to use this inheritance as collateral to release significant sums of money. This money I will use to spread bets across some carefully-selected bookmakers in the city, on you, at most attractive odds. Eldridge and his team are obviously in on this little venture.

"The secret is in spreading the bets as widely as possible so as not to raise suspicion. We are looking to involve some of your Dublin bookmaker friends. There is even talk about Paris. I hadn't realised that bare-knuckle was large in Paris, but according to Mr Connor Eldridge it is. Paris, it seems, has fully recovered from its wounds of revolution and, apparently, an aspect of its renaissance is a keen interest in bare-knuckle competition. Who would have credited that four years ago?"

"I can't believe you're tryin' t'do the bookies outta money. If them boys catch up with ya they'll feed ya stones 'till ya can eat no more and dump ya in the Thames."

"The bookmakers won't do too badly out of it. There will be plenty betting on Eldridge, we just need to publicise it properly. But you leave that end of it to me, that's what I do."

Bernie noticed Partridge tilt his head at him and peer through the white eyebrows. He thought it a look of disapproval.

"I need you to do one thing for me though, Bernie."

He'd already asked him to go into the ring with Thomas Eldridge and was suggesting he get involved in a scam to rob the bookmakers, the most ruthless gang of thugs in London. But there was something more he wanted. Partridge never had enough.

"Apart from risk me life?" Bernie said.

"Stay off the old booze before the fight, my good man. You're starting to redden up and it's not from the punches. Not wishing to be offensive, but I smell you from here. And try as you might, you cannot hide that tremor in your hand... Listen Bernie, I need you in there up to snuff. You must be in tip-top condition."

"I don't believe Thomas Eldridge is going along with this," Bernie said, ignoring the last remark.

"His manager-cum-brother, or brother-cum-manager, whichever you prefer, assures me he is one-hundred percent going along with it. He needs the money... What do you say, Bernie? One last, short, say, three-minute fight, and you walk off with your pockets full of notes and coin."

"It's too dangerous," Bernie said. "I won't be doing it."

"Bernie, my good man. It's too rich not to do it."

Bernie stared at Partridge. The well-groomed hair, the expensive frock coat over a woollen suit, the manicured beard and moustache, all made Partridge easy to dislike. Partridge was trying to manipulate him into conspiring in his latest scheme. It wasn't Partridge who would be in the ring. It wasn't Partridge who would be putting his life at risk. Who the hell did Partridge think he was?

Bernie reached for his empty ale pot, trying to conceal the tremor.

Chapter 14
Farmhill, Ireland, 1823.

As far as her father was concerned, Harriet Gardner killed her mother.

The pregnancy had been difficult, the doctor having to take up residence in Farmhill House for four months, and John Gardner almost lost his wife to childbirth. Instead, he lost part of her. It seemed to him that when birthing Harriet, along with towel-fulls of blood, she haemorrhaged what he loved most about her. Her joy, her confidence, her ability to cope when he couldn't, her love of life. It all died when Harriet was born.

The depression lasted two years and caused hair loss (her eyebrows disappeared from her puffed-up face), deafness and intense fatigue. Her heart no longer wanted to go on, so it slowed until it failed altogether.

"You're going to think me callous, George," John Gardner said. He drained his glass and stared across the room at his brother-in-law.

Colonel Saint George Cuffe frowned.

"I hold the infant responsible for Elizabeth's death," Gardner said.

"John! Don't be ridiculous, man. You can't—"

"Were it not for the child, George, my wife, your sister, would be alive and well and taking a measure with us this evening."

"I know nothing of these matters, sir, but to blame the child?"

Gardner pushed himself out of his chair, staggered to the side-cabinet and re-filled his glass to the brim. "I wanted a son, George," he said, his back to his visitor. "A son and heir. I got a daughter, who killed my wife. It's my faith in God that sustains me, George. But for my faith, I would be done for. This is, indisputably, the most difficult time of my life."

"John—"

"If my sister were still alive in London, that's where I would dispatch her. Instead, I have to suffer the persecution of seeing her grow up here, with me. I am bereft of feeling for the child, and I fear that will never alter. All I wanted for was a son, George."

"John, you are still young. You will marry again. You'll marry, and you shall have your son. Fear not about that, my man."

Eight years later, Harriet's father re-married. Within ten months a baby arrived. Another daughter for her father, a new half-sister for Harriet. With a new wife and daughter to entertain him, eleven-year-old Harriet realised she needed to fight to retain any kind of position in her father's affections. It was a fight she was destined to lose. Ever hopeful of a son, her father went on to give Harriet six half-sisters.

As Harriet reached her pubescent years, what was always a difficult relationship with her father became an impossible one. He was engrossed in tending to the needs and wishes of his new wife and the ever expanding family of girls she bore him. Harriet's relationship with her father splintered further, each new half-sibling another wedge, widening the chasm between them.

Step-mother abetted her husband's behaviour. A jealous protectiveness of her own children fostered a resentment, bordering on untrusting fear, of Harriet. It didn't take much pushing on the wedges to convince her husband that Harriet had to go.

Her bachelor uncle, the wealthy Colonel Saint George Cuffe, took on the rearing of Harriet. She went to live with the Colonel at Castle Gore in the small village of Deelcastle. It was the Colonel who guided Harriet through her formative years, instructing her in the only curriculum he was familiar with.

She learned how to hunt on horses, stalk and shoot red deer in the forests, fish salmon and trout from the River Deel, and pack and smoke a pipe. During the frequent rambunctious retreats her uncle arranged for his wealthy, landed-gentry friends, her uncle taught her to drink. She was grateful, the drinking helped stupefy the pain of her father's rejection.

Meanwhile, her embittered father sat down with his legal advisors to write a will bequeathing the estate to his nephew, his only surviving male relative. He made the mistake of declaring the will to his family *ante mortem*. The children of his second marriage contested it. So did Harriet. Harriet the more ruthless, the half-siblings outdone by her mercenary determination.

Susanna Pringle was a twenty-eight-year-old evangelical Protestant fundamentalist when she arrived in Ireland during the years of the potato blight. The purpose of her journey from Scotland was to convert Catholics. She worked with the Reverend Edward Nangle, who had established a Protestant settlement on Achill Island, on the west coastline of County Mayo. The settlement, in the heart of Irish-speaking Catholicism, was where Pringle commenced her evangelical mission. She wielded the soup-filled brachán pot with extreme evangelical fervour, providing sustenance only to those Catholics conceding to convert. A master proponent of 'souperism'.

Harriet and Susanna met at a Protestant Society meeting one wild, winter's evening in 1850. Susanna had knowledge and experience of the law, having worked as a paralegal for a firm in Scotland. She was to be of considerable assistance to Harriet in her land acquisitions.

Harriet confided her predicament over her father's will in Pringle. Pringle went to work, uncovering a recent amendment to the Poor Law Act that introduced the crime of 'neglect of dependent children'.

Harriet threatened her father with court cases on spurious charges of childhood neglect unless his Will and Testament be altered. Ill-treatment, neglect and abandonment were all cited. She manipulated her uncle, the Colonel, into bribing a County Judge to backdate application of the law so it might apply to Harriet's circumstance. The threat of public humiliation in the courts was enough to make the proud, but tormented, John Gardner reconsider.

Through audacious manoeuvres and manipulations, Harriet regained fifty-percent of the property, with management rights over the entire estate. Harriet had salvaged her inheritance.

When she repossessed Farmhill House, evicting her widowed step-mother, Susanna Pringle became her companion and took up residence with her. Together, the two women formed a formidable alliance.

By 1878, Harriet was in control of over 4000 acres of County Mayo, the vast majority of it under tillage with spade husbandry prevalent. She had accumulated considerable wealth.

Chapter 15
London, England, 1876.

The two men stepped up to the mark.
"Fight!" the referee yelled and ducked out of the way.
The first round.

By the time of the fight, the rules had changed again. Jeremiah Johnston, the proprietor of the venue, insisted some of the revised rules be adopted. He had come up with a mixture of London Prize Ring and Queensberry. There were to be an unlimited number of three-minute rounds, with one-minute intervals. Holding, kicking, gouging and butting were outlawed. There were to be no padded gloves, hands were to be wrapped in cotton crepe bandage.

It had been three months since the meeting with Partridge in *The Gun*. Bernie felt strong. His left eye had little-to-no vision and was painfully infected, but the swelling had gone down. His hand hurt, but he used an extra-long length of bandage to extend the wrapping up his forearm to support the wrist. He was sober.

He had moved back into his own lodgings. Peggy told him to "clear the hell off" the fainting-couch when he told her he was going to fight again. The ensuing row had been raucous, Peggy incredulous at his stupidity. She told him any victory would be at such a devastating cost it would be tantamount to defeat. It would be impossible for him to win. "Only a thick eejit would fight in your condition," she had said. She mentioned something about a cat having nine lives being a myth, and that he should realise he only had one. At that point in the argument he decided to drop "The Cat" handle.

There had been threats from Peggy of never wanting to see him again. Bernie hoped them hollow and temporary. If all went well, he was confident in his ability to make it up to her. What could go wrong, the outcome was fixed?

For the first time in his fighting career, Bernie stood in a corner of a roped ring, enjoying a break for a whole minute. The first round had been a tenuous affair. Bernie had tested out his left hand and it stood up to the light blows he managed to land. Thomas 'Steam Engine' Eldridge was a renowned southpaw but instead of jabbing with his right he kept it hanging in the air for much of the time. He looked to Bernie like a boy seeking permission to leave the ring to make a piss.

The second fussed over Eldridge in the opposite side. There was a brotherly resemblance between Eldridge and his older assistant, enhanced by the grizzly sideburns and tightly shaven heads. Bernie wondered when the unreliable Partridge was going to turn up. Partridge appeared as Bernie was instructed to resume fighting.

Both fighters returned to the mark that split the ring in two. Eldridge looked vacant.

"Fight!" the referee instructed.

Eldridge's muscles rippled, but his dance was broken, unrehearsed or forgotten.

Bernie stepped around the right forearm – chassé – and landed blows to the body.

Eldridge absorbed the blows and traced Bernie with crazed, furious eyes.

Bernie landed a right hook to the jaw.

Eldridge's head snapped sideways and he retaliated. A straight left. Bernie reeled backwards into the ropes. The crowd roared its approval. Bernie had been hit by a steam engine. Eldridge chugged after him.

Bernie ducked under, clear of the piston fists. He avoided getting caught again for the remainder of the round. Eldridge grew tired. Sluggish. Easier to dodge. But he showed no sign of falling over. How hard did Bernie have to hit him? The outcome had been arranged. Something was wrong.

The round ended. Bernie walked to his side of the ring where Partridge now stood, dressed in his finery. If this were a proper fight, Bernie thought, he would be pleased with his performance.

"Something's wrong. He's not inclined to go down, but nearly finished me early on," Bernie said.

Partridge pointed to the blood coming from Bernie's left ear.

"What can ya do to stop it?" Bernie shouted.

"For goodness sake, I'm not a medical man," Partridge said.

"I need a bit o' cloth to plug it," Bernie yelled.

"I am without a handkerchief my good man and you're certainly not using my neck-tie."

"Your glove. Tear a finger off your glove. Hurry."

Partridge stared down at his white gloves. "You bladdy scoundrel. These gloves are a closely woven cloth of satin and twill weave."

"I'm bleedin' from me ear. Tear off a finger or I'm climbin' out this ring."

Partridge put down his cane, removed his gloves and tore off a finger of cloth with his teeth.

"These were not inexpensive gloves, I will have you know," he said, handing the fragment of cloth to Bernie.

Bernie stuffed the silken cloth into his ear, wondering what the bleeding meant.

The referee waved them together.

Both fighters stepped up to the mark for the third round. Bernie tried to make eye contact but Eldridge's eyes dashed around uncontrollably in their sockets. It put Bernie in mind of trapped mice.

"And fight!" the referee shouted.

Eldridge's dance was a stuttering hop.

Bernie caught him with a left jab. It was hard and sent a shooting pain up Bernie's arm. "Fall."

Eldridge didn't move.

Bernie landed a right, full on the mouth, bursting a lip. He danced left and whipped in another blow, this time to the body.

Eldridge stood his ground, arms outstretched and shook his head.

Bernie ducked an arm under and delivered an upper-cut to the chin.

Eldridge's head flew backwards but he stayed on his feet, not throwing any punches.

Bernie hit him again, square on the mouth, Eldridge's lip disintegrated. "Why don't you fall?!" Bernie screamed through the squall of the crowd.

Outside the ring, Partridge looked across at Connor Eldridge. Connor Eldridge returned the stare, worry and fear crowding his face. His brother was taking too much punishment.

Bernie drove a straight right to the solar plexus.

Eldridge blew blood from his mouth but remained upright.

Bernie delivered a blow to Eldridge's face with impunity. "Fall!"

Eldridge remained on his feet. He needed to go down to declare the fight over.

Bernie stalked the ring.

Eldridge maintained his position in the centre, pirouetting like a carousel, his arms sticking out like muscled sweep bars, powerful enough to hang horse poles from, unsure if he should rotate English or American. The man they called Steam Engine would not come to a halt.

Bernie ducked and danced, left and right, sizing up a punch big enough to end it.

Eldridge was like a bloody-faced lost child.

Bernie saw his opening. He grounded his feet and rotated from the hips, swinging a right hook to the head of Eldridge. It was, what Partridge called, "a floorer".

The punch hit Eldridge full force on the bridge of the nose, smashing bone. As though a pole ran horizontally through Eldridge's middle, his head went backwards, his feet went forward. Eldridge wheeled around the imaginary central axis. As his feet rose into the air, the back of his head smashed into the hard earthen floor.

Bernie heard the crack.

The referee heaved Bernie away.

Eldridge's assistants dipped between the ropes to tend their fighter.

The crowd shrieked and waved and shrieked. The favoured fighter had been knocked down. It was pandemonium.

Bernie raised a hand to the finely-woven material in his ear. When he looked at his hand again his fingertips shone red.

"Bernie, get out of that ring, now!" Partridge shouted from behind him.

Men crouched over Eldridge's body. Bernie went over. "How is he?" he asked.

Connor Eldridge rose to his feet. "You've fackin' killed him," he said.

Chapter 16
Farmhill, Ireland, 1876.

Harriet Gardner still rode a horse, but out of function rather than boisterousness, and her strong, broad shoulders still enabled her to handle a shotgun with proficiency. She had not fished for a good many years, but was rarely without the bit of a long-stemmed pipe in her mouth. And she drank. "But only to excess," as she liked to declare when wishing to shock polite company.

The drinking and the smoking were evident in her appearance. Her skin a pale, washed-out hue stretched shiny and translucent over the skeleton of her skull, sagged and wrinkled at her neck. Peat-black eyes peered from beneath unkempt greying hair, overlooking a florid, broken-veined nose, the sole contributor of colour to her bleached countenance.

Farmhill Estate extended over several parishes in the barony of Tirawley, County Mayo. Farmhill House in the townland of Farmhill, nestling in the parish of Rathreagh, acted as the estate's principal seat. A mile-long private road served the house, guarded at the gate by the nearby Kincon Constabulary Barracks.

Oxen grazed the fields leading to the house, and peacocks and turkeys often pecked and paraded on the front lawn. A dense, mixed grove of scots pine, sycamore and horse chestnut sheltered the house to the rear. Four acres of elaborate, ornamental gardens and orchard lay to the edge of the grove, enclosed within a twenty-foot-high, stout stone wall. Harriet's mother commissioned the gardens and orchard, with their winding pathways, symmetrical beds and regimented rows of Irish Russet apple trees. Harriet's father built the imposing wall to preserve his wife's legacy. For the wealthy Gardners, labour was cheap in 1824.

Outbuildings dotted the grounds. A large hay barn doubled as sleeping quarters for seasonal land workers. There was a small lodge-house for the Land Agent and a substantial stable for the horses.

The main house, built in 1780, had a flat five-bay, southerly-facing front. Two stories high, it had an additional dormer lodging in the roof for a serving couple. The façade was a plain arrangement of nine large, double-hung windows set symmetrically around a studded, oak front door. A fanlight of stained glass (manufactured in Birmingham, England by John Hardman and Co.) sat over the door, allowing blue, yellow and red light to fall into the staircased entrance hallway.

To accommodate his growing family of girls, John Gardner had single-storey wings built either side of the main house. Harriet and Susanna resided in the comfortable confines of the west wing, the east wing given over to the grand hall. The hall, its ceiling supported by several oak summer-beams sourced from forests in Wexford, was large enough to accommodate Harriet's collection of modern and antique art.

None of these comforts were affordable without the rent from the estate's five-hundred or so farming tenants. Rent was collected in an oak-panelled room to the right of the entrance hall.

By the 1870s, almost all agricultural land in Ireland was owned by men who rented it out to tenant farmers rather than cultivating it themselves. A quarter of the largest landowners in the country were absentee landlords, living outside of Ireland.

Farmhill Estate was an anomaly. Whilst managed by Harriet, she owned it jointly with an absent landlord living in England, her cousin. Her cousin had nothing to do with the running of the estate. Harriet arranged the transfer of funds adequate to satisfy him, and he kept away. A polite, formal letter once a year their only correspondence.

Harriet employed a steward, a Land Agent. A new man to the area by the name of William 'Billy' Cuffe. Billy Cuffe hailed from Dublin and claimed to have held stewarding positions throughout Ireland, most recently in Mayo for Lord Oranmore. She had been curious about his surname, though he was disinclined to claim any relationship to her uncle, Colonel George Cuffe. It suited Harriet to employ an agent without ties to the locality and in an uncharacteristic show of affectionate deference to her dear uncle, she thought it a fitting tribute to employ a man with the same surname.

Billy Cuffe was tall with well-cut features and broad shoulders. Harriet wanted a man with broad shoulders. The handsome countenance was gratifying, but to do the things she wanted done, a man needed broad shoulders, both physically and metaphorically. She didn't believe a word of what he said about his previous experience. No matter, he seemed intelligent, polite and well bred. He had dockets to show he attended Trinity College in Dublin for a while, and he claimed to be the son of a successful business man. Though his background was obscure, he spoke well and was someone, she believed, she could trust in public. He seemed robust enough for what she wanted. She hoped he proved himself a loyal and trustworthy servant. He would be tested.

Chapter 17
Farmhill, Ireland, 1877.

Maggie accompanied Jimmy Walshe on this occasion. He was stronger with his wife by his side and he needed all the strength he could muster to face the triumvirate of Harriet Gardner, Susanna Pringle and Billy Cuffe.

They dressed down. This was not the time to portray any sign of doing better than surviving. Maggie wore an old shawl, draped over her head and veiling her face like a persecuted Madonna. Jimmy had on a frieze coat with holed pockets and his split boots.

The land agent was impervious to such displays. Billy Cuffe understood the game, exhibiting only a poisonous mixture of bewilderment, repulsion and contempt towards the tenants that appeared before him in the rent room.

When prices were reasonable and crop yields satisfactory, Jimmy Walsh met the rent from the sale of his produce. In a good year, it provided funds to live in relative comfort and invest in further improving the land and house. In the later part of the 1870s, there were no good years.

Twice a year, Jimmy made the trek up the pathway to Farmhill House. With each step, a thin slice of his confidence fell away, crumbling on the stony surface of the path. He drew no reassurance from the oxen, herd-staring, judging him as he passed.

At the House, he would wait until invited into the rent room. The same wood-lined room every time. He made his rental payment, was informed of the rent for the following period and left. The Gardners had never known him to fail to pay his rent.

They entered the rent room and shuffled their way over to the stained hessian mat, their footsteps echoing against the panelling. The room smelled of linseed and the body odour of previous tenants.

"Your earnings are good again this year, Walshe," Cuffe stated as Jimmy and Maggie halted and raised their heads.

The three-person panel sat behind a large table, their inverted reflections gleaming in the well-oiled surface of the oak.

Jimmy doffed his stovepipe hat. "T'was modest enough now, Mr Cuffe, yer honour," he said. "Enough t' be meetin' the rent and little more is all we have, sir."

"And only then 'cause baby went without," Maggie Walshe added.

Cuffe shifted in his seat and glared at Maggie. "Does your husband think you have cause to speak, woman?" he asked her.

"I don't know, sir, but his wife does," Maggie replied.

Cuffe slapped a palm down on the oak table. "I'd thank you to shut your wife, Walshe."

Maggie tensed and glared at Cuffe with narrowed eyes.

Cuffe met her stare and before they broke the connection he let her see his eyes wander down her body. His head tilted slightly as a leering smile lifted the side of his mouth.

She turned towards her husband and tightened her shawl around her.

"Is that the best you can dress her, Walshe?" Cuffe said, mocking. "You do her or yourself no justice dressing her in rags."

"Sir?" Jimmy said. His ears reddened. He fidgeted with the brim of his hat, rotating it through his fingers. "Yer honour, the earnin's were scarce enough now, Mr Cuffe. And she says a mouthful, to be certain. The youngest isn't at all well, but sickly. I've also been workin' like the Divil, yer honour, spending a lot o' me time draining the top-end field. If truth be known, prob'ly too much of me time, but there's great improvement in it. I'll've it fully done before long, I'm almost at the riv–"

"Yes, the drainage. I was intending to broach the subject with you," Cuffe said, pulling his eyes from Maggie. "Your land is much improved by the drainage. I've been keeping a watch on it." He let the comment hang in the air. It was good to let Miss Gardner know he was on top of matters around the estate, even out as far as Carrow. "But more of that later. We'll sort this year's rent first. You have it with you? Hand it to Miss Pringle who will account for it."

Jimmy reached into his hat and withdrew the money, the notes dirty with grime and sweat.

"Year's rent eight pounds eight shillings, half year's rent, four pound and four owin'," he said, handing over the notes and coins, smiling. "You'll find it all there, Miss Pringle, ma'am," he added, nodding.

Pringle counted. She signalled with her eyes to Cuffe, indicating the payment accurate.

"Walshe," Cuffe said. "I don't miss a thing that goes on here on this estate and I clearly see the improvement in your plot. In fact, did we not speak of the very same matter this time twelve month? In this very room, was it not?" Cuffe didn't wait for replies. "I am hearing reports of increased yields and your crops fetching a handsome price at market."

"Mr Cuffe, sir, market prices are low and yields is only a taste higher. But whatever increase is in it is due to me efforts on the land. I've put everythin' inta the drains over the last years. I've worked hard on it, now. We're almost at the river with nearly all the drains, and–"

"I see the improvement myself, Walshe. You are now the occupant of a valuable piece of land, the evidence is clear. It's clear to everyone that your rent is wholly inadequate for a plot of such quality. I'm sure you yourself would agree and would, therefore, be accepting and fully understanding of Miss Gardner increasing your rent again this year. I trust I don't need to labour this with you, Walshe?"

"But it's by me own efforts and at me own cost the improvements have been made, sir," Jimmy blurted. "Miss Gardner, ma'am. I've even improved the track down to the river from the house and ya know it was meself that put on the chimney-stack. Would it not be reasonable to be takin' these things inta account ta hold the rent steady for a year ma'am, please ma'am?"

"Walshe!" Cuffe yelled. "You address your comments to me. I am Land Agent for Farmhill Estate and it is in that capacity I administrate the rental agreements. Are you clear on that, Walshe?"

Jimmy nodded and wiped the sweat from his brow with his hat. "I am, yer honour. I am."

"Then that's agreed. An increase in rent to eleven pounds and five shillings for the coming year, payable in the usual two instalments. Please make a note for the ledger, Miss Pringle."

"Mr Cuffe, yer honour, please. It's only just meetin' the rent we are. Please, can ya take inta account I did the work meself and at me own expense?"

"Has not the Prime Minister, Mr Gladstone himself, put laws in place to allow for improvements without increases in rent?" Maggie asked, directing the question at Miss Gardner.

Cuffe seethed in his seat. "Walshe, I've told you to shut your wife. What she says is incorrect. Miss Pringle assures me, and I, therefore, assure you, that compensation for improvements only applies at the time of termination of the tenancy. Is that what you want, Walshe? To terminate the tenan–"

"No!" Jimmy cut in. He bowed his head. "No, yer honour. That's not what we want happen. Not at all, sir."

"Should you change your mind, let me be the first to know, Walshe. The new rent has been logged. Your business here is finished."

Jimmy and Maggie were about to turn away when Harriet Gardner spoke.

"I don't see either of you at my mission," she said, her voice deep and nasal.

"Yer mission, ma'am?" Jimmy said. "I don't think I under–"

"My Protestant mission on the Ballycastle road. Not far from here, the journey no hardship. I don't see either of you attend."

"We're practisin' Cath-lics, ma'am. We attend mass in–"

"I know where you attend mass. But I might look more favourably on rent increases were you to attend my mission."

"I… We'll hafta see, ma'am," Jimmy said.

"Make sure you do, Mr and Mrs Walshe."

The butler awaited them in the entrance hall. He pulled back the heavy door. It saved having to clean it down if he avoided tenants touching the handles.

"Thanks, Michael," Jimmy said, nodding to the butler.

Michael didn't reply.

Maggie bridled. "Michael, d'ya know what I'm nearly sure of?" she said, pausing. "You're nowt but a feckin' fart-catcher."

As they crunched over the gravelled drive, Jimmy waved and nodded a 'So long' at the two members of the Royal Irish Constabulary posted at the steps of Farmhill House.

Chapter 18
Coonealmore, Ireland, 1879.

The blackthorn stick rises and falls, rises and falls. Its knobbly length whistles as it cuts the air. Its end thumps into the head of his father. Whistle, thump. Whistle, thump. The head becomes a hand that catches the blackthorn and snatches it away. It swings the stick at an exposed ankle. Cuffe squeals in agony, hopping. Steaming liquid drips from his face as he bends, stinking of piss. The blackthorn stick strikes him in the side of the head.

Liam wakes with a shiver. His mind crawls from the dream and tries to fathom why he is in a mist-blanketed field, entwined with Aiden, both buried beneath a covering of ferns. With consciousness comes sorrow.

He wonders if Aiden still dreams his 'flute dreams'. Aiden often slept with his podgy thumb between his lips, his fat little fingers rising and falling as though playing a gentle melody on a wooden flute. His father used to study Aiden's fingering, leaning over him in the crib, working out the tune being played. His father expected Liam to believe that his baby brother learned to play *The Piper's Maggot* in his sleep. It was the same tune every time.

"Where's Mammy?" Aiden asks, waking from Liam's stirring.

"We're on our way t' find her. And Da."

The boys scramble from their fern-lined grotto and urinate against the ditch. They direct their waters over a clump of soft, green stinging nettles, united in their conviction that stinging nettles deserve to be pissed on. Revenge for their mother forcing beakers of its greeny-black sour tea into them every summer. They traipse across the field, poking two holes in the mist.

By mid-morning, the starlings have chased the mist away, slicing it to pieces with their sweeps and loops. The boys reach a narrow lane that Liam hopes it will lead them to food and drink, as well as take them a little closer to Ballycastle. They follow the lane around the shoulder of a hillock and out across a vast, verdant field. Though the late-summer sun warms the grass beneath them, Liam's bare feet are numb with the cold.

A small herd of fawn heifers with white horns, soft eyes and turned up noses greet the boys at the far end of the field. The young cows are jumpy and stare with interest as the boys pass, ready to play or dart away.

Aiden is quiet. Liam is hungry. Progress is slow, Aiden full of short rests. The lane narrows to a path no wider than their feet. Another hour passes. Heads droop, lips crack.

The sun is at its highest point in the sky by the time the boys reach the river. The water has rubbed the path away, creating a wide crevice. The path's continuation is visible through a clearing on the opposite bank.

Aiden lays himself on the grass, coughs himself into a curl and closes his eyes to rest.

The river is too wide to leap. It looks shallow but flows faster than the Cloonaghmore, the river at the foot of Da's field. Wary of the eddies and whirls, Liam crouches and cups a handful of water into his mouth. It's cold but thirst-quenching.

"We'll have to cross it, Aiden," he calls back from the water's edge.

"Aiden can't," Aiden says.

Liam smiles. "I'll have t' leave ya here then."

"Nooo. Ee-am carry Aiden." Aiden sits up and holds his arms aloft.

"Alright so, little man, I'll take ya on me back. Come here for a sip of this, first."

Liam steadies himself and his cargo and lowers his ankles into the frigid, flowing water. The fine sediment on the stream's edge pushes between his toes. 'Cowbelly' his father calls this uncertain mix of solid and liquid. He takes another step and the water tugs at his ankles. His toes splay like only toes that have not experienced the confines of boots can, curling around the stones that armor the riverbed, gripping for purchase.

Aiden's legs stick out in front of them like the alabaster horns of the fawn heifers. He clings to Liam's neck.

A couple of steps further and the water splashes above Liam's knees, soaking the bottom of his ragged trousers and pushing against his thighs. The river is noisier, annoyed at their intrusion. Pushy and noisy. The tail end of Aiden's petticoat-dress bobs on the surface, lapping up the waves.

"Keep yer feet raised. Don't give the water any pull." Liam feels for the next boulder with a foot, his legs numb with the cold, and steps deeper into the river. The icy water, up to his waist, heaves against him. His breath comes in short gasps. A foot slips off a smooth rock and they stumble sideways. He twists and yelps as he feels himself toppling. His chest folds over into the water and Aiden shrieks into his ear as his horn legs dip into the bitter-cold river. Liam drags a leg through the water to regain balance.

"Ee-am. Hep me. I code." Aiden says, into the back of Liam's neck.

Liam leans into the flow of the river as he feels for the next foothold. His clothes are drenched. The river grows angrier, shouting now. It slaps him with its waves and pushes him with its current, determined to wash him and his load over and away. It's deeper than he thought it would be, and the weight of Aiden makes it difficult to stay upright. He steadies himself and takes stock, his chest heaves.

The fall has pushed them a few yards downstream, where thorny bushes crowd the bank. It will be difficult to climb out of the river here. He needs to move back upstream, against the flow, to reach the clearing on the other side.

They centre the river, its deepest point, the water flowing freely over Aiden's outstretched legs.

"I code, Ee-am!" Aiden shouts.

"Stop it!" Liam snaps. "Shut up. You're alright."

Aiden is not alright. The waves lap up his back. His body shivers and his teeth chatter behind blue lips. The weight of the drenched petticoat drags at him, pulling him off his mount. His hands start to slip from Liam's shoulders. With a jolt, he manages to join his two hands at the front of Liam's throat.

Liam coughs and chokes and reaches up, breaking the link to breathe.

Aiden falls back, tugged by the water, his arms waving around Liam's head. He digs his nails into a shoulder and clings on.

Liam winces. He wants to rip the head off his brother for making this so difficult. He recovers his breathing and feels for a footing, leaning into the flow. The next step raises them inches out of the water. Liam blows out hard, forcing his lungs to keep expanding and contracting. His arms hover out above the splashing surface.

"Keep holding!" he manages to shout, stepping onto another slime-covered boulder.

They near the far bank when a powerful, random rush of water pushes Liam over. He topples, shuffling his feet, searching for a secure stone. His feet find one and he pushes with all the strength left in his numb legs, diving for the riverbank. He stretches for the rushes that reach out to him and splashes into the water. Fear washes over him as his entire body submerges. A shocking cold clamps his skull and his ears fill with the gurgle of a moving river.

His hand reaches the rushes and he grips. He pulls his face clear, spluttering, gasping. Aiden's face collides with the back of his head. The dread grows as Liam's legs are lifted from the rocks and swept downstream. A ravenous river-creature, long, sinuous and scaly, swims through his mind. He clings to the rushes knowing if he lets go, they will be carried away and devoured by the creature.

As he tugs, he and his cargo drift towards the bank. He scrabbles for another grip, his fingers ruffling through a patch of blue-eyed grass. Insanely, he notices its small pale-blue flowers withering to an early-autumnal brown. He grips and drags himself and his brother to the water's edge. He scrambles them both up onto the bank and lies there, like a beached mariner, exhausted.

Aiden presses his body into Liam's back. Liam feels warm. Wet and warm.

"Aiden... Aiden ya need t' get off," Liam says.

Aiden clings for another moment before pushing himself up. His petticoat dress is transparent, a wet, cold, cotton film clinging to a thin, pale-blue, shivering body. Water from his hair drips down his arms.

Ascending the embankment, they turn and glance back at the water. They share a smile and Liam places a hand on Aiden's shoulder. The river drips off them onto the grass as they resume their way along the narrow track. They walk fast, grateful for the gentle heat of the mid-afternoon sun.

"I h-hungry, Ee-am," Aiden says, his teeth rattling as he shivers.

"I know, little man. I know."

Chapter 19
London, England, 1876.

When he heard he killed Thomas Eldridge, Bernie's mind shut down. He doesn't remember how he managed to escape the clamouring crowd. Nor did he remember what happened to Partridge. It had become the worst night of his life – he had killed a man. He sought solace in the gin.

He immersed himself in a drunken daze, hiding from what he had done, hiding from everyone. Immediately after the fight he returned, drunk, to his lodgings, but he became fearful people would look for him there. He left and spent several nights sleeping rough amongst those too wretched to afford the halfpenny for a doss-house kip. A coughing, consumption-ridden underclass of the homeless, thieves and drunks.

It helped being with people. The world felt bad enough for him to *need* other people, whoever they were. He sat amongst them drinking, and watched them argue, cough, spit and die. Come the night, he himself was ready to fall over, curl up and close his eyes.

Not everyone needed or wanted *him*. By Victoria Embankment, near Hungerford Bridge, two vagrants tried to relieve him of his gin and his money. They didn't ask, they attacked wielding lumps of wood. It was the rough rasp of a dog's tongue, licking at the discharge from his eye whilst he slept, that alerted him. Though he had been lying on the ground, half asleep and drunk, his attackers were weak and thin and didn't know how to fight. He left them both nursing bruised faces. The dog watched the fight, then wandered away.

After two weeks, Bernie searched for Partridge. He visited the usual meeting places. When he staggered into *The Gun*, he looked and smelled wretched. His clothes were damp and hung off his hunched frame. His eye had swollen again and wept a white puss. A scrap of bloody cotton plugged his left ear and his pores secreted the sour, fermented smell of sweat, stale ale and spirits.

The front bar was busy with rainy-Monday men, their pockets jingling with the retrieved housekeeping money they had handed to their wives the previous week. The podgy publican stared at Bernie with disdain and refused to serve him a drink. Bernie complained, and after he toppled a table, a few of the rainy-Monday men halted their conversation and turned in support of the publican. Even the tomcat by the fire wanted nothing to do with him. Bernie staggered from the warm, dry interior of *The Gun* and returned to the wet cobbled street.

He didn't have the courage to visit Peggy. He would wait until he had his money from Partridge before doing that. He thought he should sober up first, too.

He returned to the venue of the fight.

"You've got some nerve turnin' up 'ere," Jeremiah Johnston said, looking up from his chair. "You are a fackin' wan'id man, Mr O'Malley. Officers from the Metropolitan Police 'ave been down 'ere askin' about you, ma boy."

"The police?" Bernie said. He ran a hand under his cap, through his hair. His head throbbed. He hadn't touched a drop today.

"Yes, the fackin' Peelers. Had to swerve a couple of questions myself no thanks to you. Lettin' the odd illegal fisticuffs go on now and again is one thing. When a man ends up dead because of it, the Peelers get a bit anxious."

Bernie felt nauseous, a liquid-gurgle bubbled in his belly.

Johnston sat behind a battered oak desk in the storeroom that served as his office. "The bladdy state of ya. You look like shit stirred up in a bucket. Bladdy paddies, drink spirits out of an ol' whore's bang 'ole. You are wan'id for murder, Mr O'Malley."

The police? Murder? He dashed for a small wooden crate and vomited the watery contents of his stomach into it, the taste and smell of the regurgitated gin like rancid beef.

"You dirty barstud. Get the fack out my office!"

Bernie wiped his mouth on his sleeve. "Where's Partridge? I must find Partridge," he said.

"Partridge? You wanna know where–" Johnston laughed. "Don't tell me he's stitched you right up as well...? He has ain'ee? My giddy grandma. I'm afraid Mr Partridge has done a runner, Mr O'Malley. And I must say, I care not one wet fart about your predicament." Johnston smiled. "Oh, how lovely. He's played *everyone* for bladdy idiots. Listen, the only reason Thomas Eldridge's people aren't bangin' down them doors tryin' to get their 'ands on you right now, is they 'ate Mr bladdy Partridge even more than they 'ate you. You only killed The Engine, *he* did them out a money."

"Do ya know where he's gone?" Bernie asked, his stomach deciding whether or not it had more to abandon.

"I ain't got a pot o' glue," Johnston said. "No dickie bird's been takin' t' me. Wipe yer bladdy mouth will ya? Bladdy hell. But listen up, that ain't the last of it. The bookies are after you too, and dem boys don't mess about. Heed some advice, Mr O'Malley. I'd forget about Partridge and be gettin' the hell out a London."

"He was supposed to fall," Bernie said, not caring who knew about the fixed fight now.

"Out the country would be my suggestion, Mr O'Malley. Examine your options. If the blue bottles catch up with ya, you'll be spendin' the rest of your days in 'Olloway. If Eldridge's mob catch ya first, or even the bookie boys, there will be no rest-of-your-days t' worry about. I'm even gettin' nervous ya bein' 'ere in my office. Apart from the fact yer stinkin' the place out, someone might come to the conclusion I was in on it. I might be liable for 'arboring a fugitive or some such bladdy charge."

"He was supposed to fall!"

"So I 'erd... You were fixin' fights on my bladdy premises," Johnston said. "All went badly wrong didn't it, eh? Evidently, Mr Thomas Eldridge 'imself was none too keen on the idea of takin' a fall. In fact, he was dead against it. That'd be funny if this were not so serious. Turns out, anyway, his people drugged the poor barstud before sendin' 'im out to face you. God knows what they give him, but he was completely out-of-it. Wouldn't't've been able to see a hole in a bladdy ladder. Imagine your own bladdy people druggin' you to the eyeballs before sendin' y'out to fight. Dirty, fackin' barstuds, the lot of 'em. For them to do that, though, I'm calculatin' Partridge must now owe them a lot a money."

Bernie stared into the crate of vomit. His stomach heaved. He wondered if he could drown himself in the liquid mess.

Johnston rose to move from behind his desk but gagged on the stench from Bernie and the vomit and sat back down. "You were the only one in the ring who was in on the game, Mr O'Malley. That's why Eldridge took the beatin' and didn't go down. He stood there like a true bladdy fighter." A look of contempt worked its way across Johnston's gnarled face. "You got too greedy for extra coin, Mr fackin' O'Malley, and a genuine fighter got killed. All to rip off some bookie boys. And I'm none too pleased it all took place on my premises. So, Mr O'Malley, I now want *you* off my premises, takin' that crate a guts wiv ya, before I get my gun and shoot ya my bladdy self."

After listening to Johnston earlier that day, his intention was to get drunk again and throw himself into the canal. When he arrived canal-side, he lost courage. He convinced himself the water was too cold and too filthy to cast even his broken, wretched body into.

He stood on the bank, still as a heron stalking fish, arms hanging from slumped shoulders, clinging to a gin bottle. He gazed at his shadow in the stagnant, still water. He glanced up at the horse lumbering into view on the opposite bank, the horse leaning against the drag of a barge brimming with seaborne cargo. The Regent's was quieter since the Suez Canal opened, traders no longer dependent on using London as an intermediary port, but still it was busy. He turned and staggered to a small grassy verge. He dumped his drunken body down and thought about Thomas 'Steam Engine' Eldridge. He thought about Peggy. He thought about the swindling swine Partridge. He lay back on the grass and started to laugh.

It wasn't a happy laugh. It wasn't triggered by sensations of joy or humour or relief. It was a dark maniacal laugh. It was a laugh born out of shame, confusion and fear. A paradoxical laugh, brought on by dire circumstance and an alcohol-altered state of mind. When he stopped laughing, he cried. He, Bernie O'Malley, had killed a man. How easy it is to kill a man, how hard it is to live with it.

He took another swig of solace from his bottle.

Having avoided ending his life in the Regent's Canal, he checked off the other causes of death he was susceptible to. He had to avoid getting picked up by the police, if the Peelers caught him, they'd hang him. Hanging ceased to be carried out in public almost a decade earlier, but that comforted him not one bit. Hanging is hanging. Eldridge's people wanted revenge. It's unlikely they'd hang him, but hanging might seem the more favourable option when weighed against what they would do to him. The bookie boys were the main threat. Harder to avoid, they could be anywhere and will not allow a stunt like that to go unpunished. No. They will certainly kill him if they find him. And he needed to shake himself loose of the drink, it was already killing him.

What about Peggy? She might want to kill him. He wouldn't blame her. He couldn't go to her now. Whatever they had was lost and ruined. He ruined it. He needed to forget Peggy. If he could. What if he cleaned himself up? Could he clean himself up? What a damned mess. What a waste. The loss of something that was good. The only thing in his life that was good. 'Fine' is what they'd say at home. But 'beautiful' is the right word. Peggy was beautiful.

As the ripples from the barge slapped against the bank, he made up his mind. He knew what he had to do. He examined the gin bottle. The first step in his new plan was to cast it into the canal. He raised the mouth of the bottle to his lips.

Chapter 20
Coonealmore, Ireland, 1879.

A half mile after the river, the track redeems itself. Liam and Aiden hunker down behind a sparse gorse bush to peer at a straw-covered house.

The house looks drowsy. Grasses sprout up along its ridge like unruly sleep-hair and the thatch droops low over the door and window. The whitewash is cracked like the broken-veined face of an alcoholic banshee and a sparrow flies to and from its nest tucked in the eaves. The house resembles the turnip-head of a large scarecrow in need of a smarten-yourself-up haircut. If Da saw their hair falling over their eyes like that, the sheep clippers would be out.

A short, shaggy creature stands next to the house, secured to a stake. Liam can't tell if it's a horse or an ass. A frisky cock drops its wing, running a hen a merry dance within the pointed shadow of the gable.

The boys wait, and watch, and shiver.

Twenty cold-minutes later, the door opens and an elderly man appears. A plume of grey smoke pushes out past his hat. He places both hands on his hips and stretches, relishing the sunshine on his upturned face. A shove moves him clear of the doorway, and a small woman emerges behind him. They move towards a stack of turf, the woman lumbering as though carrying a great weight on her back, the man hobbling. This house looks perfect.

The boys watch the couple return to the cottage, each carrying half a dozen sods. Aiden turns to Liam, his face asking, "why are we hiding?", and he sneezes.

Liam shoots a hand over Aiden's nose and mouth, stifling another sneeze. He peers through the gorse. The man and woman have stopped and look about them. The boys remain still. The old woman stares in their direction. Liam hopes the scant yellow flowers of the bush are enough to keep them hidden.

The old couple speak, and resume their distinctive walks.

Liam releases Aiden's mouth. Aiden stares at him wide-eyed, panting. They've got away with it. Liam hatches his plan.

Aiden scurries down the shallow incline towards the house, his black, shoulder-wide head swaying above a damp, billowing petticoat.

Liam told Aiden that when the man and woman come out, Aiden is to run back up the lane as though Theron the Viking invader is chasing him with his axe swirling around his head. Liam is confident of the little man's ability to run fast, he has chased him often enough. When the old man and woman give up the chase, he is to meet Liam back at the river they crossed earlier.

Aiden halts close to the door. Too close, Liam thinks. He wants to shout him to move away, but it's too late. Aiden takes a deep breath.

"Mammy!" he screams at the top of his voice.

Liam skulks from behind the gorse bush down to the side of the house, interrupting the frolicking fowl, keeping out of sight of the door and small window. He's ready to nip inside as soon as the man and the woman go running after Aiden. He's uncomfortable about taking the food, but he and the little man are hungry.

The door opens. Half a second later the old man has made a giant limp forward and has Aiden in his arms.

"Ee-am!" Aiden screams, squirming to get free. "Ee-am!"

"I have ya young fella-me-lad, don't wriggle," the old man says.

The old woman is beside them, trying to stroke the writhing out of Aiden, "It's alright, laddeen" she says, rubbing his damp hair.

"Leave me brother go!" Liam demands, emerging from his hiding place, arms straight at his side, fists clenched.

"Hello, young man," the old woman says, without bothering to turn. "Whatever it is brings yez to our home, a thousand welcomes?" She turns to study him. "Not from these parts, no? I wouldn't know ya. Unless yez're Kathy O'Donnell's two?"

"Alright boy, don't be stirrin'," the old man murmurs, calming Aiden. "I won't harm ya. S'alright boy."

The woman is tiny, Liam standing more than a foot taller. She wears a tattered brown shawl over a brown petticoat and a striped apron. Her eyes are as dark as blackberries, her face a lined, smoke-stained grey with high cheekbones.

The man looks taller than her in his hat. Wisps of white hair poke from beneath it. He has a red, wrinkled face. Aiden stops wriggling and hangs off him by a leg and an arm. He lowers Aiden to the ground.

The woman lumbers towards the door. "Don't be tellin' me yez fell inta the river up the hillock. Is that it? Like a pair of drowned pups. Come inta the fire 'til we warm the shiver off yez."

Liam hesitates. Aiden darts in after her. Liam resigns himself to follow.

A turf fire flickers in the centre of the floor, throwing out an enveloping ball of heat. Smoke from the fresh sods puffs up around a hook-and-chain suspended over the fire. Liam follows the smoke up to the rafters, black with a life-time of soot. Trapped smoke gathers in the blackened-straw apex. He ducks his head to avoid the suffocating cloud. If his father was here, they could build them a chimney. They inch towards the fire, comforted by its smell, mesmerised by its flames, the heat bouncing into them.

The woman fusses over Aiden, drying his hair with two corners of her apron, needing to touch him.

Aiden gives another sneeze.

"The blessing of God and the Holy Mary be upon ya," says the woman, as she edges Aiden closer to the warmth.

The old man pulls a three-legged stool under him and settles the other side of the flames. He surveys the boys through the smoke as he stokes the bowl of a pipe with curled tobacco.

It's not long before wisps of steam rise from the boys' clothes.

"Tis said there's no fire like your own fire," the old man says. "But I'm thinkin' ye'll be glad of *our* fire today. You'll stay for the taste of a potatie, ye's will?"

Aiden looks up at Liam.

"We're goin' t' Ballycastle," Liam says.

"Are ye's in such a canter as ye's don't have time for a potatie?"

"Ee-am."

"Shush, Aiden."

"Aiden, is it?" the old man says. "Aren't you the grand little laddeen? Would *you* like a potatie? Ya would, I can tell it in ya. We've just to cajole the brother inta it, too." He tamps the tobacco with a calloused finger.

"We're goin' t' Ballycastle," Liam repeats. The thought of food makes his stomach gnaw. "But we'll have a potato."

"We've two wet gossoons here," he calls to the woman. "And they're hankerin' for a potatie. I'm thinkin' they'll be hungry enough to eat the balls off a low flyin' duck." The old man gives a braying laugh, his face contorting into a wrinkled, toothless gurn.

"Enough of that dirty chat out o' ya!" the woman shouts. She tuts. "I'm pickin' them now." Whilst she bends over a creel in the corner of the room, the old man raises his white eyebrows in admonishment until they disappear under his hat, smoothing out his face. He winks in conspiracy at the boys.

Liam smiles. His first for so long.

"Young people are nice to be havin' round agin," the woman says, filling a pot with water. "'Tis a nice change from old Father Billy Bellew."

"Ballycastle yer headin' ya say?" the old man asks, gazing into the fire, selecting the means to kindle the pipe.

"Mammy and Da are there," Liam says. "We're goin' to find them." As he speaks the words for the first time, doubts surface about his plan. His plan, having said it out loud, seems ridiculous.

"Ya sure it's not runnin' away from them ye's are?" the old man says. He plucks an ember from the flickering flames with his fingers and sits it on the bowl of the pipe. As he sucks, the tobacco glows red. He blows out a plume of grey smoke and hands the prepared pipe to his wife. He retrieves a second pipe from his jacket pocket and restarts the lighting ritual.

Liam wishes he was running away, he'd turn and go back in an instant. This is all forced upon him. Soothed by the heat and hypnotised by the flames, his shoulders soften. As he relaxes, the enormity of his endeavours wraps him in a stifling blanket of despondency. How will he walk to Ballycastle if he doesn't even know where Ballycastle is? And he has Aiden to take care of. A four year old. To take care of on his own. He'll not find Ballycastle. He doesn't know where Ballycastle is. He knows that to go anywhere properly, you must know where you're going. If he can't find Ballycastle, he won't find Mammy and Da. How does he look after Aiden? Will they go to the workhouse? That scares him more than anything. His plan is broken. His plan is useless. He aches for Da. His eyes fill. A blink pushes a drop over the edge, down to his lips. The salty taste confirms it for him, it's too late to hold back the crying. Through gentle sobs, with Aiden holding his hand staring up at his face, he recounts the entire tale of the last three days.

Whilst Liam talks, the old man leans on his knees and listens. There's the hiss of sucked air drafting through a pipe and an intermittent click of a tongue off the roof of a mouth. The old woman hovers close by. "Dear God Almighty" and "God be between us and all harm" she says, as the boys' tale unfolds.

She unhooks the boiling pot from above the fire and drains the water onto the floor. She emerges from the cloud of steam like a grinning genie, a potato in her hand.

Liam blesses himself.

Aiden copies, the Holy Ghost ending up misplaced on the wrong shoulder.

"For Aiden," the old woman says, beaming.

Aiden hops the potato from hand to hand, blowing on it furiously. His cheeks bulge as he grins and blows. The smell torments the boys.

Liam smiles, delighted that Aiden has a meal at last.

Aiden turns and offers the potato to his brother.

"No. You," Liam says.

Aiden shakes his head. "Ee-am."

"No, Aiden."

Aiden spills the potato into Liam's hands. "Ee-am," he says.

"I've another," the old lady says. "And one more for each of yez after that."

The boys work at the skins with their nails. Hunger overwhelms them and they chomp into the flowery meal. They swallow too soon, thick lumps of scorching potato barge and sear their way down shrunken gullets. Their stomachs roar in red-hot approval. The boys share a smile before they chomp again into the wonderful, delicious potatoes.

After eating, Aiden curls up on the floor. He nestles, mouse-like, in the straw against the wall and sleeps. Liam feels obliged to explain it's due to all the walking of recent days. Aiden's sleep is light and troubled, filled with coughs and turns and twists. He sits up once to sneeze and, after checking each of the three staring faces, smiles and settles back down.

When the potato pot is rinsed, the old woman decants a jug of clear liquid into it, adds water, and hooks it back over the fire. Liam recognises the sweet, woody aroma wafting up from the swaying pot. It takes him back to gatherings at his house, when stories were told, songs sung and his mother imposed on him to dance the jig steps she taught him.

It doesn't take long to heat. The old man dips a wooden beaker into the warm brew and offers it to Liam. He tells them of how it reminds him of the story telling. He doesn't mention the dancing.

The old man smiles and raises his beaker. "They say intoxicatin' liquor is the curse of the land. It makes you fight with your neighbour, it makes you shoot at your landlord, and worst of all, it makes you miss him." He takes a slurp.

Liam grins, raises his drink to his lips and takes a sip. As the warmth radiates through his insides, he feels his mind relax. Aiden is resting. They're warm, and no longer hungry. It's his first taste of punch. He feels uncertain about its effect.

Chapter 21
Farmhill, Ireland, 1879.

The knock on the cabin door roused William 'Billy' Cuffe from his dream. He had dozed off waiting for the gombeen man, who was late. There was no respect for punctuality this far west, he conceded.

The pain in his throat, and the sting from the scorched skin on his cheek and neck were waiting for him when he awoke. Despite his injuries from the recent 'excitement' with the Walshes, Billy Cuffe had savoured his dream. It was a warm dream, like a soak in a hot tub bath, about the daughter of a former tenant. Duffy, the name. The girl had slipped through the fingers of his attention but in his dream, they had met again. He missed her. Dreams to savour were rare. He awoke annoyed he had been plucked out of it. The gombeen man could wait.

Cuffe admitted to himself he did well to gain employment down here in Mayo. He had lied to get it, but the deceit worked. The position has been his for almost three years. Land Agent to the Farmhill Estate, under the proprietorship of Miss Harriet Gardner.

When he arrived at Farmhill, he had no previous experience in land stewardship to speak of. So he invented some. Made the whole bloody lot up. Claimed three years in Wexford, four years in Cork and three years as land agent to Lord Oranmore in Claremorris. He regretted the Lord Oranmore lie as soon as he'd said it, Claremorris was relatively close. He hoped Gardner and Oranmore never have cause to meet, he had clearly impressed Gardner with his résumé and would not want her illusion of him impaired. He started his work unsure what the hell he was doing, but he learned fast enough to avoid disclosure.

It meant two solid years of sending money on. He was proud of that. The years before Farmhill were not so secure. Decent work outside of Dublin was scarce but he couldn't go back. There was nothing nor no-one in Dublin that meant anything to him anymore. During the decades moving across the country he left a trail of failed opportunities behind him. And a failed marriage. And a young son. A beautiful, fair-haired son.

She wouldn't accept his money at first. Wanted nothing of his to touch the child. She returned the first four payments, but he kept sending it. She threatened to give it away to a sanctuary for sick donkeys, but he still sent it. He decided it was up to her what she did with it, but he was doing his best to keep his son from impoverishment. The responsibility would have been easy to avoid, but his love for his son made him determined to contribute to his upbringing. If not in person then, at least, financially. Sick donkeys? He doubted she'd do it.

His job at Farmhill was a good one, the pay reasonable, better than the near starving he'd been at for the decade previous. And the position came with benefits, not least amongst them the comfortable lodge-house within the grounds of Farmhill. The three furnished rooms met his needs, with privacy from the main building courtesy of a dense avenue of mature yew trees, stretching from his door all the way to the main lawn.

He had established a tolerable working relationship with his employer, Miss Gardner. He knew how to treat her. With respect. A strong woman. Capable of being a gentlewoman. At least when she was sober. Her drinking was her ruination, he knew that much. It was hard to respect her when she was drunk, which was often. She was dangerous when drunk, likely to blow your brains out with her Perkins twelve-gauge, double-barrel shotgun if you upset her. What a sight, her with her shotgun. The barrels stretch three feet long and, upended, the weapon stands as tall as herself. It was comical to see her wield the beast, but he had seen her behead a fox with it at over fifty paces.

He cared less for Gardner's companion, Pringle. Susanna Pringle. Officious and devout, and looked you too straight in the eye. She too drank, though she was more the melancholic drunk rather than the aggressive, dangerous animal that Gardner turned into.

He changed his name, introducing himself to Gardner as Cuffe. A masterstroke. He had done his research, the old Colonel was the only one in the world she had any real affection for. Colonel George Cuffe had earned that affection raising her from a child and providing financial support whenever required. From the few crumbs of information gleaned, he doubted Gardner would have Farmhill at all but for the Colonel.

Gardner made the decisions on the estate. She had made it clear to him she was veering away from landlordism. (Or is it landladyism? He thought he should make it his business to find out.) She spoke, with increasing regularity and growing enthusiasm, about amalgamating large tracts of her land. Her plan was to introduce large pastoral farms on the estate. She was convinced there was more money in rearing cattle and sheep than in growing crops. The recent drop in the price of arable produce would support her view. What was that she'd quote? "What's bad for corn is good for horn." She was right, cattle feed would be cheaper now.

To amalgamate land, she needed to shed tenants. You couldn't do it with the estate divided up, as it was, in small plots. They had to evict, and he was the man for the job.

Fewer tenants would make his job of rent collection easier that's for sure. He used to believe their bleeding-heart excuses, poured out over the table in pained desperation. Failed crops, falling prices, poor weather, sickness in the family, dislocated hip, the ass dying, fairy curses. He'd already heard every excuse a hundred times.

Then there's the money lender to deal with, the gombeen man, who'd service a tenant's debt and then employ his own means of recovering the money. He used the gombeen man for a few of the outlying tenants, but that too was a bother. The useless slice of sewer wouldn't turn up for appointments on time for one thing.

It was a revelation to him that there was a whole industry set up around the management of who owes what to whom. The tenants seemed content to operate in this environment of non-payment and debt.

Gardner was less tolerant of non-payment. Her creed was 'give me your rent, or give me my land'. Reasonable enough, he thought. And he was sure everyone else in Ireland would think it reasonable, too. But not the people of Mayo. Here in Mayo it was thought the pronouncement of Satan.

It was adherence to the 'pay or go' approach that led to the Walshe eviction. He disliked Walshe anyhow, a bit too righteous. And as for his bloody wife. The bitch had taken him by surprise when she came at him with the pissy-smelling, boiling broth. He had relished striking her. She had that coming for a long time. She was wilful. And she had a mouth on her, obstinate bog-witch. But she could be controlled, it just took a strong man. He would have enjoyed spending a short while alone with her when she was sprawled on the ground, her limbs in the air and her skirts around her middle. Even already impregnated, she would have been a treat to savour. He wondered what stone she had crawled under, and if she'd had the baby. He had the damn scars to remember her by. He smiled when he thought of the enjoyment he would have had teaching her a thing or two about control.

Then there was Jimmy Walsh. Attacking him like some god-forsaken lunatic. Almost choked him to death. Still can't swallow without wincing. He was fortunate the acting-constable returned when he did. He took his revenge. That's how you deal with people who hurt you, he had learned that long ago. Walshe won't be choking people as they go about their work anytime soon. If ever.

81

He wondered about the two boys. In the workhouse, no doubt. A pity, the small one caught his eye.

He was still unsure about Acting-Constable PJ Huddy. He knew where he was with Constable Neild, you had some control over a man who took payments so readily. There was work to be done with Huddy. Miss Gardner will fund the means to bring him around to their way of thinking.

Cuffe yawned as he opened the door. It wasn't the gombeen man. He sighed down at the crooked old woman wrapped in a dirty red shawl, her weathered face brown from the onslaught of sun, wind and dirt. A shrewish woman, with dwarfed eyes. Her arm looped through the splintered handle of a wicker basket. Behind her, stood Ann. Cuffe raised an eyebrow, awake. Aroused.

"Mr Cuffe, sorr, your honour, it's only meself it is, Mrs Henessey. I was after hearing about yer troubles wit' the Walshes th'other day and I am come thinkin' a fresh loaf'd make ya feel a bit better. May I be givin' it to ya, sorr? I walked the way here wit' it so I did. There's no reason a gintleman like yerself should have ta go through all that, not at all, sorr. I was sorry t' be hearin' it about yer good self."

The Henessey's were behind with their rent. Cuffe had visited their tenancy three weeks ago to remind them of the consequences. He had asked to see the man of the farm, but Joseph Henessey was nowhere about. He unleashed his threats on the old woman instead. Whilst listening to her excuses and empty pledges, Cuffe spotted Ann, sowing seed potatoes from a creel carried on her back. He stopped listening, and stared.

The girl he saw in the field was rake thin, wisp-like, and skipped and dipped between the drills with a lightness that said to Cuffe she was not from this place. He imagined her world to be one of magic and sorcery, one of fairies, elves and wild beauty. She was not new to him, he had noticed her about a year previous. But she had grown, stretched into a lithe being.

"I'm awfully sorry too that that useless son o' mine has no poteen left in the house or I woulda brought ya a measure. I did bring me grand-daughter, Ann. I know ya have a regard for her, sorr. She might help sooth yer injuries for ya and provide a comfort for yer good self for a small wee while."

The Duffy girl had escaped him, but here stood Ann, delivered to his door. His fingers tingled and he felt the urge to laugh out loud. He roamed his eyes over her as the old woman spoke. She looked to be somewhere in her early-teen years, tall, and feral. Straggly hair hung like long, black icicles from her stooped head. Through the hair he saw a freckled nose, moist with tears, and pert young lips. She wore nothing more than a ragged sack, hung over her gaunt, naked body. Likely the same garment she wore when he noticed her in the field. The swell of her small breasts pressed against the material. Thin legs stuck out underneath. Her bare arms were bone-thin and she clutched the wrist of her grandmother with long fingers. He knew it would not take much to make her compliant, to take control of her.

Cuffe glanced over the old woman's head. There was no sign of the gombeen man, he would have to come another time. He opened the door wide.

The old woman looked away from Ann as she picked the fingers free of her arm. She bent and kissed the back of Ann's hand, and squeezed it gently. Blinking her small eyes, she ushered in the girl.

Ann sobbed.

Too hoarse to talk and still unable to swallow any food, he closed out the door on the old woman, saying nothing and ignoring the offered loaf.

Ann paused in the room and turned to face him. She raised her head as a tear dropped free from her chin. She shivered at the shrivelled burn on his cheek and the yellow bruising around his neck. He raised a hand to touch her hair.

She pushed it away.

Cuffe sent her reeling across the floor with a savage slap to the face.

Chapter 22
London, England, 1876.

Bernie found it difficult to leave London. He conducted a final drunken sweep of the public houses in search of Gregory Partridge. He knew it was dangerous. If anyone connected with Thomas Eldridge heard him asking about Partridge he'd be done for. So, too, with anyone linked to the bookmaker syndicates. The police, he reasoned, were easier to avoid. They wore uniforms for a start.

He bought a handgun for protection, a Colt Peacemaker wooden-handled revolver. The seller had it smuggled over from America. Bernie felt like a cowboy. He went to the bother of buying a licence to carry it, for ten shillings, from the post office in St. Martins Le Grand. He thought they'd refuse a licence to a drunken Irishman but, apparently, a gun doesn't care who owns it.

Along with a degree of protection, he reasoned the pistol also provided him with the means to put a bullet into Partridge when he eventually tracked him down. He wanted his money.

He found no trace of Partridge. He resolved *The Bunch of Grapes*, the public house where he first met Peggy, would be his final port-o-call. There, he staggered into Marcus Morrell, a friend from when Bernie first arrived in London.

Morrell had worked in a carriage house out of Camberwell, south of the River Thames, cleaning and maintaining London's horse-drawn hansom cabs until the end of the 1830s. At the dawn of the new decade, his wife inherited a house with a sizeable plot of land in County Waterford, Ireland. He and his wife moved to Waterford immediately.

Settling down, in what Morrell referred to as 'the old country', was the realisation of a dream for him and his wife. "London's no place to raise children," he contended. A decade later Morrell returned to London, alone, his wife and young baby having perished during the potato blight that struck Ireland in the mid-'40s.

His reputation for hard work survived his absence. On his return to London he resumed both his previous role on the carriages, and his east-London Irish accent. He worked his way through the ranks to Senior Hackneyman, hiring out a fleet of carriages and horses to other coachmen who operated across the city. Despite his status, when the need arose, Morrell was not above climbing up on a carriage and delivering a fare himself.

Bernie recounted his drunken story of the last three weeks. Something sounded familiar to Morrell.

"You won't believe this, Bernie, but I reckon I had that toe-rag on board with me two weeks ago."

Bernie was barely sober enough to register Morrell's statement. "What're ya sayin'?" he slurred, rocking forward in his seat.

"What's his name? Partridge, ya say? I think I had that shagger in me carriage. 'Bout two weeks ago. I only 'member him 'cause he came stormin' inta stable yard shoutin' and roarin' like a bull with an 'ard on. He was ragin' 'bout how he'd been tryin' t' flag a carriage for the last half hour and how he had a train to catch from Crystal Palace station. He was rantin' and rearin', he were. Chargin' round me yard, unsettlin' horses. He nearly went for one o' me footmen he did. Threatened him with his cane. Poor man was only takin' his tea in the harness room. Near me go over and shove his cane up where trains don't run."

"And ya think it was him?"

"Maybe. Ten minutes later we had a carriage rigged up for him, his bags loaded, and I took him to station meself. I charged him plenty mind. A wealthy man in a hurry and his wad of notes are easily parted, eh? Good enough for him, he were a right Jack Brag he were. 'Do you know who I am?' he kept ranting, proper posh. 'I have royal connection.' He kept shoutin' that, as if shoutin' it'd make the carriage go faster. Sure, I get that shite all the time from posh buggers and took no heed of him. However, when we got to the station, I was liftin' off his bags and I caught sight of the luggage tags he had on his cases. Smart little leather things they were, and thinkin' 'bout it, I'm sure they said 'Partridge', or somink like it. Maybe 'Pheasant'. I just recall thinkin' he could do with a pellet or two up his jacksy. So yes, I think it could've been your man I took to Crystal Palace station that morning."

"D'ya know where he was headin'?" Bernie asked.

"He was doing enough shoutin' on the way there, right enough. But I think... I think he mentioned catching the train to Dover. It *was* Dover now I recollect. He was shoutin' that if he missed his train, I will suffer the consequences of him missin' his steamer to Calais." Morrell gave a laughing shrug. "He probably would've expected me to take him over the Channel in me carriage!"

Bernie was unable to raise a smile.

Morrell leaned forward. "Bernie, pardon me for askin', but what happened yer eye?"

On the narrow footpath outside *The Bunch of Grapes*, Bernie straightened his bruised body and swayed. He looked up and down the street. London was happening around him, but his intoxicated mind thought only of Peggy. He imagined her walking the footpath towards him. Two horses lolloped past, pulling a clanking cart laden high with baskets of wooden pulley blocks destined for a shipbuilding yard on the Isle of Dogs. Bernie was oblivious to them, Peggy was beside him.

His mind rehearsed the meeting.

She smiles. She asks where has he been and says she misses him. He should come home with her. She'd take care of him, look after the eye. She understands why he had not come to see her. "I forgive you, Bernie," she says. "I understand why you had to do it. Your brother, your father. Us. I understand it was for us." Back in her room, Bernie tells her everything that had happened. Peggy agrees to leave London with him. She undresses him and drapes his clothes over the line strung across the corner of the room. She climbs into the single bed beside him.

Peggy didn't walk down the footpath.

Past the bend in the street, a driver was shouting and cursing at a group of determined street urchins. A basket of blocks had fallen off the back of his cart and the urchins were trying to steal away the scattered pulleys.

Bernie's mind ached for the want of her. His body ached for the want of her. The turmoil in his stomach was for the want of her. His head drooped and he chuckled. "I love you so much, I can't shit properly." He would tell her that, if he gets the chance. He wondered would she laugh.

He raised his head, stuffed his hands into his pockets and stared back at London. The furious cart driver walloped a boy around the head before wrenching a stolen pulley block from the lad's grasp.

Bernie knew Peggy would not be as understanding as he imagined. He doubted she would even be pleased to see him again. She wouldn't understand and would be incapable of forgiving.

The beat of another craving resounded in the front of his brain. If Peggy had been more understanding about his need to fight, to have one last big-money-earning bout, he knew he wouldn't be in the mess he's in now. The pulsing beat of the craving. He knew if Partridge had stayed and paid him his share of the money, he wouldn't be in the mess he's in now. He knew who was responsible for his present predicament. He turned back into *The Bunch of Grapes*. Damn them both.

Chapter 23
Kincon, Ireland, 1879.

"Constable Neild, you wanted to see me?" Huddy closed the door and rummaged for the handkerchief in his pocket.

"I think it's still customary to salute your superior officer when you enter his office, Huddy," Neild said.

Acting-Constable Huddy smiled. "Nothing works as hard to strengthen weak authority as custom," he said, under his breath.

Neild raised an eyebrow at the insubordination and fidgeted with his pencil under the desk. The office was small and sparse. Constable Neild sat spread behind a small table that was bare apart from a narrow jotter. A Constabulary Medal hung on the wall behind him, in pride of place but looking lost in its oversized, gloomy glass case. He earned the decoration for 'Distinguished Police Service and Exemplary Conduct' at the Battle of Dolly's Brae in 1849. The high number of casualties made the Battle of Dolly's Brae the most notorious of all 12th July parades. During the furore, Neild was inadvertently stabbed with a bayonet by one of his fellow sub-constables. The one-and-a-half-inch scar, about the same size as the silver Constabulary Medal, remains visible on his left buttock.

"What on earth were you thinking, Huddy?" Neild said.

"With regard to what, sir?"

Neild stared at the tall man standing the other side of his desk. The drawn, cadaverous face with its skeletal features belied a strong, muscular frame. Neild despised the man's categorical ambition. Huddy was due a dressing down, this was Neild's opportunity.

Neild's position gave him financial security, access to what he considered legitimate supplementary payments, a good standing in the community, authority and respect. But all that was challenged, put at risk on a daily basis, by Acting-Constable PJ Huddy. He needed putting in his place. He was the only downside to a job with so many upsides. The truth was, this disfigured, insubordinate subordinate-officer both offended and frightened Neild.

"Yesterday. With regard to yesterday, Huddy. You nearly killed that man yesterday. And I shudder to think what harm you've done the woman. She was with child. Was it necessary to be so extreme?"

"With respect, sir, I was saving a man's life."

"The man did not regain consciousness!"

"I mean the land agent, Mr–"

"And I mean Walshe! You nearly killed Walshe! That's why I had to send him and his wife to the Union Workhouse Hospital. God knows what a fever hospital will do for them, but what other choice did I have? You see the predicament you placed me in, Huddy?"

Huddy stared over the constable's head at the encased Constabulary Medal. Condensation smeared the inside of the glass, obscuring the citation. Huddy didn't reply. He crushed his handkerchief in a clenched fist. A bulb of water built on the lid of his damaged eye.

"The children," Neild said. "Where are they about? What did you do with them?"

"Left them there, sir."

"Left them? The house was levelled, they couldn't stay there."

"Then they'll be walking, sir. Until someone takes them in or they reach the workhouse in Killala."

"Acting-Constable Huddy, I charge you with finding them. Set about it as soon as we finish."

Huddy's arms went taut.

"We need them apprehended," continued Neild. "We can't have two young gossoons roaming the lanes on their own, they'll perish. It's sloppy and doesn't reflect well. I'm beyond measure, vexed, Huddy. I'll have every teacher, priest and damned workhouse mother-superior in the county knocking my door enquiring of their whereabouts."

"From what I hear, they'll be safer on their own than in the workhouse, sir."

"Huddy, find them! The woman, why were you about striking her?"

"I didn't have to. It was Mr Cuffe hit her."

"Then why allow Cuffe to strike her? That Dublin man expects too much for his..." Neild let the sentence fade.

"She attacked Mr Cuffe, sir," Huddy said, as though reading text.

"The woman was carrying a child, Huddy. You let the situation get out of hand. The Royal Irish Constabulary were there to keep the peace and you failed in—"

"Sir—"

"Interrupt me again, Huddy, and I'll have you stripped of rank and patrolling fields guarding hares from foxes before you can catch breath." Neild showered his jotter with spittle as he spoke. His eyes were tight and glaring. "Don't imagine I'd hesitate, Huddy. It'd pay you to remember your station. You've let the constabulary down."

"Sir! I'll tell you what I've done. I have done a good thing, a very good thing. I've saved a land agent from being throttled to death, less than two miles from these barracks. You, sir, should be congratulating me, not trying to find petty, irrelevant fault. Now I'm not claiming what I've done warrants the Royal Irish Constabulary awarding me a medal to blow smoke up my arse, but I would thank you for holding back on the denunciations."

Neild reddened in his chair. Sweat gathered on his top lip.

"Acting-Constable Huddy! I'll be submitting an account of the incident to County Inspector Lynch, in my weekly report. To be forwarded on to Dublin Castle. I will be making it clear you exercised excessive violence. And as for your insubordination..."

Huddy's face gnarled. He sprang forward like a wild dog and grabbed the shoulders of the constable. He hauled his bulk off the chair and pulled him over the small table. His hollow face stared into the fleshy face of the constable, inches apart. The saltwater bulb quivered on its precipice.

Neild was unable to pull away from the red ectropic right eye.

"A good mind, Constable Neild?" Huddy spat. "You're an incompetent slob, Constable Neild, abusing the position you hold. I am aware of what you're up to, sir, don't think I'm not."

Neild felt the point of his pencil sticking his stomach. Sweat bled from his armpits.

"So far, I have been patient," Huddy continued. "I've spent the last year and a half seeing out your time in this backwater of Ireland, covering for your incompetence. I have been patiently waiting for you to retire back to your small, wee plot of land in whatever spot of bog water you're from up in Donegal."

Neild wondered, wide eyed, at the strength of the man. At that moment, Donegal sounded like an attractive option.

"But you continue to try my patience," Huddy said. "And now you have the effrontery to talk of disciplinary hearings. Let me tell you that excessive violence, sir, is no stranger to me. If you can't cope with that insight, you will want to be readying for that retirement. In the meantime, Constable Neild, there will be no disciplinary hearing."

A teardrop sailed past Neild's upturned chin and splashed on an open page of the jotter.

Huddy released Neild.

The constable collapsed back into his chair, trembling.

Huddy saluted. "Sir."

As Huddy turned and walked out of the office, Neild reflected on his report to the commissioner.

Chapter 24
Coonealmore, Ireland, 1879.

His mouth is dry. Water trickles over hidden rocks above him. He needs to climb higher. He knows it's there, he hears it, tapping on the stones. A little higher. Tap. Tap. There it is. A tapping trickle but enough to quench his thirst. He'll have steady sups. He lowers a cupped hand into the trickle. It stops. A lagging drop splashes into the crease of his palm. The thirst gnaws at the back of his throat. His mouth is dry. He must go higher. Over the next boulder he finds the acting-constable, his deep cheek brimming with fresh spring water. He stoops to slurp it out.

"So. It's Ballycastle ye's are headin' for it is?" the old man asks.

Liam had woken from his dream to the tap and buzz of a mob of bluebottles bashing their bodies against the small window. Their attempt to flee the first smoke of the fire was futile, the upturned bodies of dead mob members lay on the sill in testament.

The ass-horse lay at the opposite end of the room, rolling a mouthful of oats between black-crested teeth. Liam didn't remember it coming inside last night. Even with the beast in the house and up close, he was unable to determine its species.

He felt he had spent the whole night in a nocturnal quest for drinking water, trying without success, to quench his punch-induced thirst. His head throbbed.

"That's where they took Da and Mammy. We'll be there soon."
The old man shrugs and sniggers.
"Why ya laughin' at me?" Liam asks.
"Don't be gettin' all vexed now. It's not laughin' at ya I am." He pressed the opening of his pipe bowl with a finger. "I don't know where's Ballycastle, but I knows it's not near hereabouts. There'd be fierce walkin' in a journey like that and even more in it if ya haven't a notion of how to get there. I'm thinkin' it might take ye's long enough. I know a boy's best friend is his mother and there's no spancel stronger than her apron string, nevertheless..."
Liam bites into a hard-boiled egg and stares into the smoking fire. His head aches.

"Young Aiden is sickenin', Leemeen," the old man says. "When I caught 'im yesterday outside the door, sure there was more weight in that boiled egg. Why don't ya leave 'im tarry here wit' us?"

Liam stops chewing and stares at the old man, reading his face. Like everyone else, they want to keep Aiden. But he reads no malice in the ruby wrinkles. "Aiden must come with me. He needs his mammy."

Man and boy stare into the flitting flames.

Liam casts the shattered egg shell into the fire. He watches it blacken and bubble. "Have you an agent that ya pay the rent to?" he asks.

"I have of course," the old man says. "That I do...And I'm thinkin' ya know 'im. Ya see, near to getting' ivicted like yerselves we was too this year. It's been tough. Poor weather this year and last, the rent goin' up to the heavens, and any price ye can get at market goin' down to hell. A fella in town was tellin' me about cheap grain from Amirika, but I don't know if that's the cause in it. Everyone's findin' it hard going to meet the rent. It's the way o' the world." He pauses, nods his head, and presses his tobacco.

"You're not the only iviction to take place, Leemeen. I've heard talk of others. The tale of your father upset me, but it didn't surprise me. I know the land agent, Cuffe, ya speak of. I've the pleasure of havin' to deal wit' him meself. Likes to think he's a smart man. He dresses himself well and he's big and handsome enough, but there's often the look of an angel on the Divil himself. A heart of flint in him he has. And he knows nothin' 'bout land, not a bloomin' inklin'. He's a tough man to deal with, Leemeen. A horse of an ass of a man, ya might say."

Liam glances at the beast lying at the far end of the house.

"They say that alright...The look of an angel on the Divil himself. No, I hate to see him come to the house. If I'd a dog, I'd cut its tail to make sure there was no sign of a welcome for him. I don't like the big nose he has on him either, nearly big enough to smell round corners!" They both chuckle. "And he has a scowl on 'im that would drive rats from a barn!"

Liam laughs, hunching his shoulders to his ears, mirroring the old man.

"Will y'ever go back, Leem? To yer home I mean."

"I don't know. I've a fear of it. I'd go back with Da."

"Don't let it poison ya, Leem. They say yer allowed to forgive yer enemy, just don't forget the bastard's name."

Liam leans back, his mouth gaping.

The old man stares into the fire, mouthing his pipe from one side to the other. "Despite the weather, the two of us make it through on what the farm grows," he continues. "We've a middlin' house, and we've each other to share the talk. We sell enough for a shillin', and sure, if I do be getting' a smell of a shillin' at all, it'll do us, we don't need much. She wouldn't eat what a mouse eats and as for me, my father useta say, 'He who has water and peat on his own farm, has the world his own way'."

"How long've ye been here?" Liam asks, looking up into the smoky blackness of the straw.

"Oh..." he chortles. "I could count maybe twinty generations of me family been livin' in this house. I dare say the last will be us. Both the childer died young, God love them. 'Bout your ages too they was. 'Tween me, you and the gate post, young Leemeen, dead is the only way I'll be walkin' out of this place, too. But I've spirit left in me yet, so I have."

The old woman and Aiden crash through the door, laughing. Her Aiden-induced smile wipes years from her face, like an alchemist's elixir. Aiden juggles with the two thick sods of turf cradled in his arms.

"Ya can be certain sure this laddeen's a great little worker," she calls to her husband. "He'd be a great one to have 'round the place. Bringin' turf in an' all, to keep the fire goin'." After a pause she adds, "Did ya have a speak to Liam about Aiden stoppin' here and welcome?"

Liam leaps to his feet. "Aiden's comin' with me!" he yells.

Aiden drops the turf and shuffles closer to the woman, tilting his head into her.

"It's alright petteen, it's alright," the old woman says, shielding his head, cupping his chin in her fingers.

Liam moves towards the open door.

"There's no need to be makin' ready to go yet," the old man says. "Sure bad as I like ye, it'll be worse without ye." He giggles. "Yer as jumpy as a young cock hen on a heated griddle."

"Liam," the old woman says. "Liam, listen to me awhile... Aiden's not a well laddeen... He spent the whole o' last night coughin' in his sleep. It isn't a good cough... He should rest here. He's too ill to be stirrin' far. He has no proper clothes an' he'll perish with the cold and the wet. Yez should both stay here until the spring by rights, but you're older and a headstrong one and I don't want ya vexed. But how's about Aiden stays? How's about ya collect him on yez way back, say? Give him a chance to rest and heal. When ya comes back with yer father and yer mother, Aiden'll be here waitin' for yez."

Aiden raises the back of a small fist to his eye.

"Aiden," Liam says. "D'ya not want t' find Mammy? Don't ya care about Mammy anymore? You'll be cryin' for Mammy next."

Aiden gives a small-boy blub.

"Aiden's comin' with me," Liam states. He takes Aiden's hand.

"Liam!" The woman stops him. "I seen the blood in his spittle."

Liam shrugs. There's been blood in Aiden's spittle as long as he can remember. They pause at the door. Liam turns back to the elderly couple, who return his intent stare with long, drawn, sad faces. The bluebottles buzz and thump at the glass. The ass-horse has stopped chewing but looks away, avoiding eye contact. "I don't know yer names," Liam says.

"Be God in heaven, aren't ya right," the old man says. "Kate, isn't it a quare thing we didn't introduce ourselves prop'ly to our visitors?"

"T'was the height of ignorance us not to," she says, with reluctant gaiety.

"Mullins," the old man says. "Sean Mullins and this is me darlin' wife, Kate. Now, we've managed to work out that you're Leemeen, and you're Aiden, but what's your family name? Would ya tell us that?"

"It's Walshe. Liam and Aiden Walshe...I wanted to...Thank you, Mr Mullins. And Mrs Mullins. For looking after us...I'm grateful t' ye both." Liam and Aiden step out of the house, herding out smoke.

The old man rises from the stool and limps to the doorway, the old woman beside him. They stare as the two boys walk away. He drapes an arm around his wife's shoulders.

"He'd never leave 'im," he says. "And tryin' to keep both o' them would be like minding mice at a crossroads. Sure ya never know, often the raggedy colt made a powerful horse."

The old woman shrugs and sighs.

"I know that," she says. "But that young fella won't ever make no powerful horse."

"Liam Walshe!" the old man shouts.

Liam stops and turns.

"If God sends ya down a stony path, may he give ye both strong shoes!"

"We've no shoes," Liam says, confused.

"I see that." The old man smiles. "Ye can both rest yer feet here whenever ye need."

Chapter 25
Farmhill, Ireland, 1879.

Billy Cuffe pointed to the back-room.

Mrs Henessey pushed the wooden wheelbarrow through the house.

He hated listening to old women crying. The sickening sobs made him want to slap their faces. He heard wood scraping on the flagged floor, old-woman-straining noises, and the crash of the wheelbarrow as it toppled onto its side. Damn it woman!

He strode into the back-room as she tried to right the barrow. He pushed her aside and grabbed the handles. He dropped the barrow and bent over to pick Ann off the floor. Her weight was familiarly light. He placed her in the barrow, tucking in the bare legs and folding the arms across her naked chest.

Ann's head lolled to the side.

Mrs Henessey, weeping, moved towards the barrow.

Cuffe raised an arm to halt her. He picked Ann's sack-cloth off the floor, stained with crimson patches, and dropped it on top of Ann. He strode out of the room, returning a moment later with a sheet, thin and threadbare, to enshroud Ann. He withdrew two shillings from his pocket and offered the money to Mrs Henessey.

She stared at the two shiny coins sitting in Cuffe's blood stained palm, the reflection of the glimmering lamp dancing off the two chubby-cheeked profiles of Queen Victoria. She sniffed, reached towards his hand, and she pushed it away. She lifted the barrow handles and reversed out of the back-room.

As she reached the door, Cuffe croaked, "Wait."

Mrs Henessey lowered the barrow.

Cuffe grabbed a shawled shoulder and twisted her around. Her head was bowed, her grey hair parted along the middle of her head, flakes of skin lifting from the scalp.

"You brought her to me," he said. He scrunched his eyes and swallowed hard. When the pain in his throat passed, he said, "Remember, it was you brought her to me. You're to blame. If you want to stay on the farm, you'll say this is an accident. Make up a lie, you'll be good at that. A farm accident. Do you hear me?"

The grey head nodded slowly.

Cuffe watched her leave the house.

A short way along the yew-tree-lined avenue, she let the handles of the barrow drop, and swayed. She howled into the black night-sky. It was an almighty, screeching howl that filled the air with grief. Breathless, she folded forward over Ann, snot, dribble and tears dropping on the threadbare shroud. She drew in air and howled again. Gritted fingernails scraped her face as the mournful cry passed out over the trees, over the gardens, past the lawn, into the dark fields. She collapsed to her knees and fell on top of the barrow. Sobbing. Convulsing.

Cuffe closed out the door.

Chapter 26
Knockduff, Ireland, 1879.

After a day walking, they spend a cold, sleepless night huddled in a ditch. The morning brings them a drizzle that becomes a downpour. Intimidating black clouds roll in from the Atlantic Ocean, dirtying the sky and drenching the fields. They trudge through the mud, the rain making their clothes heavy. They shiver when the breeze blows. There's an ache in Liam's empty belly. He holds an open mouth up to the rain to quench his thirst. Other than coughing, Aiden has been quiet since leaving the Mullins'. Ballycastle seems far away.

By mid-afternoon the rain relents and they come upon their first opportunity of food of the day. They're chased from the house. A man and a woman, about the same age as their father and mother, threaten to tie them up and call the constabulary if they catch them begging for food again.

The dark of the clouds segues into the dark of the evening. They gorge on berries and find shelter in a deserted cow-barn with a tree growing through its wall. Liam didn't sleep much, kept awake by the rustling of rats.

Aiden is sick during the night, coughing, and spilling berry-black vomit over the barn floor.

Next morning, the sky is filled with white clouds. Progress is slow, Aiden needing to make frequent stops. "I tired, Ee-am," he says on one occasion.

During a pause, Liam recalls one of Mammy's rhymes. He starts it off. "Ring-a-ring for Mammy, Da / Touch the ground and touch a star / You bring home an egg for me / Ring-a-ring for Mammy, Da."

Aiden doesn't join in.

They are several hours into the day before they happen upon another building. Liam crouches with Aiden in a clump of trees. He counts over a dozen children, sitting and lying around the yard of a dilapidated mud-shack of a cabin, waning and starving. Their clothing is a variety of faded-red petticoats, flour sacks and rags. Filthy, ribboned and revealing. This house is too impoverished and too desperate to ask for or take anything. Liam grabs hold of Aiden's wrist and the boys continue on their way, their hunger burning in their stomachs.

He is hopeful about this house. After reconnoitring its yards thoroughly, he spies only one woman. She spends time at an upright machine, turning handles to crush water from wet clothes before carrying her washing around the back of the house. One adult. That's good.

A whiff of baking bread taunts him. His mouth makes a watery gurgle. He goes back to retrieve Aiden from behind the wall to find him curled into a ball, asleep.

"Aiden. We've found something. Come on, Aiden. Get up."

Aiden wipes the sleep away. He coughs several times and swallows.

"Ee-am, sore," he says, rubbing his chest. "I tired." The skin around his eyes is a dark grey, as though smeared with ash.

He needs Aiden to distract the woman, but Aiden lays himself back down, closing his eyes. Liam strokes the round head.

Back at the bush, he spies a dome shaped cob loaf, cooling on the shelf of the machine. Liam cannot believe his good fortune. There's enough in the loaf to last him and Aiden for three whole days. He is going to take it.

He fears getting caught. He nearly got caught yesterday. Tied up. Taking is a sin. No-one would listen to his excuses. He'd end up in the constabulary barracks and then the workhouse. And hell?

But they may be in Ballycastle in three days. Three day's food. He's not prepared to risk asking the woman for it. The loaf is as good as his.

He crouches his way to the gable end of the house. His stomach rumbles. He tries to trap the noise with his hands, but the growl escapes. With the stealth of a hungry cat, he moves along the gable and peers around the corner to the rear of the house. The woman drapes damp clothes over a fuschia bush. She wears a flowery skirt, a brown corset and a white bonnet around her serious face. He darts his head back and makes his way back along the gable. He must pass two windows and a doorway to reach the machine. He crouches low beneath the first window. Moving fast, he shoots past the half-door. He crouches again to pass under the second window. He's beside the crushing machine, his prize on offer to him. The yeasty aroma assaults his nostrils, reminding him of home, of Mammy. He wells with joy.

As he reaches for the cob, two hands appear around it. Thin, long-fingered hands, with dirt under the nails.

He shrieks, jumping back.

The hands remain fixed on the loaf as their owner steps from around the corner of the house.

Chapter 27
Ballina, Ireland, 1879

"Don't stand there like a dumb statue of uselessness, pour another drink!" Harriet Gardner shouted, squeezing the words out around the bit of her pipe in her deep adenoidal tone. She slammed her empty jug down on the counter.

"You'll be havin' had enough, ma'am. And I've closed the bar now," Jarlath Whealan said. He remained at the far end of the counter, beyond striking distance.

Harriet picked up her jug and launched it behind the bar, shattering it against a line of large, tan ceramic barrels. The barrels rocked but none broke. The crash halted all the fair-day conversations in the small bar.

A curve of jug rocked itself to rest on the stone floor.

Jarlath had been in a good mood. The day of the Ballina Fair is always good for business. Brings people into town, even when it's raining. If it coincides with a visit from Aloysius O'Connor's Country Fair, all the better. The town do be rightly packed when the Country Fair is here. It was time for the red-headed monster, O'Connor, to pass through again. Jarlath looked forward to seeing him in his pub. In better form than last year, he hoped, when O'Connor barged in the door and dragged one of his own 'employees' out into the street. The employee was stupid drunk. A stupid, Dublin drunk, Jarlath recalled. O'Connor was intolerant, kicked him up the arse and told him to get back in the booth. Jarlath enjoyed visiting O'Connor's fighting booth, though he'd never be daft enough to climb up into the ring himself.

There was a good crowd in. The fair-day talk was catch-up chat and about prices, down again this year.

"Is it buyin' or sellin' y'are?"

"I'm tryin' to sell a beast, but it's an 'apenny-lot day. Sure I might as well be donatin' it."

Every seat in the pub was taken, and apart from the two men in earnest conversation by the window, almost everyone had a connection with the land. Hungry-looking dogs curled around the legs of tables, dozing.

Jarlath's dinner had gone on to boil, he was waiting for his wife to give him the nod. He checked on the two women drinking at the table next to the counter. Harriet Gardner and Susanna Pringle. They had been in all day, drinking as much as two men, never mind two women, ever drank. Intent on lavishing everything they had on the drink, by the look of them, he thought. But he regretted serving them in the first place. Not every public house in Ballina allowed women in, fewer still served Harriet Gardner.

They had been quiet, sociable even, to start with. Bought Jarlath a drink. But as the jugs of porter went down, their volume went up. Pringle wasn't a worry, she drank her fill and fell asleep. A sleeping patron spends no money, but he would tolerate her if she was quiet. Gardner wasn't inclined to be quiet.

"Five-hundred tenants and not one o' them worth a pig's fart!" Gardner shouted, directing the observation across the table at the dozing Pringle. Loud enough for everyone in the pub to hear. "Lazy laggards the lot o' them!"

She took a rapid sip from her ceramic pot.

Jarlath could see the frisky fidget in her, her knees jerking up and down beneath her skirts. He knew it meant trouble. "D'ya think it's because they're Catholics?" she said, to no-one in particular.

A few heads turned her way.

Jarlath saw it build. Any other customer, he would have thrown out, but Gardner was different. She had money and land, a lot of each, and a Protestant with money and land was a protected species around these parts. Protected by no less a body than the Royal Irish Constabulary. She was free from having to answer to anyone, including the constabulary. She was the landed gentry, lording it over everyone else.

Jarlath had decided she wouldn't lord it over him. Not in his own pub.

"Now, ma'am," he said. "Can ya keep yer voice down, please? There's no need for that shoutin'."

Harriet raised the pot to her lips and drained it. She scraped her chair back, stuck her pipe in her mouth and stepped up to the counter.

"I think the two things are related," she had said, her pipe still stuck in her gob. "Catholic and laggard. Ya can't have one without the other. Two more drinks, Mr Whealan."

Jarlath disliked her standing up, especially with a jug in her hand.

"I'm sorry, Miss Gardner," he said, the sweat beading on his upper lip. "I've finished servin' for today."

Harriet scoffed. "It's a Fair day. Ya can't stop on a Fair day. Yer dreary little place is full."

"I'm sorry, there's no more today."

That was when she flung the pot.

Susanna Pringle, slouched in a wooden chair against the wall, raised her chin from her chest and forced open her eyes. "Harriet, what's wrong?" she slurred, before her head drooped. She fell back into a drunken doze.

"That dumb eejit over there doesn't want to serve me!" Harriet shouted, pointing at Jarlath with the stem of her pipe.

The shouting stirred Susanna again. She blinked around and pushed herself upright on her chair.

Jarlath looked down at the shattered jug and shook his head.

"I... Ya can't call me like that in me own pub," he said. "Didn't I say the bar is closed? There'll be no more drink today. And I've a mind to bar ya entry again."

The other customers watched from their seats.

"Did I upset you when I started about Catholics?" Harriet asked, mocking Jarlath. "Serve me a drink, Mr Whealan, and I'll temper my attitude. I wouldn't want to be upsetting the Catholics now, would I? Hang the whole affair!"

"The bar's closed."

"Closed? Then tell me this, Mr Whealan." She swayed and grabbed the counter with both hands. "Tell me straight because I won't be haggling with the likes of you." She leaned in over the counter. "How much do you want for your pubbeen?"

Susanna burst into a snorting giggle and listed forward, almost toppling off her chair.

"What're ya sayin'?" Jarlath asked.

"How much? For your unpleasant, horrible little pub. I'll buy the bloody place off you, here and now." She stuck the pipe back in her mouth and sucked.

Jarlath was confused. "Why would ya do—?"

"Because you won't give me a drink!" she yelled, bowl of the pipe bouncing up and down in the air.

"Harrie', please. Please listen," Susanna slurred, shaking her head and pointing a drunken arm. "Harriet, we don't need a pub. No. We don't need a pub." Susanna lolled back in her chair laughing, a drunken, derisory, mocking laugh.

"Shut up, you," Harriet said, glaring at Susanna, training the bit of the pipe on her. "Useless," she said under her breath. "Can't drink like you used to. Father ruined you, that's your problem. Too bloody smug." She raised her voice so Jarlath could hear. "This is a transaction between me and Whealan. Don't need your bloody interference. I can buy a shitty little pub on my own, can't I?"

"The pub's not for sale," Jarlath said.

"Come on," she drawled, feigning disappointment. "I'll be the first pub-owning Protestant in Ballina, will I? And if you do me a good price, I'll keep your name on the front for a year, how about that?"

"It's not for–"

"Typical Catholic. A shame you didn't convert more of them when you were at it over in Achill, Susanna. Grow them a pair of Protestant balls."

Susanna giggled and shook her drooped head.

"Shower of Fenians." Harriet was talking at Jarlath, but what she said was for everyone in the bar to hear. "Think you can rule Ireland without the Crown? Never. Two reasons. Church of Ireland will never give in, and you Catholics will never have enough. Only ever want more. Like dogs fed scraps from the table, given half a chance you'd be up on top of it eatin' yer fill."

"Lookit, it's time you were leavin', now," Jarlath interrupted. "You need to go."

"I'll go when I'm ready!" she said and stuck the pipe in her mouth. She leaned her back against the counter. Harriet had everyone's attention.

Susanna reached for her jug. Her face fell towards it as she brought it to her mouth.

The men in the bar stirred in their seats, unsmiling.

"Maybe the nuns will save you," Harriet continued. She swayed as she addressed her congregation. "I hear there's a great shower of your women going on to take your holy vow. Why would that be? What are you doing that's driving the women to seek refuge in a convent?"

Jarlath squirmed behind the counter. "That's enough now, Miss Gardner, please," he said. "You've talked enough. I'd be grateful of you leavin'. Please."

The air in the pub smelled of damp grass, sour porter and boiling cabbage. Harriet had shot a bolt of lightning through it, charging it with tension. She smiled.

"I'll tell you." She stared around the room, catching the eyes of the men. "You can't be looking after them in the bed. That's what's wrong. The whole way you treat your women. Like the dirt on your shoe."

"Shut yer mouth, woman!" An anonymous call from the corner of the room.

"Who was that?" she spat, scanning the shadowy room, her eyes narrowing. "Who said that?"

The bar was silent.

Jarlath was the first to speak. "Lookit, Miss Gard–"

"Who said that?!"

Susanna straightened up in her chair and looked out at the men. "If Harrie' had 'er shotgun wi' 'er, there'd be no calls," she managed to slur. "She'd shoo' the bloo'y lot o' ya. Harrie's good wi' 'er shotgun."

"Scared of a woman," Harriet said. "Catholic, Fenian cowards."

Chairs scraped as two men at a corner table rose from their seats. Both long and thin, a generation in the age difference. The older man's face was pocked and pitted, the younger one's a mask of pustules of delayed puberty and dirt. They tugged their caps down low over their eyes.

"No. Marr," Jarlath said. "Don't. Not here. Don't do nothin' here." Jarlath moved along the bar, pleading with the older man.

Harriet watched the two men approach. They stopped in the middle of the floor, facing her, hands at their side. The bar was hushed and still, like a prelude to a shoot-out in the Wild West.

Susanna stared from her seat and sneered.

The older man said, "I'm of the mind you'll've drunk your fill, Miss Gardner,"

"Will you look at this?" she said. "Two men anyhow, who don't seem scared. Where are you from, Marr?"

"Worry not 'bout that, missis. It's time you and your drunken friend left this establishment."

"Oh, it's an establishment now is it? If I didn't know better, I'd accuse you of trying to inflate the value of this shitty little hole before I buy it off Jarlath."

Susanna snorted another mocking laugh.

As the two men made a move towards Harriet, the door of the pub swung open. A cool blast of damp August-air rushed in. From the dim interior it was difficult to identify the face in the doorway. The shape cut an intimidating silhouette against the daylight.

Harriet recognised the man in the shoulder-caped overcoat, tall and broad with a bowler hat, leaning on a blackthorn stick. "Ah, Mr Cuffe, so glad you can join us," she screeched. "I was explaining to these Catholics why their women are all running away from them."

Cuffe's creased his brow at the remark. As he strode in, the two men moved aside, the elder tugging his cap down further. Cuffe clutched the blackthorn like a weapon, its large round cudgel-handle ready to crush skulls. He passed the men, placing himself between them and Harriet.

"Miss Gardner, Miss Pringle," Cuffe croaked. "A carriage awaits to take you home as requested." He reached down to help Susanna Pringle to her feet. Her chair toppled with a clatter to the flag floor as she rose. He held her arm.

"We'll carry this conversation on another day," Harriet said. "I have plenty more to say about your women, if I had but the time to say it. It'll wait. I'll bring Mr Perkins with me next time. He can be quite persuasive in getting his point across."

Cuffe raised an eyebrow at the reference to Miss Gardner's Perkins twelve-gauge shotgun. He led the two drunken women out of the pub, eyeing the two standing men as he passed, clutching his blackthorn.

Eamonn McHugh, the editor of the Castlebar-based 'Mayo Telegraph', an ailing regional newspaper, sat at a small table under the window. McHugh had been scouting the fair for stories and had taken the opportunity to interview a youth by the name of James Daly for a reporter's job. James Daly was nervous and unconvincing.

"Listen, I'll be straight with you," McHugh said. "I think you're literate enough, but you seem... a bit too decent a young fella to make a good reporter."

Daly looked devastated.

"I'll need convincing you'd have what it takes, James. To put a story across, I mean. We're expecting people to pay good money to read it, after all."

McHugh explained to Daly that the Telegraph did not employ reporters as such, it couldn't afford to, but it was always interested in hearing from anyone with a good story to tell. If that person was capable of writing it down, then so much the better.

"For example, I've a man in Dublin, works in a bank. Travels back and forth to London. He sends me stories about all the corruption that goes on. There's people want to read about corruption, James. Then there's others that want the local story. They want to do something, then be told about what they did in the newspaper. You see, James?"

They stood up to leave when they heard a woman shouting at the bar. A crash of ceramics told them to resume their seats. They sat down, and a story featuring a wealthy, local landowner played itself out in front of Daly.

"Whealan!" shouted Harriet, as she stopped and swivelled in the doorway. She pointed at Jarlath with the long stem of her pipe. "If I come in here again, don't *ever* tell me when I've had enough."

Chapter 28
Knockduff, Ireland, 1879.

"I think I was here first," the girl says.

She looks older than him, but it could be the dirt.

"D'ya live here?" Liam asks.

"No, not at all, I'm here to steal the cob."

"That's my cob. Now it's bein' robbed o' me," Liam protests.

"Think about what you just said there, 'That's my cob'. I'm sure that if you think about it carefully even you would have the brains to realise that what you said is a mortal lie."

"I need it," Liam says, his face creased in panic. "For me little brother."

"You have a little brother? So you think that because there are two of you, you should get the bread, is that it?" The girl gives a relaxed smile.

He frowns and looks around to check for the serious woman in the white bonnet. "Give me the cob, or I'll push ya over," he says. He doesn't remember ever pushing a girl over before, nor a boy come to that, other than Aiden.

The girl lifts the cob from the mangle shelf and hugs it to her body. She closes her eyes and inhales the warm aroma. "Mmm," she sighs.

Liam isn't sure if she made the noise deliberately to rile him, or if she couldn't help herself.

She starts to sway her body. No rush. Prepared to stand and argue all day.

"I don't think you could," she says, opening her eyes. "You're tall with a bit of meat on you, but your shoulder muscles haven't started to grow yet. Me, on the other hand, have been wrestling sheep to the ground for almost five years. I can hold a sheep down for as long as needed 'til my brother is ready to shear its wool. I'd hold it still too. There'd be not a move from it."

The girl doesn't look strong to Liam. The arms that cradle the cob are like the twigs of a young tree, frail enough to snap with your hands. He hesitates, turning again to check for white-bonnet.

"Lookit," the girl says. "She'll be around any time now. This is what we'll do. I'll take the loaf, we'll go and find your little brother, and we'll share the loaf between the three of us."

His mouth wants to open in surprise. His eyes want to stretch wide in wonder. He wants to ask her why she's prepared to share when she holds the loaf. Instead he stares at her, giving no reaction.

"Hey, there!" the serious woman in the white bonnet screams, her head poking out over the half-door. "Put that back where ye found it, ye whelps!"

Liam and the girl dash around the back of the house and slip between the cloth-clad bushes. They scramble over a high, grassy ditch and gallop away over the black tilled field. White-bonnet doesn't give chase, but Liam is too scared to look back to realise.

Chapter 29

The Mayo Telegraph, Saturday, August 17, 1879

(Specially written for The Mayo Telegraph)

By J. Daly

Never in our days have we seen the likes of it and no decent man amongst us wants to witness it again. It is bad enough for a woman to behave outrageously, without any courtesy to those present, in a public place, but to do so in a hostelry, on Ballina Fair Day with the hostelry patronised to the full, is beyond reproach. So it was, this Monday last, with regard to her known as Harriet Gardner, when she was accompanied by her intoxicated companion Miss Pringle. Both of these women (to use the term recklessly) were thoroughly inebriated, having consumed far more than a social amount of alcohol, Miss Pringle to the point of unconsciousness. If it were the same with Harriet Gardner, I would have a lesser report to make, but Gardner was repulsively conscious. After behaving discourteously to the proprietor, Mr Jarlath Whealan, Gardner went on to upbraid the tenants of her Farmhill Estate and then went further to chastise the women and the men of this great county. What was said is inappropriate for this publication to replicate, as this organ is no conduit of Harriet Gardner's spleen, but let it be said that what took place was a thoroughly objectionable, ungentlewomanly display. Such was the condition of the two, they had to be escorted from the public house by a lackey in Gardner's employ, but for whose intervention the situation could have seriously deteriorated, such was the bile she emitted.

Eamonn McHugh raised his thick eyebrows and peered over the frameless rim of his spectacles.

"You took it upon yourself to have a go at writing a story?" he asked.

"Yes, sir," Daly said.

"I see you've chosen the date you'd like it published."

"Yes, sir."

"It'll need an edit. But I like the attitude," HcHugh said.

James Daly let out a breath, sat back in his seat, folded his arms and blushed.

Chapter 30
London, England, 1876.

"I thought you'd be dead by now. You only smell as if you are."

The man in front of her looked a bedraggled mess. Incapable of standing up straight, his legs buckled, his head hung down. His once-strong shoulders had withered on their frame. A wiry black and grey beard ran riot across his face.

"My heart is broken twice, Bernie O'Malley. Or Kelly, or whichever it be. Twice–"

"Peggy," Bernie said, lifting his head. "I know what you're about to say... I just... I had to see ya."

"Why, Bernie? Why did you have to see me? You haven't wanted to see me for almost a month. What were you about all this time?"

"Don't be shoutin' me in the street, Peggy. Can I come in?"

"Shouting you in the street?! Your worry is about shouting you in the street? Why is that, Bernie? Is it your pride? Are you a proud man? Are you embarrassed? Ashamed someone'll see you being shouted in the street?" Peggy stopped yelling. "Me shouting you in the street is the least of your worries. Look at you. Look at the state of you... This is like a dream, some ruinous nightmare. I told you not to do it."

Bernie stepped back and stretched his arms out, like a drunken Jesus. He staggered, and reached for the doorframe to avoid toppling.

"Even when yer rarin' up on me, I love the sound of West Cla–"

"Damn you!" she said.

She sniffed back the tears. There would be no tears.

He propped himself against the frame.

"Peggy, I had to have that last fight. The money would've set us up. *Us.* Ya know Partridge did me over wit' the money, don't ya? Oul' posh-man Partridge, with his top hat and his walkin' cane. He did me over with the money. Might've skipped to Paris, France. It wasn't my fault."

"Not your fault? It wasn't your fault you've spent the last month on the drink?"

Bernie's head drooped again. "You told me go."

"Bernie you've a problem," she said, to the top of his head. "You're broken. Torn. I can't go on loving a man as broken as you are. I'm not able for it. I'm far too old for such a bloody carry-on. I can't be all the things I want to be for you, Bernie."

"D'ya love me, Peggy?"

Peggy drew breath. She regretted her indiscretion. The man she loved was damaged. She exhaled. "I thought I did."

"Peggy, I killed a man. I killed a man with me bare hands."

Peggy tutted and squeezed her eyes closed. She folded her arms and leaned against the doorframe, crossing her legs. "I heard," she said. "I knew no good would come of it, Bernie. I told you not to do it... I'm surprised you haven't been arrested or murdered or something, yourself. Instead, you turn up here like a... what's that they say here? An arf'arf'an'arf? You look like you've had a few 'arfs alright." Her bended knee rocked from side to side. She was pleased with her sudden humour, tears averted.

Bernie gave a hopeful smile. "I apologise, Peggy. I'm sorry for not listenin' to ya. And I'm sorry for turnin' up in this state."

"I don't want to know where you've been hiding, Bernie, but you should've come to me first. We could have resolved matters. Gone somewhere."

"It's not too late," he said. He took a step closer.

His left eye was a swollen, infected clump, connected to the beard on his cheek by a white line of puss. The sour, fermented stench of ale and spirits made her gag. She drew away and gave a loud laugh into the street. It began a full-throated belly laugh, tapered off through nervy-laugh, ended up a laugh through closed lips, the sound like the humming of pigeons.

"It is too late, Bernie. You're too unfaithful. Drinking and fighting are your mistresses." She jerked herself away from the doorframe.

"Peggy, come with me," he pleaded. "I've to leave London, come with me."

Peggy smiled through tears.

It must have been Partridge in Marcus Morrell's carriage, he thought. He resigned himself to never seeing any of his money. Partridge had taken the London, Chatham and Dover railway service to the port and caught a steam vessel to Calais, France. What was that Partridge had said when he had spoken of his plans for the final fight? "Paris is going through a renaissance." Partridge would surely be in Paris now, enjoying its renaissance. Paris's rebirth. Bernie thought he needed to go through his own renaissance. He had to leave London.

Peggy hadn't agreed to go with him. Damn Peggy. Damn Partridge. He was better off without them. Peggy may still leave with him. There was nothing else here for him. Only danger.

Chapter 31
Knockduff, Ireland, 1879.

"The name's Eileen. I know you didn't ask, but I'd say it's because you're shy."

Liam rips at his portion of the loaf. His ears burn.

"Aren't you going to tell me yours? I know this is Aiden, I heard you wake him." Eileen smiles at Aiden and touches his round head. Aiden returns the smile with a crumb-covered flash of teeth. "How old are you, Aiden?"

Liam swallows and says, "I'm called Liam. Liam Walshe. Aiden's only four."

"Ee-am and Aiden," Aiden says, pointing each of them out with a tiny finger before returning his attention to the bread.

They chew on the dry loaf.

"It'd be better with a bit a butter," Liam mumbles.

"T'would yes," Eileen says. "That's what you should've been doing back at the cabin."

Liam furrows his brow into a question.

"Going in and stealing some butter," Eileen says. "Instead, of standing outside looking as nervous as a sheep queuing for the dip, gawping at me."

Liam's jaw drops. "I didn't...I wouldn't steal butter. I wouldn't steal anythin'."

"No?" Eileen says, smiling. "So what were you going to do with the loaf on the mangle? Were you going to ask the woman for a cut of it?"

"No, but... I don't steal." He pauses to consider what it is he does. "I'm only *takin'*... not *stealin'*." The red flows from his ears into his cheeks.

Eileen edges him towards the sheep dip. "So what's the difference, Liam Walshe, big brother of Aiden?"

"Takin' means... I'll maybe... I don't know, give it back some day."

"And where will you get a loaf from? Are you going to bake it? You're good at baking bread are you?" she says, swilling him around in the dip, his face glowing. "Isn't baking women's work, Liam Walshe? I didn't think–"

"Me mammy can bake."

Aiden stops chewing.

"Where is your mammy?" Eileen asks.

Aiden gapes at the girl.

Liam rises to his feet. "Is that what it's called? A mangle?"

"What?"

"The crushin' machine. Ya called it a mangle."

"Yes. We've one at home. They're new things."

"Right... Lookit, it's gettin' dark and I need t' gather fern and look for a place t' shelter." He passes what is left of his bread to Aiden. "Don't eat it all, Aiden. We've t' save it."

"Sorry," Eileen says, looking up. "I didn't mean to annoy you. I was only teasing. My brothers say I do that sometimes. Listen, I've hoked a hole out of a mound two or three fields away. It's big enough for three of us. But fern will help, it's going to be cold this evening."

Liam weighs up the proposal. She was suggesting the three of them stay together tonight. A girl, with him and Aiden. "I suppose that'll do." He turns to go, then halts. "Will ya look after Aiden for me?"

"I will of course," she says. "We'll be lovely here, won't we, Aiden?"

"I stay with Ei-een."

"He can't say—"

"L," she finishes. "Not to worry, we can soon teach him that."

"No, he useta be able but...Ah nothin'."

Liam patrols the field's edge, gathering fronds in his arm. He glances back over the brow of the field, through the dimming light of the late afternoon. He wonders why the girl he left sitting with Aiden is on her own. Eileen. He liked the sound of the name. It sounded grown up, but not. She's smart enough, her talk not thick. Was she evicted? Where's she headed? From the state of her, he'd say she's been wandering for a while. The dirty face. The long, red hair, thick and ropey, like twine twisted from strands of dirty hay. If his mother got hold of her she'd sit her in the tub in front of the fire in no time. Mammy'd scrub that grime out of her skin until her back glowed like a candle.

He imagines Eileen's naked back, hunched in the small tub of water, his mother kneeling, kneading knots from her hair. The ribs sticking through her skin like a curved washboard.

Beneath the dirt, the face is pretty. Dark brown eyes, the colour of leaves in Autumn, below arched red eyebrows. There's a trace of freckles, dotting her cheeks like a pinch of brown salt sprinkled from between thumb and forefinger. She has an eye that refuses to look at him straight. After a while, it prefers to veer inwards towards the nose. He couldn't blame the eye for that, she has a good nose.

When Liam returns, Aiden is asleep leaning against Eileen, her arm around him. He has grown used to people, men and women, fawning over Aiden. A jolt of jealousy passes through him this time. He drops the fern.

"I don't like his cough," she whispers. "He's been at it since you left."

"He's fine, he's always had it. He's tired is all. We've been walkin'. The truth is I'm more worried about him not bein' able t' say me name properly."

"Not say your... What? Why? He's coughing like a sick lamb and his brother is worried about how he says his name?"

Liam feels his ears warm up again. He's glad of the dimming light. "No, it's just... He useta be able t' say it. Liam. As clear as ya like. After everything happened... then he couldn't say it. Callin' me *Ee-am*. When he speaks at all, that is. Ee-am. I don't know why, is all."

"You were evicted, weren't you? That explains you going around stealing loaves of bread."

"I don't stea—"

"Where's your mother and father now? Did they send you away?"

"No!" Liam's shout disturbs Aiden who shifts, nuzzling closer to Eileen.

Another jealous pang.

"Shhh!" she says. "Don't wake him."

Liam fusses with the ferns.

"Look, don't be ashamed," she says. "It's what people have to do sometimes, let their children off. When we were going to be evicted my mother and father knew they couldn't take care of us, so they sent us off. To look after ourselves. We'd only be taken to the workhouse anyhow." Eileen lies her head back against the grassy ditch and stares out into the dimming evening. Her voice slows, a sadness colours it. "My parents were...old. And my father... Mother said we'd be better off without them. My mother would never leave him. She stayed. We were on our own."

"Mammy and Da'd never do that t' us," Liam says.

"I've four brothers." She wipes at an eye and struggles to lift her voice.

Liam narrows his stare.

"They're all older than me," she continues. "Ryan's thirty-one years and married to a second cousin, Dirdre. There's Thomas, their son, who's a lot bigger than Aiden. Five he is. I miss Thomas, he's beautiful and never shuts up. He's certainly not as quiet as Aiden."

Liam scoffs. "He hasn't always been—"

"Then there's Cathal, James and Michael. My other brothers. Michael's the youngest, he's twenty-five. I'm fifteen. So we're old enough to look after ourselves, and too big for Father to do it. And anyway, when Father lost the farm he had nothing, nothing at all. Nothing for him and Mother even, never mind us."

"You're fifteen and they sent you away?"

"They sent my oldest brothers first." Her talk is confident again. "Then me and Michael. We went after we... They had nothing remember, and they wouldn't be able to cope. My father was dying."

"Was he old?"

"My father? Losing the farm broke his heart. Everything he—"

"Was it big? The farm."

"We worked sheep. My father had hundreds. It was big, I suppose. He was the biggest sheep farmer in the area, for sure. That's how I learned to wrestle sheep to the ground. I *can* do that you know. I'm good too."

"How comes ye were evicted?"

"The payments my father had to make to the landlord. He couldn't do it. I useta catch him whinging to my mother about how high they were getting. The landlord wanted him to make the farm bigger, take on the farms of others who were being evicted. Me father said no, so the rent started rising. One day, they came and said they were going to take the farm off him. Broke the heart of him. Mother told me he wanted to die after that. He took ill. Didn't leave his bed. Wouldn't eat nothing. I told Michael, father wanted to die but Michael just said 'Yer talkin' shite again, Eileen'. Do you mind me saying 'shite'?"

Liam shakes his head.

Eileen stares out across the field, a finger twirling strands of Aiden's hair around itself. "I didn't know people can do that, die of a broken heart. But if you wait long enough, they can... It's a slow death."

Liam thinks back, his own father lying on the floor of their house, his hair matted with fresh drying blood. Was he dying slowly? It hurt, the pain sitting in the pit of his stomach, beside where the hunger lived. He thinks back to Cuffe beating his father, the dull thuds, like thwacks on a stubborn ass, the up-swings launching blood into the air. The tiny wet splashes on his legs.

"Hello, are you still here?" Eileen says. "I've been talking to myself for the last minute. You went someplace else."

"Hah?" Liam says, his tone uncertain. He had been here all the time. His fingers ache when he releases his fists. His nails leave small arcs in his palms.

"I was asking what happened to you. Did your parents send you off?"

"They didn't send us off, I told ya. They was taken by the constabulary men."

"They were arrested?"

"They was beaten, and taken away. And me and Aiden left on our own."

At the mention of his name, Aiden coughs. A globule of grey phlegm lands on Eileen's outstretched leg. She leans forward to inspect it in the dimming light. It's not grey, it's red. Blood red.

"Jesus, Liam, do you see this? He coughed blood, look!" She points at the red jelly.

Liam leans over her. "He's done it before. Does it mean anythin' bad? People says he's sick. Do you think he's sick?"

"Jesus, I don't know, Liam. I know that when a sheep coughs up blood at home we normally kill the poor thing before the others start it too."

"Ya kill it?"

"Ryan would slit its throat and bury it up in the corner of the field, beside the fairy well in the clump of trees."

"Stop it. Jesus," he says. It's the first time he has used the name in vain. "Why'd'ya say that? Slit its throat? He's alright, look. It's just tired he is. We've been walking. He's tired. He's still sleeping. Ah God. He just needs a good sleep is all." Liam raises both hands and pushes back his hair. "He needs t' rest. Leave 'im now tonight. We'll sleep here. We got fern. We'll stay here tonight."

"That's alright, Liam. Easy," she says. "I'm sorry. I didn't mean...We'll stay here...We will stay here. This little man'll keep us warm anyway, he's boiling hot. My old dug-out wouldn't be half as warm."

Eileen wipes her leg with a fist-full of grass and squeezes Aiden closer.

Liam's heart races. Nothing must happen to Aiden. Mammy'd be mad if anything happens to Aiden. He must get Aiden to Mammy, safe. He calms himself by spreading out the fern and settles down the other side of his brother. A final adjustment of fern and he rests his back against the ditch. He takes a breath. Eileen's arm is warm against his. It sends an unfamiliar frisson of confused emotions through him.

"Where're yer mam and da now?" he asks.

The grass rustles as she turns her body away. Her arm leaves his. "I don't know," she says. She's talking to the field. But it's a lie. He knows from her voice. Not smart anymore. A lying croak had appeared in it.

"Will he be alright?" he says, letting the lie pass.

Eileen doesn't answer.

"Aiden'll be alright, Eileen, won't he?"

"He will of course," Eileen says, but her voice weeps.

His breathing is rapid, staccato. The blackthorn stick rises and falls, rises and falls. Whistle and thump. As it thumps, Aiden coughs. The cough is beaten into Aiden. Aiden's mouth gapes, his eyes like saucers, his little chest pulling air into itself.

Liam shakes awake. He sees only blackness. His heart echoes off the ditch. He twists his head to see Aiden pressed next to him. There's Eileen. Did she hear his heart beating? He blinks out at the blackness. Black field, black sky, blended. No stars. He tries not to think about what might be lurking out there. In the dark. Aiden snores. A deep breath, a long hold, then hissing, like a steaming kettle. Liam's breathing eases. His heart calms. He turns his head to the side as he lies it back against the bank. A spider sleeps at the centre of a web. He moves an arm to swipe it away but remembers how, only a few days ago, his own house was swiped away. He turns his head.

Will Eileen want to come with them to Ballycastle? He has enough to look after with Aiden, he doesn't need a girl to take care of. She talks a lot too, but not in a bad way. Did she lie? She'll have her own plan. He'll find out what it is before they go their separate ways in the morning.

His eyes feel heavy, but he can't sleep. He notices dark patches of sweat pushing through the thin material of Aiden's petticoat dress.

Mammy'll be mad if he lets anything happen to Aiden.

Chapter 32
Kincon, Ireland, 1879.

Sub-Constables James Jackson and his brother, Jeremiah, collected her on the back of a cart. Huddy had sent the ashen-faced Jeremiah home after finding him vomiting against the back wall of the barracks.

The arc of purple on the inside of her arm told him the tightness of the grip. He had seen such bruising before. Her arm was thin enough for the thumb to overlap the fingers, there was no mark for the thumb. Moving down the table he noted similar bruising above both ankles. Her thighs were scratched raw by rough cloth, or leather, or metal. The ileum bones of her thin hips crested into the air, flaring like pale, creamy plough blades. Her pubic mound was smeared ochre by dry blood, and cuts and bruises were visible through the downy triangle of hair.

He moved around the table and looked for grip marks on her other arm. There were none, but he detected dried blood under her fingernails. Her thumb had been bent back to breaking point and lay flat against her forearm, leaving her hand twisted around her wrist. She had struggled. The marking around her throat was livid, discoloration leaked down over her chest and back behind her ears. A blue hand mark, four full fingers, saluted him from a cheek beneath a swollen eye.

He finished his inspection and cloaked the body with the blanket.

The grandmother was never taller than short, but recent events had shrunk her further. She uncurled her frame as Acting-Constable Huddy approached.

"Mrs Henessey," he said.

The small eyes of the woman looked up into the flame-red eye of the man. Deep creases lined her face.

She had a resigned, beaten look about her. He had never seen such tiny eyes before. Perhaps on a field mouse, he thought. "Where's the girl's mother? Or her father, where's Joseph?"

She bowed her head. "Father's not right, sorr," she squeaked. "Took to poteen when he found out. Can't stand up in his boots, sorr. Gone off the head of himself, he has."

"What of the mother, Mrs Henessey? What form is she in?"

"Hopeless, sorr. Blitherin' mess, she is. Couldn't come here this morning she couldn't. Not able to rise herself to come. Never no good for nothin' the mother. A mess, sorr".

"Mrs Henessey, tell me what happened."

The old woman stared at the flag floor whilst Huddy waited.

"'Twas an accidint, sorr," she said.

"How, Mrs Henessey? This was no accident. Someone did this to Ann."

"An accident, sorr...A farmin' accident," she sobbed.

"She was wrapped in a sheet, Mrs Henessey. In the corner of an empty field. What sort of accident would cause that?!" His arms were open in question.

She sobbed.

He held her by the shoulders, raising her head. "Mrs Henessey?"

She lifted two small fists, leaned into him and beat on his chest. "An accident..." she wailed. She fell against him. Her small frame shook as she wept into the green uniform. "Nooo...My Aaann." she wailed.

Huddy let her sob until the shaking eased.

"You know, don't you?" he said. "You know who did this." He held her away from him. "Look at me..." He bent down to her face. "This was no accident. I can't do anything unless you tell me...Who?"

She stared up at the acting-constable, her lined face a smudge of tears and dirt. Her head trembled from side to side, a slight, almost imperceptible movement. She shook her shoulders loose, turned and shuffled out of the barracks.

Chapter 33
Dublin, Ireland, 1876.

Dublin had changed.

Thirty years. What's that song? 'It's been thirty-odd years since I wandered through Dublin'. He couldn't remember the next line. Some of the changes were obvious, slapped him right in the puss, others he had to search around for.

He arrived back in Ireland, the Island of Saints, as he had left, having given up everything. He had money in his pocket. And a handgun. His heavy little revolver. He laughed to himself at the thought of it. Eldridge's men, the bookie-boys, the police, had all failed to catch up with him, and he was delighted about that. But would he have used the gun? If he got in a tight spot, would he have cocked the hammer and pulled the trigger and killed *another* man?

That reminded him. There's something else different, of course. He has the death of a man on his hands.

The revolver must go. Dublin didn't need another cowboy. Now, at home - yes, it still felt like home - in Dublin, he'll launch it into the River Liffey at his earliest convenience. Good riddance to the revolver. And good riddance to the streets of London and the dangers that stalked him there. Good riddance to that damn Partridge too, may he die of the pox in a brothel in Paris.

Fighting? Good riddance. Too old now, opponents too young and too strong. He is still fast if he stays off the drink. 'Fast hands' the Gypsies called him. Thirty years ago.

Good riddance to the drink. No more drink.

He travelled from the port on a rattily horse-drawn tram, sitting upstairs to take the air in the hope it might settle the nausea in his stomach after the sea crossing. He also thought it a good way to see the sights, like on a charabanc ride. He caught it at the North Wall and it took him to Nelson's Pillar on Sackville Street. Bernie looked up at Lord Horatio and told him he used to drink in his old pub.

Dublin was travelling in horse-drawn *buses* when he left. The bored driver was happy to explain the tram workings to Bernie.

"The rails are sunk inta the road, like, d'ya see that? So's a man won't trip, like. A big job that was. The carriage so, is biggur and carries more people. It's the friction that does it, like, there's no friction in them rails.

Smoothest ride in Dublin so it is. And that includes them women out at the Wall. Trimmin' minutes off times we are. Minutes, like, not seconds."

There was a bit of craic about the seats on the upper deck, too.

"See them boards up there with the writin' on, around the side o' the bus? They call them 'decency boards'. D'ya know why we need them?"

Bernie looked blank.

"They're stuck around the railings to stop the men lookin' up the women's skirts! Aren't they the bloody gurriers?"

Bernie took lodgings in Dalymount, north of the River Liffey, close to Mountjoy Prison. He wanted to avoid Temple Bar for fear his father still drank there. It suited him to be far away from Ballsbridge, where he grew up. He wondered if his father and mother were still there, or even still alive? He wouldn't be calling on them to find out. How would he be as some latter-day prodigal son? Best he avoided them. That's why he had to move on, out of Dublin. As soon as he worked out where to go.

When he left the lodgings, he didn't know what to do. It would be easier if Peggy were with him, he could rediscover his home city as he introduced it to her. They would explore its parks, its streets and alley-ways, visit hotels, its dance halls and eating houses. He'd gone back to her, asked her again, but she hadn't agreed to come with him. Citing no room for her and his two mistresses. Funny. Tragic. But there was hope. There was always hope. With Peggy around, it would be easier to remain off the drink.

From his lodgings, Bernie walked straight over the Royal Canal, crossed the railway line and entered Cemetery Road. At the far end of the street, he eased open the green door of a public house known as *The Grave Diggers'*. Grave diggers didn't own the pub, they only got drunk there. Its proper name was *Kavanagh's*, next door to the gates of Prospect Cemetery. Welcome home.

After three days heavy on the drink, and a sleepless night fending off black beasts flying out of the bedroom walls towards him, he decided again to address the drinking issue. No more drink.

When that didn't work, he tried to restrict it to after six o'clock in the evening. Abstinence until six o'clock. He was amused when he realised he had curfewed his abstinence. No abstinence after six o'clock.

To help stay off the drink during the day, Bernie walked, rediscovering his home town on foot. He walked for hours, his strident perambulations helping control the incessant pulse in his head. He walked for miles through the smells, the slums, the wealth, the filth, the flowers, the grass, the cobbles and the poverty. He took in parks, ports, the river, and offal-strewn streets of backyard abattoirs. He walked in the sunshine, the sweat pushing out of him. He walked in the rain, the drops flushing the ashen air, throwing the dirt back down on top of him. On a walking day, he behaved like a functioning drunk. Yet come mid-night in *Kavanagh's*, even on walking days, he barely functioned at all.

He met up with Dermot O'Leary, a hurling friend since the days before Trinity-College. O'Leary butchered for a living and travelled over the river to meet Bernie in *The Grave Diggers'*.

"I see ya like ta drink in the dead centre o' town, Bernie," O'Leary said, winking. His fleshy cheeks shook up and down when he laughed.

After the customary interchange of pleasantries, O'Leary was keen with the questions. He wanted to learn what Bernie had been up to since leaving Dublin. Bernie didn't tell him everything.

"Boxin'?" O'Leary replied, his brow furrowed. "Wit' bare knuckles? All dis time? Holy God. Dat explains the ugly puss on ya, so. Is the beard to hide the scars? Don't hide the flat nose on ya, though. Can y'even see outta dat eye? I'd say y'were takin' more blows than ya were givin' out, am I roight?"

"I blocked a few."

"Yea, wit' yer jaw be the looks o' ya! And why're ya twistin' yer head? Ya deaf?"

"I have one good ear."

"I could never do dat now, fightin' I mean. With me bad back an' all. Don't touch the hurl now, either."

Bernie asked about his brother, Philip.

"Yer brudder? Dat's roight, ya had a brudder. Not seen him in years. I'd forgot about him. He musta pulled outta Dublin 'bout the same time. Did he not go to England?"

"Don't know," Bernie said. "How's Dublin?"

"Fuck Dublin, how's London? Did ya marry?"

"They're diggin' enormous tunnels under the ground and running trains through them."

"In London?! They are in me arse! Yea, an' Her Royal Highness rides my oul' father instead of John Brown when she holidays in Killarney."

Bernie didn't want to talk about London. "Tell me about Dublin."

"Dublin's buggered so it is. I'm serious, don't be laughin'. The whole country's buggered. It's on its knees it is, with its arse in the air.

Buggered. Ridden ta death like an oul' hoor. No need me tell ya who the jockey is. No real buildin' work goin' on at all, and dare chuckin' all the farmers off the land. On me solemn. The culchies, the only ones able t' till a field at all, are revoltin'. Yer just back in toime to see the whole place go up like an explosion o' shite from back pressure, j'understand me? Dare are matters needful, me good man, matters needful."

"Ever the optimist, Dermot."

O'Leary's laughing shoulders made his belly shake. "Never moind about it. How's about we drink a few porters, and the country can go t'blazes? What's yer plans so, Bernie Kelly, now yer back on Éirinn's green shore?"

For a moment, Bernie wondered who O'Leary was talking to, he had been O'Malley for so long.

"No fixed plans, now. Stick around Dublin for a while. Become reacquainted with the Pale. Then maybe get meself down the country, see what the rest of the country's like. Not sure where to, but."

"Dublin's changed since ya were here last, so it has. Be sure to call inta the art gallery, we've an art gallery now. An' a dead zoo, full o' stuffed creatures. Have a good look 'round, haven't ya lashin's o' toime? Outside Dub, it's still all about the tilled field. The country's still all agriculture, j'understand me? 'Tatoes and turf. But you'll need t'be careful if you do go down the country though, Bernie. I wasn't jokin' 'bout the revoltin' culchies. We're on the brink of an agricultural uprisin', j'understand me?"

"No," Bernie said, smiling. "I don't understand ya at all. But I'll order two more porters, and ya can tell me all about the agricultural uprisin'."

O'Leary turned out to be Dublin's self-proclaimed leading authority on agricultural issues, holding stringent opinions on everything land related. He had pedigree. His father owned vast swathes of County Cavan before selling up in the late '30s and moving to Dublin to establish what became the country's largest meat processing and slaughterhouse business. O'Leary told Bernie how his father, alive and well in his eighty-second year, still took an interest in Irish land matters. He laughed when he explained how his father got frustrated by his son's unwillingness to accept that things have never been as good as when the land was allocated to loyal subscribers during the Cromwellian settlement, two centuries earlier.

During hours of strident argument within the cosy confines of *The Grave Diggers'*, and whilst consuming enough porter, Bernie thought, to flood the Liffey, he grew to admire the grown-up fervour of his old friend. He was pleased to see that arguing with passion was still obligatory in the pubs of Dublin.

He was intrigued to detect from his old friend that the ancient anti-British sentiment had survived his absence. It soon became clear to Bernie that there were still only two real points of debate in Dublin in 1876, Irish rule and Irish land. Everything had changed, nothing had changed.

It was a Friday evening. O'Leary trounced into *The Grave Diggers'* reeking of dead meat. He carried a headless carcass of lamb over his shoulder, its feet bound at either end with butchery bands. He leaned the cadaver against the wall. When he sat down, Bernie challenged him about the smell.

"Confound ya man. Haven't I slaughtered fifteen sheep since I broke me fast? The back is stranglin' me. I can hardly straighten."

"Isn't yer father doin' the slaughterin' for ya?"

"Not payin' what he charges. Anyways, isn't meat a good smell?" O'Leary looked offended. He cheered himself by sinking two jugs of porter in quick succession and steering the conversation back to his area of specialism.

"Didn't ya have an agricultural revolution in England? Four-field crop rotation, all dat bollocks."

"I believe so," Bernie answered.

"The Irish got involved in that, too. We had our own revolution, j'understand me?"

O'Leary waved his arms when he spoke, as though herding sheep. Excepting the smell, Bernie enjoyed the monologue. He told Bernie all about the Irish Agricultural Revolution. He described the new cultivation techniques, the introduction of new crops and a plough they borrowed from the Chinese.

"I couldn't believe me ears, a bleedin' Chinaman, showin' *us* how to plough a field, j'understand me?"

Bernie had a finger up his nose, using the nail to scrape the dead-meat smell off the inside of a nostril.

"Then dare's the other thing, the livestock." O'Leary took a slug of porter. "The landlords are wantin' tenants to be rearing sheep and cattle dese days. And it's causin' ructions. On me solemn." O'Leary poked a finger at Bernie. "Ya need to take heed o' dis if yer riskin' goin' down the country, Bernie. It's all hoggs and heifers as the oul' fella would say. And dey started dis selective breedin' t'ing where only the best lookin' animals get ta ride one another, j'understand me? Sure dat's what enticed the oul' fella to go into slaughterin'. He saw all dis comin' years ago. Shrewd oul' malcontent that he is."

Bernie had listened for almost an hour when O'Leary rasped his chair closer and leaned towards him. Bernie's nostrils flared and his right eye stung.

O'Leary lowered his voice. "All dese improvements," he whispered, "benefited everyone in farmin' except the smallholder. The smallholder was left behind. Dare's a minimum size ya have t'be before ya see any of the benefits, j'understand me? Ya had t' have a farm of a certain size for the sheep and cattle. Big fields o' pasture, j'understand me? So what did the landowners do? They started evictin' smallholder tenants to make the bigger farms to rear livestock."

O'Leary sat back, letting the enormity of his statement ferment.

Bernie gave an underwhelmed tug on an earlobe and ran a thumb and forefinger over his beard.

"Are ya not shocked by what I just said, Bernie? Smallholders getting' evicted. Especially in the west of Ireland."

"What d'you care about smallholders in the west of Ireland?" Bernie said, and took a sup of porter.

"Hey now, Bernie Kelly. Ya had kin dare yerself once, I remember. An uncle was it? Anyone listenin' to ya would think ya never stepped outside o' Dublin. It's the injustice, Bernie. The God Almighty injustice."

"They're smallholders," Bernie said. "That's the way it is. No injustice. To be an injustice there has to be a violation of a person's rights. There was no violation of their rights."

O'Leary gave out a loud roar of a laugh but checked himself, looking around the small room with wide eyes. He leaned in again, the meat-stench emanating from his pores. "These smallholders have no bleedin' roights!"

"Aw, come on, yer not goin'—"

"It remains the case today," O'Leary explained to Bernie. "Rents are rackin' up and tenants are still getting' thrown off... I'm buyin' a drink before I depress meself." He raised his bulk off the chair and pressed a fist into the small of his spine. "No one knows but meself the sufferin' I'm goin' through with this back," he said, and limped to the counter.

Whilst O'Leary waited for the drinks to be poured, the sound of revelry came from the back parlour. It was a funeral party, but sounded like a come-all-ye. There was laughter, swearing, singing and salutations to the man they were waking. He carried the pots back to the table.

Bernie watched the cooling carcass in the corner weep a bloody fluid over the floor.

"Dere's a wake goin' on in the room beyond," O'Leary said. "I wonder why I'm not at it."

"Because you're here with me. Yer oul' friend."

"The room sounds full o' people, I wonder whose wake is it?"

"Prob'ly the dead man's," Bernie said. "Are ya listenin' to me?" He waited until he had O'Leary's attention before continuing. "Agricultural output was up to blazes in the first half of the century? I remember studyin' that."

"Jases Chroist, Bernie," O'Leary said, laughing. "In what part of yer battered brain did ya find that shite? Tell me this, did y'ever hear of the potato blight?"

Bernie didn't think the question worthy of an answer.

"Ya remember that? Good," O'Leary said. "How many people died durin' the blight?"

"The famine? Don't they reckon about a million," Bernie said.

"One-and-a-half-million. How many smallholders died in the potato blight?"

"Wait now. Your argument is a nonsense. There were a lot more–"

"One-and-a-half-million."

"Cop on to yerself, Dermot? We can argue 'bout the numbers, but what're ya tryin' to say? That the famine was some kinda... I don't know, some kinda victimisation of the smallholders?"

"Then dare's the big question. Could it've been avoided?"

"Oh, I see. The ship-fulls of food being exported. Is that yer point?" Bernie stood up. "You'll be tellin' me next the famine was all me father's fault. I'm makin' a piss, before ya sicken me arse." He circumnavigated the smell on his way out.

"I'm just sayin' dare's food for thought dare," O'Leary called after him. "No pun meant," he murmured.

Chapter 34
Knockduff, Ireland, 1879.

Eileen has disappeared.

"Aiden. Aiden, wake. We need t' head on." Liam nudges his brother's shoulder. "Aiden, come on."

Aiden unwraps from his foetal curl against the ditch, and yawns.

Bubbly clouds, the colour of dirty sheep fleece, sprawl across the sky.

Liam looks for signs of Eileen. Which way did she go? He finds no clues in the grass, downtrodden from last night. Why did she leave? It's as well she's gone, they don't need her, and he has enough to look after with Aiden.

"Aiden, is the bread still there? Aiden?"

Aiden slumps, limp and lifeless, against the ditch.

Liam kneels beside him. "Aiden, what's wrong? Are ya ready to go?" He strokes his brother's bony back.

"I code, Ee-am. Tired."

"Ah, come on now, you'll be grand in no time. Look, it's a lovely warm day. Ballycastle may be just over that hill. We might be almost there."

"Hode me, Ee-am."

It's an unusual request. Liam wraps his arms around his brother, who feels damp and clammy. "Yer fine, little man, yer fine, I'll hold ya... I'll look after ya." Liam hopes gentle rocking will make Aiden better.

"Hello."

"Where'n the hell d'ya come out of?" Liam asks, spinning around, Aiden mounted on his back. "We were about to go."

Eileen is cloaked in a blanket, her hair damp. She smells of spring water. More freckles have been washed into the open. "Aiden, what's wrong?" she says, ignoring the question. "You look grey."

"I thought you'd gone. Where've ya been?" Liam asks.

"I had myself a wash. There's a brook near where I hid the blanket. It's alright smelling like a shit-matted sheep when you're travelling on your own, but now I'm not. So I had a wash. I'm cold, mind."

"Does that mean yer comin' with us?" Liam says.

"He's not well, is he? Is that why you're carrying him?"

"Why didn't ya wake us before ya left?"

"We must get him to a town, Liam. He's poorly, God love him." She reaches up and combs Aiden's hair with her fingers. "You'll be alright, Aiden. We'll look after you."

"Where'd ya get the blanket?"

"'T'was left in the dug-out I told you about."

"There was a blanket in the dug-out? Who left that there?"

"Me. It's my blanket. I've had it a while. I'd left it in the dug-out."

"Why not get it last night, when—"

"I didn't think we needed it. Look, we were fine. You gathered some...leafy things and sure Aiden was like a boiling kettle. Anyway, I'll bring it with me now, for sure. I'm cold after the wash. We must get some help for this little fella."

"And where'll we get that? He'll be fine. I'll carry him. He's just a bit tired." Liam shuffled his feet. "Eileen, ya didn't answer me question. Are ya wantin' t' come with us t' Ballycastle?"

"Do you want me to?"

"Only if ya want to. It's just I've Aiden to look after."

"I have a blanket. That might help keep him warm."

"Eileen, I won't be able t' look after ya."

"I can see that. You're barely able to look after yourself."

"No. That's not what I meant. I mean—"

Aiden coughs into Liam's hair. He swallows and rests his head back down on the nape of Liam's neck.

"Come on," Eileen says. "If we're going to Ballycastle, you better lead the way."

The day continues dry, a warm wind pressing at their backs. They pass through several flat fields. Progress is faster with Liam carrying Aiden. Eileen carries the blanket over her shoulder, the bread wrapped within its folds.

Though Liam is supposed to be leading the way, Eileen strides out in front. Her red hair is no longer ropey but billows over her shoulder. "Where are we going, Liam?" she asks.

"Aren't you doin' the leadin'?" he chides, grinning. "Ya know well where we're goin'. Ballycastle, t' find—"

"Why are we going this way, I mean? How do you know Ballycastle is this way?"

"Well..."

"Are you sure it's in this direction?"

"It could be."

"It could be?!" Eileen stands still, the boys catch up.

Liam, his back aching, takes the opportunity to stoop and allow his brother to slide off. "We'll have a bite o' bread, will we?" he suggests.

"Liam, you're not sure Ballycastle is in this direction are you?" Eileen asks.

Aiden sits himself down and coughs. He turns to the side and dribbles red phlegm onto the grass.

"Not completely."

"Glory be to God, Liam. How do you know going this way'll take you to Ballycastle if you're not sure?"

Liam notes the use of the word 'you'. Not 'us'. 'You'.

"We've walked this way every day since the eviction," he says.

"Why? What made you walk in this direction?"

"The truth?"

"For sure the truth."

"The sun. In the mornin's, me and Aiden are usually still cold from the night's sleep. So I head us into the warmth. I walk towards the mornin' sun."

"East," Eileen says.

"What?"

"You've been heading east. And you've done that every day?"

"Yea."

"And you've stayed walking that direction all day long?"

"I mostly follow the sun. It's warmerer that way, for the little man."

"South-east. You've probably been walking south-east, following the sun as it moves across the sky. Let me think, see if I can... Did you pass Lough Cloonagh?"

"Lough Cloonagh? I've been there with Da. No. I'd know Lough Cloonagh if we passed it."

"Did you pass through any towns?"

"No. No, no, no. We've passed through no towns and we passed no Lough Cloonagh." Liam busies himself pulling the blanket off Eileen's shoulder and unrolling it for the bread.

"Ballina then."

"What about–?"

"I'd say we're heading for Ballina. There'll be someone to help Aiden in Ballina, for sure. My father took me there once. A busy place, hundreds of people."

"How do ya know all this? About where we're headin' and all?" Liam asks.

"Because I went to school. My mother insisted I did the reading and writing. And speaking properly so folk respect you. The schoolmaster used come to the house. Geography he called it. We were shown pictures of–"

"I betcha yer wrong!" Liam says.

Eileen stares at him. "I've seen lads do this, on my father's farm. It happened when I worked out the correct sheep for lost lambs. Boys don't like being corrected by a girl, do they?"

They eat bread in silence.

The lane is wide, the surface even and clear of grass. It's not the sort of lane to lead you nowhere, or into a river. Liam gazes back over the fields they crossed. Acres of brown, black and green land splays out before him. There's not a cottage nor a shed nor a path in sight. They have been walking for hours and have met no-one.

"We'll rest," Liam says. His back aches, his shoulders throb, and his neck is raw from Aiden's fingernails. He collapses his legs for Aiden to dismount and examines his brother's eyes, unsure what he is looking for – a sign he won't die on him?

Eileen hears it first and points.

"Liam, look."

In the distance a huge, white-faced horse trots towards them, hooves clopping on the smooth surface of the lane. The horse has their scent and veers itself sideways as it approaches, reluctant to meet them head on. Apart from the white face and long white feathering around its fetlocks, the horse is mottled grey. Its mane is extravagant and flicks back over its withers. Muscles in its shoulders bulge and contract as it trots. It pulls a flat-bed cart.

There are two strong-looking shapes sitting on the front edge of the cart, four legs dangling.

"Tinkers!" he says and grips Aiden's arm. "Stay near t'each other 'til they pass. Don't look 'em in the eye and say nothin'."

The horse draws closer. As it bears down on them, Eileen steps out into its path. The horse jerks back its heavy head in equine dismay, black eyes glaring down at her. "Whoa, there, boy," she says.

"Hey, girl!" the driver shouts, yanking on the reins. "Y'll get yersel' killed. What possessed ya t' do that?"

Liam wraps an arm around Aiden's shoulders and draws him closer. Why did she halt them up?

"I didn't think you were going to stop," Eileen says. "Where're you headed?"

Now she's talking to them. Leave them go past, there'll be trouble.

"I nearly didn't. Nearly us trample ya t'death. What's wrong wit' ya?"

"I know horses," Eileen says. "Where are you lads headed?"

The cart driver gazes at Eileen.

Liam thinks he detects a leer.

The driver lifts a foot onto a shaft and rests an elbow on his knee. "Goin' our own way," he says. "Who're you t'be askin' us anyhow?"

His companion, riding coach-gun, giggles.

"We'd appreciate it if we could have a lift," Eileen says.

If she thinks we're getting up on that tinker's cart...

"The laddeen has no need of the petticoat," the driver says.

"Which? What did you say?" Eileen asks, frowning at Aiden.

"The laddeen," the driver says. "I see ye have 'im dressed in a petticoat to be makin' 'im look a girl. Lots do that with the baby boys so's the fairies don't make away with 'em. You're right in thinkin' fairies only take the little boys, but they don't take the sick ones."

Liam and Eileen glance at each other. Who are these people?

"And he looks like a sick one." The driver stares at Liam. "By the way, mister, ya can stop chokin' 'im. We're not goin' to eat 'im on ya."

"That's why we need the lift," Eileen says. "He's poorly. Where are you going?"

"Why don't ya tell us where you're goin' and we'll see if we're any help to ya?"

"Ballycastle," Liam says. "We're goin' t' Ballycastle. But we don't need no lift."

"Liam!" Eileen says.

"So one ofs ya do want a lift and one ofs ya don't want a lift. Is that it?"

Coach-gun laughs, parading a mouthful of decayed teeth, and rocks backwards on the cart-bed.

"We do want a lift," Eileen says. "If we're going the same way."

"We ain't goin' t' no Ballycastle, I know. And I'll bet ya me horse, Max, here, you all ain't goin' there either. You'll never make it with that sick child. He's a nice enough laddeen, but he won't make no Ballycastle walkin'. And anyways, I seen ye come out o' that field and I think yous is headin' the wrong way."

Coach-gun hides his laughing face in his hands.

"Ballina will be good enough," Eileen says, gambling. "Are you going to Ballina? The little lad is poorly. We need someone to look at him."

The strong chest of the driver rises as he considers his response.

"Right, so. I'll tell what we'll do with ya. And I'm doin' this for the laddeen, God love 'im, he looks ailin'. We'll give ye's a lift as far as Ballina. We're camped in Ballina, but you'll have t' be makin' yer own way to Ballycastle cos dat's the other way."

"We'll take the lift, and thanks," Eileen says, before Liam can speak. "Ballina will be grand. Thank you."

"Nice to see manners on a young girleen," the driver says. "Jump up on the back there, so. That laddeen can't be walkin'."

Aiden sits between Liam and Eileen, six feet dangling. For the first time today, he smiles.

Liam smiles, too. Aiden's magical powers know no boundaries, even traveller strangers are susceptible.

Eileen notices the grinning brothers. "You said I was wrong about Ballina?" she says. She twists her body and calls out to the front of the cart. "What're your names?"

Coach-gun giggles, turns, and speaks for the first time. "I'd be Martin McNulty and this big fella by the side o' me'd be Christy Sherridan."

129

Chapter 35
Dublin, Ireland, 1876.

Bernie blinked when he returned to the table.

"Listen to me, Dermot." He took a long slug of his drink to wash the taste of raw meat from his mouth. "The famine was not caused by anyone. You seem to've forgot it was caused by a simple blight in the potato."

"Such is the fiction fed to us, Bernie. My argument, is how could the failure of just one crop, the humble potato, lead to one-and-a-half-million people dyin'? Dare musta been people in powerful positions lettin' it happen."

"It wasn't an abdication of responsibility that caused the famine."

"I have a theory, roight?" O'Leary said.

"Right," Bernie said. "Go on so. Tell me how it happened. Explain to me yer theory." He took a sustaining slug of porter. The question of who was to blame for the devastation during the 1845 famine in Ireland had troubled minds, and caused arguments, fights and murders for almost thirty years. Bernie looked forward to Dermot O'Leary's version of events.

"When d'ya leave Dublin, Bernie?"

"Forty-six."

"The blight started a year before dat, roight?"

"I remember the workhouses fillin' up with all the bog-splicers comin' up to Dublin."

"Ya remember that ya do?" O'Leary smiled. "Like cattle dey were, smell o' cow shite off them. What else ya notice 'round that time?"

"There was a lovely lookin' girl livin' out in Sandymount who attracted me attention. She'd a fine pair of–"

"Soldiers."

"Shoulders? I wasn't goin' to say shoulders?"

"Soldiers, Bernie. Soldiers."

"A pair of soldiers? I doubt she had any–"

"Shut up and listen. I asked ya, what else did ya notice? I'm sayin' 'soldiers'."

"You'll need to say more than 'soldiers'. Explain yerself."

"The country was flooded with British soldiers. Passin' through Dublin like gas through a flatulent cow's arse. The bad smell o' them passin' out inta the countryside. Settin' themselves up in small barracks in every corner."

"Nothin' unusual about British soldiers. They've always–"

"No, Bernie. This was unusual. It started about a year before forty-six. Discreet like. Just passin' through Dublin. All jolly and polite." He attempted a London cockney accent. "On our way down the country so we are. No bovver. How d'ya do dare, mister? I'll have a top o' reeb wiv ya."

Bernie gave a broad grin. "For a moment there, I was back on Narrow Street in London, being lured into The Bunch o' Grapes by an alcoholic costermonger."

"I've more talents than just the ability to fillet a pope's eye steak, ya know," O'Leary said.

Bernie chuckled. "So why were the soldiers spreadin' out inta the country, setting up–"

"'Cause they feared the potato blight."

"The soldiers?"

"No, ya ass, the Government. They feared the blight. Dey had to protect the sales and profits o' the landowners."

"But there were no potatoes to sell," Bernie said.

"Let's assume, for a small while, dat the Irish didn't give every acre of land in the country over to the potato. Let's assume they were capable of plantin' wheat, and barley, and rye, and oats. And let's assume dey were still capable of rearing hens, and sheep, and pigs, and cattle. We'll go madly outrageous and even assume dey were still capable of making butter."

"Right," Bernie said.

"Not unreasonable assumptions, now?"

"Right."

"So where did all dat go when the potato crop failed?"

"Thousands o' small tenants, labourers, cottiers, all them, were livin' off plots o' land just big enough to park a barrow in," Bernie said. "It was subsistence farmin', no more. On marginal land, good for virtually nothin'. They had to choose a crop that would feed them throughout the year."

"Yer not answerin–"

"Nothin' tolerated poor soil like it," Bernie said. "And on top of all that, they fell in love with the bloody taste. Ya stuck it in the ground, and it grew. Easy. The lazy man's crop. They became totally dependent on the potato. That was the problem, Mr O'Leary. And when the potato became blighted, year after year, they were doomed."

O'Leary slammed down his pot and wiped his mouth on his sleeve. "The soldiers escorted it over to England," he said, slowly.

131

"What?"

"I'm after havin' to answer me own question. The crops and the meat dat was grown here was escorted by the soldiers, t' the ports. For export to England. To make sure the English didn't starve from dare own potato blight and to preserve the sales and profits o' the landowners."

"The English didn't suffer the potato blight," Bernie responded, shaking his head.

"Why didn't the Government close the ports t' exports, so? I'll tell ya now, Bernie, and this is on me solemn, the people couldn't have been more resentful or more fearful. Imagine watching food leavin' the market towns for the ports, with its own military escort. And you and yer family starvin', the children mouths stained green from eatin' grass. I'm not kiddin' ya, Bernie, dare were herds o' cattle sailin' off on every tide from every one of the Irish seaports."

"That's the ravin's of a porter-soaked mind."

"So the hunger years were not the Government's fault at all? Is dat what you think, Bernie?"

"They didn't cause it, no."

"Ya know nothin', Bernie Kelly. What about the bloody evictions?"

"Evictions? What–"

"The Government made landlords provide relief for their smaller tenants. So what did the landlord do?"

"You'll be tellin' me."

"Evicted them," O'Leary said. "Cleared them off the land. No longer a burden."

The mood had turned sombre. Both men took a reflective swig from their pots of porter.

"Ya know what sticks in the craw o' me throat the most?" O'Leary said, scratching his neck. "The evictions are startin' up again."

"You're livin' in the past, Dermot. Who's been fillin' yer head with this stuff?"

"I'm glad ya raised it." O'Leary pointed a finger at Bernie. "I was meanin' t' say. I have a polite invitation for ya. Listen, dare's a meetin' next Monday evenin'. A few friends o' moine. How'd ya like t' come along? I'll introduce ya. Ya must come along. Meet a few people. Important people. Clever people. If ya still don't agree with what's bein' said, that'll be yer opportunity t' bamboozle us wit' the cut 'n' thrust of yer Trinity education."

"No, I'm not inclined."

"Not inclined t' be proved wrong? I'll meet ya here beforehand. If ya don't want t' stay, I'll leave with ya, and we'll come back here for a skinful. I can't be more accommodatin' than dat?"

"We'll see."

"We'll see alroight, Mr Kelly. It's one of our biggest issues is evictions. The whole place is goin' t' go up in flames. The landlords and the bullocks are drivin' the people off the land, Mr Kelly, the landlords and the bullocks. The country is becomin' nothin' but a cattle-pen for the English, and Dublin a mere transit point."

O'Leary drained his jug. "Listen, I'm away. I'll meet ya here Monday. Now pass over that lump o' lamb till I drop it 'round to Bridie O'Sullivan. She'll be needin' it to feed dose t'ree hungry little terriers o' hers over the weekend." He tucked the carcass under an arm. "I'll nip inta the back room first, see if yer man was someone I knew."

Chapter 36
Kincon, Ireland, 1879

"Enter!" Constable Neild called.

Huddy stepped into the small office. "It's about the Henessey girl."

Neild pushed himself back in his chair. "PJ, hello. What do you... How can I assist?" He wrung the pencil in his hands, beneath the desk, then coughed into a fist. "Yes. Lamentable, PJ. Most regrettable."

"You've recorded it as an accident, a farming mishap. I suspect something more sinister, sir."

"You...I spoke to the grandmother as, I believe, you did yourself."

"I think she's lying, sir. There's clearly something not—"

"Why would she lie, PJ? Why would she lie about a thing like that? Surely not. The girl was her granddaughter. It's all in order."

"She's scared. Someone frightened her, threatened her."

"No-one has threatened her, PJ. Nor frightened her. You're letting—"

"Sir, she was found in the corner of a field." Huddy edged closer to the desk and peered down on the constable. "The corpse was wrapped in a sheet. There's no sign of an accident that would leave her like that."

"We have a witness, Acting-Constable. She seen it happen."

"The grandmother is hiding some—"

"I had her sworn testimony, Huddy, her mark at the foot of it. I've submitted the documentation. It's gone. There's nothing else to be done." Sweat beaded Neild's brow. The snap of a pencil came from beneath the desk. Neild swallowed hard. "This matter is closed, Acting-Constable. I have requested Mr Cuffe, the land agent for Farmhill, to be so kind as to meet the funeral expenses. It would be a benevolent gesture on his part, I thought. The honourable gentleman that he is, Mr Cuffe was only too happy to oblige."

'The honourable gentleman that he is', thought Huddy, back in the mess room. Cuffe was no honourable gentleman. Cuffe was implicated in Ann Henessey's death, and Neild knew it. Neild was on the make. Taking bribes. And was going to brush the matter away. He had probably been up at Farmhill House already, to negotiate his fee. Cuffe shouldn't escape free of consequence.

A rat scuttled along the edge of the floor. Huddy grabbed his baton and flung it at the rodent, crushing its skull against the blockwork.

Chapter 37
Ballina, Ireland, 1879.

It's easier to ride on the back of a flat-bed cart, being lulled by its gentle rocking and the squeak of the axle in the hub, than it is to carry your brother on your back. Even a light load gets heavy before long.

Aiden slept on the cart's bed, swayed to sleep shortly after they set underway, Eileen's blanket tucked around him.

They roll alongside fields that undulate in contours and colours of green and brown. They rumble past a lea of gaunt cattle who stare at them over a stone wall with cowed eyes. A sloping field of blond wheat waves them a welcome in the wind. They pass flocks of browsing sheep, dotted over verdant pastures - a Galway breed according to Eileen - and empty, keen-green fields shut within ditch embankments.

Liam lowers his gaze and watches the lane reveal itself between his long feet from the rear-underside of the cart. In his fatigued imaginings, the cart itself unravels the lane, hammered into place out front by the clapping hooves of Max, laying it over the boggy land for others to travel its surface forever more. He blinks his eyes awake and turns to Eileen. "How long ya been on yer own?"

"Not sure," she says.

Liam watches her search for a time mark in her head. Nothing. "Seems like forever. It's more than weeks. A few months maybe."

"An' are ya headin' anywhere? Is there someplace you're goin'?"

"I thought I was going to Ballycastle with you?"

The answer pleases him. He wants to ask about her parents again, but mindful of her reaction last time, he asks about his own, instead. "Do ya think I'll ever find Mam and Da again?"

Eileen lets out a long breath. "You told me they were beaten. Who bet them?"

Liam calls to mind the horror of eviction day. It too seems like forever-ago, but he remembers every painful detail.

"Mainly a fella called Cuffe."

Eileen stiffens.

"The land agent," Liam continues. "He belted Da. Lots o' times. When Mam tried to help, he belted her. Only stopped beltin' them when the acting-constable fella came back. Cuffe's a big fella, and he belted them with this lump of a blackthorn stick he has." Liam's fists clench. "I'm goin' t' kill Cuffe one day."

"Hey! Stop." Eileen glares, wide-eyed. She turns to check if the traveller boys overheard him. "Ya can't go saying things like that, Holy God above," she whispers. "I don't blame you thinking that, Liam, but you can't go saying it out loud."

"You don't think I'll do it, do ya?"

"I just know it's dangerous to be thinking like that. Killing's not—"

"It can't be right he hit Mam and Da, batter them, and nothin' happen to him for it."

"For sure, but…"

"You're prob'ly right, though. I don't think I'll do it either. Kill him I mean. I can't even find Ballycastle. Can't even find me own mother and father. I'm not getting' anythin' right, Eileen. Da said always have a plan and so I made a plan. But it's broke. I'm afraid 'cause Aiden's sick. And I'm afraid I won't find Mam and Da for them t' make 'im better. I don't think I'll ever see them again. And what'll I do about Aiden? He needs them." His cheeks are damp. "And I keep cryin' like a baby when I think about it all."

She reaches over Aiden and places a hand on Liam's shoulder. He wants to flinch, but doesn't. The squeeze of her fingers feels warm.

"I'm never goin' t' cry in front of ya again," he says, staring at the blurred road.

"My mother used to say, 'That's boys for ya', about my brothers. They'd rather break something than cry." She removes her hand.

"What'll I do if I can't find Ballycastle?" he asks. "If I can't find Mam and Da?"

"We'll find them, we will."

"I don't think we will… And, don't be worryin', I won't be killin' Cuffe, either. I don't know how t' be fightin' with no-one, never mind be killin' them. I'm just a boy. I've a little bit o' meat on me but I've no shoulder muscles yet."

Eileen smiles.

A humped bridge takes them over the babbling stream that runs through Rosserk. Approaching Ballina, they pass close to a group of men in caps huddled around St Patrick's Well, arguing. By the time they enter the town, the sun is past its meridian. At a T-junction, Christy Sherridan whoas Max to a halt. The stillness of the cart wakes Aiden.

"There's a travellin' fair suppose' to be startin' up today down that way, towards the river," Christy calls back, pointing down a road signed 'Garden Street'. "The young fella might enjoy it if ye've time."

The three passengers dismount and walk to the front of the cart. Max swings his great head to look back.

"Thanks for the lift," Liam says. "We'd not walk it." He reaches up to shake Christy's hand. "You were born in the same place as me."

"Hah?" Christy says. "How d'ya know where it was I was born? Sure you're no older than me."

"Me father told me the story of when ya were born. Your family camped near our village. They was scared of ye all. Me father said the weather was bad and you were near being born, so ye camped. He said there was snow about."

"That's right! Me mother always says I was born in the year of the big snow. Reckons it's why I'm never feelin' the cold. It was in Kincon. Is that where you're born?"

Liam nods. "You was born in Rathoma, near Kincon. I'm from next t'ya in Carrow."

"Well there y'are now, me and you is townies."

Aiden sidles up beside Liam, wiping sleep from dark eyes.

Christy shakes his head. "Listen, if ye've no place to be stayin', you can camp with us," he says. "Ye'll need ta sleep under the cart, mind, but at least ye'll have shelter. Ya need be watchin' out for the constables, they're fierce around these parts for wantin' to fill the workhouse. If they see ye sleepin' on the streets they'll nab ye, and ye'll be sowin' buttons onta shirts the rest of yer lives."

"We'll do that," Liam says, looking at Eileen, who gives the slightest of nods. "Where's yer camp?"

"Opposite way out o' town," Christy says, pointing. "Out that road, towards Crossmolina. Past the workhouse on the right. Ye'll not miss us."

"Is there still a woman there who can tell yer future from readin' cards?"

"Good God, you know more about me than I do. No, that was me granny. Passed now. But Martin's father gives us a tune on the ol' fiddle now an' again. That's good for the craic too."

Chapter 38
Carrowkeel, Ireland, 1879.

Five days after Ann's funeral, half-a-dozen green-uniformed members of the Royal Irish Constabulary assembled outside the front door of Joseph Henessey's cottage. Acting-Constable PJ Huddy was commanding.

Constable Neild had ordered him to oversee the men on this occasion.

"The supervisory experience will do you no harm," Neild had said.

"Condescending cyst," Huddy thought.

The lane beside the cottage was cart-wide, rough under foot, long and straight. To one side, the damp soil was overrun by a thick forest of aspen. The other side was lined with heaps of hawthorn, the deep-red haws glistening in the September sun. The Henessey cottage sat hidden behind the hawthorn.

Billy Cuffe approached the front door with Mr Hogan, the Magistrate, at his side. Cuffe had employed a gang of three heavy, thickset brothers as driver-men. Sligo men, from over the county border. He said they were there to assist with 'the removal of belongings'. He had armed each with a crowbar.

What with payments to Constable Neild, the Magistrate, the driver-men and the undertaker, the cost of the brief encounter with young Ann Henessey was mounting up.

Huddy had his men lined up between the cottage and the lane. There were no spectators, the eviction had been arranged quickly and discreetly.

"Henessey," Cuffe said to the door. "There is a magistrate here with an eviction order for you. Open the door now, man." He slapped the blackthorn into the palm of his hand.

The door creaked ajar and Joseph Henessey shuffled into view. Drunken tears tracked over gaunt, soiled, freckled cheeks. His eyes glowed red beneath bushy brows, barely visible in the shadow of a tattered stove-hat brim. His button-less vest was open, exposing a dull grey simmet stained with soil and spilled poteen.

"Joseph Henessey," Magistrate Hogan said. "By the powers invested in me through the County Courts of Ireland, I hereby serve this civil bill of ejectment for non-payment of rent to the Farmhill Estate. This notice has immediate effect. Now accept this notice and vacate the premises."

As the words fell against the half-open door, mournful cries of distress were heard from inside. The driver-men stiffened in readiness for physical confrontation and inched up behind Cuffe.

Henessey raised his blood-shot eyes and glared. It was a glare filled with all the hatred a drunken, broken man was capable of mustering. The glare was all he had to assault Cuffe with, his final outpouring of abhorrence. His last pathetic means of showing his contempt for the man.

"She comply?" Henessey managed to ask.

Cuffe took a half-step backwards.

"Or fight…? I teached 'er t' fight."

Cuffe raised a hand to the facial scratches that Ann inflicted.

"Come now, Mr Henessey," Magistrate Hogan said. "Gather your accoutrements, we need you vacate the premises." Hogan stepped away and signalled with a flick of the wrist for the driver-men to move in.

Henessey swung the door open wide and stepped into the gap. He stretched himself tall, drew back his chin and clenched his fists. The heavies stayed their ground. Henessey stared at each of them. When he was sure they wouldn't enter without his consent, he turned, and disappeared into the wailing and sobbing.

A twin-wheeled cart and horse crunched on the lane. Huddy raised a hand to ease his men and walked towards it. The cart slowed as it drew near. The young cart driver stared over him at the cottage. Huddy called up to him. "There'd be nothing here to see. Move on, like a good man."

The man sitting on the box seat tipped his hat to the acting-constable and clicked his horse. The cart rolled on between the aspen and the hawthorn. On passing the cottage, the driver gave a look back and flicked the reins. The horse trotted. Half a mile down the road, James Daly pulled up his carriage. Like a real newspaper reporter, he reached into his inside pocket for his pad and pencil and made his notes.

The family stood around the grandmother in front of the cottage. Joseph Henessey stood alone, away from the crying and the sniffling, his hands stuffed into patched pockets. He watched the driver-men drag and throw his belongings onto the grass. He itemised the objects he would take back in when that gobdaw of an agent, his lick-arse men and the constabulary cleared off and left them in peace. He knew he shouldn't enter the cottage once evicted, but he had to put his family somewhere for a few days until he decided what he was going to do. He couldn't be put to thinking now, all he wanted to do was vomit. He wished he had a bottle of poteen with him, to stave off the turmoil in his stomach. As soon as this was over, he intended to head for the still in the mountain. There will be poteen there, enough to drink this problem away for a while.

"Everything out?" Cuffe asked his men. He turned to Henessey. "Anything else, now? If so, better you get it quick, you won't be going in there again."

Henessey shook his head.

Huddy's men were lined up, ready to march away.

"The curse o' Jesus and ruin to ya, ya lyin', thievin' rascal," Mrs Henessey called out over the heads of the children gathered around her.

Cuffe glowered. He strode over and dragged the old woman by the shoulder from the midst of her family.

Huddy noticed it and marched towards them.

Cuffe bent level with her ear. "You'll hang by the neck before I do," he said.

The harshness in his voice made her wince.

"You brought her to me," he said. "Remember that."

Huddy arrived beside them, his brow furrowed.

Cuffe glanced at him and walked away. "Right you men!" he shouted. "Burn it down!"

Within seconds, the tinder roof of the cottage blazed. Billows of grey, acrid smoke mushroomed into the air. As the flames grew, crackling, burning straw dripped between the rafters. Hay bedding and thin net curtains shrivelled and combusted. A wooden box the driver-men had not bothered to remove peeled, twisted and burnt. A forgotten jar of poteen was found by the flames and exploded, spraying liquid fire across the floor. The roof timbers moaned as they contracted, and collapsed with a crash. Sparks swirled into the air. Flames licked the walls, smearing them sooty.

Joseph Henessey waved away a charred flake before it alighted on his vest. His family clung to each other like a fall of lambs, and watched their home burn. The hiss and snap filled their ears, the orange and yellow flares stung their faces.

The grandmother stood alone, the blaze warming her tears.

Chapter 39
Dublin, Ireland, 1876.

When he and O'Leary were not presenting their opposing cases like two drunken barristers called to the public-house bar rather than the wooden barrier of the courtroom, Bernie walked.

He was back at the North Wall. The late-morning was bright and blustery. He stood and watched the steamships docked in the deep-water berths exude their cargoes. As the gulls screeched overhead, he wondered if Peggy's name was on the ship's manifest. He waited. It wasn't.

A small group of prostitutes shivered by a warehouse wall, sheltering from the wind. He assumed them tenement women, forced into their line of work to survive. They looked expectant, ready to welcome newcomers to Ireland with open legs. Arrivals might ride them into town to save the tram fare, thought Bernie.

One of their number ambled over to him with a proposition but caught him in the wrong frame of mind. "Ya lonely, soldier?" she asked, with the admirable perceptiveness of one skilled in peddling companionship.

The gulls glided on the gusts and shrieked their mocking laugh down on them all.

From the North Wall, he walked a route along the river, past Customs House. At Carlisle Bridge, at the bottom of Sackville Street, an old, thin man with one-and-a-half legs and wearing a greasy flat cap, stopped people crossing. The man leaned on a crutch telling everyone to, "Walk bastardin' 'round." Bernie asked him why he was guarding the bridge.

"Day're t'inkin' a widenin' it," the guard said, and scowled at Bernie.

Bernie turned and surveyed Sackville Street. The impressively wide thoroughfare was lined with lofty buildings. Awnings draped like scalloped skirting from busy ground floor shops. The pillared portico of the General Post Office, like a discourteous grandee, ignored any agreed building line and jutted itself out onto the footpath.

Nelson's Pillar dominated the vista, with Nelson gazing down on the flower sellers, the trams and the tramps, his armless sleeve tucked in between the buttons of his jacket. Bernie wondered now long it would be before friends of O'Leary toppled Lord Nelson from his plinth and dragged his carcass into the Liffey.

"How wide'll the new bridge be?" he asked the guard.

"An extra couple a foot dey're t'inkin'. That's th'engineer's over dere. In the hat. Lookin' at his drawin's. Don't t'ink he knows how wide ta make it at all. Bastardin' eejit."

"Tell 'im it needs to be as wide as Sackville Street."

The guard laughed. "Yu'll never build a bridge dat bastardin' wide," he said, pointing up Sackville Street with his crutch.

"Jus' tell 'im."

"I will. But he'll take no bastardin' notice. Now walk 'round."

He paid a ha'penny and passed through a turnstile to cross at a footbridge further along the river. He wound his way through cobbled lanes to Dame Street, crossing into St George's North. He took a left towards St Stephen's Green. Another turn and he was on Merrion Street Upper, outside the National Gallery.

He stepped in and spent an afternoon there, distracting himself from alcohol. He was drawn to the landscapes, particularly those of William Ashford and Thomas Roberts. He unnerved the guards with his intimate inspections of the brushstrokes, the materials and the colours, as he leaned in over the cord barriers. He lost himself for minutes at a time in the rich rural scenes. The skyscape in a George Barret picture moved him to tears. He recalled a visiting French artist from school days, telling him that you can learn a lot about yourself from how you react to art.

As the time approached five o'clock, Bernie thought he had resisted long enough. He made his way to the exit. As he descended the grand sculpture-gallery staircase, he heard a hollow cry echoing in a side vault. He crept inside the packed room to find an auctioneer in full voice, chanting the bid-calls in an indecipherable stream of words.

Bernie stayed long enough to see a painting by Hugh Douglas Hamilton sell to an absent bidder for £302 and 10 shillings. It was a staring portrait of Francis Seymour Conway, Marquess of Hertford and former Lieutenant of Ireland. The buyer's name was Harriet Gardner. As Bernie returned the stare, he thought the Marquess smiled at him. It was a friendly enough portrait, but the price was a lot more than Bernie would want to pay.

Bernie attended the meeting on Monday evening with O'Leary. It turned out to be the first of several meetings he attended. It didn't stop their arguments in *The Grave Diggers'*.

He missed Trinity College Library when in England. It was in one of its secluded corners he shared his escape plan with Philip. He visited it now on his return, several times. It proved his favourite distraction.

Bernie discovered the Liffey had a renovated bridge. A steel plate informed him that, in 1859, what he had known as Bloody Bridge became the Victoria and Albert Bridge. When he lifted his head from the plate he found a young street-arab leaning against the corner of the granite abutment, staring up at him.

Bare feet crossed, hair over eyes, heavily-sooted face, a hand plunged deep into a liningless pocket, the boy raised a fist to wipe his nose. Behind the urchin sat a box of coal fixed into a rusting perambulator frame. One side of the frame missed a spoked-wheel.

Bernie flicked him a coin. The street-arab plucked it from the air before it reached the top of its arc. The lad had the makings of a good fighter, Bernie thought. He would have enjoyed tutoring him if he had the time.

After almost two months of walking, meetings, arguing and drinking, Bernie had rediscovered all he wanted of Dublin. It already pressed in on him, as London had done after thirty years. The guilt and shame associated with his family festered inside. He hadn't bothered to seek out his father and mother, and all his enquiries about Philip came to nothing. He thought it time to escape to the countryside depicted in the works of art he admired in the gallery. All part of his renaissance.

Though ready to leave Dublin he acknowledged the characteristic pattern of inertia, wasting time in a city for no productive reason. He did it in Liverpool for his brother, and he did it in Dublin for Peggy Deagan. Both waits equally futile. His brother hadn't descended a steam-ship gangplank and materialised beside him, and nor would Peggy. He thought of her every day, often reliving the drink-induced scenarios of her sauntering down a footpath towards him, smiling and forgiving, as he swayed, submerged in a drunken state of self-pity.

It took another two weeks for him to work out where to go.

Browsing the newspaper archives in Trinity College Library, his hands trembling from the alcohol, he discovered a copy of an American newspaper from 1865, *The New-York Tribune*. In it, its editor, Horace Greeley, had penned an editorial headed, 'Go west young man, and grow up with the country.' Greeley, of course, referred to the westward expansionism of America. Bernie smiled when he read it and said out loud, "I wonder how Roscommon is this time o' year?"

"Shush," the usher said.

Chapter 40

Written Especially for The Mayo Telegraph.

By James Daly.

Saturday, September 14th, 1879

It has been noted, without little concern, that we are in a time of an ongoing increase in the deplorable actions of one or two of our regional Landlords. This paper has written of the misdemeanours of one Miss Harriet Gardner in the past, but I myself witnessed another outrage on the Monday of this week. It took place at the home of Joseph Henessey, a small-holding tenant of the Farmhill Estate, the estate owned by none other than the notorious Gardner. The woman was absent herself but instead sent her henchman of a land agent, William 'Billy' Cuffe, to do her dirty work. Mr Cuffe and a gang of thugs, summarily evicted poor Joseph Henessey, along with his family, leaving them destitute. No sooner had the Agent removed the family from the house than he set it to fire, razing it to the ground. The flames were so ferocious, smoke was visible for miles around, sending a clear signal of terror to other tenants. The Henessey family consists of husband and wife, a teenage daughter, two younger sons and an elderly grandmother. At least half-a-dozen members of the Royal Irish Constabulary were present at the scene, ostensibly to prevent any disruption to the peace. To this reporter's eye, it was Cuffe and his gang of thugs that were the ones disrupting the peace and in warrant of incarceration. This is the second of a double tragedy for Mr Henessey and his wife. Only last week Mr Henessey buried his eldest daughter following a fatal accident on the farm. Our condolences for the sad loss of their daughter are with Mr and Mrs Henessey. The family are now destitute from the inconsiderate actions of the agent, Billy Cuffe. Cuffe is thought to be a relation to the deceased uncle, who bore the same name, of Miss Harriet Gardner.

"You witnessed this yourself?" Eamonn McHugh asked.

"Drove past it on me dog cart," James Daly said. "I was gone by the time they set fire to the cottage, but I was only down the lane and I could see the clouds of smoke. I left it a while and walked back to the house later. It was there I spoke to Henessey's mother. I refer to her as the grandmother in the piece. Henessey himself was gone. She didn't know where, or at least she wasn't inclined to let on to me. It was the grandmother who told me about the daughter's death last week. It's a tragedy so it is."

"I need to work on your copy," McHugh said, "but we'll run the story. Good work, James."

Chapter 41
Ballina, Ireland, 1879.

The fair is alive with remarkable people doing remarkable things. Two jugglers spin long lengths of wood into the air, high above their heads, and catch them behind their backs. They toss the planks to each other, performing flic-flacs whilst the wood is in flight. They drop nothing, clean catches every time.

Next to the jugglers a big sign introduces "The Irish Singing Clown". The clown stands on an upturned galvanised-steel wash tub. He blows into a small, black piccolo, his fingers dancing over the shiny keys. The tune has an impressive stridency for such a small instrument. Liam sways his head to the music, but the clown is not funny at all. Nor is he singing.

Behind the clown, they find a big man with no hair, dressed in a sleeveless simmet and short trousers. The man stands amongst a collection of farming paraphernalia. Anvils, chains and sledge hammers lay strewn around him. He lifts a pair of cartwheels above his head, black muscles beaming like giant beetles as they bulge. Liam has never seen a black-skinned man before. "Francois Bertran - World's Strongest Man" says a painted sign propped in front of him.

Francois winks at Liam and smiles, parading a mouthful of yellow-white teeth around a thick, pink tongue.

Liam takes a step back, pulling Aiden with him.

An exotic woman with shadowy, Romani features, sits half-in-half-out of a pointed tent. Her small stool is almost hidden beneath the layers of her colourful dress. Her dark eyes flicker over the three of them as they approach. Stars and a crescent moon sparkle off the surface of the tent, on which the words "Temple of Knowledge" slope upwards behind her.

"I'm Zena," she says, bowing her head.

They shuffle past.

Eileen spies a bareback rider. The horse trots in a tight circle, the woman standing aloft on its back whirling a wooden hoop around her middle. Her arms are outstretched. She resembles a bird circling in the sky warning people of bad weather. Eileen calls Liam over so that Aiden sees from his position on Liam's back.

"What in God's name's that?" Liam asks, indicating with a nod of his head.

Eileen turns to see. "Aiden, look," she shrieks. "A little monkey dressed as a cowboy. And look, he's riding on the back of a sheepdog! How'd they do that?"

"Is that what it is?" Liam says, laughing. "Aiden, see it? I've never seen a monkey before. Or a cowboy, I'm thinkin'."

Aiden rocks with laughter. He screeches into Liam's ear, "Ee-am, monkey has hat!" His wriggling fingers beckon the monkey closer.

The dog gallops past them. Eileen turns to Aiden and drums the ground with her feet as she gives rapid small claps of excitement in front of him.

Aiden bucks with glee on Liam's back.

Liam delights in the little man's joy. It's good to feel him happy again.

After watching the sheep-dog-riding monkey-cowboy for a few minutes, Liam's attention is caught by a tight crowd of men further down the field. The men shout and move as a group. He kneels to allow Aiden off his back.

"Eileen, keep Aiden a minute, will ya? I wanta see what's the noise about."

Without taking their eyes off the monkey-cowboy, who rears the sheep-dog up onto its hind legs, Eileen and Aiden clasp hands.

Liam gives Aiden a final check and is disheartened by the dark circles around his eyes, distorted though they are by his monkey-induced smile. He ruffles Aiden's hair.

Liam cannot see what the men crowd around. They move in a harmonised flock, like land-bound starlings in a murmuration, shifting in random directions. He climbs a stone wall nearby. When he straightens his long frame, he has a view into the middle of the mass. Two men, each wearing oversized gloves, square up to each other.

One fighter has a beard and wears a bright-red shiny vest. The other is younger and dressed like the other men, in a cap and shirtsleeves, braces crossing his shoulders. Liam watches, open-mouthed, as the two fighters move around each other, gloved-fists aloft.

Braces takes a swing at Shiny-vest. The crowd shout, but Shiny-vest dances clear of the big glove.

"Get into 'im Dominic, good lad," comes a clear shout from an old man in the crowd.

The crowd gives a nervous laugh.

Braces lunges with another punch. The oversized glove hits air. Shiny-vest heaves him away across the small space, into the perimeter of people. Braces recovers and unleashes another swing. Shiny-vest allows it to come close, but there is no contact.

There's murmuring in the crowd. Expectant, smiling faces, exchanged glances.

Shiny-vest is toying with Braces, Liam can tell.

In frustration, Braces gives a loud, angry roar and runs at Shiny-vest who ducks under the outstretched arms and counters with a punch so fast Liam barely sees it. Braces falls to the grass and the crowd moans and shouts as it shifts shape again.

A tall, ginger-haired man with a thick curly beard and wide hairy nostrils appears at the crowd's centre. Liam has never seen a man with so much ginger hair on and around his head. The giant grasps Shiny-vest's gloved fist, raises his free hand and waits for decorum.

"Gentlemen," he bellows over their heads, nostrils flaring. "Go home tonight, limber up and flex yer muscles." He draws the syllables out as he shouts. It sounds to Liam like singing. "But make sure ya come out tomorra and visit Aloysius O'Connor's Country Fair. The fightin' booth will be set up for you all to get a better view of the action. It's an open-ring competition gentlemen and we'll be here for five more days. Pit yourself against my champion over two rounds. If ya knock my man down, ya win the prize money. If you're still standing after two rounds, ya get your fight fee back, and you win my immense admiration."

The crowd laugh.

"Tomorrow gentlemen, I'm looking for the cream of County Mayo to take to the ring and step up to the mark. You all look like fine fighting men to me. Even you, sir, with the crutches."

"Barney'd mollicate 'im wit' the wooden leg!" someone shouts.

There's laughter.

"We may even see some of them Sligo men from across the river in town," says O'Connor, "fine fightin' men that they are. But the Mayo man takes some beatin'."

Another laugh of acknowledgement from the crowd.

"If any of ye want to buy me a drink, I'll be in Whealan's within the hour. Otherwise, until tomorrow afternoon, gentlemen. Before ya go, please give a clap for Aloysius O'Connor's boxing champion, a Jackeen, all the way from the heart of the Pale itself, Mr Ber-nie Ke-lly!"

The crowd give brief applause and disperse in many huddled conversations, some wanting to reach in for a hand-shake with the Dublin man before they go.

"What was all this, Liam?" Eileen asks as she and Aiden approach the wall, hand in hand.

Liam stares, Shiny-vest is helping Braces remove his gloves.

"There's a man who can fight, Eileen. He moves like he's been fightin' all his life. He didn't need t'—"

"Oh, you missed something with the monkey," Eileen says. "He was amazing. He was jumping the dog over fences and everything, wasn't he Aiden?"

"Monkey came to Aiden," Aiden says.

"He did, Liam. It was as if the monkey knew him. I think that monkey loves you, Aiden, d'ya think?" Eileen laughed, a hand at her mouth.

"I 'ove monkey," Aiden says.

"Come on now so, Liam," she says, smiling. "We'd better start walking up to find the traveller camp, it's getting dark."

Liam jumps from the wall, pleased Aiden is talking again.

"You'll be fine now, I only swiped ya gentle," Bernie Kelly says to Braces, patting him on the shoulder. Movement by a stone wall catches his attention. The blow is as fast and powerful as anything he can deliver himself. His senses spin and he holds on to Braces's arm or he, himself, will topple. Peggy Deagan stands beside the wall holding a young child's hand, smiling and talking in her usual animated way to a thin young man. Bernie had dreamt it a thousand times, usually when drunk. But he is sober, has been for some time, and it has become reality. Peggy Deagan has found him. She isn't walking towards him along a pavement, smiling and waving, but she is here. He blinks and stares.

The disappointment of reality crests over him. It's not Peggy Deagan. How could it be? It's a young woman with the same red hair, the same round face, an identical proud nose, the same postures. But it's not Peggy Deagan. This woman is a child, what Peggy grew from, what Peggy was like twenty or thirty years ago. The resemblance makes the hairs on the nape of his neck tingle. Who is she?

Chapter 42
Farmhill, Ireland, 1879.

"Who calls at this hour?"

Acting-Constable PJ Huddy kicked with the heel of his boot.

The door burst its latch and struck Billy Cuffe on the forehead with a thick thud, knocking him onto his back.

Huddy lowered his foot and strode into the lodge-house. Before Cuffe got to his feet, Huddy was over him, brandishing his baton.

"Forgive me for not answering, sir," Huddy said. "I wasn't sure you would open the door, and I'm not wasting time explaining why I'm calling."

"What in the name of God!" Cuffe yelled, assessing the damage to his forehead with his fingertips. He looked up into the cavernous face of the uniformed man, the moist red eye glaring down at him.

"Don't mention God, Cuffe. I believe you know nothing of Him."

"What is the meaning of this?" Cuffe yelled.

"The Henessey girl."

"What of her?" Cuffe asked.

"She was but a child," Huddy spat.

Cuffe pulled his hand away from his harried face. "What is it you infer, man? Speak to Constable Neild. The Henessey girl was nothing to do with me. Ask the grandmother, she'll tell you." Cuffe wriggled himself onto all fours, about to stand.

He knows, thought Huddy. He knows that I know. Huddy drew back his foot and swung it into Cuffe's ribcage.

Cuffe let out a rush of air as he lifted and slumped down on top of a footstool.

"Fourteen years old!" Huddy said. "I think it has to do with you and I've a mind to batter and kick you to death, you warped, unholy savage."

"Wait," Cuffe gasped. "Wait." He held up a hand as he rolled himself into a seated position. "Let me speak... Talk to Neild." He held his ribs. "By God that hurts. I cannot tell you what happened her, I know nothing of it. And you have no evidence linking me to any crime."

Huddy paced the floor in short strides, his knuckles white around the corrugated grip of his baton. He already knew what happened, he examined the girl's body, he recognised the marks of molestation. Cuffe didn't have to explain to him what had happened.

"The grandmother was here with the girl the day before the body was reported," Huddy said.

"You can prove nothing. What is your evidence, man?"

"You refused her loaf. The men tell me she dropped the loaf off at the constabulary barracks on her way home. She was here alright."

"She will deny it," Cuffe said, rubbing his ribs. "And your men have no doubt eaten any evidence you had." Cuffe gave a sinister, mocking cackle as he threw back his head. "Who the hell do you think you are coming here, making accusations with no ev–"

Huddy turned and pressed the point of his baton into the healing scratches on Cuffe's cheek. "Cuffe, if you repeat an act like that again, so help me, I will beat you and see you in shackles. They'll be holding your broken body up in the dock of the court whilst the Judge condemns you to a life sentence. Do you hear me? Do you hear me?!"

Cuffe pushed the baton away. "Curb your threats and lower your voice," he said. "You have no evidence. Now, if you value your position in the constabulary, you will let me stand." He scrambled to his feet and adjusted the line of his jacket coat.

Huddy stayed his ground.

Cuffe stood inches away. He spoke into the ruined face of Huddy. "This is assault, Acting-Constable. If you have any evidence of my involvement in the Henessey girl's death, arrest me."

They held a stare. Huddy's fingers fluttered over the handle of the baton. He could finish Cuffe now. Retribution for what he did. Retribution for everything. One blow, and it would be over. He felt water build on his eyelid. His fingers fluttered, regripping the handle.

"I thought not," Cuffe said, and smirked. "You have no evidence. You do, however, have a statement to the contrary from the grandmother." Cuffe stepped away. "Neild will hear of this outrage, and I'll see you are destroyed. Your time with the constabulary is finished, Huddy. You will come to realise who it is you are dealing with, Acting-Constable."

Huddy turned towards the open door.

"That's right leave, Huddy. And ready yourself for dismissal."

Huddy paused at the door. "I won't be dismissed."

Cuffe cocked his head.

"You've no evidence," Huddy said, and left.

Chapter 43
Ballina, Ireland, 1879.

He wakes to the sound of ripping grass and snorting.

Max's huge horse-head nibbles dew-drenched blades from between the spokes of the cartwheel.

Liam realises he has spent the night in a traveller camp. He hasn't had his throat cut and all his eyes are accounted for.

When they arrived from the fair, Christy Sherridan introduced Liam, Eileen and Aiden to a few of his family. They were fed a small taste of a pig's trotter that Christy had brought back from Killala and shared the remaining bread. Aiden didn't eat anything, preferring instead to sleep. Liam had spent the rest of the evening sitting close to the campfire, with Christy. He listened to a man scratch out a tune on a badly-chipped fiddle whilst telling Christy about Rathoma and Carrow, and about Kincon, the regional town that was a link between them.

Christy asked Liam about the people of the area. He heard about Spinster Kennety and how she had frightened the life out of Liam with her card reading. When Liam told Christy about the eviction, Christy shook his head in dismay.

Whilst Liam talked to Christy, Eileen nursed Aiden. The coughing had become persistent. With each cough, Aiden spat out runny, bloody mucus. His breathing sounded like an old-man rattle and he complained of a pain deep in his chest. Overcome with exhaustion, he had fallen into a sweating, wheezing sleep, cradled in Eileen's rocking arms. When Liam returned, they laid Aiden between them under the blanket, sheltered beneath the cart.

A blaze of pure white runs the full length of the horse's long face. Fluttering lips gather the blades for teeth to tear.

Liam extends a hand between the spokes and his fingers glance off the dangling head as it sways back and forth over the wet grass. "Hello, Max," he says. He twists to check on Aiden.

Aiden is swamped in sweat.

"Eileen. Eileen, wake up," Liam says.

Eileen wakes and stretches. She pushes herself up on an elbow. "Liam, I don't think he slept many winks last night," she says, through a yawn. "He was coughing nearly all the time, God love him. We must get him seen to."

"How? Where?"

"Ask your friend, Christy. Who would he go to if he was sick? There must be someone."

A maroon silk scarf encases her silver hair. Her complexion is dark-skinned and smooth with remnants of a striking former beauty. A dark-brown mole rests to the right of her nose, drawing a beholder's eye like candlelight draws a moth. Though her face hides the secret of her age, her body confesses the truth. Her spine is twisted and she has to be held up as she shuffles towards them. Two women lower her down to the grass beside Liam.

Liam sits on his heels with Aiden laid back over his thighs.

She rocks her body back as she raises her elegant face to appraise the child. An unsteady arm uncoils from her black shawl and she reaches for Aiden's hand. The small, white, smooth hand of Aiden contrasts with the large, brown wrinkled hand of the woman. Her head quivers. The examined hand is returned, and she extends her wiry fingers to the side of Aiden's neck where they pause. She grabs a fist-full of her shawl and covers her mouth before leaning in close to his face. Liam expects her to topple over him and he tries to see what she is looking at. She straightens and reaches down to Aiden's leg, gliding a wrinkled hand along the length of the limb to a soiled foot, its sole callused and leathery.

She flicks an arm to indicate she has finished and is lifted to her feet. Before she walks away, she turns to Liam.

He stares up from his kneeling position into the young face of the old woman. Her face shifts, but Liam finds it inscrutable. A smile? A look of pity? He wants to ask, but nobody has spoken to the woman since her arrival, and she's so terrifying he says nothing.

Christy follows the old woman as she limps away on human crutches.

Liam looks at Eileen, who shrugs.

"Liam, I'm the one dat bringed ya to the camp," Christy says, perching himself next to them on the fallen tree. "So they asked me t'tell ya what Granny Ward do be sayin'."

"Christy, what is it? What did the ol' woman say?" Liam asks.

"We call her Granny Ward. I wouldn't let her be hearin' ya callin' her 'ol' woman' or she might boil yer bones and eat ya for her supper."

"I'm sorry, Christy. I meant no offense. Granny Ward. What did Granny Ward say? Will he be alright? When will he be able t' move on? It's just that we're supposed t' be findin' Da and Mam. They'll be—"

"Liam," Eileen interrupts. "Let Christy talk."

"I'm sorry, yes... Sorry, Christy. What did she say?"

"I must be tellin' ya straight that Granny Ward is no doctor, d'ya hear me? She's not a doctor. Well at least not to buffers, the town's people I do be meanin'. She's not a doctor to everyone. But she is a doctor to us Pavees. Us travellers come from all over to see 'er. Most say she's betterer than any buffer doctor."

"I understand, Christy. What did she say about Aiden?"

Christy looks Liam in the eye. "She says he's not goin' to make it, Liam."

Make what? What is it he's not going to make? Is he not going to make it to see Mammy and Da? Will he not make it home to see Da's tilled field? Is he not going to make it to Ballycastle? Will he not make it back to see Sean and Kate Mullins? Is he not going to make it back to see the monkey-cowboy riding its Border Collie over fences? Is he not going to make saying my name right again? Liam leans forward, props his elbows on his knees and hangs his head. No matter how many alternatives he thinks of, he knows what Aiden is not going to make.

"Christy, if she's not a doctor, how does she know?" Eileen asks.

"Jases, I'm goin' t' be missin' somethin' out, but she rattled off a load a reasons. She was talkin' about... about Aiden's fingers. His fingers are a bit clubbed, I think she said. And his toes are, an' all. His neck is all swelled up t' hell. And she listened to his breathin'. She says his breathin's all wrong. She says there's a cackle or a crackle in it, and that's a bad sign, she says. She called it consumption. She says Aiden has the consumption. She told me t' tell ya he's too sick to move anywhere."

Liam doesn't want Aiden to be sick, certainly not too sick to move anywhere.

"Listen, both o' ye," Christy continues. "Granny Ward has told two of the girls to be stayin' with Aiden until... well, until the end. The two're with him now. She says it could be soon, like today or tomorra. I'm sorry t' have t' be tellin' ya this, Liam. She sent a message to the fathers tellin' them that the camp stays here until it's all over. No-one else is to go near the child other than the two women. She told you two to stay away, an' all, but she says ye'd've probably caught it by now if y'were goin' to be catchin' it. Does any of this make ense to ya?"

"Catch what?" Eileen asks.

"The same," Christy says. "The same sickness. The consumption."

"Like sheep," Eileen says.

Liam stands. Without speaking, he stomps away through the damp grass.

"Liam!" Eileen calls. "Do you want me to come with you?"

Without looking back, Liam raises a hand, signalling, "No."

The red, shiny vest in the distance hops up and down, shimmering the sun in faint gleams around it as it approaches.

The runner's gait is awkward, uneven and heavy footed, his arms cross the front of his body making him twist at each stride.

Liam wipes his face dry and gazes out over the river. The wide expanse of water rolls and whirls its great liquid bulk past him towards the sea. He wishes it would take him with it. He wonders what the fighting man is doing running along the river bank, wearing a ridiculous pair of short trousers.

The runner's arms flap as he slows to a walk. "Howaya, young fella?" he gasps. "I think you've found the best way... to enjoy the River Moy." He sucks in big gulps of air. "You're relaxing whilst I'm puttin' the red o' me arse out tryin' to keep meself active."

The runner leans on his knees as he recovers his breathing. The bridge of his nose is flat, its tip bulbous and a darker red than the rest of his flushed, bearded face. One eye looks full of milk. His sweat glistens like film, coating his body and beading his forehead. A dark crescent arcs down from the neck of his vest. "I saw you watchin' the scrap yesterday, didn' I?" he says. "You were up on the wall. Was you, wasn't it? Tell me this, who was the comely young one that was with ya?"

Liam jumps to his feet and faces the man. They are of equal height.

"Ah, listen, sorry. I'm sorry, right? Let me start again, I didn't mean aught." The runner holds up open hands, the fingers gnarled and twisted. "My name's Bernie Kelly, howdyado?" He extends a hand to Liam.

Liam shakes the sweaty palm. He feels lumps and ridges that he wouldn't expect to feel in a hand.

"I fight in the country fair that's in town," Bernie Kelly says. "I'm just out for me mornin' constitutional. Thought I'd take in the river. The runnin' helps with the boxin', or so Mr O'Connor tells me. But I'm sure it's for the best. It's the only thing I can do to ward off the ravages of age. Apart from not drink... I'm sorry young fella, I only asked about the girl 'cause she looked like someone I useta know, that's all." He pauses for breath. "So, there we are, so. Heh there, why ya cryin'?"

Any jealous anger over mentioning Eileen had left him. Liam's contorted face turns towards the manic waters of the Moy, his mouth a thin horizontal line, his eyes moist slits under a furrowed brow. His stomach tightens in spasms, his chest rises and falls as he sobs.

"Heh there, young fella," Bernie says. "What is it troubles ya?"

"I don't know what t' do," Liam wails, burying his face in his hands. He hasn't met the runner before, but Liam doesn't care. The runner happens to be here, now. Someone big enough to look after him as he spills the hurt, the rage, the sadness, his pent up painful emotions, onto the bank of the River Moy.

"That's it, young fella," Bernie says, placing a hand on Liam's back.

Liam sobs. A gasping, broken sob.

"That's it."

The two strangers remain standing on the riverbank until Liam cries himself out.

"Where I'm from, they say talk's the cure for every sorrow. But ya don't have to talk, or say anythin', if ya don't wanta... Sit yerself down again... Talk away if ya want and are ready. If not... Are ya alright?"

Liam wipes his face on his arms. "I'm sorry," he says. "I don't know ya and... I'm learnin' meself not to carry on like a small babby."

Bernie runs a thumb and forefinger over his sweaty beard. "Ya don't need to know me, young fella. The world sometimes gets so full o' shite, ya just need someone. Doesn't need be someone ya know. Believe me, I know all about shite-filled times. I've been in shite deep enough to drown in."

Liam snuffles through a snotty chuckle. "Her name's Eileen... The girl by the wall. She's called Eileen and I'm glad she's not here now. She's goin' t' be the only person I've left in the world. I've lost me da and I've lost me mam and me baby brother's about t' die with the consumption. I'm not good at lookin' after people."

"Holy God... What's your name, young fella?"

"Liam." He is unsure if he needs to shake hands again. He decides they are past that.

"Where's yer brother now so, Liam?"

"The traveller camp, far end of town."

"A traveller camp? On his own? What'n the hell–"

"No, it's alright," Liam says. "They're alright. They're lookin' after 'im for me. Eileen'll be there as well. They're lookin' after all of us. I wouldn't know what t' do if it wasn't for them. It's because of Aiden. They're lookin' after us because of Aiden. Everyone loves him, ya see? He has a big head and a little body and a magic that he sends out t' people. People take the magic and fall in love with 'im. He's only four.

You're prob'ly fallin' in love with 'im now and ya haven't even met 'im. He's four and he's dyin' of the consumption."

"What about a doctor? Has a doctor seen 'im?"

"No. We've no money for a doctor and Granny Ward has seen 'im. It's too late t'do anythin'. Granny Ward thinks he'll die in the next day or two."

"Granny Ward? Liam, there's a medical fella workin' in the fair. I could get him t' come and have a–"

"No. No, it's fine. Granny Ward's better than all the buffer doctors."

"My man's no doctor either. Prob'ly only good for bandagin' broken limbs. I've never seen 'im cure anyone yet."

"Bernie, I better be gettin' back. I'm sorry for cryin' an'all."

They stand up.

"Listen, young fella, if ya apologise for that again, I'll box ya inta the river as tall as y'are. I'm a fighter ya know, and good too."

"I know you are, I've seen ya."

"Well, when I say 'good', I'm good for me age that is." Bernie gives Liam a slow-motion swipe across the jaw. "Listen, Liam. I'll be back here again tomorrow at the same time o' day. That O'Connor's a bit of a slave driver but he's savin' my life at the moment so when he says run, I run." Bernie winks.

Liam smiles at the light-hearted humour.

"If ya want t' meet up and let me know how Aiden's doin', I'll be here. If not, it's been a privilege meetin' ya, Liam. And I wish ya all the best."

They shake hands.

"I'm gettin' stone cold here, I'll be on with me runnin'. Good luck, Liam." Bernie turns and after a few stumbles, resumes his awkward gait. The red, sweat-patched vest hops up and down, shimmering the sun in faint gleams around it.

Chapter 44
Ballina, Ireland, 1879.

Maggie blinked open her eyes and stared up into the wood-clad void of the roof. She was unsure if the words painted in white lettering on the side of a beam were there to warn or reassure her. GOD IS JUST.

The boys? Please God, let them be safe.

A window, set deep into the wall above her head, allowed a beam of light to pass through the dusty air and spot the half-open door of the dormitory. She turned her head to see other occupied, cast-iron beds. Apart from a regular wheeze to her right, the dormitory was quiet. A heady odour of stale sweat, rotting meat and disinfectant pervaded the air, so thick she could discern the tastes.

She tried to remember how she got here, wherever here was. She sifted through brief snatches of broken conversation lodged deep in her memory.

"He said we've to take them to town, at the double..."

"As sure as hell this baby'll be born here on the bed o' the bloomin' cart..."

"Has he stirred? Take a look at 'im. Any breath in him at all...?"

"The baby! Holy Mother o' God and all the saints, help me...!"

"He's done for..."

"Get a shift into us, or she'll be done for too..."

She raised her head off the flock-filled mattress, but her head was heavy and the pain in her abdomen severe. She eased it back down and took deep breaths. Her eyes focused on the sign decorating the stone wall below the window above her. She read the upside-down words. Rules, of, Ballina, Poor, Law, Union, Board, of. Then a word she couldn't read. More writing, underneath these words, was too small to make out.

The workhouse. She was in the workhouse. In Ballina.

Her furthest journey from home, her first time in Ballina, and she landed up in the workhouse. She heard footsteps in the hallway carrying a shrill voice towards the dormitory door. "...can be satisfied, Mrs Brannigan, the Guardians are ensuring that everything is being done to..." The footsteps and voice faded as they swept past.

Maggie had no hint to determine how long she had been there.

The boys. Liam would look after Aiden, but Aiden needed her. She had to find them. She had to get out of this bed and find them. She ground her teeth as a cramp crushed her abdomen, the pain searing through her middle. A tear trickled onto the mattress.

The baby? Her hands moved beneath the sheet to her stomach. The baby had gone. The burning pain was there in its stead. A hopeless, too-familiar pain. She remembered Cuffe striking her. She reached a hand down lower. When she raised it in front of her face, her fingers glistened with vivid, bright, burgundy blood.

Chapter 45
Ballina, Ireland, 1879.

Noreen is with them.

Eileen lifts the lamp and dabs a damp rag to Aiden's forehead.

The small boy sweats and shivers in an unsettled slumber.

Unsure what's best, Liam has the blanket folded across Aiden's middle.

Noreen strokes a naked small-boy foot. The soothing, soporific action pinches her eyes closed. Her head droops.

Liam gazes down on Aiden's consumed, pallor countenance, the eyes ringed dark, pained from the struggle of staying alive.

The camp is still, the others asleep under cover sheets. The only sound is of intermittent snores and farts. On the other side of the field, Max also sleeps, standing upright, dreaming horse dreams.

Liam wonders if Aiden is dreaming.

"Why did Granny Ward tell everyone stay away from Aiden?" he whispers.

Noreen jolts awake. "Huh? Granny Ward?" She blinks her eyes wide. "Oh... She thinks ya can catch the fever off each other, ya see? She raves a bit does Granny Ward, but don't be tellin' anyone it was me that said that t' ya, promise?"

"How do you catch the fever?"

"She's great is Granny Ward, she is, but she's ideas no-one understands, ya see? She's good, mind. She does cure folk. Our people come from all over the country to her when they're sick 'cause she knows the ancient cures, ya know? She told me once that to cure a sprain, a young girl of under fourteen years of age needs to spin a thread dry, without using any spit. They hafta tie it round the leg or arm with the affliction, ya know what I'm saying? When the cure is completed the thread just disappears. Like that. Ya see?"

"Aren't you scared you'll catch it?" Liam asks.

"The fever? Me? Notatall. He's a beautiful little boy and his fever is hectic but if I could catch it, Granny Ward wouldn't have told me to stay up wit' yez, ya understand me? Gillian and me's the healthiest in the family, we're never sick, ya know?"

"Gillian's the other girl?"

"She is yea. Gillian'll be here in the mornin', then I'll be back later in the day and we'll carry—"

Aiden's breathing interrupts the talk.

They glance at each other for explanations, for reassurances that the laboured, deep-guttural rattle is normal.

Aiden's shoulders pull on his small chest, heaving like tiny bellows, struggling to draw in air. As his lungs fight for breath, his ribs stick through the flimsy, damp material of the petticoat. He coughs. Blood seeps from the side of his mouth and down over his pallor cheek, dark on light in the dimness.

Eileen mops it with the rag.

A cough comes again, a racking cough that shakes Aiden's small body. Bright-pink flushes on his cheeks glow in the lamplight.

Liam straightens his back and scrapes his hair back. He doesn't want to cry, He wants to cry. He bites hard on a lip. His brother is dying.

Another cough. Enough blood to fill a spoon spills from his mouth. Another convulsive cough. Aiden moans as he curls his body sideways.

Liam wants it to stop, it's too sore for his brother, the little man. The quantity of blood worries him. He bends forward, wipes it away and slides a shaking hand in under Aiden's head.

Aiden turns his face to Liam and opens his eyes.

Even in the dull light of the lamp, the irises of the little man look bluer than daytime sky. The pupils, blacker than peat, draw Liam into their darkness. It's in that darkness Liam sees the fear. His brother is scared.

"Aiden, I'm here. I'm here, Aiden," Liam says, bending closer. "Aiden you're goin' to get better and we'll find Mammy and Da and everythin'll be alright. I promise, Aiden."

Aiden's lips move, but there is no sound.

"Shhh," Liam whispers. "It's alright. No need to talk, little man."

Liam lifts his brother to him, wrapping his arms around the thin, light body, holding him firm. As he rocks, Aiden's heart beats against him. Aiden's chin stirs against his neck.

"Aiden love Liam," Aiden says.

Liam feels the heart stop. Aiden becomes heavy in his arms. A dead weight.

Chapter 46
Ballina, Ireland, 1879.

"Bernie Kelly!" Liam screamed, his hands cupped to his mouth to funnel the yell.

In the distance, the shiny red vest of Bernie Kelly stopped running away and turned. Bernie waved a hand above his head in acknowledgement and headed back towards Liam.

"I thought I'd missed ya," Liam said, as Bernie slowed to a walk.

"How's the brother?" Bernie said, through heavy breaths, extending a sweaty hand for Liam to shake.

"Aiden died last night."

"Holy God in heaven, I'm sorry. I'm sorry for yer troubles, Liam." Bernie kept shaking Liam's hand. "Do ya want to sit and talk?"

"No," Liam said. "I think I'm alright now. This mornin' was odd though. I wanted t' talk this mornin', needed t' even, but no-one else did. Frightened maybe 'bout what they'd say. I think they were afraid of makin' it worser for me. Thing is, it couldn't get any worser."

"Astute for a young fella."

Liam smiled. A sad smile. "No, I think I'm alright. I was with Aiden when he died. He looked... happy afterwards. I'm alright if he's happy. He'll be up in heaven now anyway, pullin' the hearts out o' people. Do ya go t' heaven when ya die or at yer funeral?"

Bernie shuffled his feet and looked out over the Moy. He concentrated on recovering his breathing. "I er... I'd say it's right away," he said, at last. "No delay. God wouldn't want 'im hangin' round, worryin', would he?"

"That's good, so. I feel better now."

Bernie nodded and gave a flicker of a smile.

"You've no need t' worry, anyway. I won't cry on ya," Liam said.

"Lookit, I don't mind the cryin'. I've cried enough meself. But if you're alright, well then that's a good thing." Bernie stared, his posture stooped, his hands on his hips. "I lost a brother meself a long time ago," he said. "Not dead as far as I know, but I lost him all the same. I cried about that."

"I'm lookin' for me mam and da, maybe we'll find yer brother, too?"

"Ya might be right," Bernie said, nodding his head.

"I'm stoppin' the cryin'," Liam Said. "But I cried a bit with a horse called Max. Last night."

"A horse? Called–"

"I want ya t' learn me t' fight," Liam said.

"Hah? What did ya say?"

"I want t' be able t' fight. I need t' be able t' fight. I seen ya fight. And I want you t' learn me."

"Hold on. Hold on now, young fella... Why are we talkin' about fightin'? I think maybe things–"

"Bernie, listen to me. I want t' be able t' fight. I'm alright, but I want you t' learn me how t' fight. If ya won't then say, but I must be able t' fight."

"And can I ask ya why ya must be able to fight, Liam?"

"Ya can ask, but it's a personal thing, and I'd rather not say. Will ya do it? Will ya learn me t' fight or not?"

"Lookit, slow down, now... The thing is, young fella...The thing is, Liam, it's not a five-minute job. I can't just teach ya to fight that easy."

"I know that, I'm not thick. How long? I've time. How long does it take?"

"Lookit, Liam. Aiden has just die... passed away, and you're talkin' about learnin' to fight."

"Bernie, please don't try t' make sense of any of this. It's somethin' I need t' do. I thought you'd help me because ya seem like someone who would, that's all. Ya helped me before. I need t' do this for Aiden, and I need t' do this for Mammy and I need t' do this for Da. Don't ask me t' explain 'cause I'm not sure I can now. But I know I've t' do this for them. So will ya help me? Please?"

Liam watched Bernie weigh up the request, frown, shake his head, smile and then frown again. Why should Bernie help him? He felt guilty forcing this stranger into a position of having to refuse him. He was about to tell Bernie to forget he asked, that he didn't mean it, when Bernie spoke.

"How old are ya, Liam?"

"Nineteen."

Bernie gave a slow nod and wiped the side of his beard on his shoulder. He looked down, as if to find the real answer written on the riverbank. "Are ya going to stay livin' with the travellers?" he asked.

"No. I expect we'll have t' leave tomorrow or the next day. They're good people but they don't want us around them. We're not like them and we all know it. They'll move on, travellin' again, anytime, and we'll be left t' go our own way."

"I'm assuming the 'us' and the 'we' ya refer to is you and the girl, Peggy is it?"

"Eileen. Yes. Me and her spoke about it this morning."

"And where are ya goin' to go?"

"We were goin' t' Ballycastle, but... Well, I've given up on that now. I don't think I'd ever make it t' Ballycastle. It was mainly for Aiden, anyhow. I still don't know where is Ballycastle."

"Someone'll tell ya where Ballycastle is, that's not difficult."

"No. I don't need t' go there now. I've decided."

"Where do ya want to go, Liam? 'Cause I have to go with–"

"The fair," Liam finished. "I know ya do. I've nowhere t' go and I need t' learn t' fight, so goin' with the fair'll suit us."

"Us? Arrr now. That might not be so simple. You'd have to work, and O'Connor might not take two of ye on."

"He will. He'll take both of us on, me and Eileen. We'll work for nothin'. Sure we've nothin' anyway and it'll help us stay clear of the workhouse."

"I see ya've it all worked out. What about Aiden? What are ya goin' to do with Aiden's..." He left "body" unsaid.

"Taken care of," Liam said, matter-of-factly. "Christy and Noreen'll arrange a funeral. Make out he's their brother so's the priest won't ask questions. If I go t' the priest, we'll likely end up in the workhouse and we don't want that."

"So ya think you've everythin' sorted, do ya?"

"Will ya learn me t' fight, Bernie Kelly?"

"Yer a bloody headstrong one aren't ya, young fella? How old d'ya say ya were?"

"Nineteen."

Bernie smiled. "Lookit, I'm not goin' t' say yes now, and I'm not goin' t' say no. You and I'll consider it. I'm continuin' me exercise, and if we meet here again tomorrow, we'll talk more. Right?"

They shook hands again.

"Thanks for runnin' back t' me, Bernie Kelly," Liam said, to the sweaty back of the shiny red vest.

The funeral was simple by Irish traveller standards. No word was sent out to families across Ireland notifying them of Aiden's death. There were no keening women, no long procession of horse-drawn caravans through the streets of Ballina and no concerned sermon from the lectern by a priest warning the traveller men in the congregation to behave themselves during the wake.

St Muredach's Cathedral, sitting in splendid solitude on the far bank of the River Moy, was the tallest building Liam had ever seen. They had to travel over the five-arch bridge into County Sligo to reach it, but he spotted the point of its cross-topped spire spearing the sky long before they reached the river. Liam wondered what spirits lived behind the windows that shrunk in size the higher up the spire you looked.

The uniform-grey steeple rose like a broad bluff, a sheer cliff holding back the ocean waters of the Moy. The blackening of its southern flank by the blown drizzle enhanced its forbidding facade. Liam admired the grim grandness of the great building.

When he peeked inside, the grimness fell away. His head nodded as he counted the slew of wooden bench seats, lined up, extending as far as he could throw a stone. There were over a dozen fluted pillars holding up the ceiling. The wind nudged a cloud out of the way, and the vast Cathedral was filled with a magical kaleidoscope of light from its coloured-glass windows. He thought it a church worthy of the funeral of his brother.

Christy, his mother and father, Noreen and Gillian went inside to meet the priest. The small funeral-party, silhouetted in the glow of the stained-glass alter window, looked lost in the enormity of the nave. Liam remained outside, sheltering from the showers, with Eileen and Bernie Kelly. Bernie was dressed in a suit and wore a cravat the colour of dry moss. He tried to console the weeping Eileen with handkerchiefs.

Father John O'Keane kept the ceremony short.

Whilst the brief service went on inside, Liam sat alone, wallowing in the failure of his plan. He had failed to look after his brother, failed to keep him alive, failed his father and mother. The first part of his plan had come undone with terrible consequences. It made it all the more important that he seen through the rest of it. He knew whom he shared the blame with.

From St Muredach's, Aiden's body was carried, without fuss, back over the river and out the Killala road past St Patrick's Well to the cemetery. Three hundred years earlier, St Olcan, under instruction from St Patrick, let his axe fall to the ground in the corner of this cemetery. The cleaved spot was marked by the centuries-old ruin of the Kilmore Church of St Patrick, now cloaked green with foliage. Aiden was buried beside the ruin, in a grave marked only by the freshly-turned, damp soil. In time, the grave would become less obvious, blended into anonymity by the daily wipe of the shadow of the crumbling, ivied chapel.

PART TWO

Chapter 47
Ennis, Ireland, 1879.

A thick glove crashed into the side of Liam's jaw. He felt no pain.

Adrenaline coursed through his veins. It helped him breathe, fuelled his muscles and anaesthetised his body.

"Get the hell out of that corner," Bernie yelled, from outside the ropes. "Ya damn fool rake of an eejit ya!"

Several in the small crowd grinned in expectation. They sensed an upset. The fair's fighter was taking a beating, the local man might win.

Liam shoved his opponent away and stood in the centre of the ring, his arms open wide.

His opponent snarled at the goading gesture and leapt in with a punch.

Liam took the blow to the side of the cheek and rocked back onto the ropes. The joy. The ecstasy. What did he hear someone say recently? "An Irishman is not at peace unless he's at war."

His opponent failed to follow up.

Liam had a fraction of a second to savour the moment. He rolled away from the ropes and glanced at Bernie.

Bernie glared back and punched his palm. "What did I teach ya!" he yelled.

'If it's not working do somethin' different.' That's what Bernie taught him. He knew Bernie would be anxious. He smiled. He knew Bernie understood, Bernie had lost a brother. But oh, the relieving hurt. 'I hurt, so I am healed.' Was that another of Bernie's? It felt good to be rid of the numbness, alive again. He decided the time to do something different had arrived. Time to dance.

His opponent held his breath between gasps of air, a fledgling's error. Bernie told him this will happen. "They can be big, strong monsters of men, but it's natural for them to hold their breath. Are you familiar with 'instinct', young fella? Well let them carry on, you have t' train yerself to breathe."

Liam side stepped and skipped around his opponent, arms raised to the front, fists poised. His opponent detected the change in demeanour, Liam watched confusion and disappointment flood the face. Liam tip-stepped forward and slammed his foot down. His left fist hit a jaw. Thud! His opponent didn't even see...

Bernie climbed between the ropes, dragged Liam into the corner of the ring and shouted into his face. "What was that carry on? You're not ready. It's my fault, I put ya in there too soon. I shouldn't have listened to meself, yer just not ready."

"Bernie, I'm good, I'm alright. I think you'll find I won, didn't I?"

"Don't give me that shite, ya cheeky whelp. I'm in charge here don't forget. If you want to go riskin' yer life ya do it at another fair. I'll have no part in it. A man the size of that big lump could've done damage if he caught ya right."

"Bernie, it's alright, I'm good. I'm sorry if I frightened ya. It–"

"Frightened me? I couldn't give a shite about ya getting' hurt if that's what you want, but don't do it when I'm witchya."

Aloysius O'Connor entered the ring.

"Gentlemen, gentlemen! Gentlemen, a remarkable bout!" he bellowed in his singing voice. "Well done to… what's yer name? What's his name? Aloysius? Sure that's the same name as meself! Well done to Alo-ysius for coming so close. I thought we had a tie on our hands there, yes I did. We've another bout comin' up for ya in a while. So if you'd like to exit the booth for a short break, I'll see you again in thirty minutes, gentlemen. Be sure and be back in thirty minutes. Make certain to sign up for a go yerself, I see we have the cream of County Clare with us today. Ya all look like fine men to me. Even you, sir, with the arm missing. Here's yer chance to show just how fine a man y'are."

By the time O'Connor had finished yelling, he was addressing the backs of two old men, shuffling towards the arch in the booth-board. The board around the arch was decorated in poorly-painted, larger-than-life images of a red-vested Bernie Kelly, in fighting pose.

Eileen walked in through the arch, directly beneath a threatening black glove, returning from a meeting in Ennis town. She rid herself of her frown as she twisted past the two old men.

Aloysius O'Connor's itinerant Country Fair had been home for Liam and Eileen since the consumption took Aiden.

From Ballina, it took them to Claremorris, then on to Athenry in County Galway. Liam spent the time learning his new craft.

"Can ya dance, young fella?" Bernie asked.

Liam's ears blushed. "A bit."

"Fightin's like dancin'. I learned that nugget from a beautiful woman in London."

"A wom–"

"It's two people, movin' in harmony, with the leadin' man dictatin' the steps. You must become the leadin' man, because it's the leadin' man that wins the fight."

"In harmony?"

"Not familiar with 'harmony', young fella? If ya want to learn to fight prop'ly, ya must learn to dance properly. Go on at it so, show me what ya know about dancin'."

Liam pulled off the boots Bernie had given him and set off, hopping and skipping over the ground. A national dance with taut torso and fluttering feet.

Bernie grinned. "I see ya can move alright, young fella. But you'll need to start swingin' those arms when ya climb inta the ring."

When Bernie agreed to show Liam how to fight, he explained it was because he thought he recognised and understood the conflict Liam was going through. Liam thought he won Bernie's agreement when he told him of the eviction and had explained again that there was nowhere now for him, or Eileen, to go. Bernie's enthusiasm told Liam that Bernie might actually look forward to teaching someone to fight.

Liam postponed the search for his parents.

Bernie introduced Liam and Eileen to O'Connor and explained the situation. O'Connor was suspicious and reluctant. When he heard the girl had worked with animals, he conceded that as Maeve's previous groom had ran off to marry a farmer from Bangor Erris, Eileen might be of help to the vaulting equestrian acrobat. He agreed to give Eileen a trial. He said another ginger head about the place would be a blessing bestowed on the fair.

O'Connor had no need of the lad.

Bernie lied about Liam's age and about him being a good fighter. He argued that as Bernie himself wasn't getting any younger and was having difficulty seeing out of his left eye, he would train the lad as his successor. He tried to convince O'Connor that with his strong, long and wiry frame, Liam had the makings of a good fighter. O'Connor wanted rid of the lad unless he could fight straight away, "If it's trainin' he needs, he can sod the hell off and do it elsewhere. I'm not runnin' a bloody nursery for destitude bog crawlers."

Liam had nowhere to 'sod the hell off' to. Bernie decided he would support him with his own meagre resources, and he trained him to fight. He trained Liam hard and praised him on his commitment. "Channel the anger, young fella," he'd say, "and I'll make a scrapper of ya yet." Within three months, Bernie thought Liam was trial ready.

In late September, they rolled into Ennis in County Clare. Bernie thought this the opportunity for Liam's his first fight.

Bernie found Ennis torturous, his mind persecuted by thoughts of Peggy. As he walked over O'Connell Square admiring the column and splendid statue, he felt it. As he ran with Liam along the banks of the River Fergus, he felt it. As he stood beside the Gothic tower of the Catholic Church, he felt it. Her presence was everywhere. If she was ever going to walk up to him, it should be here, in the town she called home.

Eileen approached the ring as the two old men passed out through the arch. "How'd it go, so?" she asked, her smile fixed.

Liam grinned back, though he noticed the blotched rose-red of her face.

"Nearly got 'imself knocked to bejases is how it went," Bernie said, pulling off a glove.

"Take no notice of him, I won. My first fight and I won."

"Don't try that again, son," O'Connor shouted, heading for the arch. "Or I'll have ya picking the hairs out of the elephant's arse for a month."

"We haven't got any elephants," Liam shouted back.

"I'll buy an elephant."

"Is he any good, Bernie?" Eileen asked, laughing.

"He's good, but he's not brilliant."

"As long as they don't disturb the handsome face," she said.

Bernie winked at Liam, who blushed as though he'd just been caught on both ears with a double-glove slap.

"There's potential. Are ya familiar with 'potential' young fella? But I won't be paintin' his handsome face over my beardy one on that boothboard anytime soon."

The Fair moved on without Peggy walking up to Bernie.

Chapter 48
Ennis, Ireland, 1879.

Eileen paced back and forth alongside the gate, biting her bottom lip. Liam was having his first fight in the booth ring today, she would miss it. But she needed to be here. Knowing he intended to go to Ennis, she had looked for him and found him. She wanted to meet.

She paused and leaned out to peer down the lane. She recognised him by his strident march and the way he wore his cap askew. The sun glared off the ground behind him. She wrung her hands and rubbed them into her thighs. He looked angry. She took deep breaths, hoping the queasiness would pass.

"Why did you do it?" he shouted, before he even got close.

She waited until he stood next to her, his hands on his hips, his chin in the air. "How's little Thomas?" she asked the ground.

"Why did you do it?" he repeated.

"Why? I did it because they asked me," Eileen said. "Mother did. Father'd never ask anything like that. Too weak."

"Holy Jesus, you've a heart in you like the top-face of an anvil."

"What would you have done? Hah? As mother asked? Or are you too weak as well?"

He raised a hand to strike her. "God in heaven, you'll burn in hell for what you did?" he said.

"That's why I did it. So's they wouldn't."

"What? What in God's name are you sayin'?"

"I did it so they wouldn't go to hell."

"I've a mind to slit yer throat," he said. "The Devil is within in you."

"'To take your own life is contrary to love for the living God.' That's what it says in the Catechism?"

"Don't be quotin' the Catholic Catechism to me you unholy little briar. You didn't save their souls by what you did, you condemned them!"

"I saved Father's. And Mother believed I saved hers. As long as she believed, isn't that what matters? The rest will happen or it won't."

He slapped her.

She glared back at him, the glow growing on her cheek.

"How dare you doubt the word of God," he said.

Ryan was her eldest brother but she continued to glare and clench her fists.

He stretched out the words, "You set fire to them." He shook his head.

"You should've gone on to be a priest, Ryan," she said. "Why did you not? Was it Dirdre that stopped you? Was it? Her falling for little Thomas and you having to wed her? Was that what stopped you?"

He raised a hand to strike her again.

She screamed at him. "They had nothing left! Nothing! Mammy sent you all away so she could ask me and Michael, on our own." A strand of red hair, bonded to her cheek by tears, looped to the corner of her mouth. "She knew you wouldn't allow it, so she sent you away. But you think I'm not scared for what I did? Do you not think it keeps me awake at night-time? It bedevils my dreams. All of them. Every single one. Horrifies me all the time, haunting... But Mammy asked me... She asked me." She collapsed into him, sobbing. "Amn't I sick thinking about it...? My dreams make me sick... And that Michael shouldn't have told you what we did."

He looked up to the heavens.

She wept against him, convulsing, catching her breath.

His arms went around her. He stroked and patted her hair.

"And you weren't there when I needed my big brother!" she wailed.

Chapter 49
County Galway, Ireland, 1879.

It moved in a cavalcade of carts, trailers, animals and people. A spectacle that brought families to their doors, drew children to run alongside and enticed loquacious latchacos to hurl colourful verbal abuse from street corners. From Ennis, the fair set-off north, its destination the October Horse Fair in Ballinasloe.

It wound its way through the county of Galway pausing only to rest for the night beside the speckled-grey lake at Loughrea. Some of the fair-people poached trout from the lake, others bathed or rested. Bernie walked Liam into the town, pointing out to him the ancient crannog built on the water as they passed.

Loughrea was a farming town and a victim of the downturn in the economy. Poor potato and oat crops had affected pig and poultry stocks, an important source of income. The ailing British economy deprived the people of their supplementary earnings from temporary work abroad, and news of the American slump had cut off that major emigratory route.

Trapped men gathered at street junctions, in small groups, with little to do but argue, their hands heavy with time. They openly denounced the poor prices their produce fetched at market, the land rents they were still being forced to pay and, to Liam's chagrin, the evictions they were being subjected to. Loughrea looked to Liam like it had given up, spiritless, beaten to a standstill.

He joined one huddled group and learned of organisations that were 'secretly' being set up to "once and for all tackle the injustice". A small fellow, speaking through dark brown teeth clenched on the bit of a long clay pipe, told Liam, "We shouldn't have anythin' to do with them rent-racking agents, by rights. Let them get on wit' their cursed work on their own. Should turn our backs on bloody land grabbers, too. Useta have four pigs in the house, meself, at one time." Liam thought he smelled like he still did.

Liam heard talk of "home rule" and the "Irish Republican Brotherhood" and "agrarian agitation". Phrases that were to become regular topics of discussion and argument with Eileen and Bernie in the months ahead.

A day later they were in Ballinasloe, preparing for the commencement of the greatest fair in Europe.

The nine-day Horse Fair began on the first Saturday in October. Bernie permitted Liam to fight on more than a dozen occasions. Bernie fought too, but Liam's bouts were the most thrilling to watch. His lanky, lean frame made him look an easy and tempting conquest. Bernie had Liam fight vest-less, and in an elaborate display of showmanship paraded him around the ring, arms aloft, ribs grinning through his skin. It was an effective ploy, luring a steady flow of confident challengers.

When the fighting started, Liam was in complete control. His confident grew with every bout. His speed mesmerised opponents and a bout lasted two rounds only if he, under instruction from Bernie, allowed it to. To Bernie's consternation, Liam forfeited one bout without his permission, to a stocky lad called Christy Sherridan.

Christy and his family had made the annual pilgrimage to the Fair in Ballinasloe, in common with hundreds of other travelling families. Christy spotted Eileen leading a freshly-groomed horse to perform. She arranged for Christy to meet up with Liam, who suggested Christy step into the ring.

"Are y'any good, are ya?" Christy asked.

"He's good, but not brilliant, according to Bernie," Eileen said, glancing a smile at Liam.

"You'd prob'ly beat the head o' me," Liam said. "So let's rile Bernie by makin' sure ya win."

"For the love o' God," Christy said, rubbing his hands together. "Wha'do I have t'do?"

Christy shared his winnings with his two friends, treating them both to a plate of cally, the small mountain of mashed potato topped off with a crater of butter and warm milk.

The second Saturday is the biggest day of the Horse Fair. Tradition names it Country Fair Day, the day that draws the most local people. Liam boxed on four different occasions. One permitted loss and one draw ensured a steady flow of, what O'Connor called, 'punters'. When the fair closed for the evening, Liam retired to bed, nursing a scar on his cheek where a lanky, long-armed lad called Cosgrove had removed a layer of skin with the seam of a glove.

Bernie and Eileen woke him before mid-night. Without explaining where they were going, Bernie marched them through the town. On Dunlo Street, he led them across the wide thoroughfare to steer clear of two drunks arguing over the ownership of a white stallion. The stallion looked on impartial. They turned left up a steep incline, into a street lined both sides with terraced stone houses. They stopped outside a black-painted door.

"Are ya familiar with 'courteous' young fella?" Bernie whispered.

"I–"

"Both o' ye keep yer mouths shut," Bernie said. "Say nothin' and listen. Ye might just learn somethin'."

Liam and Eileen shared a bemused look.

Bernie ran a thumb and forefinger over his beard as he waited for his knock to be answered. "Bernie Kelly. The Schoolmaster invited us," he said, into the cracked opening.

The door swung wide to reveal a large man, wearing a cap several sizes too small for his enormous head. His jacket looked unbuttonable around the belly.

There was an awkward, comical bump of bodies as Bernie and the man both attempted to manoeuvre their bulks through the doorway at the same time. Bernie squeezed past the man and the man stepped out to check the road up and down.

"Hey, hold on. Who's the girl?" he said.

"She's with me," Bernie said.

The man reached for Eileen and turned her head to let the moonlight to her face.

"There's no women in here, and I don't trust anyone with a gammy eye," he said.

"She's with me," Bernie said again. "They're both with me. The Schoolmaster knows they're comin'."

The man softened.

"And I'd be careful what ya say about her eye," Bernie said. "Her *buachaill* there might give you a gammy eye of yer own."

The man swivelled towards Liam. Looking at the scrawny, scarred youngster he giggled at the ridiculous suggestion, his bulk gyrating.

The big man directed them down a dull hallway. A man's voice grew louder as they approached an open door. They stepped into a large room filled with almost two dozen silhouettes of men standing with their backs to them. It smelt of tobacco and oily flames. An array of kerosene lamps sent up a yellow glow the far side of the room. In the midst of the glow stood the speaker, flanked by men either side. Behind the speaker, nailed to the wall, hung a banner declaring this gathering a meeting of the Ballinasloe Irish Tenant Defence Association.

Chapter 50
Ballinasloe, Ireland, 1879.

"So you're my boy now are you?" Eileen teased.

"According t' Bernie I am," Liam said. "I'm yer buachaill and I didn't even kiss ya yet." His ears blushed, hot and red, at his own audacity. He was glad of the darkness.

"I'm not sure you ever will, Liam Walshe."

They carried on walking along the empty streets. What did she mean? Had he offended her? What if he kissed her now?

"Did ya hear what Michael O'Sullivan said at the meetin'?" he asked, instead.

"Why does Bernie call him 'The Schoolmaster'?"

"He reckons everyone calls him that. A codename or somethin'. He used t' teach yer man's kids, Matt Harris. He's the real leader of the Defence Association, the Matt Harris buck. It was Matt Harris that set it all up, here in Ballinasloe."

"Who's the fella in the corner, the one doing all the writing?"

"That's Daly, James Daly. Has a newspaper or somethin'."

"He's handsome."

Liam glanced at her.

"At least The Schoolmaster was more... enthusiastic than Mr Charles Parnell," she said. "What did Matt Harris say?"–she lowered her voice an octave–"'I'd like to welcome Mr Parnell back to Ballinasloe.' I'm not so sure Mr Parnell wanted to be here at all."

"His name's *Parn*-ell, not Parn-*ell*. Bit of a dry bollocks, alright."

Eileen giggled. "Mr *Parn*-ell didn't smile much. I don't think he even blinked those black eyes of his. Did you notice he was the only man in the room without a cap? He's losing his hair, too. The beard makes him look like his head's upside down."

"Cut out that talk," Liam said, laughing. "Parnell's an important man."

"I saw you talking with him," Eileen said. "After Bernie telling us to 'keep yer mouths shut, say nothin' and listen'."

Liam smiled at her mimicry of Bernie's east-coast accent.

"You made him look even more miserable. What did he say to you?" she asked.

"The talk was all one way. He ignored me completely, never said a word. The bollocks. Matt Harris couldn't wait t' move me away."

"The Schoolmaster seemed concerned about the small tenant farmers and labourers though, didn't he?"

"He was tellin' them t' stand up and fight back," Liam said. "Reminded me of a fella I met in Loughrea. Small man with a pipe and bad teeth. He wanted t' fight back. What's that word, subju...?"

"The Schoolmaster said, 'Your powerlessness has led to you remaining subjugated'."

"Bernie'll tell me what it means."

"Controlled. And a bit submissive, maybe," she said. "He means you're inclined to give in too easily because you think there's nothing you can do. He's talking about the evictions and the rent increases. People give in too easily because they feel there's nothing they can do."

"I don't think Mam was subjugated."

"No, it don't sound like she was."

They plodded the rest of the way to the fair ground through deserted streets, without talking. It was peaceful, still and black out on the edge of town this hour of the morning. The only sounds were those of stirring horses and a late-emigrating nightjar chirring from a prickly bramble bush.

Bernie remained at the meeting. Dermot O'Leary was there, down from Dublin, and he was keen to introduce Bernie to Matt Harris and the others.

They reached the wagons. Before they parted, Eileen said, "You know how you haven't kissed me, Liam?"

"Who?"

"I'm going to kiss you." With a step and a rise onto her toes, she kissed him.

He felt the soft lips on the cheek with the graze from the Cosgrove lad. She didn't kiss the graze, though. It was nearer his lips. He thought she might have touched his lips. With her lips. Then she left him, listening to the chirring.

Liam climbed into the covered wagon he shared with Bernie. He was exhausted, but an hour passed before he fell asleep with his boots still on. He grinned for that hour.

The stick whistled. Not a tune Aiden would play on his sleep-flute. Not a set of notes in an agreeable succession. Just the one note. A note of discord. As it sliced the air, the stick whistled. Before the thump. Whistle, thump. Whistle, thump. His father's head like the hide of an ass, rocking at the thump, then quivering to stillness. Ready for the next blow. In his dream, Aiden played a melody to drown out the whistle. But he couldn't drown out the whistle, because there was too much blood.

O'Connor varied the duration of the Fair depending on the size of the town, careful not to outstay his welcome. "Leave them wanting more," he liked to declare. As the fair rolled out of town, he'd misquote the Thomas Bayly ballad, *Isle of Beauty*, shouting it from his seat on the wagon, "Absence makes the heart grow fonder; town of beauty, fare thee well."

From Ballinasloe, the fair rolled and rattled its way into Athlone, a border town linking counties Roscommon and Longford.

After four days, O'Connor guided the procession north, parallel to the boat trips of Bernie's youth, to Roscommon town for an early-winter fair. Bernie took them to his uncle's cottage. It was mantled with ivy, the windows and door boarded up as he'd left them two years earlier, before he joined O'Connor's fighting booth.

It stormed for the week they were in Roscommon, the weather defying the people to venture out of their houses to attend a travelling fair. A bitter north-westerly threatened to cut the nose off anyone brave enough to try.

O'Connor called a halt. He decided it was to be the last fair of the year. He sensed the troupe were ready for a rest and he himself was looking forward to hibernating until spring. "It's like draggin' an oul' cow up a hill backwards," he claimed. "It's hard work and for nothing. Winter weather freezes pockets shut".

It suited Bernie to spend winter in Roscommon. He made good use of his uncle's cottage, carrying out the necessary repairs to make it habitable for himself, Liam and Eileen. He assumed it now belonged to his mother, nevertheless, he was relieved no irate landowner descended upon them as they saw out the wet winter months.

Winter turned to spring and by March the following year the fair had regrouped, its performers returning from their places of winter refuge. The Irish Singing Clown was a notable exception. During the cessation, he met a woman on the eve of the New Year who enticed him to England with a proposal of marriage.

Two new performers joined the fair. A French man performed gravity-defying manoeuvres on, what he called, a 'high-wheel bicycle'. The two-wheeled machine had a small wheel at the rear. The rider sat on a leather seat high up above the ground, his legs forcing pedals around to propel the large front wheel. The height and speed of the contraption worried Liam, and it gave him no reassurance to see the Frenchman crashing into the ground whilst practising and performing his stunts on the bumpy fields.

The other newcomer was an Irishman calling himself 'The Diddy Man'. He performed hilarious novelty tricks whilst milking either of his two cows. Such was his skill with the beasts' teats he could fill any receptacle or quench the thirst of any bystander within a six-yard radius with fresh, warm milk. Liam particularly liked the trick where he squirted milk from one cow into the slurping mouth of the other as it ran around them in a circle.

Satisfied he had "all aboard who's comin' aboard", Aloysius O'Connor led his entourage of entertainers out of Roscommon in early March. The 1880 tour of Ireland was to be Liam's last.

From Roscommon, the procession of performers moved throughout the midlands, working through Aloysius O'Connor's carefully planned itinerary of Longford, Mullingar, Kells and Cavan.

Liam travelled through scores of bustling towns and belittled villages. He wondered at much of what he saw, and was saddened by much else. He saw wealth and poverty, he met dignitaries and laymen, spoke to successful farmers and evictees, shook hands with working labourers and the unemployed. He listened to all their stories.

By autumn, they reached the small river-trade depot town of Carrick-on-Shannon. Their visit coincided with the annual regatta of the August holiday. Aloysius O'Connor's Country Fair fitted right in, adding to the carnival atmosphere of the regatta.

Liam trained alone, Bernie no longer able to keep pace, his runs taking him along the water's edge. He had time to marvel at the build-up of racing and pleasure boats that skated back and forth across the harbour. Away from the riverbank, Liam noticed a more worrying sight.

Chapter 51
Rathreagh, Ireland, 1880.

"Th'oul' woman's nearly dead, yer honour," Brendan Cahill pleaded. "It'd be the endin' of her to be stirrin' her now. Plase, sir, yer honour."

"Dead my arse hole," Billy Cuffe said. "You need have taken heed of that before you refused to pay your rent. Now shift her, or I will,"

Acting-Constable PJ Huddy stood back from the cabin with his body of six sub-constables. He dabbed his eye. Constable Neild had opted out of supervising evictions from now on, delegating them to his subordinate. Huddy knew it was because Neild was afraid. Afraid, and the man too lazy to yawn.

Two weeks ago, the Sub-Inspector had sent a missive to all constables warning them to be watchful of a resurgence in Irish Republican Brotherhood activity. "With particular regard to evictions," the memorandum stated. Huddy knew the source of that intelligence would be a constabulary man who had infiltrated the brotherhood, but he doubted the IRB would be active here in Tirawley.

Three people had turned up to witness Cahill's eviction. Two brothers he knew by name (having only last month penned a letter from them notifying a sister in Philadelphia that their father had passed away), the third he was more suspicious of. The unknown man dressed well and had a vague familiarity about him. He didn't look like a farmer to Huddy. Nor, to his relief, an IRB man. An IRB man wouldn't have pulled up on a twin-wheeled dog cart.

Huddy surveyed the fields, noting locations of ditches and bushes that might shelter men. He also watched Cuffe. He had made enquiries about Cuffe, but other than learning he was from Dublin, he knew little else of any certainty. He heard rumours of a good education and a father a business man. A wealthy business man. It made him all the more curious as to why Cuffe was here in Mayo? A falling out with the father, maybe? He knew it could happen. Running from a damaged relationship? There was talk of a wife in Kerry.

He longed to catch Cuffe falling foul of the law, to provide an excuse to detain him, free from Neild's interference. The visit to Cuffe's lodge had been dangerous, impetuous, but he had heard nothing from Neild about it. He wondered how many more people he would end up assaulting. He had searched for Ann Henessey's family, to speak with the grandmother, but the family had disappeared without trace. Dead, or holed up in some temporary scalpeen shelter in the hills, no doubt. Without the grandmother he was unable to link Cuffe with Ann Henessey's death, he had nothing to contradict the grandmother's statement. But he was sure there was a link.

"Mr Cuffe, sir, I'm not refusin' to pay. On me solemn oath. I have oats to harvest that I can be after givin' ya. That'll be a dacent instalment on it, yer honour. I'm unable–"

"Shift her!" Cuffe shouted.

Cahill surveyed the forces of justice amassed in front of his home and sighed. "Yer honour will be after givin' me time to coax her out." He turned into the mud cabin.

Huddy heard sobbing as Cahill gathered his family.

Cuffe signalled the men with the battering ram to ready themselves. "As soon I clear it, Mr McManus."

McManus stood with his arms folded, a leg cocked. The tripod towered over the shabby mud cabin, ready to wreak devastation.

The stained back of Cahill's jacket appeared in the cramped doorway. He carried his mother in his arms, papery-skinned and wrapped in a torn, tartan blanket. He manoeuvred through the gap with no sign of effort, his mother's flesh-riven body as light to him as a spring lamb.

Cahill's wife, Nora, emerged next, herding out four whimpering children small enough to shelter inside the tails of her tattered coat. She bowed her head as she passed Cuffe, downtrodden, her spirit worn away.

Cuffe stepped into the cabin. It smelled of decaying bodies and burnt turf. A dull fire glowed in the grate with a stool to one side. A depressed truckle-bed of straw lay against one wall. He stooped back out through the doorway. Cahill's family were gathered on the grass. A muddy sky hung over them. A grey drizzle descended, the fine drops jostled by a breeze that blew from over the fields. Cuffe glanced at the three onlookers on the road, and across at Huddy who stared back at him. He turned up his collar and nodded to the man in charge of the battering ram.

McManus and his assistant did their work. The shelter caved in on itself with the first blow. They made a show of lifting the heavy tripod of logs into different positions. It helped justify the charge McManus had made for its use.

"Killala's the nearest workhouse," Cuffe called down to Brendan Cahill, as he passed on his horse. "It's that way," he said, pointing with his shillelagh. Cuffe smiled.

Chapter 52

The Mayo Telegraph.

By James Daly, Editor.

Friday, 15th August 1880.

Organised resistance or retaliation? The outrages continue. Two days ago, at the tenancy of a Mr Brendan Cahill, in the parish of Rathreagh, near Killala, another disturbing eviction took place. A reporter from this organ was present to witness the heinous eviction of Mr Cahill and his family, carried out without the merest hint of compassion or humanity. Mr Cahill, made wretched by oppressive rent demands, was forced to carry his ailing, elderly mother from her sick bed to clear the dwelling. Regular readers will not be surprised to learn that the estate on which Mr Cahill was a tenant is the Farmhill Estate, owned by none other than the notorious scoundrel, the money-grabbing miser, Miss Harriet Gardner. Choosing to be absent from the scene herself, Mr William 'Billy' Cuffe, who is thought to be a bastard son of her uncle, 'Colonel George Cuffe, executed the deed. The eviction leaves Mr Cahill, his elderly sick mother, his wife and four young children destitute and destined for the county workhouse. Will landowners ever show compassion again, or are we of an era when the only course for the powerless tenant is one of organised resistance or even retaliation?

Chapter 53
Carrick-on-Shannon, Ireland, 1880.

The Carrick-on-Shannon regatta of 1880 was notable for its extravagance. Town dignitaries hailed it as the most successful ever. Its success was in contrast to the depressed state of the country's economy, still in the doldrums.

The regatta drew crowds from all over Ireland and abroad. The Midland Railway carriaged people in from stations in Sligo and Mullingar. Flags of every nation adorned the banks of the River Shannon. Large boats and barges threaded their way along the river, their bows and sterns bedecked with banners and streamers. The six-oared gig race drew a large, excited crowd, with people four-deep along the bank. A brass band from Europe played beside the bridge. *Captain Finch's Quickstep* and *Free and Easy* and *General Taylor Storming Monterey* were trumpeted out in loop.

Away from the grandeur of the riverbank, Liam noticed the underlying layer of poverty. Out-of-work farm labourers were already reduced to begging at makeshift soup kitchens set up around a huge brachán pot, reminiscent of potato-blight days. The authorities, keen this should not detract from the pageantry of the regatta, had been swift to move the kitchens on, well away from the river.

For the first time, *Aloysius O'Connor's Country Fair* outstayed the exuberance of the event, remaining in Carrick for a full week after the boat races had ended. O'Connor had no regrets, August was the driest month so far in a miserably-wet year, and he had a feeling that people's attitudes to the frivolity of fairs was about to shift. By the middle of the last week, Liam, Eileen and Bernie had time to spare.

"...he lay himself down and fell asleep, drunk, exhausted and his clothes in tatters." Bernie approached the climax to a story about a man called Malachy and a púca.

"No wonder he was tired," Eileen said, "walking all night."

"Eileen, you're not believin' any of this?" Liam said. "It's nonsense. Bernie's only trying to frighten me. Us."

"When morning came," Bernie continued, "Malachy opened his eyes. The sun had lifted back the fog and a small swallow sat on a tussock of reeds, eyeing him warily."

"Is that the end of it?" Liam asked.

"Not thirty yards away was a building Malachy recognised as his own shabby house. When he stood up, he saw a clear path in the bog that circled out to the road." Bernie was on his feet, drawing large circles in the air. "On the road, he saw a muddy trail crossing it to the bog on the other side. The trail disappeared behind the house, then wound back over the road. The path then arced its way back to where he stood."

"He'd been walking in circles!" Eileen said.

"Exactly. The púca had just been up to its oul' mischief with poor Malachy."

"See, a load of rubbish," Liam said.

"Did he ever see the púca again?" Eileen asked.

"Eileen! Púcas aren't real. They don't exist," Liam said. He swiped her on the arm.

Bernie sat back down on the rock, grinning.

They were quiet for a moment, savouring their bathe in the sunshine. Liam said, "I don't know how Madam Zena does it, but I once knew a woman who told ya yer future by readin' cards."

"Oh, now," Bernie said. "This from the man who thinks my púca story's a load of lies."

"No, this is the truth," Liam said.

"Who, Liam? Who was she?" Eileen said. "Was it the traveller woman?"

Liam hesitated. "Her name's Spinster Kennety," he said. "She lived near us. She learned this thing off travellers where you laid cards out on the floor and she'd read them for ya. She'd tell yer past, present and future. With numbers. Never understood the numbers thing."

"Was it Christy Sherridan's grandmother?" Eileen said.

"Christy Sherridan?" Bernie said. "Not that big little gob-shite. He caused enough trouble when you threw that fight to 'im. Ballinasloe, wasn't it?"

"Christy's grandmother taught her, yea."

"And, no doubt, Spinster Kennedy would relieve you of a copper or two in the readin'," Bernie said.

"Kennety. No. At least I don't think we gave her any money. A hen egg, maybe. She told me my future once."

"Go on," Eileen said, propping herself up on an elbow. "Did she say anything about meeting a beautiful, red-haired girl?"

"My, my," Bernie said, smiling. "Would ya look at the ears on 'im."

"No!" Liam glared at Bernie. "She told me... She did say, I'd have to look after the baby. She meant Aiden. He was tiny then, his arse the size of a coat button. She said I'd be in some sort o' trouble." The flush subsided.

"Trouble? How?" Eileen said. "What sort of trouble?"

"She left then. Before tellin' us. But she mentioned someone dyin'."

"Stop, Liam. You're making it up."

"She told us she saw *death* in the cards. That's what she said, danger and death. Do ya think she seed the house bein' knocked down? And Aiden... Aiden dyin'?"

"How could she know?" Eileen asked. "Right. Liam, stop. You're frightening me more than Bernie's púca story. That's enough."

"She mentioned evil. A man made evil by his own kin. And she said I'll have help when the danger comes."

"What evil?" Eileen asked, sitting up, blessing herself with the sign of the cross.

"That's alright then," Bernie said. "If you're gettin' help with all that danger and evil, aren't ya safe enough?"

"I'm sure it was the eviction she saw in the cards," Liam said. "And Aiden's death. I don't know the evil bit. I know the help... She meant you, both of you."

A flock of gulls glided overhead, their screeching like the cry of a small child.

Despite the warmth of the sun, small bumps formed at the base of the hairs on Eileen's arms.

Liam and Eileen stared at each other.

Chapter 54
Ballydonnellan, Near Westport, Ireland, 1880.

Sydney Smyth flicked the reins. His father, John, wrapped in a heavy overcoat and his hat pulled down over his face despite the mild evening, was in no mood for conversation.

The jaunting car rocked as it rolled over the deep recesses in the road. Near-naked gorse hedgerows lined the route, screening the fields like dirty net curtains. Sydney remembered one of the many country sayings learned during his time in Westport, "When the gorse is out of blossom, kissing's out of fashion". He knew his wife, irritable of late, would be angry with him for getting home at this hour. Kissing would certainly be out of fashion.

As the evening darkened, the only evidence left of the October sun was the red underbelly of the clouds to the west.

The journey had been a waste. His father, land agent for the Marquess of Sligo, had called on four rent-defaulting tenants. From each, the claim was the same, "We've no money to pay the rent." His father had been tolerant at the first call and had agreed a grace period. But his patience had waned with each subsequent stop. At the last, his father grabbed the tenant by the vest-collar, swiped the hat off his head and threatened him with eviction. The tenant was alarmed, but Sydney detected a look of helplessness in the tenant's eyes. A look that suggested he harboured a fear of something even more perilous than the land agent's ire.

George John Browne, the 3rd Marquess of Sligo, owned over one-hundred-thousand acres of Mayo. His residence, Westport House, had been in the family for over three-hundred years. It was to Westport House Sydney and John Smyth were returning.

Sydney heard the crack of rifle-fire a fraction of a second before he felt the buckshot smash through the louvered side panels of the car. The impact opened up a hole the size of his fist and littered the air with splinters.

He stood up on the footplate and scanned the field to his right. A bulky, crouched figure, carrying a rifle low and parallel to the ground, scurried away from a conical cloud of gunshot smoke.

"Take these," he said. "Go, go!"

His father took the reins and reached across his son for the whip.

Sydney reached into the back of the car for the bolt-action hunting rifle. The car jolted him, but he knew it was best to take his time loading the weapon. Slow is smooth, smooth is fast. His father had drummed it into him on every hunting trip since he was an eight-year-old. That knowledge could now save his life. He withdrew a cartridge from his jacket pocket and guided its tip into the breech. He released the bolt and cocked the hammer. He needed to stand to get a clear shot over the hedging.

"Slow down. We'll outrun no-one on this excuse for a road."

His father pulled back on the reins.

Sydney stood and held the rifle to his shoulder.

There were four men. Armed, grey, anonymous silhouettes, bunched and running to head them off at the road.

"Do you see him?" his father asked.

"I see four of them. Armed to the teeth and out to murder us."

"Well let them have it!" his father called and halted the horse.

Sydney's heart raced. He had never hunted men before. He took a breath, steadied himself and squeezed the trigger. As the rifle recoiled against him, the bass bang of the discharge filled his ears and the familiar smell of gunpowder swirled around him. When the smoke cleared, he saw three of the men run back to their fallen comrade. He swallowed hard to readjust his eardrums.

"Let's go. Fast as you can."

The dead man was later identified as Charles Howard, a former member of the North Mayo Militia based in Ballina. At the time of the shooting, he was without land and without employment. The court heard of Howard's 'bad reputation' and his associations with the underground Irish Republican Brotherhood. Sydney Smyth was charged with his murder but found 'not guilty by reason of self-defence'. The three unknown gunmen fled the scene and remained at large.

Chapter 55
Ballaghaderreen to Castlebar, Ireland, 1880.

After Carrick-on-Shannon, Aloysius O'Connor steered his fair across County Roscommon to Ballaghaderreen for a three-day stop. From there, they rumbled over the county border to Swinford in County Mayo. Swinford was a wash-out. The rain fell in slanting sheets to the misery of the performers, and the tenant farmers.

"I wanted me own circus, truth be told," O'Connor said to Liam. They sat in a covered wagon, wondering if the downpour would ever stop. "Yer not dependin' on the weather as much with a circus. The 'big top' they call the tent. I'd love them exotic animals all around me. Especially the elephants, I'd love ta have an elephant."

"Ya nearly bought an elephant for me, once," Liam said, smiling. "Ya'd miss the fightin' if ya left this for a circus."

"You could be right, there. I use ta do a bit you know?"

"Bernie said that. Said ya were handy too."

"'Swhere I met him. Roscommon, I think. He paid his money and stepped up inta the ring wit' me. Knew right off he was good, like. Afterwards, we got talkin' and he told me he did a bit of it in London, over in England. I asked him ta work for me. I was getting old and slow, anyhow. He was old enough too, but he still had all his buttons on, as they say. He was still fast. Even though he was a drunk, had only one good eye and was deaf in one ear, he was still fast."

"He never told me he fought ya. Who won?"

"That's for us ta know lad, for us ta know."

"Was that when he stopped the drinkin'?"

"Mostly. I put 'im to trainin', with Francois. Liftin' stuff, runnin', that sort o' thing. I've had ta drag him out of a couple of shebeens and public houses, but I don't think he's touched any liquor since you joined. One of the reasons I put up wit' ya."

Liam considered revealing his plans to O'Connor. He decided he'd leave it to Bernie.

From Swinford, the troupe wound its way to Castlebar. O'Connor contemplated not setting-up in Castlebar because of the rain. He intended to announce the closure for the winter when the weather turned, and they were greeted on the edge of town by glorious sunshine. He opened the fair, determined to keep it open until either the patrons petered out or the rains returned.

Liam limbered up in the ring.

O'Connor was installing the next contender into the oversized gloves. He glanced over to the arch of the booth-board where a small man in a top hat stuck his thumb in the air to indicate there was no-one else waiting to pay their way in.

"What did ya say yer name was?" O'Connor asked.

"Me name's Doonigan, Val Doonigan," the big man said, in a slow, polite drawl.

"Are ya local, ye are?"

"I am, sir."

O'Connor pushed against the huge hands of Doonigan to fit the gloves.

"Right, Mr Doonigan, no dirty punches now, or I'll be up on yer back in a flash."

"I'll fight fair, no bother."

"Make sure ya do, he's only thin."

"He's in for a thumpin', mind."

"You thump away. Just thump clean, that's all, you're three times his size."

With the gloves squeezed on Doonigan, O'Connor moved to the centre of the ring and glanced at Liam who looked smaller than ever. He was grateful the lad moved like a rattlesnake. He raised his arms into the air for attention.

"Ladies and gentlemen of Castle-bar," he sang, his red-haired nostrils flaring. "You have a fine representative for this next bout. I want ya ta show your appreciation for the valiant Mr Va-al Doonigaa-an."

There was a brief flutter of applause from a few in the crowd of about three-score and ten.

An old man in a braided-cloth cap withdrew a pipe from his mouth and called out, "Go on Doorframe, crack 'im in the chops. But try not ta hurt the laddeen too much, good man yourself."

The crowd chuckled.

O'Connor, the showman, responded. "Doorframe? Ladies and gentlemen, I give you Doorframe Doonigan against Whippet Walshe. A contest of might versus speed!"

Bernie shook his head at O'Connor's rhetoric. Doorframe Doonigan and Whippet Walsh? Holy Christ. "I don't need tell ya he's big," he whispered to Liam. "Stay nimble, keep dancin' on yer toes. He won't be breathin' so just tire him out. If he's not inclined to go down, make this one a draw, it'll do no harm. And remember what I taught ya."

"Not a bother," Liam said.

"Here's the bell!" O'Connor yelled. He clanked a hammer against an oblong metal sheet. "Fight!"

The fighters moved to the middle of the ring and squared up to each other. Doonigan looked enormous, in woollen trousers, rolled shirtsleeves stretched over bulging biceps and a greasy cloth cap, next to Liam's naked, stick-thin torso. It looked, to Bernie, like a mismatch made in the Valley of Elah, Doonigan the uncircumcised Philistine.

They danced with their fists up. Liam hopped to the side. He slung a fast left hook, hitting Doonigan on the forehead. The blow dislodged Doonigan's cap sending it spinning into the crowd.

The crowd grew animated, a few shouts of acclamation went up.

Liam smiled. He liked to dispose of the caps as early as possible. This must have been one of the quickest.

Doonigan swung a massive right glove at Liam's head.

Liam ducked and danced around the ring – a lead around, like his mother taught him. The crowd oooed the near miss.

Doonigan took steady breaths.

Liam shot a left fist into Doonigan's jaw and followed with a rapid right to the big man's liver. Doonigan absorbed the punches without consequence.

Liam ducked and dodged. A familiar, concerned voice scythed its way through the crowd to him. "Be careful, Liam!"

Liam was eight-years-old again. He stretched off the top rung of a ladder, handing a flat stone up to his father. His father straddled the straw-ridge of the roof, reaching down. The chimney was almost complete, built by the two of them from the ground up. Liam knew his father was pleased to be nearly rid of the task, he was behind with the tilling, he was neglecting his field. "I'll never till that field turnin' it over in my mind," he repeated. Liam didn't fully understand what he meant.

Throughout the build, his father complained to him that the land agent would probably use the chimney as justification to raise the rent. If it wasn't for his mother's insistence, the chimney wouldn't have been built at all. She had demanded it be finished before the winter set in. This winter will be a special one, with a baby due. (Liam never did get to see his sister. She tried to leave her mother's belly long before she was ready.

Mammy buried her with all the other children who were born too early, in the baby graveyard, further up the Cloonaghmore River where it's shallow and the water gurgles and chimes and tinkles over the rocks.)

"A little higher, good lad," his father said.

They strained to make a transfer.

Liam repositioned his feet, gripping the rung with his toes, and stretched up.

"Be careful, Liam!" his mother called, surprising him from around the corner of the cottage.

Liam turned to look and his toes slipped their grip. His leg shot down through the top hole in the ladder, grinding against the stones of the chimney stack. He fell backwards, letting go the stone. The ladder toppled, vaulting Liam into the ground. He heard his mother scream.

The next he knew, his mother was wrapping her apron around a deep gash below his knee. It didn't hurt, it only stained the grass a dark red.

Liam stared out at the faces in the crowd, searching. They all carried the same wide-eyed, open-mouthed, concerned expression. He saw her. She wore a lacy bonnet, quite unlike anything she wore before, but it was her alright. He fixed on her face, different but familiar, the first face he knew.

"Mammy?" he said.

The right glove of Doonigan crashed into the side of his jaw. He didn't hear the crowd gasp.

Chapter 56
Ratheskin, Ireland, 1880.

With a contingent of six armed sub-constables of the Royal Irish Constabulary, Acting-Constable Huddy had all routes into the small glen guarded. The area around the three cottages was secure. He remained wary and stood part way up a boggy slope, scanning the landscape for signs of danger. Neild had briefed him on a recent firearm attack against the land agent for the Marquess of Sligo, near Westport. The attackers came at him from a field at the side of the road, armed with rifles. The land agent survived it, but his son killed one of the attackers in self-defence. Land disputes were escalating into a war.

Within the sealed-off area, Billy Cuffe moved from one cottage to the next, evicting tenants.

Cuffe claimed that all three tenants were significantly behind with the rent and had obtained the eviction orders necessary for him to clear the land. The three plots amounted to over seventy acres of dry, flat land. Ideal for pasture and the rearing of cattle.

Cillian Moriarty argued at his front door that Cuffe had caused the backlog of rent by excessively racking it up year after year. He accused Cuffe of setting it at a cost where he had no hope of meeting the payment.

Cuffe checked the whereabouts of Acting-Constable Huddy while he listened to Moriarty. At his first opportunity he dragged Moriarty from his house and threatened to fire it with his family still inside if Moriarty didn't call them out at once.

Moriarty, his wife and seven children gathered on the road, carrying what they could of their belongings. By the time Magistrate Hogan had read the eviction notice to the closed door of the next cottage, a stone's throw away, Cuffe had men levering the Moriarty home apart with crowbars.

Cuffe strode up beside the Magistrate and walloped the door with the end of his blackthorn stick. "Dawney!" he shouted. "I don't mean to be indelicate but open this door now or as God is my judge, I'll break it down and then I'll break you."

Magistrate Hogan slinked away, it was all getting a bit too abrupt.

"Mr Cuffe, yer honour, please," Dawney called from within. "Sir, ye knows I'll gladly be payin' what I can of the rint. Ye knows it's the best I'm doin' ta meet th'increases."

Cuffe signalled for two of his driver-men to come forward. "We are past that stage now, Dawney. I have no more time for your excuses."

"Mr Cuffe, yer honour, please. Amn't I givin' ye all I have to be givin' ye."

Cuffe stepped aside.

A large axe struck the door dead centre, the boom echoing across the glen.

Acting-Constable Huddy turned to look from the slope.

As the driver-man worked the blade-head loose, a second axe smashed into the door beside it. The axe men swung again. With only a few blows, they had opened up a gaping, splintered hole in the door of the cottage.

Huddy stood with hands on hips and observed proceedings.

Cuffe instructed the two men to step aside and he hit away the remnants of the door. He stepped into the cottage, his hands in front of his face. The smell assaulted his nostrils, his eyes watered. He coughed, thinking the stench thick enough to dig out with a shovel.

Dawney, his wife, four teenage children and a sow pig huddled in the far corner of the room.

The sow snorted in rage.

The youngest son clutched his mother.

Cuffe's heart quickened when he seen the child. He thought the youngster a beauty. He regretted not spotting him before. A rose from shite grows. "Out!" Cuffe demanded. "All of ye, out!" He swung a boot at the sow as it passed. As the boy drew level, Cuffe stopped him, his blackthorn under the boy's chin. The cheeks were smeared pale where tears had washed the dirt away. Cuffe smiled but only with his mouth.

The boy's mother pushed the stick away and shielded her son with her shawl.

"Leave that, come with me," Cuffe instructed his men, outside. When Cuffe and his axe-men arrived at the third house, the family were already gathered on the track. Magistrate Hogan had finished serving them notice.

Seamus Burke, his wife and two children stood around their belongings. A bench seat, a stool, two pots, three wooden beakers and two delft plates decorated with scratched hunting scenes lay stacked on the ground.

Cuffe ignored them as he strode past. He held his breath and paused in the doorway of the cottage. He gazed into the empty, dim hovel. "Get the crowbars," he called to the driver-men. "Take it apart."

Chapter 57
Castlebar, Ireland, 1880.

The icy shock of the pale-full of water woke him from his stupor. He heard vague voices. A man's voice, angry at him. A woman's voice, angry at the man.

"Don't touch him," the woman said.

Liam opened his eyes. Before him, Bernie's bearded face was next to the bonnet-clad face of his mother. Liam smiled and passed out.

In the drawing room of the town house, Maggie interrogated Bernie on all that had happened since the eviction. He told her what he could. He had been uncomfortable informing her about Aiden, but she had been insistent. She thanked him afterwards. When Liam regained consciousness, Bernie left him and his mother alone together.

"Here it is you are, now. I feared I'd never see ya again. I feared I'd lost everyone. You, Aiden, your father, everyone. The baby too." For the briefest of moments, Maggie let go one of his hands to wipe her eye. "Liam, I don't blame you for what happened to Aiden. Ya mustn't burden yerself with thinkin' it was your fault."

"Mammy, but—"

"No listen. It's important to understand the way of it, or it'll tear the heart outta ya." She shook his hands and stared into the handsome, bruised face. She sniffed. "Aiden was sickenin' before the eviction. He was months with the fever, God have mercy on him, a long time poorly. Whatever chance we had of keepin' him alive at home for a while, you had no chance in the fields. D'ya hear me?"

They looked at each other, she trying to convince him of his innocence with the stare of her eyes and the squeeze of her fingers, he thinking of things he should have done to save his brother. She pulled him to her. Their arms wrapped around each other.

"I thought I might never see either of you again," she sobbed over his shoulder. "But you're safe, thank God. Here it is you are, yes. I looked for the two of ye everywhere. I went back to Carrow. The house was a ruination. I checked the constabulary barracks at Kincon and the workhouse in Killala. No-one had seen ye. James Jackson from the constabulary said everyone in the barracks had been out lookin' for ye. I feared ye'd both perished. But I didn't give up hopin'. A mother never gives up hopin'."

As the sobbing subsided, she pulled herself away and they surveyed each other at arm's length.

Her smell was familiar, of his mammy, with a leathery tinge of carbolic. There was a lop-sidedness to her face where her lower jaw refused to line up properly. Liam suspected the misalignment was the cause of the slight lisp. Her hair was flecked with unfamiliar flashes of grey.

"Would ya know me, Mammy?" he asked. "Have I changed?"

"Oh, I would... I did, didn't I? You've become a man, Liam, in only a few brief seasons. Look at you." She laughed more tears as she ran her fingers over his rangy face and pinched at the fine hair pushing out on his chin.

Liam dodged his head away, a blush spreading from his ears.

"And look." She clasped the musculature of his shoulders. "I could get angry about missin' seein' ya become a man, Liam. To see that was mine by rights." She kissed him on the forehead. "Your father'd be proud."

"What happened t' Da?"

"Yer father, God rest be to his soul, I don't think ever stirred again. I was told he passed away before they got us to the hospital in Ballina."

"Ballina? You were taken to Ballina?"

"To the workhouse hospital. They saved me there, they did. I owe me life to the Sisters of Mercy. We were too late to save the baby. It was poor James Jackson delivered the baby on the cart, but..."

"He said Ballycastle! That bastard said they were takin' ye to Ballycastle. I heard him!"

"Liam, stop it. Stop..."

"Sorry, Mammy." He felt his toes curl at his outburst. "But he said–"

"We were probably too hurt to take to Ballycastle. If we hadn't gone to Ballina I don't think I'd be here now meself. The nuns saved me life."

"I thought ya were in Ballycastle. Ballina? Jese, all that time lookin' for Ballycastle." Then it occurred to him. "It doesn't much matter, I didn't find me way to Ballycastle anyway."

They both smiled, Liam noticed his mother's missing side teeth.

"Mammy, I think me, Aiden and Eileen might've been in Ballina the same time as you! For the love of–"

She held a finger to his lips. "Enough," she whispered. It was a delicate gesture, so beautiful and familiar to him, unique to his mother. His mouth stretched into a smile beneath her touch.

"It's gone," she said, and smiled back. She stood up and walked to the ornate, wooden surround of the empty fireplace. "I'll take ya to his grave one day, Liam. It's the paupers' cemetery. In Ballina."

"It's maybe the same cemetery as Aiden, Mammy. They might be buried beside one another."

"I hope so," she said.

"Is the baby buried there too?"

"She is."

Another sister, thought Liam. Another sister he never got to see.

"I'm not the best at holdin' on to babies, am I?" she said, staring into the empty grate.

"It wasn't your fault. That bastard hit ya with his stick. T'was him killed the baby. T'was him killed Da and t'was him killed Aiden in the end."

There was venom in his voice. She turned to face him.

"Listen," she said, smiling. "What's this ridiculous boxing thing that ya're at? Do ya work for the fair or what is it?"

"Have done for over a year. A long story that I'll tell ya sometime, but Bernie teached me to fight. I'm good."

They both laughed at that.

"Bernie told me somethin' of it. Ya put the fear o' God on me today when I noticed ya up there in the fightin' booth rope stage thing. And the clatter that horse-of-a-man gave ya? I honestly thought I'd found ya and lost ya on the same mornin'."

The broad smile made Liam's jaw hurt. He held a hand to it.

"So who's this girl, Eileen?" his mother asked. "Should she be introduced to me?"

"You'll meet her." He tried to hide the red flush with his hand. "Mammy, we're stoppin' doin' it now. I mean meself and Bernie... and Eileen. We're pullin' away from the fair. We've been plannin' it and we mean to do it here, in Castlebar."

She returned to her chair, curious.

"Bernie's been findin' out about somethin' called the Land Leaguers, Mammy. We heard they're based here in Castlebar and we're goin' to join them, the three of us. Bernie knows some of the men involved through friends in Dublin. I think they're good people, Mammy. They're tryin' to stand up for–"

"I know what they stand up for, Liam. I know of them."

"Ya do? The Land Leaguers? And are they here in Castlebar?"

"My God, even though I think your character is more me than yer father, I'm still thrilled to be able to touch and stroke ya again."

Liam smiled back at her.

"We must find the Land Leaguers, Mammy. The three of us want to join them. Bernie has letters to introduce us."

"I can help with that," she said.

"You, Mammy? God in Heaven, how? If ya know them that's wonderful." His expression went from glee to gloom. "And then I want the two of us t' think about Billy Cuffe?"

Chapter 58
Ballina, Ireland, 1880.

"You're all nothin' but a shower of damned Fenians. God damn the lot o' ye!"

The waxing moon filled Knox Street with a silvery-grey gloom, throwing black shadows against doors and into alleyways. The long avenue of three-storey terraced buildings was still, its residents sleeping, or hiding behind curtained windows.

Harriet Gardner staggered along the middle of the mud road, her Perkins twelve-gauge double-barrel shotgun cradled in the hollow of her arm.

"Comeonoutun' face me, Ballina Catholics!" she shouted, the drunken slur making her almost incoherent. "Or ye all 'fraid of a womun?"

At the corner of Pawn Office Lane, Mickey Marr stood with his back flat to the wall, shielded by shadow. The Gardner woman had plagued this town for too long, thought Marr. His town. Never any respect for no-one, only contempt. Her and her drunken rants.

"The Church of Ireland'll never shurrender!" she roared down the deserted street.

He was delighted when the name 'Harriet Gardner' came up at a brotherhood meeting. She had evicted the tenant he and his father worked for almost nine months earlier. At the time, nothing was said. Why wasn't it mentioned at meetings back then, straight away? He had been angry for a while. No work meant no food. The old fella half starved to death. But labourers don't count for much. He should have raised it at the meetings himself, but he wasn't bold enough. Not brazen enough. He knew his place. "Soon or Never", they like to say at brotherhood meetings. He had thought it would be never.

After that incident in Whealan's Bar last Fair Day, when he thought the old fella was going to swipe her across the puss, her name *was* mentioned. The brotherhood was *Irish*, and *republican*, to the heart. He knew it wouldn't let him down. Old ball scratcher himself, Seamus MacGuire, even arranged a sack of vegetables for the old fella. When the others talked about Gardner, he discovered he had been right all along, she was to blame. For everything. She was even worse than he thought. Racking the rent, intimidating tenants into changing religion, evictions. Wanting every earthly thing for her own profit. Good God above, she was responsible for it all.

And she's a drunk. Her and that leech that sucks off her, Pringle. Both drunks. They say Gardner gives Pringle the odd clatter around the head when she has the mind to. She sleeps with the devil, this woman. Probably sleeps with Pringle too, the dirty old cow.

Some in the brotherhood are frightened of her. He wasn't. Even when she stalked the streets with her shotgun. If he'd his rifle on him now, he'd down her where she trod. Right this minute. He's a good shot with the rifle. He wished he had it with him. But no bother, he had something else that would serve as well.

"When I wus lasht in this town, some dirty whore struck me 'cross the face. 'Cross the face! With a teapot! Where're ya now, teapot whore? Come and strike me now if ya dare!"

Even the constabulary guarding her have felt the force of Gardner's blows. She clobbered a member of the constabulary! What happened to her? Nothing. Up at the petty session court but nothing more than a warning or a shilling fine. Nothing that would make her mend her contrary ways. There's one rule for the tenant and the labourer and the cottager and quite another rule for the landed class.

"Mr Muffeny. Mr town-commissioner Muffeny!" she yelled. "Where're ya, Mr Muffeny? Shun me in yer shop, will ya? Decline my custom? Well ya won't decline Mr Perkins here."

There's no constabulary guard with you now, Harriet Gardner. We won't be denied a fair shake this time. I'll dispense your proper justice. The brotherhood will be proud. They won't overlook me and my father again. My father will be proud. It's time for me to be bold. They may even pen a song about me. Harriet Gardner, by the power invested in me, I'm going to cut your throat.

Harriet Gardner staggered towards the junction with Bridge Street.

Marr palmed the twine-wrapped handle of the hunting knife tucked into the rope-belt of his trousers. Bridge Street could have a few walkers this hour of the night, there would be a greater chance of being seen. He needed to act fast. He slipped from his cover and ran in a diagonal across the street to where the moon shadows were fattest. He stopped in the doorway of P. Flanagan, Family Grocer, Wholesale Wine and Spirit Merchant, Estd. 1865.

If Flanagan caught him hiding in his doorway, trying to make sense of the writing on his signs at this hour of the night, he'd have some questions for him. "I'm makin' meself famous," he'd explain. "I'm goin' to kill that drunken bitch up the street. Ya might even be in the ballad yerself, now you've spoke to me."

He left the doorway and slinked along the shadows towards her. The night was mild, dry and moonlit. A good night for the killing of Harriet Gardner.

"Ya called me vile names!" Harriet shouted. She stopped and stood swaying in the middle of the street. "You all enjoyed the yellin' and the hootin' didn't ye!"

Mickey Marr picked up speed, running.

Harriet shuffled towards the junction. "I'd rather than ten pounds in me hand to know ye wuz all set off from me!"

Marr held his breath. He sprinted, drawing down on the staggering Harriet. Fast as a fox. A trail of her alcohol lingered on the moonlit air. He drew his knife, the street so quiet, he feared she might hear the beat of his heart. Almost upon her.

"Miss Gardner, come wit' me." Sub-Constable James Jackson rounded the corner from Bridge Street. "I'll escort ya to your hotel... Hoy boy! What are y'at?!"

Marr kept running, veering past Harriet and the uniformed man, over Bridge Street and on to King Street. He leaned into the hill as he ran past the empty shops, predator turned prey, arms and legs pumping.

"Hoy! Stop, there!" Jackson yelled after him. "I know who y' are!" he lied.

Mickey Marr didn't stop. He dipped into an arched alleyway half-way up King Street, clambered over walls, leapt gates, ran through backyards and along narrow streets. He ran until the pain in his lungs forced him to stop. He stared back, wide-eyed and gasping, hoping the sub-constable had given up the chase.

Chapter 59
Castlebar, Ireland, 1880.

"So you're Liam? I've heard a lot about you. I'm delighted to make your acquaintance at last. Your mother speaks of you in such exemplary terms I was beginning to think you were a figment of her fancy."

She was flattering, confident, with no smile in her humour. She was tall and willowy. Her long face had a straight nose and was curtained at the top by auburn hair pulled so severely down each side it reflected the light from the window. She wore a day cap, with a white ribbon that matched her complexion. Her speech was deliberate.

"I'm Mrs Brannigan. Welcome to the Irish National Land League."

"I've heard about the Land League," Liam said. "We've met people that work for ya, as we've travelled 'round the country."

The statement startled his mother, but she remained silent.

"The 'we' you refer to? I presume this is your gentleman friend and the girl your mother informed me of?"

"Bernie and Eileen. Dublin and Mayo. We've seen people handin' out food and money. We were in Carrick-on-Shannon there recent. They were doing good work. And we've often times seen the shelters ye've built for evicted families and the likes."

"We're in turbulent times, Liam. Crops are failing, the blight has been seen again in the potato, and we have rent and eviction concerns. The perfect nightmare. We believe in tenants paying a fair rent for their holdings, Liam, but no more than that. A fair rent, free sale and no evictions if rent is paid, that is all we ask. Full implementation." She paused, as if waiting for a reaction from Liam.

Liam stared. She had a beauty about her. A severe beauty but a beauty none the less. Liam guessed she might be several years younger than his mother.

"The League's leaders are under attack," Brannigan continued. "They are harassed by the Government and their function impeded. The men need help. It's time the women of Ireland be mobilised, give the men some much-needed stimulus. Tenants are bolder with the support and encouragement of their women, Liam."

Liam glanced at his mother.

"In America they have a Ladies' Land League. There are funds being raised over there to establish the same in Ireland. It will complement the male Land Leaguers. A Ladies' League will operate out of the limelight, freer from the attention of Government forces. We will be better organised than the men's League and with the scope for... shall we say, a more resolute approach."

Liam knew he had found what he had been looking for.

"We are fearful it will be 1845 and the famine all over again. It's our mission to avoid a repeat of 1845. I assume you are aware of–"

"I know about '45. Though, I'm not sure I'd call it 'the famine'."

"Nevertheless, it is our belief that some landlords are racking rent deliberately. Elevating them to intolerable levels. You see, there's a move from arable to pastoral farming. Fewer, larger farms, Liam. They think that to make pastoral farming cost effective you–"

"Need the big fields," Liam inserted.

"Hence the evictions."

Maggie beamed. The introductory meeting between her son and her employer was going well.

"Charles Parnell leads the National Land League," Liam said. "Who will lead the Ladies' Land League?"

"Can I trust you, Liam?" Brannigan said.

The question made Liam snort.

"It's because I know and trust your mother, I am meeting with you at all, Liam. The Ladies' Land League will be an open organisation, but we do have enemies. It seems that in some quarters there are people who question our methods."

"You can trust me, Sheila," Liam said.

"Liam," Maggie said, leaning forward on her chair. "It's Mrs Brannigan."

Liam gave another snort. "You can trust me, Mrs Brannigan. To be sure."

"That's good, Liam." Brannigan slowed her speech. "That's very good. I am pleased." She stared at Liam for a long moment, a close and searching stare.

As her dark, unblinking eyes roved over him, Liam felt scrutinised. He turned to his mother.

"Now listen," Brannigan said, snapping out of her reverie. "I have important League matters to attend to with your mother. It's monotonous administration so I won't detain you. If you want, you can talk to your friends. Everything I've told you so far could be learned in any public house in Castlebar for the cost of a pot of porter. If you're still wanting to get involved, come and speak to me again, tomorrow."

Brannigan hadn't revealed the founder's name. She still didn't trust him.

"I suppose–"

"Until tomorrow, Liam."

The sleep chased him. His mother had told him Mrs Sheila Brannigan was a regular visitor to the workhouses in the north-west corner of Mayo. A well-connected agitator, she made a habit of inspecting workhouses and making the lives of the Guardians uncomfortable wherever she found conditions wanting. It was during a visit to Ballina workhouse Brannigan first met his mother. Over several visits, a friendship developed. It was Brannigan who took his mother from the workhouse, giving her work, a little money, good clothes and a place to live. It was Brannigan who assisted his mother in her fruitless search for him and Aiden.

His mother surprised him with the news she was able to arrange a meeting with the head of a branch of the National Land League. Bernie had been right in thinking Castlebar the place to make their introductions. Castlebar, where it all started a year last October in the Imperial Hotel.

He hadn't expected to be meeting a woman. The Ladies' Land League was news to him. He knew of Parnell, Andrew Kettle, Thomas Brennan and Michael Davitt, the grand council of the National Land League, but which of them will head up the Ladies League?

That Brannigan was a curious one. He could see why his mother would be loyal to her.

The sleep caught him.

They struggled to pull his father's dead head away. Welded to the floor with congealing blood, the hard earth reluctant to let go at the lift, tugging it back down with tiny, maroon ropes. The ties stretch to breaking and snap back, melding out of existence. A ridged ring remains, separating the mess of splashed blood from the clean patch where his head had lain.

Chapter 60
Castlebar, Ireland, 1880.

"You told me about these people, Liam. Take a look. It's an old article, but I warn you, it's not good news you'll be reading." Eileen handed the newspaper to Liam.

Liam hunched his head in over the folded pages. His lips moved as he slid his finger under the words.

The Mayo Telegraph.

Friday, 17th September 1880.

It was the brutal behaviour of a mad dog. I am indebted to Parish Priest Fr. William Bellew for the comprehensiveness and accuracy of his account. It seems that day upon day, the calamity increases as poor, wretched tenants are evicted with impunity. On too many occasions, the repercussions are fatal. So it was, two months ago, when Mr Sean Mullins met his death whilst being evicted from his home in Coonealmore townland. Mr Mullins was a man of at least 70 years, with a wife of equal maturity. The land agent for the landowner Harriet Gardner, is Billy Cuffe, and he was about the heartless business of evicting Mullins when an altercation broke out. Despite the intervention of Fr. William Bellew, who was present at the scene and who pleaded for clemency, the fracas proved fatal for Mullins. It is unknown what caused the death, but Cuffe is known to have been wielding a long stick, similar to a blackthorn fight-stick. The calamity was not to end there. Mrs Kathleen Mullins was taken to Killala workhouse in a state of profound despondency. She was but to last a fortnight before dying. If grief be a fatal affliction then, from witness accounts, it was from grief she died. Fr. Bellew conducted both funerals. Two lives for the price of one for Billy Cuffe, and all under the supervision of the Royal Irish Constabulary. Organised resistance is called for. If Cuffe is Gardner's mad dog, she needs to keep him on a tighter leash.

Liam's shoulders slumped as he collapsed the paper. "There ain't even a decent track t' the house," he said, his voice flat, monotone. "The arse end of nowhere. Had nothing. But they were content. And they shared what they had, with us." He closed his eyes and took a slow, deep breath.

Chapter 61
Castlebar, Ireland, 1880.

"I've seen ya feed the starvin'," Liam said. "That helps, but changes nothin'. Evictions still happen all over. Yer organisation is in a powerful position to take action."

"People will be talking, Liam," Sheila Brannigan said, relaxing back in her seat. "A handsome young man calling to see me on two consecutive days?" A slow smile worked its way across her face, transforming it.

He shuffled in his seat and felt the heat of a blush spread from his ears. She wasn't wearing her bonnet. Her hair gleamed. Liam thought he detected its vinegary perfume.

"What action are you suggesting?" she asked, tilting her head, maintaining the smile.

They were alone, sitting opposite each other on padded, high-backed chairs. The room was warm. It was the first time he drank tea from a china cup with a saucer. The American Irish were, seemingly, generous benefactors.

"Me mother will've told ya what happened t' us," Liam said. "The country needs t' take the fight t' the landlords. Attack their property."

"Fight? Attack? Liam—"

"Tell tenants t' withhold rents and support those bein' evicted. Are ya familiar with 'boycotting', Miss Brannigan? We should boycott the landlords. And the land grabbers. As for the graziers, with their air of superiority, boycott the lot of them, too. They're nothin' but shoneens, anyway, with their English ways."

Her eyes were wide. "Where did you learn about Mr Boycott?"

"I suggested the shunnin' idea to Mr Parnell when I met him in Ballinasloe last year."

"You met Charles Stewart Parnell, Member of Parliament and the President of the Irish National Land League?"

"Some late-night meetin' in Ballinasloe, yea. Parnell was at the Horse Fair, though I don't think he was buyin' livestock. I told him and his friend, Matty Harris, they needed t' be tellin' people t' shun the landlords who're evictin' folk. Not serve them in the shops. Not work for them. Don't even deliver their post. And I told him land grabbers should be treated the same way."

"Would he remember you, Charles Parnell?"

"Unlikely, he was in a miserable enough mood that night. And that was before I started proddin' him with a finger, tellin' him what he should and shouldn't be doin'."

Brannigan giggled behind a hand and leaned forward in her seat.

Liam smiled at her. She seemed to enjoy the thought of Charles Parnell getting accosted in conversation.

"Fair play to 'im, though," he said. "I think 'boycotting' is a better word for it than 'shunning'. He's smart enough, t' come up with that one."

"I beg your pardon, Mr Walshe," Brannigan said, with mock irritation. She flicked a hand at him, her fingers glanced his knee. "It was I who coined the phrase 'boycotting', in an innocent conversation I had with a priest from Neale. It was not Charles Parnell."

"Then all the fair play goes to you, Mrs Brannigan," he said.

They held a stare. All was quiet in the well-furnished, well-lit room. The beam from the window passed behind her, throwing her features into a complementary shadowy softness. Liam considered reaching for his tea but feared the cup might rattle out of its saucer.

"It would be scandalous," she whispered.

"What would?"

Brannigan looked away. She inhaled deeply, raised her head and stiffened her back. "Attacking the landlords' property. We must remain legitimate. We can't break the law."

"The law's not equal. Laws need to change. Politicians need t' sit up and take notice if there's t' be change, and we won't get their attention by handin' out food and buildin' shelters. You know that. We've t' cause a disturbance. It's revolution we need, Mrs Brannigan, a revolution."

"What age are you, Liam?" Brannigan asked.

The question caused another blush.

"As near twenty years as makes no difference," he said, talking at the tea cup on the table.

Brannigan raised an eyebrow and gave a knowing nod. She rose from her seat and reached into a tall wood and glass cabinet. She plucked a thin cigar from a pewter box and lit its end with a white-phosphorus match. Her cheeks hollowed as she sucked. She exhaled a grey cloud of smoke. She didn't offer Liam a cigar.

"We prefer to call it 'agitation', Liam," she said. "Our founder's name is Miss Anna Parnell."

"A lady? And a Parnell?"

"Don't be so surprised, Liam. Anna Parnell is Charles Parnell's sister. We will be the Irish Ladies' Land League and Anna Parnell will lead us."

Brannigan sucked on the cigar and blew another cloud of smoke into the room.

Liam thought the smoke smelled musty. It reminded him of drying piss.

"Anna Parnell has her own method of working, Liam. Arguably, she's a lot more... actively radical than her brother."

"I understand what yer sayin'."

"We have links with some of the more militant groups in this region. Unofficial, of course, but, let us be candid and say, you're not alone in your thinking. There will be work for people like you, Liam. Operations, missions, whatever it may be. Something will come up before long."

They lock stares through the smoke. Liam senses an unwritten, unspoken contract being drawn up between them.

"In the meantime, I will arrange for you and your friends to be provided with supplies. I do this because I trust your mother, Liam. She says I can trust you. Don't let your mother down."

"No, ma'am. And me friends will be only too glad to meet ya."

"If you and your friends join us, Liam, you need to be aware of what you're getting involved in. It will be dangerous."

"We're prepared for danger, Mrs Brannigan."

Chapter 62
Castlebar, Ireland, 1880.

"It's been a while in the planning," Sheila Brannigan said, stretching the truth. "We must move on it soon."

"And has it received the requisite sanctioning from above?" Seamus MacGuire asked.

"Now what do you expect me to say to that?" Brannigan answered. "That it's Mr Parnell's idea? You can rest assured that it's as sanctioned as any action is ever sanctioned."

MacGuire reclined his thick frame in the chair and scratched at his groin with his stubby fingers. His face had an unruly black moustache that spilled over his mouth and his hairline, though closely shaven, ended at the expanse of his shoulders. There was no neck to be seen.

Though based in Ballina, MacGuire was originally from Killala. His father had eked a livelihood fishing the deep waters off the continental shelf close to the Killala coastline. His grandfather had also been a fisherman but was deported to Botany Bay for his part in the failed French rebellion of 1798.

Although he was a senior member of the North Mayo Irish Republican Brotherhood, Brannigan disliked the man. She thought him unkempt to the point of crudeness, a bath was in order after being in his presence. "If he were hanged for handsomeness," her mother would have said about him, "he would die an innocent man." Yet the Brotherhood stood alongside the Land League, and he was loyal, so she tolerated him.

"We've a problem that's slight in its nature, however," he said. "I'll be in need of additional men."

"Or women, MacGuire. Don't forget the women."

"A'right, so," MacGuire said, laughing. "If ya've women ya think are fit and able and can do it, it's additional women I'll be needin'."

"Don't mock, MacGuire."

"Ah, come on. Don't be so touchy, will ya not? Amn't I only here wit' ya 'cause ya want t' carry out an operation on my patch. I'm doin' you the good turn, remember."

Brannigan drew a breath, tilted back her head and looked down her long nose. She conceded him a hard smile. "We have people," she said.

"I'll be needin' at least three more," MacGuire said. "I'm afraid the landowner has a reputation that's fearsome and I'll have me work cut out to get anyone meself. Three more, from out the area, would be my recommendation."

"I hope you will not get any of them shot and killed?"

MacGuire bridled at the barbed reference to an ambush he led on the Marquess of Sligo's agent. He and three others tried to ambush the agent from a field. MacGuire fired off a shot but one of his accomplices, Charles Howard, was mortally wounded in return fire. He calmed himself.

"There'll be no guns involved in this one, I can assure ye of that."

"We want you to source only one other," Brannigan said. "Find us someone who knows the lie of the land and won't get us lost. We have the three other people we think we'll need."

"I'm sure I can find one. If ye've three more, I'm thinkin' that should be ample enough."

"Three people," Brannigan said, looking to Maggie sitting beside her. "I have three people for you."

Maggie smiled, her smile made crooked by the misalignment of her jaw.

Chapter 63
Lecarrowanteean, Ireland, 1880.

The soot stains were still there, scorched into the stones forever, scant evidence that the Walshes ever lived hereabouts in Carrow. Any shred of charred blanket or shirt or curtain had long since been carried off by the wind. The furniture had gone. Burnt, no doubt, in a cottage hearth to keep the cold away or to heat a pot of stew. The house had been taken too. Or large portions of it. Where had that gone? To repair a wall? Fill a hole in a track to nowhere? Half a gable wall was all that remained, the gable without the chimney. The roof, under which Liam and Aiden had sheltered that first night on their own, had gone. The rafters for firewood, he knew well.

Liam lifted his finger from the burnt stones and looked around to where he had stood watching the workmen, Aiden sitting on top of the chest of drawers leaning against him. If he closed his eyes he could still hear the dull thud of the battering ram as the thick pole demolished their home.

He walked to where the rear of the cottage used to be and looked out over his father's field towards the river. The river seemed closer than he remembered. The bushes and trees that lined its bank looked taller and, with no-one to beat them back, were invading the field like a rampaging army. The army of Theron, perhaps, the Viking invader on a raid from the land of the lakes. Have it, army of Theron. Rape, kill and pillage as much as you want because, Jimmy Walshe, his father, tiller of this field, would not want this land now.

Liam had convinced himself that his family had been evicted from their farm so that Billy Cuffe could turn the field from tillage to pasture. So that another farmer, a land grabber, took it on, joining it with his own, to raise cattle, or sheep, or horses. The quality of the soil would not be in doubt. He had envisaged a slope of rich verdure, from the track down to the river. Some churning of the ground around the gates, maybe, from the inevitable concentrated stomping of a thousand hooves. But the field? He expected to see the field set to lush grass. A feast for any beast.

Or was it a hope? Did Liam want the field to be put to pasture? It might have served as paltry justification for what had happened. For the misery, the violence, the deaths. What else could it have been for? He'd resent the land grabber, but his father might, at least, draw some comfort. Comfort from the fact his legacy, the field he tilled until he could till no more, was put to good use.

What Liam saw, tensed his body and churned his stomach. His father's field had been untouched since the eviction. It was green but not the green of grass. The green of abandonment.

Chickweed smothered acres of the field in small, oval, pale-green leaves. A murder of crows had descended and picked at the tiny white flowers. There were ranks of cleavers along the bottom edge of the field, what his father called 'Robin-run-the-hedge', with their whorl of petals. The cleavers were the advance party for the raiding river bushes, reconnoitring the landscape, preparing the terrain and then calling the main troops forward when the way was clear. Through another patch of the field swept a swathe of willowherb, late remnants of its mauve flowers dying off in the winter cold. Clumps of hard rush, large and thick, their stout stems sprouting into the air, littered the field like a school-full of unruly, scraggy children. Ragwort, three-foot-high, that Liam knew to be poisonous to cattle and disagreeable to sheep, stalked the line of turned soil that marked where his father was burying the next run of drains.

His mother had been right, the house was a ruination, and so was his father's field. His father's work had come to naught. This untilled field was good for nothing. Abandoned. Liam found no reason for his family's eviction here.

He wiped at a cheek, the solitary tear chilled by the wind, and pulled his cap down to his ears. He tightened his jacket around himself and worked up the collar. He sniffed and turned away.

Mickey Marr drummed his feet on the ground. He breathed warm air into his cupped hands and rubbed it into his palms. When Liam approached, he bent and shouldered the sack-wrapped bundle propped against the ditch. The two men set off walking, their necks tucked into their shoulders.

Chapter 64
Kincon, Ireland, 1880.

Mickey Marr was the first to raise his hand when the mission was proposed. Seamus MacGuire had hesitated before agreeing his nomination. Not that he doubted the lad's loyalty, Mickey couldn't do enough for the cause, but he thought there might be something not quite right about the Marr lad. Too keen. Simple, even. Not the sort of lad you'd bring home to meet your sister, anyhow, thought MacGuire.

There were few alternatives. Joesy Heffernan put himself forward, but when Joesy heard the details, he confessed to being afraid of the dark. Marr was selected. After what happened to his father, he probably deserved this chance. Having no other to choose from, MacGuire was relieved when the Walshe woman and her son met Marr in Ballina and agreed he was the right man for the job.

It was an eclectic group, made up of Marr, an old man called Kelly, the youngster Liam and a girl, dressed like a Protestant in cap and trousers, by the name of Eileen. No matter, the job was simple enough. Set fire to the hay barn and get the hell out of there.

"Right, have ye everythin'?" MacGuire asked.

They nodded.

"Then you'll be about yer business on yer own from here lads. Beggin' yer pardon, miss, and you. So may yer wits be about ye and careful, right? Ye know what ye have t' do, and ye know how t' go about it." MacGuire had his hand buried deep in his pocket, scratching. "I'll be on me way. The height of the castle of luck to ye. I'll look out for the glow in the sky."

He dropped down off the roadway and clambered over the gate. His bulky black shape rushed off across the field, his progress lit by the red of the setting winter-sun reflecting off the rolls of thin cloud.

Marr, his face ablaze with acne, stared after him. If he had his rifle on him now, he thought, the moving MacGuire would be a good test of his shot. A bullet in the arse would give him something to scratch at.

Marr would have opportunity to test his shot soon enough. He tried to catch Liam's eye.

"Come on," Bernie said.

Marr led off, towards Farmhill House.

Chapter 65
Farmhill, Ireland, 1880.

"A straightforward enough job, as ye know. There were the two constabulary men guardin' the house to worry about, but we had chosen early evenin' so's we were there at the time their shift changed over.

"I hadn't met the Marr fella until that night, but I felt fairly confident nothin'd go wrong. I trusted the other two. I hadn't figured on that bollocks of a lackwit, Marr, goin' off on his own damn quest for immortality. Beggin' yer pardon ladies."

"Liam. Come 'ere I need to talk to ya." Bernie beckoned Liam back with a nod of his head.

"What d'ya want?" Liam said.

Bernie waited until Eileen and Marr had gone on.

"Here. Keep this on ya," Bernie said, handing Liam the handgun.

"What in the name of God, Bernie? What's that? I know what it is, but what do ya have that here for?"

"I want you to carry it, Liam. For protection."

"Protection? Bernie, I don't need it. Where'd ya get that yoke from, anyhow? How long've ya that thing on ya?" Liam stared at the handgun as if he'd been asked to take a warm, bloody, beating heart that Bernie had freshly cleaved from a man's chest and put it in his pocket.

"Liam, there's no time to argue this. I got it in London for protection. I'm givin' it to you now for protection. I nearly threw it away several times but didn't, I kept it. You're the nearest thing I have to family, Liam. I didn't protect the family I had. I want to protect you."

"Bernie, I don't know what yer sayin'. What're ya talkin' about?"

"Liam, listen. These guards might be armed. MacGuire says they're not but what the hell does he know? Take this in case ya need it. I'm tellin' ya to take it. I need ya to take it."

"Bernie? Bernie, I don't even know how t' use somethin' like this."

"It's not bloody difficult. Ya cock that thing on top back, point it and squeeze the trigger."

"Holy God, Bernie. Listen, keep it you. I'm alright, I've all I need."

"Take it. We've got to go."

Liam weighed the gun in his hand as Bernie scuttled off to catch up with Marr and Eileen. A gun? What was Bernie thinking? You could kill a man with one of these things.

"When MacGuire left us, we crossed the field handy enough. The field slopes up towards the big garden wall so we had a bit o' cover. By the time we got to the wall we were pantin' for breath, but everyone was alive with excitement. Lookin' forward to seein' the barn light up the sky, no doubt. Prob'ly lookin' forward to the bit o' heat out of it as well. The cold that night'd cut ya in two.

"Anyways, we made our way along the wall. God, that's some wall they had built. Around a bloody garden! An orchard is it? Built in 1824 according to a stone set in the corner. Must be golden bloody apples they're growin'.

"We could see the main house from the end of the wall. A Tilly lamp outside for the sub-constables, bright lights on inside for her ladyship. Then there was Cuffe's place, nearest us, with its small light on.

"All we had to do was sit an' wait. We were all excited, but Marr was bouncin'. I should've known then he'd somethin' stupid planned."

"They should be changing over soon," Eileen whispered.

"That's the barn, the far side," Bernie said. "Have ya the matches?"

Bernie's warm breath plumed in the backlight of the house. "I have," Liam said, tapping the jacket pocket containing the sticks of white-phosphorus.

"Liam," Bernie said. "I thought I should warn ya."

"What?"

"Look out for the púca."

"For feck sake, Bernie, this is no time for jig-actin'."

Eileen nudged Liam.

Liam tugged at his collar, feeling warm despite the temperature.

"C'mon lads," Bernie coaxed, in a low, slow voice. "Feck off back to the barracks. Yer shift is over. You've done enough. C'mon, before I piss in me trousers with excitement. They're movin'! Stay low."

They crept from the wall and weaved their way between the heavy branches of scots pine. They had glimpses of a faint-yellow glow from the outbuilding window in the distance, but it was lightless amongst the trees. They groped their way through and crouched at the edge of the grove. Bernie saw the Tilly lamp flash on and off in the distance as it swung between the retiring sub-constables.

"Have ya noticed how only wealthy people have big trees?" Bernie said. "A status symbol. Are ya familiar with 'status symbol' young fella?"

"No," Liam said.

"Only the wealthy have big trees," Bernie said, by way of explanation. He turned to make checks. "Where's Marr?" he asked.

"I...I didn't see him go," Liam answered.

"The bastard's made off scared. Eejit. He shouldn't have come. I knew I was right to be wary of 'im. Think I frightened 'im with talk of the púca?"

"I'll find him," Eileen said.

"No!" said Liam, but Eileen had already crept away, faded into the fir trees.

"I'll kill 'im. As sure as there's a God, I'll take his life," Bernie declared. "We must go. Now."

"Marr wasn't frightened of no púca. He had other plans. I didn't know where he'd disappeared to and I wasn't too bothered. Liam had most of the fire-starting paraphernalia on him. I should've stopped Eileen going to find him, though, that was a mistake. I'll have trouble livin' with that the rest o' me days.

"Just as meself and Liam were about to cross in front of the house to the barn, things started to go seriously wrong. We found out where Marr had disappeared to."

"Lookit!" Bernie said. "Is that yer man? What's he doing? What's that he's with 'im? Where'd he get the rifle?"

Marr's silhouette ran across the open lawn towards the house.

Bernie and Liam crouched and stared.

"What's he doing?" Bernie said. "Oh God. Please no."

Marr found them where he and Liam had buried them, next to the gateway in the garden wall. He wiped sweat from his brow and unwrapped the rifles with care. He looked around for Liam. No sign. He covered his father's rifle with the sacking and replaced it in the hole.

"Up to you now, Liam. If ya want to use it, it's there for ya," he said. He ran a hand along the barrel of his own weapon and checked the chamber. He had pre-loaded both rifles. He allowed himself a self-congratulatory smile and sped off across the lawn towards the light in the window.

He had no concerns about the constabulary men disappearing towards the barracks. He didn't care if they saw him and came back, he only needed to get into a good position. Seconds is all it would take.

Forty paces from the sitting-room window, he saw the figure of a man move inside. He halted, cocked the hammer and shouldered his rifle. He steadied his breathing as he took aim.

She stood with her back and hands pressed against its cold face. Her heart pounded in her chest, her mouth was dry. The garden wall was mentioned several times in the planning meetings, but Eileen never envisaged it would be so imposing. She found it disorientating in its dark dimensions, as high as four men, stretching a country mile into the black field, its surface a silver, monolithic mass of mortar and stone.

All around her seemed as black as a tinker's pot. She had to decide which direction to take. "Where are you, Marr?" she breathed. Had he gone back or gone on? She turned right and ran, moth-like, towards the reassurance of the pale-yellow light of the outbuilding.

"We've to stop 'im, Liam. He'll get us hung by the neck," Bernie said.

Liam didn't answer.

Bernie's pulse raced. He had to act fast. He ran from the cover of the grove, scared to shout, scared not to.

"Move out o' the way or damn you, too," Marr said, his sight set dead-centre between the shoulder blades of the man in the window. "Move."

The man moved, revealing the profile of Harriet Gardner, sitting-on-a-chair height, illuminated by lamps, framed by darkness.

"You escaped me before ya bitch, not this time. Balladeers, you've a new hero to write about."

Bernie ran into the periphery of his vision, arms waving. He was almost between him and the house. Marr squeezed the trigger.

The rifle-shot resounded through the estate.

The sub-constables stopped and turned.

"Get Huddy, quick. Tell him there's shots comin' from the big house. Run. Fast!"

Jeremiah Jackson set off at a brisk rate down the path, happy to be running away from the sound of gunfire.

His elder brother, James, looked back at Farmhill House and waited. James decided nothing would be gained by rushing into an armed conflict when all you're carrying is a two-foot baton. "Small loss anyway if the cantankerous bitch got a bullet in her hole," he mumbled.

Billy Cuffe had his boots up on a footstool. He was three-quarters through a bottle of 1856 Chateau Lamothe Guignard. A sweet Sauternes, made sweeter by the fact it was an unexpected gift from Gardner that afternoon. "Fresh from France," she told him.

He felt warmly drunk. He felt warmly lascivious.

His arousal was spawned by thoughts of the son of a tenant from the far side of Kincon. The boy was delicate, pretty beneath the grime, rake-thin and hard working. He reminded Cuffe of himself at that age. As Cuffe enjoyed the wine, he contemplated the different ways he would enjoy making the boy compliant.

The jolt of the gunshot caused him to splash wine in the stiff lap of his trousers.

"Who in hell has she shot now?" he said, rising.

He gave a quick search for the Wedley revolver Constable Neild had sold him but couldn't find it. He grabbed his blackthorn stick, the shillelagh always to hand.

He pulled open the door and rushed out. The winter chill cut through the thin material of the open-necked evening shirt and shocked his senses.

Something, or someone, crashed screaming into the side of him and sent him sprawling on the gravel avenue. He rolled onto his feet and brandished the blackthorn, clutching it near its middle, the shorter length protecting his forearm, ready for combat.

The slight figure stood in front of him, hands covering an open mouth, eyes full of shock.

He jabbed the bulbous end of the stick into the exposed stomach and punched the intruder on the jaw.

The intruder groaned and dropped to the ground.

Cuffe bent down and pulled off the cap, certain he would recognise an aggrieved tenant. A girl. They were in the moon-shadow of the yew trees, but as his eyes adjusted he saw the round face, the freckled proud nose, the red hair tied-up high on the back of her head. He liked the look of her and she looked familiar. Where did he know her from? He felt light headed from the alcohol and the sudden exertion but he knew this girl. It's a year or two, but he never forgot a face as pretty as this. Duffy. For fuck sake, Thomas Duffy's daughter! The girl that burnt the bloody cottage down.

"Oh, my sweet little thing. Eileen Duffy. I'd thought I'd lost you forever."

He gazed down the avenue and held his breath. Nothing moved. He heard only the faint hiss of a breeze as it passed between branches of yew.

The shooting had stopped. Had Gardner shot at the girl? God Almighty. He decided Miss Gardner was more than capable of looking after herself on this occasion.

"Come on, my sweet one," he said. "I've dreamt of this many times." He scooped the girl off the gravel and carried her into the outbuilding, closing out the door with the flick of a foot.

"He nearly took the head off me. I swear to God I felt the fizz of the bullet as it passed me. I didn't think the gobdaw would shoot with me there. I gazed after the bullet, in through the glass, and I saw Harriet Gardner fall in the lighted window. I was that close I nearly heard her fall. A figure of a gentleman then moved over her and looked to the window to see where the shot had come from. That's when I recognised my oul' friend."

Liam thought Bernie had been shot. A tiny tinkle of glass told him the bullet must have reached the window, but he was relieved to see Bernie run towards the front door of the house.

He twisted his head and stared back into the grove. He was torn. What should he do? Help Bernie set fire to the barn? Carry out his own plan? Or search for Eileen? She could be anywhere in these trees. She was certainly not with Marr.

The hay-burning wouldn't happen now. But that was not why Liam had suggested this 'operation', as the Brotherhood men called it. It was not the hay he wanted to destroy.

He watched Marr turn circles on the lawn, gazing up at the stars, arms held aloft in victory celebration, rifle gripped in one hand.

"Damn!" he said, through clenched teeth, and searched for Eileen.

Acting-Constable Huddy charged up the path towards Jackson, bearing a lighted torch that gave a precarious flicker in the flurry of running air.

"What happened, James? Who's shot who?"

"Up at the House, sir. One gunshot. Don't know if anyone was hit."

"I don't suppose you'll find out either, standing here like a useless prick."

"No, sir."

"Follow us."

"Yes, sir."

Jackson gave an anxious check for his brother, Jeremiah, in the faces of the three rifle-bearing sub-constables that ran off behind Huddy. It was his mother's dying wish that he care for his younger brother. Relieved, he took his time examining his baton and straightening his uniform before he strolled after them.

Bernie tried the big brass knob, but the oak front door was bolted shut from the inside. He moved along the front of the house until he found what he needed.

A winged, stone gargoyle with large ears crouched in front of the house, sneering out over the lawn at Marr.

Bernie plucked it off its plinth and set it to flight towards the dark window.

Cuffe let the blackthorn rattle to the floor and arranged Eileen on the table top, unconscious. He pulled off his flannel shirt, rolled it up and tied it around her mouth. Ann Henessey had hollered. Best he took precautions.

"Your brothers aren't here to interfere now, sweet one."

She moaned.

He tore at the front buttons of her trousers and ripped at the material until the weak seam separated from front to back. He pushed both parts of the trousers down her legs and stood between her thighs, pinning her to the table. He panted, sweating, and as he stared down at the girl his arousal recovered from the blast of cold air.

"Set fire to the mother and father? You're some girl."

She opened her eyes, lifted her head and glared into the face of Cuffe. She snorted a lung-full of air and screamed. Only Cuffe heard the muffled cry.

He watched the brown eyes fill with fear as recognition came to her. "It's me, alright," he said. He smiled at the slightly-turned eye and punched it.

Her head ricocheted off the table top and she groaned.

He grabbed her throat high under her jaw and squeezed, pushing her head back, extending her neck.

She choked, breathless. Her hands flailed his arm, grabbed his wrist and flailed his arm.

"Dug their charred bodies out myself, I did. Wouldn't know them," he said. He reached for the buckle of his belt.

Bernie held an arm across his eyes as he beat at the broken window mullion and splintered glass with a fist. He lifted himself onto the sill and swung through the gap.

The floor of the grand hall was at window level. The gargoyle lay on its side, curled up asleep, a chipped ear pointing into the air. He scrambled to his feet, the crunch of glass reverberating in the hollow, spacious room. His nostrils filled with the musty smell of old oils, turpentine and charcoal. He inhaled the aroma.

Francis Seymour Conway, Marquess of Hertford and former Lieutenant of Ireland, smirked down at Bernie. The Marquess followed Bernie with his eyes as Bernie stepped towards the door-shaped line of light in the distance.

They surrounded him on the lawn, ready to stick him with their bayonets.

"They're gonna write songs 'bout me, and you'll be in them!" he shouted, laughing at the moon, his arms still aloft.

Huddy strode up to Marr and snatched the rifle out of his hand, the barrel still warm.

Marr tore his eyes away from the moon to see the butt of the rifle rise into his face. He yelped and fell to his knees, his hands clutching his nose. Burgundy blood glistened in the torch flame as it seeped through his fingers.

Huddy dabbed his eye.

"Lock 'im up, Davey. You two, with me."

Bernie heard a creak high on the staircase of the limply lit entrance hall.

A man and a woman, dressed like ghouls making for bed, stared down at him from the shadows like a pair of inquisitive illusions. He locked stares with them, and took a moment to convince himself they were real. He raised an index finger to his lips.

The man and woman turned and spirited themselves away.

Bernie tiptoed to the sitting-room door and pushed it open.

Susanna Pringle sat next to the window, ashen-faced and bleary-eyed with her back to the wall. A Perkins twelve-gauge double-barrel shotgun stood upright on the floor between her legs.

Harriet Gardner sat away from the window, shielded in a high-winged chair. She looked flushed, her hands clenched in fists on her thighs.

Holding a handkerchief to her brow was the small hand of Mr Gregory Partridge, his snowball-head of brilliant-white hair luminous in the lamplight.

Partridge snatched up his cane. He looked down his nose at Bernie. "Come no further my man. Stay where you are. The police will be here any moment, so don't do anything rash. What do you want? Was it you shot at my cousin here? What were you thinking? Who the hell are you anyway?" He pointed his cane. "What's your name, eh? Your name, man!"

Bernie waited for Partridge to stop asking questions.

"I believe you owe me some money," Bernie said, and scratched at his beard.

"I owe you money?" Partridge said, glancing around at Harriet wide-eyed.

Bernie said nothing.

"O'Malley...? Is that you Bernie? Bernie 'The Alley Cat' O'Malley? My God man, it is you. With an awful beard, no less. I thought you would have drank yourself into the soil by now. What on earth...?"

Bernie smiled at the familiarity of the conversation. "I believe you owe me some money," he repeated.

"Who is this damned laggard?" Harriet shouted. A line of red crept its way around her eye to her cheek. "And what the hell's he doing in my house?"

Partridge gave a miffed sniff.

Bernie edged towards him. "What brings ya to these parts, Partridge? A social visit, is it?" Bernie said. Then it came to him. Partridge wasn't the type to travel to the west of Ireland during these turbulent times for a social visit. "Your inheritance. You inherited something 'round here didn't ya? You inherited somethin' in bloody Ireland! Well, I'll be damned. You, of all people, inheriting a lump of my oul' country. Yer determined to have every last bit o' me, aren't ya."

Partridge raised his nose and puffed out his chest. "Irish roots, my man. Someway back, but there all the same."

"Cromwellian-settlement roots, more likely," Bernie said.

"As maybe."

Bernie took a small step.

"My God...," Bernie said. "I'd never have believed it. Where is it? Where's yer estate? Is it nearby? Hah?"

"You're, stronger, than, you look, you, little bitch."

Eileen had worked a leg free and wriggled like a wild-cat on the table. Her hair had worked loose and fell over her face. A red mask to hide behind.

Cuffe's grip on her neck eased as he struggled to regain control of her leg.

She took a deep breath, pulled at the shirt-gag and screamed.

"Shhh girl. Shhh," Cuffe said. "You're all fire aren't you? By God, I've missed you."

Eileen strained to look around her. A yellow-green glass bottle, that she couldn't help notice glowed with warmth and lustre in the soft light of the kerosene lamp, stood on a small, single-leg table nearby. She stretched for it.

"You had the smell, of sheep on you, when we last, met, sweet one," Cuffe said, through gritted teeth. He grabbed her throat, lifted her head and, leaning his weight over her, drove it down on the table.

She gave a choked moan. Her leg fell limp. Her arm lolled over her head, glancing the edge of the small table.

He tore at her jacket and shirt.

Liam didn't find Eileen amongst the firs. He emerged from the grove, panting out clouds of warm breath, at the end of a straight path lined with yew trees. At the far end stood the lodge-house, a yellow light in its window. He didn't know whether to continue the search for Eileen, or retrieve the rifle and come back to find Cuffe? He was running out of time.

A scream came from the direction of the lodge.

"Eileen?"

He walked towards the small building.

The smash of glass and a dull crash of toppled furniture.

Liam ran for the lodge-house. His boots clattered on the gravel, the handgun knocked against his chest. "Eileen!" He ran. The handgun jumped his pocket and scraped across the gravel into the shadows. He crunched to a halt, arms flailing, and went back to retrieved it. He found it in the shadows, and dashed towards the scream.

He charged at the door with a shoulder. Latches buckled as the door burst open. Liam halted inside, the gun behind his back

Cuffe spun around, a hand down the front of his trousers. He snatched the blackthorn stick off the floor, gripping it in its middle.

Liam thought he looked like a macabre fair-clown. Scarring on cheek and neck, wild hair, naked torso, brandishing a blackthorn stick like a Viking axe. There were two half-trousered legs appended to his hips. A black leather belt with a metal buckle arced away from his middle. His trousers hung unbuttoned and damp, to reveal where the stream of hair running down his chest and over his belly gathered in a bush. Comical yet menacing. Liam recognised the man immediately. This was the man he wanted to kill.

"Who in hell?!" Cuffe glared at Liam. "Does no-one ever knock my bloody door? Who, by fuck, are you…?" He lowered a hand and fastened the top button of his trousers. "Have I met you before, lad?" He cocked his head, like a confused dog. "I know you, too, don't I? More recent. Where…? You're Walshe. Jimmy Walshe's lad. You've grown, Jimmy Walshe's lad. I hear your father didn't make it. Farm accident we call that. And there's your mother, of course. And didn't you have a brother? Is it you been firing rifles tonight?"

Liam wasn't listening, he was staring at the stirring shape on the table, its legs hanging either side of Cuffe, the cloth of the trousers crumpled around booted feet.

"You know this one then?" Cuffe said. "She your girleen is she? Far too good for a long-streak-o'-piss of a boy like you. Well, I knew her first, so what you should do is turn around and step back out that door. Close it gently after you. You're very-much in the wrong house, at very-much the wrong time of the day, as I'm not of a mind to apportion her. So go on. Go!" He pointed at the door with the blackthorn.

Liam noticed the bare thighs on the table quiver. He pointed the handgun at Cuffe.

As the gun came into view, Cuffe lunged forward and chopped down with a swing of the stick. The heavy root-knot knocked the pistol from Liam's hand.

Liam lunged with a punch and hit Cuffe on the side of the mouth. The speed and strength of the blow caught Cuffe off-guard. "You big, long streak-o'–"

Liam punched again, catching Cuffe square on the nose. Flexing his knees, he lowered, and felt the swish of the blackthorn as it swung over his head. He punched Cuffe in the solar plexus.

Cuffe blew out breath and fell back against the pair of legs draped over the table's edge. He held up the palm of a hand as he gasped in air, his eyes bulging. "Wait!"

Liam hesitated.

Blood seeped around the ridge of Cuffe's lip. He wiped it across his face and swung with the blackthorn.

Liam was fast enough to raise an arm to block the stick hitting his head, the root-knot bludgeoning into his elbow. At the crack, intense pain shot up and across his shoulders, paralysing his arm.

Cuffe whirled the stick and planted the cudgel in Liam's ribs. Another snap.

Liam saw the near-naked body stirring on the table. He launched himself at Cuffe, knocking the blackthorn out of his hand. He punched with his working arm, catching Cuffe once, twice, a third time.

The table scraped across the flagstones as Cuffe fell against it, spinning it around. Eileen rolled onto her side, pulling a thick white collar off over her head, alabaster skin from shoulder to knee.

Cuffe lashed out high with a black boot and caught Liam on the broken arm. He grabbed a handful of Liam's hair and pulled the head down to meet a rising knee.

Liam's nose sprayed blood. He was unable to see. He was unable to breathe. He was bent double, the room tilting and revolving. He didn't know how to straighten up. One hand dangled, damaged and useless, towards the floor. The other held his face together, failing to stem the spurting from his nose.

Constable Huddy heard the crash of the door travel through the night air down the yew-tree corridor and out along the driveway.

"Carry on, both of you, and make sure Gardner's alright. I'll check the agent's place." He set off running.

"You're standing in it," Partridge said. "This is my estate. And I must say, if it weren't for the financial irregularities of late, I would not be standing in it myself."

Harriet shifted in the chair. Her eyes were cold, dark and flinty. Bernie thought he heard her teeth grind.

"Farmhill is yours?" Bernie asked.

"Half of it, yes. I don't mind confiding in you Bernie, we go back a long way, but my cousin seems intent on running it into the ground. All of it. My half as well."

Bernie edged closer. Partridge had embarked on a eulogy.

"The strategy appears to be increase the yield by evicting all the tenants. Please don't take offense, but that seems very Irish to me. Pastoral farming appears to be the next big thing. I know sod all about pastoral farming, but I do know the yield coming to me has not increased. It has decreased. So either the strategy is not working, or something else is amiss."

"Ya know nothing about it," Harriet said. "You've not the faintest idea of what we've to go through to make this place work. Can you not see they're even prepared to shoot at me through my own window?"

"It's a nick on the brow, woman. You will survive," Partridge said, dismissing the almost fatal attempt on her life.

Bernie edged closer.

Cuffe clenched his hands in a combined fist and brought them down on the back of Liam's neck.

Liam crumpled to his knees. He couldn't lose this bout. Aloysius O'Connor would rear up if he lost this one. Bernie would be yelling at him from the corner by now, cursing him, damning him. "What did I teach ya?" he would be screaming. "What did I teach ya?!" His vision cleared. He spotted the grip of the handgun protruding from under a footstool. He fell over it, tucking the gun inside his jacket as Cuffe rolled him onto his back.

Cuffe dropped on top of Liam, brandishing a long shard of the broken wine bottle in his hand.

Liam drew the handgun for a second time and cocked the hammer with his thumb.

As Acting-Constable Huddy ran in through the doorway, Cuffe slapped at the gun, deflecting it away. It fired. The explosion deafened Liam, smoke filled the gap between him and Cuffe.

The bullet struck Huddy, poleaxing him. The rifle he carried clattered to the floor.

As the gun smoke cleared, Cuffe turned back to Liam.

Liam had the revolver re-cocked and pointing at Cuffe's blood-smeared face.

Cuffe stared into the black hole of the barrel.

Liam squeezed the trigger.

The gun clicked.

Cuffe snorted snot and blood in relief, and smiled.

Liam knew that smile. The hateful, bruised and bloodied smile of triumph. The same smile Cuffe had before he struck his mother. The same smile Cuffe had as he beat his father to death. The same smile that marked the death and destruction of everything that ever meant anything to Liam. Aiden, his home, his unborn sister, Sean and Kate Mullins, even his father's field. All victims of that smile. And now him and Eileen.

Cuffe drew back the shard of glass to plunge.

Liam recognised the whistle before the thump happened. The fist-sized root-knob of the blackthorn stick, seasoned to hardness in butter and hot ash, glistening like polished brown marble, thudded into the side of Cuffe's head, plugging a space where his temple used to be.

Liam stared, open-mouthed, as Cuffe's face warped.

The side of Cuffe's head collapsed and his eyes rolled back in their sockets. Cuffe, his blank eyes staring down at Liam, waited. He was dead, but he waited. Then, without smiling, he slumped onto his side, the blackthorn shillelagh stick still lodged in his skull.

As Cuffe fell away, Liam glimpsed Eileen, standing over them, her face anguished, bruised, wild, strewn with red hair, shaking. Her face disappeared.

The stick's golden ferrule gave two taps on the flags as Cuffe landed.

Liam worked his body out from beneath Cuffe's legs and scrambled to his feet.

Eileen had turned away and wrapped herself into Cuffe's oversized evening shirt, her red hair visible through the material. She dipped her head as she worked at the buttons.

"I intended to get close enough to give Partridge a few slaps in that well-manicured puss of his, but when the revolver went off, I recognised the sound immediately. It was me who let in the two sub-constables that were knockin' on the front door. I told them they were needed in the sittin'-room and ran off. I'm lucky they didn't stab me, or shoot me in the back.

"Not that I knew where I was runnin', it took me a while to come across Cuffe's place. The door was wide open and I could see a man lyin' in pain, his head propped up against the jam.

"I didn't believe the sight that met me when I reached the door. I didn't expect it. Not at all. I hadn't seen me brother in thirty-four years. A lifetime, and...Well he'd been put through some shite as a boy, growin' up... And he was goin' bad after it. When I last saw him, he was being dragged away by police on Kingstown dock in the pourin' rain. I thought then his life was ruined. Not his fault, at all, he'd had it tough. Awful, truth be known. He had every cause to go bad, the hell-shite he went through.

"But I knew it was him on the floor, straight away. I'd know that cheek-scar and ectropic right eye anywhere. Me father burnt him in a drunken rage, one night, with a hot poker. He was fifteen years old. I didn't expect to see him in a constabulary uniform."

"Howaya, Philip?" Bernie said.

"Yer safe," Liam said to Bernie. Liam was pointing the pistol at Huddy. "Come on, we must get out of here."

"I've been better, Bernie," Huddy said, from the floor. "And I'll be a lot worse if this young buck lodges another bullet in me."

"Liam, it's alright," Bernie said, holding up a hand.

Liam hesitated before pointing the pistol away.

"But then you don't look like you've escaped the ravages of aging, either," Huddy said.

Liam gaped at the conversation taking place in the doorway.

Eileen hitched up the legs of the trouser and tied the shirt around her. She placed a trembling hand on the table for support.

"I think I look pretty damn good," Bernie said. He crouched to examine the bullet wound in his brother's shoulder. "I look better than that young fella with the revolver, I know that." He turned to Liam. "What the hell happened ya?"

Liam rocked back his head and pinched his nose.

"So what brings ya to these parts?" Huddy asked, wincing. "With your flat nose and old-man beard."

"Oh, I'm with these two. We were supposed to be lightin' a fire here tonight, but it all went a bit…ya know. And you? What are you doin' here all dressed up in yer smart green sub-constable's uniform?"

Huddy smiled. "I'm only here apprehending bullets that are trying to escape the house…" He paused to let the pain pass. "And I'm an acting-constable, ya cheeky bastard," he said, raising an arm to show the chevrons sown onto the sleeve.

Liam struggled with the removal of his jacket for Eileen, the revolver caught in the sleeve.

"I think you'll live," Bernie said. He stood and looked over the scene. "Cuffe?" he said.

Liam nodded.

"Who…?" Bernie asked.

Liam stared at him. Bernie glanced at Eileen. She had her back to them, slouched over the table, taking in deep, silent breaths of air.

"Ya know these two, then?" Huddy asked from the floor.

"I do," answered Bernie. "But I still can't believe it's you. I see the eye still looks disgustin'. And still leakin' like a burst sewer."

"Damn you, Bernie. Have ya seen yer own eye? Jesus, what a pair we are. What happened it?"

"Philip, I want to tell ya I'm sorry," Bernie said. "For everything I let happen ya."

"Ya bollocks ya!" Huddy said. "Ya sound like I'm about to drop dead."

"I know, I'm sorry. I do sound a bollocks, I know it's thick. I think it's because... It's because it's all I've thought about for the last thirty years. And then I find ya here in the midst of all this...and, well..."

"Now you've found me, you'll have plenty time to make reparation. For now, you better go or those two jackasses I have with me will be upon us. The three of ye, go. Be away. I saw what happened here." Huddy looked past Bernie at Eileen. "If he's dead, the world is no worse a place for the lack of a man such as Cuffe. You should go. If we're caught like this I'll have no choice in it."

"Gimme yer hand, I'll help ya up," Liam said.

Huddy stared past the proffered hand to the bloodied face. "I don't know who you are, lad," he said. "No, if they find me on me feet they'll think I should've stopped you. I just hope I don't have to lie here all bloody night, I'll either bleed or freeze to death."

"He let us go... We were lucky. It was as well it was him, we could've all landed up in Kilmainham. That or we'd have to shoot 'im." Bernie ran a thumb and forefinger over his beard.

The two woman stared at him. The debrief had stunned them both into silence.

"The girl'll need lookin' after, Maggie," Bernie said. "For a spell at least. You might be the best one for it, d'ya think?"

"Of course, Bernie," Maggie Walshe said. "She's stoppin' with me a while now, anyway. She's bruised cruel. I hope it's the only harm he's done her."

Sheila Brannigan blew a cloud of foul-smelling cigar smoke into the room. "I think it best we get all three of them away from Mayo for a while," she said. "Introduce them to another branch down the country. There's plenty going on in Galway, they're in need of help. The movement is only gathering pace, we have a long way to go. We've only just begun. I have plans for Liam and Eileen. And you, of course, Bernie. Setbacks are to be expected, but the cause is greater than any setback. They'll be plenty operations to get involved in elsewhere."

"Sheila, no," Maggie said. "I mean, I agree with the move. But I think they should steer well clear of operations for a while."

Brannigan sucked on the cigar and scowled.

Chapter 66
Castlebar, Ireland, 1880.

"So when were ya goin' to tell me?" Bernie said.

They were standing on a patch of risen ground on the outskirts of Castlebar, Liam's arm strapped to his chest under his shirt. A biting breeze fought against them the entire way up the steady climb, but Liam found the chill helped numb the fiery throbbing in his elbow. They had been silent during the ascent.

"What?"

"Feck you, ya little shite! Don't give me 'what?'!"

"He had it comin'," Liam said, staring out over the patchwork of fields.

"Why didn't ya tell me you had a plan to kill 'im?"

Liam spun around. "'Cause you'd have stopped me... At least I thought ya would've. Then ya gave me a bloody pistol, Jesus. Which only had one bullet, by the way!"

"Where is it now?"

"The bullet?"

"The bloody gun."

"Below in the house."

"Did Brannigan know?"

"No."

"Yer mother?"

Liam answered with a stare. Bernie's left eye was closed, the eyelid shielding it against the chill of the air, lest the milk inside froze.

"I tell ya now," said Bernie, reading the silence. "She's some woman to be arrangin' a thing like that with her own son."

"Subjugated, she is not," Liam said.

"Subjugated? No, she isn't. But to send you in there—"

"He had it comin'," Liam repeated.

Bernie stared at the grass, and kicked some blades. "I can't believe ya trusted Marr ahead o' me. The man's as mad as a bag o' wasps."

"Bernie, whisht. I didn't want ya involved. I didn't want ya involved in killin' a man. If it went wrong, I'd get shot or gaoled or somethin'. I didn't want you involved in any of that. Haven't ya been like a... Like a big brother, a father even, t' me these last years?"

"I know all about killin', Liam, don't you worry. But that's for another hilltop. When'd ya plant the guns?"

"Beginnin' o' last week. Me and Marr walked t' Farmhill and buried them by the wall. We stopped by me father's house on the way. House is gone now. Field's ruined too. "

"Some walk."

"Three days there and back. He stole his father's rifle for me. I knew when we first met 'im he'd do it. He hated Gardner more than I hated Cuffe. He was delighted with the plan."

"That's where ya were, was it? Whilst I was meetin' my local painter friend outside the Linen Hall, you were off plantin' guns at Farmhill. 'Twould make a fine gallery one day, that Linen Hall."

"What's Linen Hall?" Liam asked.

"Anyways, he's the reason we must get out of Mayo, Marr. He'll be squealin' to the authorities like a stuck pig right now."

"And that was yer brother?" Liam said. "Who'd've thought it? An acting-constable an' all."

"Yea, that's the brother. The one ya were about to shoot again." Bernie softened the sarcasm with a grin. "Always did like the police did Philip. Seems to be doin' well."

Liam assumed 'police' a Dublin word. "I was only tryin' to get us out o' there, keep him lyin' down. My one bullet was stuck in his shoulder, anyway. I hoped he didn't realise I had no other."

Bernie smiled.

"He's not 'Kelly' though?" Liam said. "Your brother."

"Long story," Bernie said.

Liam gave him a slow smile. "Go on."

"The short version is when we were young, we ran away from home and planned to change our names. He chose Huddy."

"Why?"

"We had a favourite uncle. Frank Huddington. Uncle Huddy."

"No, why'd ya run away and want t' change your name?"

"Ya don't want to know."

"Another hilltop? Did we spend last winter in his old cottage? In Roscommon."

"We did, yea."

"He recognised me," Liam said.

"Philip? Nonsense. How would–"

"He was at the eviction. Ours. It was him first struck me father."

Bernie fumbled in the pockets of his jacket for something he didn't need.

"He came over to us, after. The eye. The cheek. I remember all that. He remembers, too."

"He won't do anythin'. Didn't he let us go?" Bernie said.

Liam turned back to the panorama.

"You'll be givin' me back the pistol, Liam, ya will?"

Liam snorted. "Don't worry. He'll be safe enough, Bernie... Does it seem queer, you and him on opposite sides?"

Bernie chuckled. "Nothin' new about that. Irish history is riven with split family loyalties. Anyhow, I'm not on any side, Liam. I'm not inclined to think headin' around the country as an agin' rapparee will suit me after all. I feel tired. Old. Too bloody old for these shenanigans. Like an oul' horse, I'm long in the tooth. No, I'll meet up with the brother again and if I don't go back to London, maybe try to catch up with Aloysius O'Connor. I might talk 'im into buyin' 'imself a circus and I'll run the fair."

"What about that other fella, Cartridge?"

"Partridge? I've decided to leave him be. Don't sound like he has any of my money left now, anyhow. Him and Gardner deserve each other."

Liam looked doubtful. "This is only beginnin', Bernie. The Land League hasn't got goin' yet. There's a job o' work here needs doing. You remember Matty Harris, from Ballinasloe?"

"Matty's makin' a name for himself, alright."

"Harris is out to pull the institution of landlordism down. And I agree with him. The time has come when the land of this country, confiscated from our forefathers, shall be confiscated once again t' us."

"Yer soundin' like a public speaker, Liam,"

"It's only what Matty Harris said himself, Bernie... Ya'll not stay for it? After all we've seen and spoke about?"

"Are ya sure you'er for it yerself, Liam? It'll be dangerous enough."

"Anna Parnell's back from America. She'll have a chest full o' dollars and a head full o' plans."

"You know MacGuire's IRB?" Bernie said.

"The Irish Republican Brotherhood. I know that."

"They're dangerous bastards to be getting' involved with, Liam. That man lives his life as entirely outside the law."

"That I know, too. But it suits the Land League does it not? Havin' the IRB stirrin' up hell for them? Anna Parnell can handle the IRB. They'll be runnin' t' her whistle like sheepdogs."

"I wouldn't be so sure, meself," Bernie said.

"Don't worry about Miss Parnell. She talks and writes but that's not all. She can make a difference. We can make a difference. The three Fs, Bernie. Ask Brannigan about the three Fs." Liam counted on flicking fingers. "Fair rent. Free to sell on. And fixture of tenure. Anna Parnell won't rest until we have them."

"It's you I'm worried about," Bernie said.

Liam looked down over the fields. Large, well-manicured rectangular strips stretched off far into the distance, patching the countryside like a quilt his mother would use to wrap Aiden. He stroked his throbbing arm. His nose ached. He couldn't understand how Bernie was prepared to walk away now. "Brannigan says Marr's destined for the asylum," he said.

"Bag o' wasps, I'm tellin' ya."

"It's tough, but it helps us. He's in there writin' a song or somethin'. They're not sure if the names he's tellin' them are ours or just names he come up with to rhyme with the rest of the verse."

"Not right to laugh, but."

"Dundrum. D'ya know it? An asylum near Dublin."

"Good luck to the poor sinner if it's there he's going."

"Don't ya think it funny, Bernie? Them buildin' that big asylum close and handy for Dublin. What does that tell ya 'bout you Dubs?"

"Yer not too big yet to have yer arse kicked, ya rip. It was prob'ly cheaper than puttin' a wall around Mayo."

Liam smiled. He preferred it when he and Bernie were provoking each other. He didn't like it when the old man was quiet or solemn. Bernie reminded him of Aiden that way, innate blitherers the two of them. When either were quiet, something was wrong. He wondered if now was the right time to ask. He'd ask anyway.

"Have ya ever been in love, Bernie?"

"Hmmm. Can you tell me a better way to take the air than this? A crisp, dry day in late November?" Bernie said.

Liam sniggered. "Bernie. Did ya not hear–"

"Did ya father ever tell of the charge of the Light Brigade?" Bernie said. He didn't wait for an answer. "It happened a while back when the British and the French and the Turks were fighting the Russians. At one point, near a place called Balaclava - and they say the Irish have queer place names - anyways, near Balaclava, the Russians routed a Turkish battalion. And didn't they steal away the cannons.

"This wouldn't do at all. So the British high command sent an order for the Light Infantry Brigade to go after them, to harry the retreatin' Russians. That's what soldiers do, pester the bejases out of the retreatin' enemy. Harry they call it, seemingly. The main thing was to get the cannons back, ya see?

"The order came scribbled on an oul' scrap o' paper and wasn't it misinterpreted by the cavalry commander. Didn't the Light Brigade attack the main Russian gun positions further down the valley instead?

"As they say in England, "Twas a warm day to the British'. Sticks and swords up against cannons. But, theirs not to reason why. The Light Infantry were mightily slaughtered by the Russian cannons."

Liam snorted. This was the Bernie he enjoyed, story-full, benevolent. He just needed to push a bit more. "Are ya goin' to get 'round t' me question?"

"Six-hundred men, with a lot o' regrets. They made a poem about it."

"Marr'd be pleased. Now, back to my–"

"Now, d'ya see that lodge down there. See where I'm pointin'? There. That's Lord Lucan's lodge. And they're Lord Lucan's fields. They say he spent over a hundred-thousand pound getting his fields to look that good. He has a Scottish fella down there lookin' after the place. Simpson or Stimson he's called. A decent enough man, now people have got to know 'im. But d'ya see that Lord Lucan? A meaner, more heartless landlord ya won't find in Ireland."

Liam focussed on the lodge.

"One reason I share these, seemingly unrelated facts with ya, Liam, is because the man who lives in that lodge down there, is the same man as gave the wrong command to the Light Infantry Brigade. Lord Lucan denies it of course, but it was him alright. Whole o' London knows it was him."

Liam stood still, counting the outbuildings. His stomach fluttered.

"But think about them British infantry soldiers for a minute. Ridin' their fine horses inta battle. Scared for the life o' themselves. I bet ya, all o' them dearly wishin' they were home instead, with their loved ones. Havin' a few regrets I'd say. Wishin' they'd done some things better when they had the chance.

"I guarantee ya, they'd be girls at home who should've been courted, others who should've been proposed to and some that should've been wed. And them lads would've given their sword arm to be at home at that moment, doin' just those things.

"But they missed their opportunity. They didn't do it when they had the chance. Now, some eejit has given a wrong command and they're chargin' on their horses, as fast as they can gallop them, straight into round after round of cannon fire. Into the valley of death. And yes, is the answer to your question."

"What was her name?" Liam asked.

"Aren't you the nosey one? Peggy Deagan."

"Where is she now?"

"Ah, she could be anywhere by now. But the way I'm meetin' up with people lately, I wouldn't be at all surprised if that's her down there heardin' cattle. Dressed in the wellingtons and the Mackintosh."

Liam laughed.

"London, last time I saw her," Bernie said, staring at the grass.

"She's why you'd go back there?"

"It all seems a long time ago. Too long. Yet, at times, it feels like yesterday."

"How did ya know ya loved 'er?"

"Holy God in heaven. Me own mother wouldn't dare ask me these questions. Why d'ya need t'know that?"

"Just answer me."

Bernie crouched and lay back on the damp grass, propping himself on his elbows and crossing his legs.

"You're indebted to me for this, Liam Walshe." He cleared his throat. "When she spoke, every word sounded like a symphony."

"A what?" Liam turned his head over his shoulder to show Bernie his bruised and blank expression.

"Orchestras play them. Ya familiar with 'orchestra', young fella, no? Musical instruments playin' together. Violins, cellos, cymbals, lots of them, playin' together. They play beautiful, sweet-soundin' symphonies. Why're ya laughin'?

"Symphonies're full of colour, full of character, moody, strong, gentle, melodic, lots of expression. Intricate yet simple. Firm but kind. If ya don't stop gigglin' I'll get up and punch ya in the elbow.

"A fella by the name of Beethoven useta write them. That's how Peggy Deagan sounded to me, like the sweetest symphony. She asked me to take her dancin'. Ballroom dancin' mind, none of your oul' straight-armed, flickety feet nonsense. We went to a small church hall in Shoreditch. We were a good partnership, we picked it up fast. She was a gracious dancer, loved it she did. She also happened to be lovely to the eye. I might've said it before, but Eileen reminds me of her every day. I useta think they might be related there's such a likeness, but no. Anyway, Peggy Deagan had all that and then one night, she kissed me. I knew then I was in love with her."

"What about Maeve?" Liam asked.

"What about Mae–"

"Eileen told me she saw ya creepin' into Maeve's trailer a few times. Did ya not love Maeve?"

"Ah now, it was a different type o' thing with the lovely Maeve. We just provided a small service for each other. A sort of physical service. She useta say I was a pleasant change from ridin' horses all day."

Liam jarred his arm laughing.

"Right, enough from me. My turn now, kiddo. Why all the questions?"

Liam waited.

"The red's crawlin' up the back o' yer neck to yer ears," Bernie said.

"Ya know why…," Liam said. "It's just… After losing Aiden, I didn't want t' be that close t' anyone ever again. I just wanted t' batter people if the truth be known. There was a while I just wanted t' be battered meself. Is that the sign of an amadán?"

"No, you're not an idiot. But if yer intent on carryin' on with your land war, have ya thought ya might have to choose between Eileen and the Land League."

"She has choices too," Liam said. "It won't be just up t' me. Me mam says she's pretty shook up at the moment, but I'll wait. She's recoverin' well and I'll see her soon. When she's ready, then she can decide. We'll decide together." He took a deep breath of cold air. The chill filled his lungs. He stared down on Lord Lucan's lodge, noting the layout of the buildings, the stables, the storage sheds. There were tall trees there too. The lodge was vulnerable to a strike. He could organise an attack on Lord Lucan's lodge, easily enough. If he were asked. He felt strong. Ready to fight. "I almost lost her at Farmhill, Bernie. She was nearly stole from me."

"I think ya shouldn't miss yer chance, young fella. Remember what I said about them Light Brigade lancers. Tell me this though, how d'ya know ya love her?"

"It's when she speaks," Liam said, still talking at the lodge and the tapestry of tilled fields.

"Oh?"

"Yea, she sounds like a Beethoven."

Chapter 67
Castlebar, Ireland, 1881.

"Happy new year to you, Eileen," Maggie said. She chinked her glass against Eileen's.

"I haven't bled, Maggie."

THE END.

Acknowledgements and Sources

To the authors of the following publications, thank you. Joseph Lee, *The Modernisation of Irish Society 1848-1918*; Roy Douglas, Liam Harte and Jim O'Hara, *Ireland since 1690 A concise History*; Caesar Otway, *Sketches in Erris and Tyrawley (1841)*; Lady Francesca Speranza Wilde, *Ancient Cures, Charms and Usages of Ireland*; Brian Casey, *Matt Harris and the Irish Land Question, 1876–1882*; Elizabeth Lynn Linton, *About Ireland*; W. R. Le Fanu, *Seventy Years of Irish Life*. W. Rahbone, M.P., *Great Britain And The Suez Canal*; Desmond Keenan, *Ireland 1850-1920*; Bernard H. Becker, *Disturbed Ireland - Being the Letters Written During the Winter of 1880-81*; Brendan Hoban, *Kilmoremoy Parish*.

I am grateful for information provided by the following websites: Leabharlann Chontae Mhaigh Eo, Mayo County Library; Museums of Mayo; Family History in North County Mayo; History Ireland; Waterford County Museum; A Web of English History; Maggie Land Blanck; LiveStrong.com; University College Cork, Multitext Project in Irish History; The People History; Irish Memory; New Advent; Irish Newspaper Archives; London Pubs in the 1890s; SWilson.info.

Thank you to Paddy and Mary O'Boyle for facilitating a visit to the location of Farmhill House and its gardens, and to Gerry Murphy and Michael Ruddy for sharing their knowledge of Harriet Gardiner and the House. The wall, built in 1824, still stands.

I am grateful for the historic artefacts provided by the proprietors of Rouses, formerly P. Flanagan's, one of the oldest and most welcoming public houses in Ballina.

Thank you to Noel Rafferty, bodyguard to the stars, for his comments on the fight scenes.

I owe a debt of gratitude to those who took it upon themselves to read through and feedback on early drafts: Joan Carey, David Sykes, Bill Branson, Jem Lough, Ellen Lessner, Carole Kane, Eamonn O'Sullivan, and Lorraine Morrell. Thank you all.

Many thanks to Elisha Kane and Jade Sawden from Elk & Owl Photography (www.elkowlphotography.co.uk) for their work on the cover and portrait photographs.

And lastly, thank you, dear reader, without whom the process would be a lot less fulfilling.

Dennis Carey

Author's note

The storyline is fictitious. So too are all the characters. Where I have used the names of real people from history, the storyline has no connection with them in any way. There was a landowner called Harriet Gardiner who owned Farmhill Estate in Tyrawley, County Mayo. If accounts of her are accurate, that Harriet was at least as notorious as the Harriet depicted in the storyline. William 'Billy' Cuff was a Land Agent to Harriet Gardner but I have taken liberty with the spelling of his surname, his lineage and his character.

Thank you for reading *An Untilled Field*. If you can, please post a review on Amazon, I would be delighted to receive feedback.

About the Author

Dennis Carey was born in County Mayo, Ireland. His family moved to Coventry, England when he was very young and they were responsible enough to bring him with them.

He now lives with his wife in Northamptonshire.

For 30 years he worked in education, teaching for a short while in Secondary Schools and more substantially in Further Education.

Connect with Dennis Carey

If you are able to post a review on *An Untilled Field* book page on Amazon, please do.

Email: *denniscarey999@gmail.com*
Find me on Facebook: *http://www.facebook.com/dennis.carey.378*
Follow me on Twitter: *http://twitter.com/dmpcarey*
Like and comment on *An Untilled Field* book page on:
http://www.facebook.com
Follow my blog: *http://dmcarey.wordpress.com*
Connect with me on LinkedIn.

Also by Dennis Carey

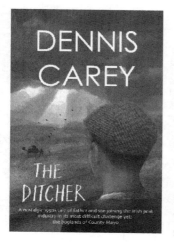

The Ditcher

An Irish historical novel about family. A story of love and hate, romance and betrayal, humour and tragedy, community and family, people and machines. A nostalgic, informative and humorous insight into Ireland in the 1950s

The burden of debt does not sit easy with Willie Casey, especially when the debt is to a dangerous man. For the solution, he relies on his young son, Sean, who takes on the challenge with fervour. But will all of Sean's dreams be realised?

Set in 1950s Bangor Erris in County Mayo, Ireland, this is a fictional tale set around a factual event.
http://mybook.to/theditcherbydenniscarey